NO TIME TO CRY

James Oswald is the author of the *Sunday Times* bestselling Inspector McLean series of detective mysteries. The first two of these, *Natural Causes* and *The Book of Souls*, were both short-listed for the prestigious CWA Debut Dagger Award. *No Time to Cry* is the first book in James's new Constance Fairchild series.

James farms Highland cows and Romney sheep by day, writes disturbing fiction by night.

Praise for James Oswald and his novels:

'The new Ian Rankin' *Daily Record*

'Oswald's writing is a class above' *Express*

'Crime fiction's next big thing' *Sunday Telegraph*

'Oswald is among the leaders in the new batch of excellent Scottish crime writers' *Daily Mail*

'A master of his material . . . an unusually competent and humane police procedural' *Scotsman*

'The hallmarks of Val McDermid or Ian Rankin . . . dark, violent, noirish' *The Herald*

JAMES OSWALD

NO TIME TO CRY

WILDFIRE

First published in 2018 by WILDFIRE
An imprint of HEADLINE PUBLISHING GROUP

1

Cataloguing in Publication Data is available from the British Library

ISBN 978 1 4722 4989 0 (B Format)

Typeset in Aldine 401BT by Avon DataSet Ltd,
Bidford-on-Avon, Warwickshire

Printed and bound in Great Britain by Clays Ltd, Elcograf S.p.A.

Headline's policy is to use papers that are natural, renewable and recyclable
products and made from wood grown in well-managed forests and other
controlled sources. The logging and manufacturing processes are expected to
conform to the environmental regulations of the country of origin.

HEADLINE PUBLISHING GROUP
An Hachette UK Company
Carmelite House
50 Victoria Embankment
London EC4Y 0DZ

www.headline.co.uk
www.hachette.co.uk

For all the readers, without whom I'd just be shouting at cows

1

It's the scent of smoke that tips me off.

Sure, the unlocked back door's a big clue too, but it's the smoke that really has me worried. I've come here alone, checked I'm not being followed. Must have done it a hundred and more times. Never been anything wrong before. But now the back door's unlocked and there's a smell of smoke in the air.

Wood smoke? Coal? I can't really tell. Maybe it's the scent of a recently gone cigarette. London's ruined my country-born senses. All I know is there's smoke and there shouldn't be. So where's it coming from?

I'm in a quiet courtyard at the end of a dark alley, tucked away in a forgotten part of the city centre. You don't have to go far to find hipster cafés, old Victorian pubs and all the other stuff the tourist board loves about London, but this is well hidden. We chose it for that reason, among others. Not cheap to rent, but not so expensive it looks suspicious either. Just another business trying to make its way in the capital, struggling to pay the bills and maybe open to a little dealing under the counter, as it were. We set it up to fish for contacts, get someone into the local organised crime scene. It was working fine too. Until now.

I pull out my phone and stare at the screen like a lost tourist. Pete's text is there in front of me.

Come to the office. Something's up. Usual protocols. P.

It's unlike him not to just phone, but not so odd I'd thought to bring backup. We're a small team anyway, and this is meant to be deep undercover. Dragging anyone else along would risk blowing the whole thing before it's really started.

Except there's that faint whiff of smoke, and the back door's unlocked.

Despite everything the press and politicians say, most of us in the Met aren't armed and don't particularly want to be. I wish I was right now though. All I've got is a can of mace and a rape alarm. It's small comfort as I nudge the back door wider with my foot, try to peer inside. Foolish, really. There's just the narrow hallway, piled up with old cardboard boxes and a couple of bin bags waiting to be taken out. Then the stairs climb up to the offices on the first floor. Can't see anything around the corner. Do I shout?

No. That's being stupid. Come on, Con. Get in there and find out what's happening.

I thumb a quick text to DS Chambers anyway. Not that she'll do anything about it, but at least it covers my arse. A quick look around the tiny courtyard, and then I step inside.

The smell of smoke is heavier, but I still can't see any fire. I take the stairs as quietly as I can, back to the wall for support. Wary. At the top, I peer over the parapet, nervous ears straining for any sound over the ever-present rumble of traffic. Time was I loved that sound, the noise of progress, of sophisticated living. Now I'd happily trade it for the bored silence of my youth.

There's no one in the outer office, but then I wouldn't have expected there to be. This place is a front, usually only Pete here going through the motions of being an unsuccessful business-man. Waiting for the right person to start taking an interest in what we're doing. I don't notice the chair on its back at first, my gaze drawn by movement at ceiling level. That's when I see the smoke clinging to the plaster, easing out of the gaps in the doorway through to the front room. Pete's office. The top half of the door's made from obscured glass, nothing but indistinct white shapes beyond.

'Pete. You in there?' Even as I speak the words I know how stupid they are. There's a fire alarm in this place that feeds straight back to control. Should be bells ringing, fire engines on their way. My phone should have lit up with notifications when the back door was opened without the right key code, but there was just the text. This is wrong.

I try the door, unsurprised to find it locked. The handle's warm to the touch though, and when I place my palm against the glass it's the same. Two steps back, the time for subtlety is over. I kick the door just below the handle, stagger as my foot rebounds off the solid wood frame. Try again, and this time the lock breaks. A third kick has it open, and thick white smoke billows from the room beyond. Through the fog of it, I can see the source, a waste paper bin on fire. Dark charring marks the wall beside it, but mercifully the blaze hasn't spread. The acrid smoke catches my throat, brings tears to my eyes and makes everything blurred as I hurry in and stamp out the last of the flames. Only then do I turn and see what I already fear.

There's a large desk to one side of the room, an office chair on the far side. A man sits in it, facing me but unmoving.

'Pete?' I step closer, blinking my vision clear. It's not easy to breathe, but I'm stuck where I stand, unable to process what I'm seeing.

Detective Inspector Peter Copperthwaite, my boss and perhaps closest friend in the force, slumps in the chair and stares lopsided at nothing. If he wasn't tied up, he'd probably have fallen to the floor by now. I can't quite work out what's happened to his face. Blood smears across his skin, bruises seal one eye shut. The other is red and lifeless. A line of bloody drool drips from his ripped mouth, adding to the red stains on his torn white shirt. But it's the tiny red dot in the middle of his forehead that I can't stop staring at.

That and the smear of his brains on the wall behind him.

2

'Well, this is a fucking mess, and no mistake.'
I sat and waited in the reception area outside Pete's office until the first of the clean-up team arrived. It didn't take them long to get here, but it was long enough for me to get past the shock and think. Past the initial shock, I should say. There's going to be a moment, maybe in a few hours' time, maybe a few days, when this all hits home.

'You say something, sir?'

There's a team of forensic technicians working the room where Pete's body is still sitting in its seat. Duty doctor's been, and the pathologist's only hanging around until the ambulance arrives. The only police officer here apart from me is DCI Bain, Pete's boss. No doubt there's an over-officious crime scene manager at the back door making sure as few people as possible contaminate the scene.

'I said it's a fucking mess, Fairchild.' Bain rounds on me, one leg swinging as if looking for something to kick across the room. Finding nothing, he just scuffs the carpet tile, rams his hands deep into his pockets in frustration. I don't know him well; he's not been part of the team long. Pete seemed to like him though. They certainly spent a lot of time together planning this whole thing.

'How did they find out? How did they even get in?'

'I don't even know who "they" are, sir. Back door was

5

unlocked and open when I got here. Security cameras should have something on them. I've not had a chance to look at them yet. Should probably get on to that.' I start to stand, but Bain pushes me back down into my seat. He pulls a chair out and slumps into it, runs a hand through his straggly grey hair. His suit hangs off him like it was made for a much larger man. Maybe he was, once. I don't know.

'No. You don't. You're too close to all this to be part of the investigation. You'll need to be debriefed soon as. We need to find out what happened here. How it happened. Dammit, this was always a risk, but I never thought . . .'

DCI Bain's words penetrate my muddled thoughts. 'Always a risk, sir? How? This isn't normal, even for the kind of people we're after. Someone's tortured Pete and then executed him.'

An expression runs across Bain's face that, were he a suspect being interviewed, I would label guilty as fuck. It's that look of a man hiding something but not doing it particularly well.

'There's more to this than meets the eye, Fairchild.'

'No shit, Sherlock.' I start to get up again, but something occurs to me. 'You knew this could happen, didn't you?'

Bain's silence is all the confirmation I need.

'Did Pete know?'

The all but imperceptible nod, almost as if he's trying to stop himself from telling me the truth he wants to.

'Well, don't think I'm just going to sit here and take this. We need to find them. Get the word out on the street. Someone will—'

'You're to say nothing, speak to no one, until you've been debriefed. Is that clear, Detective Constable?'

Bain's tone is so stern I daren't answer in words, just nod my head and clench my fists until my fingernails dig into my palms. Christ, they're going to cover this up. Bain opens his mouth to say something more, but a shout from the open office door has us both standing, rushing towards it. We're almost there when he puts a hand on my shoulder, stops me in my tracks. He may not be a large man any more, but he's still considerably bigger than me. And a detective chief inspector as well.

'I'll deal with this, Fairchild. You should go home.' He glances at his watch briefly as more muted cursing comes from the doorway. My best guess is that Pete's body has fallen off its chair. 'We'll schedule a debrief for the morning, OK? Just as soon as we've got the initial pathology and forensics in.'

I glance at the office door, then back at the DCI. It's clear from his body language that he's not going to let me back in there, and if I'm being honest, I'm not sure I want to go back in there anyway. I shouldn't really be going home though, and a debrief should happen much sooner than tomorrow morning. Something's very off here.

'Sir.' I nod my understanding. Nothing else I can do. I'm not going to let them hush this up though. Pete deserves better than that.

Nobody speaks to me as I leave the office. Even the crime scene manager just looks at me like I'm something the cat brought in as I scribble my name on his sheet. I'd have expected a bit of sympathy, what with my boss and friend having just been murdered, with me being the one who found him. Instead all the faces I see look at me with suspicion in their eyes, or maybe even fear. That more than anything else brings home to me just how much shit I'm in.

I should really go home. That's what DCI Bain told me to do, after all. The afternoon's moving on into evening anyway. Home, bottle of wine, try to get some sleep. Get myself ready for tomorrow's debriefing, which is going to be long and brutal. That's what I should be doing right now.

Who am I kidding?

It takes me half an hour to get to the station and let myself in the back door. I can't really think things through beyond the need to work out what the fuck's going on. My mind keeps going round and round in circles, always ending up with the look on Pete's face. That mixture of astonishment and anguish, those dead, staring eyes. I've seen death before, too much of it, but this is the first time it's been so personal.

Somehow I make it to the IT room unseen, so there must be someone up there looking out for me. I fire up one of the workstations and log in to the secure server we set up for this operation. Everything's here, even if a lot of it's above my pay grade and security clearance. Still, I know what we were doing in that makeshift office. Pete was posing as a struggling business-man, buying and selling goods that were barely on the right side of dodgy. We knew there was a gang out there exploiting small start-ups like that to launder money, and other things besides. This was meant to be the first step in getting a man on the inside of their operation. How the fuck did it go so spectacularly wrong? Unless there was more to it than I've been told, of course, which would explain DCI Bain's reaction.

I daren't go near the security camera feeds, even though that's the first thing I want to look at. How simple it would be just to check and see who came, who beat Pete until his face was black and blue, then put a bullet in his head. Every viewing of those files is logged though, and the last thing I need is someone thinking I've tampered with evidence.

Without going through any of the monitoring files, there's not a lot I can do. We've some intelligence on the gang we were hoping to infiltrate, and a more detailed plan of how we were hoping to achieve that. I pull up a list of lowlifes suspected of being part of the operation, most of whom are currently serving at Her Majesty's pleasure on a variety of charges. Going through their records is a snapshot of everything that's wrong with modern society, but I don't see any cop killers in the parade of mugshots.

I close down the window, switch off the workstation. There's nothing here that's going to get me any closer to finding Pete's murderer. There's nothing here that makes any sense at all.

3

The early morning debrief hasn't turned out quite the way I thought it would, not helped by the dull ache in my head from the half-bottle of wine that completely failed to help me sleep. I'd imagined a thorough but informal conversation with DCI Bain, and maybe another detective constable to take notes. What I've got is more like a kangaroo court.

'What the hell were you even doing there, Constable?'

Detective Superintendent Bailey's always been a bit of a twat anyway, but this time he's struggling to contain his rage. If there weren't a couple of other detectives and the union rep in here, he'd probably be swearing like a navvy and breaking things just to intimidate me. It won't work. I'm as pissed off as he is, and still in shock. And my head hurts, which always makes me grumpy. The question doesn't really deserve an answer anyway, so I keep quiet. For now.

'Is this a good time to go looking for blame, Gordon?' For once Sergeant Thomas is a voice of calm reason. I could almost hug him, except that bristly beard of his smells funny.

'Pete's dead, Barry.' Bailey's voice is the growl of a cornered bear. 'The whole operation's fucked and this—' He waggles an accusing finger in my direction, momentarily stuck for words. There's something very wrong with his eyes. Actually, there's something very wrong with the whole of him, but then I've never really got on with any of the senior officers here. Pete was

10

my boss, and he'd have been far more understanding in a situation like this.

Except that he's dead.

'Are we sure the operation's a complete loss?'

I'd been going to speak, but Bain beats me to it. Ever the optimist, he's at least trying to look for a positive side to this. I'm inclined to agree with Bailey though; the operation's fucked. In fact, it was probably fucked a week ago. Maybe even fucked from the start. I've been thinking about it all night, staring at the light fitting in the middle of the ceiling above my bed and trying not to see Pete's dead eyes. This was something far bigger than we thought, or at least far bigger than I thought.

'You tell me, Ed.' Even I can hear the sarcasm in the detective superintendent's voice. 'Detective Inspector Copperthwaite was tied to a chair, tortured, then shot once in the forehead. Whoever did that somehow disabled the security cameras and alarms and tried to set fire to the offices we've been paying a fortune in rent on for the past three months. Pete was one of our best undercover detectives and they found out who he was anyway.' Bailey's standing too close, he always stands too close, like he's Russian or something. When he turns his attention to me I can't help but take a step back. 'So I ask you again, Constable. What the hell were you even doing there?'

I stare at him, and for a moment I'm scared. I'm a little girl back at school, being bullied in front of the class by a crap teacher who really should know better. But I'm not that little girl any more. I've faced down bullies before, and I know I haven't done anything wrong.

'Pete texted me. Said something had come up and could I meet him at the office. Usual protocol.'

'Which was?' Bailey's voice drips with condescension. The bastard knows damn well what the protocol is, he just wants to show me up as incompetent in front of the other officers here.

Pick on me because I'm junior and female. Well, fuck him. Metaphorically. This was meant to be a debrief, not an interrogation.

'Always come by public transport. Walk a different route each time. Observe the building for five minutes minimum before entering. Use the back entrance and the key code that lets control know which officer is there. You know, all the basic stuff they teach you when you're working undercover. The common-sense stuff.'

Bailey stares at me, a vein in his forehead bulging ominously. Another reason why I don't much like the man: he doesn't take being answered back well. I meet his stare with one of my own. No way I'm backing down now. The tense silence is probably only a couple of heartbeats, but it still feels like an age before he breaks away, addresses the two more senior detectives.

'We need to know how they found out he was a cop. Damage limitation too. How much did he tell them about our other operations? Who's going to be next? I want a full review of everything Pete was involved in, going back five years, on my desk by the end of the day.'

'Aren't we going to try and find out who did this?' I know as soon as I've opened my mouth it's the wrong thing to say. Just can't stop myself sometimes.

'No. We're not. A different team will be looking into that. And you'll go nowhere near the investigation, Miss Fairchild. Do you understand me?'

Miss Fairchild. Now I know I'm in trouble. No one's called me that since school. I open my mouth to answer, but Bailey doesn't give me a chance. Is that a twitch of a smile on his face?

'Your warrant card, please.' The bastard holds out his hand.

'You what?'

'I'm placing you on suspension, prior to a full investigation by Professional Standards. Frankly, if I had my way you'd be out the door already.'

I can feel my temper rising, the shock of Pete's death the only thing that's stopping me from punching the smug fuck. Suspension? How can he do that? Then a hand on my arm steadies me. I glance around to see Sergeant Thomas, the union rep. He'll back me up.

'It's for the best, Con. Just for now. Don't make a fuss, eh?'

Not the words I was expecting at all. I look around the room, the collected male faces, eyes not brave enough to meet my gaze. Even DCI Bain looks uncomfortably at his shoes, shakes his head ever so slightly. That's when it dawns on me. This is it. My career as a detective is over. My career as a police officer is over. And I've done nothing wrong.

'Fine. Take it.' I pull the card from my jacket pocket and fling it at Bailey. No doubt that confirms every suspicion he's ever had about women in the police force. I can't bring myself to care. I'm too angry. Resisting the urge to spit in his face, in all of their faces, I pull my arm from Sergeant Thomas's weak grip, turn on my heels and stride out of the room. They won't get away with this, I hear myself muttering under my breath. But the cynic in me knows that they will.

They already have.

My angry stride down the corridor is broken by a loud voice behind me.

'Detective Constable Fairchild. A moment, please.'

Any other voice I'd probably have ignored, but of all the people who've treated me shittily since Pete's death, DCI Bain has perhaps been the most sympathetic.

'Sir?'

'In here, I think.' He pushes open a nearby door, ushers me into an empty room. Pete's office. It takes me a moment to recognise it; the place has been stripped of all files and folders already.

'What happened back there.' Bain hooks a thumb in the loose direction of Detective Superintendent Bailey's office. 'I'm sorry. I should have realised they'd be like that.'

'Like what? A bunch of bullying arseholes?'

Bain takes a deep breath, then holds it in. I can almost see the count of ten going on in his head before he speaks.

'From what I've heard you're a good detective, Fairchild. Must be, otherwise you'd not have been part of this team. But if you don't mind your attitude, then Bailey and his friends will throw you to the wolves.'

'I—'

He holds up an interrupting hand. 'It's not right, I know. It's not fair and it's counter-productive. But some powerful people are angry and embarrassed and probably scared shitless for their jobs right now. They're looking for someone to take that out on and, guess what, they've chosen you.'

'So what? I'm supposed to just act like a punchbag? Go home and take up knitting?'

Bain stares at me, silent, for long enough for my rage to calm to a rolling boil.

'For now? Yes. I can't say much. I probably shouldn't say anything at all. But there's more here than meets the eye.'

I remember his words yesterday, at the scene of the crime. Or, rather, his lack of them. 'This operation wasn't about infiltrating the local organised crime scene, was it, sir?'

'Oh, it was. At least, that was part of it. The other part?' He shrugs, but says no more.

'Above my pay grade. Fucking marvellous.' I walk around Pete's old desk and stare out of the window. It's not the most edifying of views: the back of offices, a yard full of badly parked police cars, distant skyscrapers knifing the clouds. London in all its murky glory. My home, or at least I thought it was.

'A month, maybe two.' Bain's words drag my attention away

14

from the dull scenery outside. 'We'll track down the people responsible, clear your name. You'll be back in no time. Just keep your head down for a while, OK?'

He's trying to reassure me, I can tell. He means well, and that's something, I suppose.

'I'll need to get a few things from my desk.'

He nods once, then turns and leaves. I linger in Pete's office for a while after he's gone, unsure whether I can bring myself to move.

I can see it in their faces. The fear. The hatred. The anger. To a certain extent I can understand it too. I'd probably be the same if some other poor bugger had found Pete like that. Everyone liked him, after all. It's just a bit fucking annoying they all blame me for what happened.

The joy of an open-plan office is that there's nowhere to hide. Everyone can see you, and watch silently as you clear all the personal shit out of your desk. Not that there's much of it, and none of it's all that sentimental. Maybe the only thing worth keeping is a photo in the bottom of one of the drawers. Me, Pete and DS Lowry. My first big case, breaking open a nasty protection racket. What was it, five years ago? No, six. Christ, the years roll into one.

'You've a nerve showing your face in here.'

It's such a cliché, for a while I think it's meant to be a joke. I'm too busy looking at the photo, remembering the good times. Lowry took early retirement, buggered off to Spain if I remember right. I wonder if anyone's told him about Pete yet.

'You listening to me, Fairchild?'

I look up. The simple answer is no, but that's not what my accuser wants to hear. Detective Constable Dan Penny isn't someone I'd choose to spend much time with unless I had to. He's always been a bit too full of himself to take seriously, and not much of a detective either. Lack of imagination probably explains the cliché too.

'What do you want, Dan?' I slide the photograph into my jacket pocket as I speak. Everything else I need is in the small rucksack I emptied the contents of my locker into half an hour ago.

'I want you to explain what the fuck you think you were doing blowing Pete's cover. Way I hear it that's not all of Pete's you were blowing either.'

'How long did it take you to come up with that joke, Dan?' I sling the rucksack over my shoulder while he's thinking how best to answer. 'Actually, I reckon you probably stole it from someone a lot smarter than you. Only, I thought you were meant to be keeping away from children these days.'

All bluster, and the insult goes way over Penny's head. I'll be out of the office before he works it out, but that doesn't stop what he said from hurting. Pete and I were close, it's true, but we weren't that close. Well, maybe that one time, but we both agreed it wasn't a good idea. Got it out of our systems and worked well as a team after that.

'Just so you all know.' I raise my voice as I walk to the door. 'Pete's cover was blown well before I went to see him. I know you don't want to hear that. Easier to point the finger at me because I was there when it happened. Only I wasn't, right? I didn't get there until after he was already dead. I didn't lead them there, I didn't tip anyone off. I followed protocol every time I had to go to that office. Can each and every one of you say the same?'

I'm at the door now, heart pumping just a little bit faster than normal, adrenaline making me jittery. They're all staring at me like I've got two heads or something, and that's when it hits me.

I'm not a part of this team any more.

4

I've always loved the buzz of London life, the energy. There's always something happening, some drama unfolding. And the people, most of the people, are great. As melting pots go, it's bubbling away. Right now I could do with a bit of space though, a chance to hear the night birds calling and breathe air that hasn't been used by half a dozen other people in the last minute already.

You don't get much space around here. At least, not on a detective constable's pay.

I could ride the bus all the way home, or probably cadge a lift from a squad car heading in that direction. Instead I take the Tube to King's Cross and then decide to walk. It's only a few miles and the weather's fine. Warm, but not too muggy. Walking gives me time to think, time to process what's happened and what's still happening.

Pete's dead.

Somewhere in the back of my mind, I always knew this could happen. To him, to me, to any one of us in plain clothes or uniform. Policing's a shitty job at times, dangerous and thankless. I know that, and still I do it.

Did it. Who knows whether I'll be able to go back, whether I'll want to go back after what's happened today? Talk about being thrown under the bus.

I still can't quite believe it. They know I didn't break protocol, know I'd never do anything to put Pete in danger, and yet they're going to use me as a scapegoat. I can see Detective Superintendent Bailey right now, toadying up to the commissioner. 'Sorry, sir, terrible business. Lost a good man and wasted half a mill' on a busted operation. All because some stupid little tart couldn't follow orders.' Fuckers. I've half a mind to take it to an unfair dismissal tribunal, but I know that won't do me any good. All those hostile looks from my supposed friends and colleagues proved that well enough. The poison's already there.

Pete wouldn't let them do this. Wouldn't matter who it was, he'd never let the rest of the team gang up on one person.

But Pete's dead.

I've been walking for hours now, the same thoughts going round and round. Damn them, but I can't stop the tears. Wipe my eyes, sniff like a teenager. Come on, Con. You're thirty years old. Don't let them make you cry. I should be home by now, but I've been circling the streets, staying away. I laugh out loud; there's protocol for you. Make sure nobody's following. Double back and go the long way round. Fuck-all good it does.

Pete's dead.

The sobs are getting harder to suppress, like there's a lump growing in my throat and the only way to dislodge it is to bawl like an infant who's just thrown his favourite toy on the floor. I don't think anyone's watching, don't think anyone would much care, but then I hear a voice nearby.

'Come on, love. Worse things happen in war, you know.'

I can tell by the accent exactly what he's going to look like, even before I turn to face him. Forty-something, white, what might be an attempt at a beard but is probably just laziness. He's wearing a grey cotton hoody with the history of his fast-food diet written all across its front, and his eyes are too close together.

'My best friend just died. Shot in the head. Sounds a lot like war to me.'

'Just tryin' to cheer you up. No need to be a bitch about it.

Should learn to take help when it's offered. Learn some fucking manners.' He takes a threatening step forward and I shove my hand into my pocket where my warrant card always lives. Except it's not there now. It's on the floor of Detective Superintendent Bailey's office. For an instant I feel vulnerable, but he's just one man. One unfit, overweight man who knows nothing whatsoever about self-defence. I could have him on the pavement and in cuffs in seconds. Only I left the cuffs back at the station too.

'Not today, OK? I'm not in the mood.' I pitch my voice a little lower than normal, despite the tightness in my throat. It's enough to make him pause, so I heft my backpack and sidestep my way past. Most people probably wouldn't notice the hand he reaches out towards me, grabbing for my arm. But I'm not most people. I've had training. Even with my backpack making life awkward, I've got his arm twisted behind him before he can open his mouth to speak. It brings me far closer than I ever wanted to be to him. He smells of grease and body odour.

'Just so you know, I'm a police officer and I've had a really shitty day. If I wasn't on my way home I'd arrest you right now and throw you in a cell.' I pull his arm up just a little further than it's meant to go. His yelp of pain is very satisfying, but it also reminds me that I've better things to be doing. As I let go his arm, I shove him in the middle of the back. Off balance, he stumbles away from me, falling to his knees. Hopefully the pavement will leave a more permanent reminder of his folly on the palms of his hands, but I'm not counting on it.

Turning my back on him, I walk away, confident he's not going to do anything stupid. I can hear his groans as he struggles to his feet, the muffled curses getting quieter as he and I go our separate ways. At least I've stopped crying now, I'll give him that much.

But Pete is still dead.

* * *

19

Old Mrs Feltham is sitting on the open stairs that lead up to my flat when I get home. Judging by the mountain of green waste and small plastic bowl of shelled beans, she's been to the market recently. I'm more the convenience food type; there's never enough time to cook. I envy her that luxury, though her old face is lined with years of hard work.

'You home early, sugar.' She shuffles to one side slightly so I can get past. For a moment I consider stopping for a chat; that's what I'd do if it was my day off. I don't want to have to explain everything to her though, don't want her sympathy even if it might mean a pot of whatever she's cooking left outside my door later.

'You know how it is, Mrs F. Some days it's all hours, others there's not much to do.' And before she can come up with a retort, I'm up the steps and gone.

The flat is dark, cool compared to the summer heat outside. Nothing special, it's just an ex-council place in an unlovely concrete block thrown up sometime before I was born. The rent's extortionate, especially given the owner bought the place off the council for a knock-down price in the eighties. God Bless Maggie Thatcher and the right to buy. Still, it's been home for the past five years, and that's the longest I've stayed anywhere since I can remember. As I dump my backpack in the tiny hall, I wonder how much longer it'll be before I have to move on again.

There's a half-empty bottle of wine in the fridge, but for once I don't feel like getting drunk. A bit more of a search produces something that might just about make a meal. A lump of cheddar cracked with age, butter gone a bit rancid, bread that's hard rather than mouldy. Cheese on toast washed down with a mug of black tea. It would have been white if the milk was maybe just a day younger, but I don't like the way the carton's bulging.

I take my sparse meal through to the living room, fall into the saggy armchair and stick my feet up on the coffee table. Sunlight spears through the blinds, shadows hiding the worst of the mess. It's not dirty, just cluttered. Life's too short to spend your free time clearing up shit. Maybe if I ever had visitors I'd make an effort, but I can't remember the last time anyone came back here.

Then I can remember. It was Pete. About six months ago when we were first starting to plan out this operation. Fuck.

There's still half of my cheese on toast left, but I've got no appetite any more. I dump it in the bin under the kitchen sink, pour the tea down the drain. For a moment the half-bottle of wine calls to me from the fridge, but I ignore it. Now's not the time. Get your life in order first, Con. Then you can get shitfaced.

Most of the stuff I've shoved into my backpack could really just go in the bin too. There's some station paperwork I'll have to fill in if I want to continue being paid, a few certificates that'll be of limited use if my police career is truly over, a mountain of cheap biros and felt-tip markers that I've been hoarding for a while now, and a bunch of keys. I set everything out on the table in front of me, each item bringing with it a memory. There's the photo still in my jacket pocket too, but for now I leave that where it is. Pick up the keys. Pete's keys.

I remember him giving them to me, making some joke about it to ease the tension. We had a history, sure, but this wasn't that kind of exchange. More a 'look after the place while I'm gone' kind of gesture. At least I think that's what it was. As it happened, he wasn't gone for long enough for me to need to use them. Now he'll never go back there again.

I loop the keyring around my finger, dangle the keys in front of me. Indecision's always been a problem, and I can hear Detective Superintendent Bailey's voice, grumpy and harsh, warning me off going anywhere near the investigation into Pete's murder. Will they have sent a team already? It's probably the first thing I'd do, visit the victim's house. But I'm not running the case.

Fuck it. What's the worst they can do? They're going to run me out of the force anyway. I shove the keys in a pocket, grab my own from the sideboard in the hall and head back out into the city.

5

Detective Inspector Pete Copperthwaite was forty-five when he died. That's another reason why we never really got together. Bad enough a DC and a DI in the same unit, but a fifteen-year age difference? Don't get me wrong, I'm not against that sort of thing. It's just that coppers are the worst gossips and there's only so much tutting I can take before I lamp someone. And Pete has an ex-wife too. Christ, I wonder if anyone's told her yet?

All these and more useless thoughts bounce around the inside of my skull as I ride across the city, south of the river. Too far to walk, it takes an age to work out the bus routes, but I'm damned if I'm taking the Tube. In the end I give up and walk the last mile.

It's a nice place. Tiny little terrace house in a quiet street just a little too far from the main commuter routes. Even so it's probably worth ten times what young Police Constable Copperthwaite paid for it when he first joined the Met. I don't imagine any PCs starting out now will have much chance of buying their own place. Not around here anyway.

Walking here's given me the opportunity to scope out the street before I get anywhere near. There's no sign of any police presence, no sign of anyone at all. The sun's making it hard to see through the windscreens of some of the cars, but I reckon they're all unoccupied. Parked up while their owners are at work in the city. I never could quite understand the point of having a car in London; it's usually quicker to walk. Still, people love their motors, I guess.

I can't find any evidence the front door's been tampered with, and when I unlock it the alarm beeps until I key in the code to disarm it. So far so normal. There's about a week's worth of mail on the doormat, but that's to be expected. Pete was working undercover, spending most of his time at the office where I found him. There's a small flat above it that came as part of the deal and that was his cover. For all the good it did him.

I've still got a pair of latex gloves wedged in one of my jacket pockets, an old habit I'm glad of now. I pull them on before going beyond the hall, aware that I've already touched the door handle and the buttons on the alarm keypad. It's not as if I've no right to be here; Pete gave me keys and told me the code, after all. We were colleagues, worked together on loads of cases. Got drunk together. I pause a moment, trying to remember him like that, pint in hand, head back as he laughs at some inappropriate joke. All I can see is his bruised and battered face, that tiny red dot in the middle of his forehead. The choking stench of smoke everywhere.

Snap out of it, Con. You came here for a reason, so get on with it.

I step lightly through the house, checking for any obvious signs of disturbance, but also for anything that might embarrass Pete's memory. His whole life's going to be rifled through for clues as to how he died, and that seems wrong to me right now. Strange, really. I can't begin to count how many times I've dug through people's personal history, often those who are still alive. Pete's dead. He doesn't care if every detective in the Met knows he wore boxer shorts with polka dots on them, or liked reading fantasy novels and comics. But I care. I want him to be remembered well.

There's a back door to the house, opening onto a tiny patch of garden that's been almost entirely paved over. A high wall at the back with a black-painted wooden door set into it, bolted top and bottom. If memory serves, there's a lane beyond, and some of the bigger houses on this street have garages. I don't bother going out; it's obvious no one has been here any time recently. The house has that feel about it, a staleness to the air. I take one last look around the hall, try to call up happy memories. It doesn't work. Coming here was a mistake, now it's time to leave.

Resetting the alarm, I reach for the front door at the same moment it swings open. I think DC Penny is as surprised to find it unlocked as I am to see him.

'What part of "stay away from the investigation" do you not understand, Fairchild? Posh public school education like yours, I'd have thought you'd understand basic English by now.'

Back at the station, back in Detective Superintendent Bailey's office. It'd be déjà vu all over again if it weren't for the absence of Sergeant Thomas and DCI Bain, replaced by a smirking DC Penny. I guess it could be worse; they could have shoved me in a cell for a while and questioned me under caution.

'I have a key for Pete's house. I know the alarm code. He asked me to keep an eye on the place while he was under-cover.' It's a weak excuse and I know it, but it's all I've got right now.

'Keep it so clean you had to wear gloves, right?' Dan Penny is enjoying my discomfort way too much, and for once I can't see any easy way to get my own back on him. He's not the one in charge here, so I ignore him.

'You're suspended while we investigate Pete's death and your role in it, Constable. How do you think it looks when we find you snooping around his house? What were you trying to hide?'

'Hide? I wasn't—'

'Picking up a pair of your old undies you'd left behind, were you?'

This time I round on DC Penny. It helps that I've got a couple of inches' height on him, but the way my blood's boiling it wouldn't matter if he was a giant.

'Pete's dead, Dan. Someone shot him in the forehead. Right there.' I poke him in the exact same spot, hard enough for him to take a step back. 'He was a better cop than you'll ever be. A better man. So keep your fucking sick fantasies to yourself, OK?'

I can see the red flush spread up his neck and across his cheeks. The anger not far behind it. Brawling in the Detective Superintendent's office isn't a good idea, but it wouldn't be the first time Dan and I have come to blows. Bailey interrupts us before we can get started.

'Are you denying that you were in a sexual relationship with DI Copperthwaite?'

There's just enough disbelief in his tone to stop me from laughing. That and the anger I can barely control at the moment. 'Of course I'm fucking well denying it. Pete was my friend, sure. But Jesus Christ, sir. "Sexual relationship"?' I almost make little bunny ears with my fingers. 'He was fifteen years older than me.'

Bailey stares at me with a mixture of contempt and disgust I'm more used to seeing on hardened criminals in the interview room. Lawyers too, now I come to think of it. He doesn't believe me, and neither does DC Penny. How many others in the station think Pete and I were together? How did I never know? I mean, there was that one time, sure. But that was years ago.

'Nevertheless, it's very suspicious of you to go round there alone. What were you doing there? What were you looking for?'

It's a very good question, and one I don't have a ready answer to. Put simply, I wanted to make sure there wasn't anything to embarrass Pete when they went in and turned the place upside down. I knew they were going to, didn't have to be part of the investigation to see that coming. I just don't know how to explain that to Bailey and Penny, perhaps the two most unenlightened men in a station dripping with testosterone.

'I wasn't looking for anything, sir. Wasn't trying to hide anything either. I just wanted to see the place one last time.'

Blank stares from the both of them, but then I was hardly expecting anything else. On the other hand, it's just the two of them. And I'm not in one of the interview rooms, not being offered a lawyer or read my rights.

'Look, Pete and I were close. You know that, everyone in the station knows that.' I've been standing to attention, on my guard, but now I force myself to relax a little. Make this feel like an informal chat rather than a dressing-down. It might work.

'I had heard.' Bailey's voice is all snark, but that's better than anger, right?

'It wasn't like that, sir. I know what station gossip's like. Two officers working closely together, they must be having an affair. Only, we're detectives, aren't we? We don't do supposition, we do facts. And the fact is Pete and I weren't fucking each other. We were friends. And we were both working on the same operation. He was undercover, I was first contact should he need anything. You know all this. You authorised the whole thing in the first place.'

For a moment I think I've got him convinced. Somewhere deep down, hidden under the machismo and management by bullying, Bailey's a good detective. Dan Penny, on the other hand, is the closest thing to a talking piece of shit I've ever met.

'Come off it, Fairchild. You were in his house wearing latex gloves. That's a potential crime scene and you were tampering with it despite being told to back off the investigation into DI Copperthwaite's death.'

'How is it a potential crime scene, Dan? Pete hadn't even been there for a fortnight. He was working undercover, remember?'

'Nevertheless, you shouldn't have been there, Constable. You knew that, and yet you still chose to disobey a direct order.'

There's something about Bailey's tone that kills my snappy retort. When I left here the last time I was still in shock, still coming to terms with Pete's death. I couldn't understand why everyone seemed to blame me for that when it clearly wasn't my fault. Stupid, really. I assumed they were all in shock too, and their anger was just a knee-jerk reaction. Now I know it's something far more serious. They really mean to make me a scapegoat for this. Bailey set me up perfectly. He knew exactly what I'd do. Christ, he probably even had Penny tailing me, ready to pounce when I crossed the line. They want me out, because then it's easy to blame me and sweep everything under the carpet. Idiot that I am, I walked straight into their trap.

6

'We have come here today to remember before God our brother, Peter Copperthwaite.'

I don't really do churches. Got that all out of my system at school. There was a time I loved the ceremony, the singing, the sense of shared purpose, but then I saw through the lie. Or I became a teenager and rebelled the way all teenagers do. Whatever the reason, church and me don't really get along any more. I've skipped out on quite a few weddings just to avoid the awkwardness of having to explain why I'm not going to accept the inevitable christening invitation a year down the line.

But I still do funerals, even if I'm starting to have second thoughts about this one.

Pete didn't have many friends outside of the police service. Those of us who worked with him are huddled together at the front. Twenty or so people in a nave built for a congregation of hundreds. The vicar's almost as old as the church, his face as grey and lined as the plaster cracking from the walls. He's wearing a simple cassock that looks enormous on him, weighing him down like the mountain of sins he's forgiven. I don't know if he knew Pete at all, but he's doing his best.

I can see the coffin from where I'm standing, near the back of the small crowd. Plain, cheap, it was carried in here by six uniformed officers who probably didn't even know Pete at all. I don't know why that makes me angry, but it does. I fight back the tears anyway. Damned if I'm going to let any of this lot see me cry.

'To commit his body to be cremated.'

I've not really been listening to the vicar, but as he speaks those words I'm reminded of the fire in the wastebasket, set to burn the whole building down and cover up the crime. Is it my imagination, or can I smell that smoke again? Two fat candles flicker on the altar, twin trails of black drifting up from their yellow flames. Maybe that's what has set me off. It's been two weeks since he died and there hasn't been a day when I've not thought about that room, that fire, Pete's bruised and beaten body. I've no idea how the investigation is coming along. Nobody will speak to me about it. I made a formal statement to DCI Bain, but nobody has come back to me for anything more. Almost as if I no longer exist.

'Let us commend Peter to the mercy of God, our maker and redeemer.'

Time slips forward and the coffin is being carried out again, a sombre line of black uniforms following on behind. A grey-haired old man, hunched with arthritis and walking slowly with the aid of a cane must be Pete's father, retired police sergeant Henry Copperthwaite. The tiny woman by his side is his wife, Marjory. They both look at me, but only briefly. No more attention than they give any of the other people here. Then they're gone, following their son's body to the crematorium, where new flames can finish what the old flames failed to do. His ashes will be buried in a small pot beside his grandparents, somewhere on the North Yorkshire moors, and in time – a short time if the look of them is anything to go by – Henry and Marjory will join him. This church service is for them more than anyone.

Detective Superintendent Bailey stares at me for longer than is polite as he shuffles past. It looks like he's going to ignore me, but at the last moment he stops. His scowl of annoyance at my presence here is a small victory.

'Professional Standards want to interview you. First thing tomorrow morning.'

His tone surprises me, and I get the distinct impression that if I'd not been here, seen in his presence by at least two dozen other police officers, the message would have somehow been 'forgotten' and not reached me. It's not as if I had any plans for tomorrow though, and this was going to happen sooner or later.

'I'll be there.' I hold his gaze until he breaks eye contact, then wait until he's long gone before joining the few stragglers.

'It's Constance isn't it? Con?'

I turn to see a woman dressed almost as inappropriately for a funeral as me. She's got a thin black woollen cardy on, but that's about it as far as mourning goes. I don't recognise her for a moment, then the young face I've seen in a few photographs at Pete's place morphs itself onto the older one in front of me.

'Veronica?'

Pete's ex-wife smiles, wrinkles spreading from the corners of her eyes. 'I don't think we've ever actually met before.' She holds out a hand and I shake it lightly. 'Peter spoke very highly of you though. I must say, I'm surprised not to see you in uniform. Everyone else is.'

'I quit.' It's not quite the truth, but it gets to the essence of it.

'Not over what happened to Peter, I hope?'

'Partly. Indirectly, I suppose.' I lean against the end of a pew, unsure where this conversation is going or why I'm even having it. The church is empty now, save for a verger tidying up around the altar. He snuffs the candles and the smell of burning flesh grows stronger.

'You going to the wake?' I ask, not really sure what to say.

'With a bunch of coppers? Why do you think I left in the first place?' Her smile is at odds with the occasion, but suits her face just fine.

'I didn't realise you were police.'

31

'Not for a long time now, but that's how Peter and I first met. We came through training together. He went through the fast track and ended up in plain clothes. I stuck to uniform.' She shoves her hands into her pockets. 'You want to get a coffee? Got to be better than standing here chatting, right?'

Mid-afternoon, I'd more likely be looking for something a bit stronger than coffee, but what the hell? This woman was married to Pete for almost ten years. Least I can do is give her a bit of my time. It's not as if I need to be anywhere else, after all.

We're in a chain coffee shop just around the corner from the church. Veronica's drinking something with ice in it, which seems to defeat the point of coffee as far as I'm concerned. My double hit of dark espresso lasted all of thirty seconds, so maybe she's onto something.

'They wouldn't tell me how Peter died,' she says after we've dispensed with the small talk. 'I spoke to his boss, Gordon Bailey. Never really liked him, if I'm being honest, and he's not changed. How he made it to superintendent I'll never know.'

'The length and texture of his tongue, I expect. He's very good at being nice to the people who matter.'

Veronica smirks into her coffee. 'I can see why Peter liked you. And why Gordon didn't.' She pauses a while before continuing, the smile drifting away as she remembers why she's here. 'I'll understand it if you can't tell me either. I know how these things are, when there's an ongoing investigation and stuff.'

'You know, no one's actually debriefed me on the operation. Not properly. I gave them a statement two weeks ago, but no one's told me what I can and can't say about it. They're all too busy trying to work out how to hang the blame on me, I guess.'

'But you don't want to talk about it.'

It's not a question, but I can see the subtle probing behind it.

I've spent enough years interviewing suspects to know when I'm on the other side of the metaphorical table.

'What is it you do?' I ask. 'Pete never said. Never talked about you much at all, really.'

'I work in security. Personal protection.'

I look at her more closely. She's about my height, about Pete's age. Not particularly bulky or strong, although it's hard to tell given her loose-fitting clothes. She doesn't have the face of someone who spends long hours in the gym or the ring though.

'Admin mostly, these days. And the agency I work for does a lot of private investigation work as well. There's a surprising overlap. Sorry about the interrogation.'

'Nothing to apologise for. You were only asking questions.' I sit back in my chair, stare at my tiny espresso cup and wonder if I need another. 'As to how Pete died, he was working undercover, his cover was blown and the people we were after killed him. Then they set fire to the building he was in to try and cover their tracks, only I was on my way there, arrived before the fire had taken hold. I . . . found him.'

Veronica's face darkens into a scowl. 'Is that why they suspended you? They suspect you of blowing his cover? Ridiculous.'

'They want a scapegoat, and I'm not exactly loved by all in the unit.'

'Let me guess. Not many female detectives.'

'There's a few of us. I'm probably a bit more free with my opinions than the rest. Less bothered about scrambling up the greasy pole too.'

'Less tolerant of your male colleagues' wandering hands and casual misogyny, I suppose.'

I think about the station banter, the rough machismo that always gets excused as a coping mechanism for the stress of the job. Not something I'll miss, if I'm being honest.

'Did you speak to Pete often?' I ask, turning the attention away from me and my story. Veronica takes a slow drink from her coffee before answering.

'Not a lot, no. We used to do Christmas cards, but that dried up a few years back. I sometimes emailed him if I needed a favour, but we've been divorced almost ten years now. Gone our separate ways. I've been trying to remember when I last spoke to him on the phone and it must have been eight, nine months ago? Can't think when we were last in the same room together.'

'And yet you came to his funeral.' I pick up my cup, turn it round and round, watching the tiny drip of dark brown liquid pooled in the bottom.

'I didn't hate him. Well, maybe for a while, but that was a long time ago. We just stopped loving each other, that's all. He had his career as a detective and I . . . didn't.'

'Why did you leave? The Met, that is.'

'Wandering hands and casual misogyny probably sums it up best. I'd had enough, and someone made me a better offer.' Veronica reaches into the small patent leather bag she brought with her, takes out a business card and slides it across the table to me. I pick it up, see a company logo, an address in Birmingham, the name Veronica Copperthwaite and a title that's somewhat more senior than admin.

'You kept his surname?'

'Call me sentimental. Also, I had enough trouble growing up as Roni Potts. People take me more seriously this way.'

There's more to it than that, I can tell. I'm more interested in why she's giving me her business card.

'I'm not looking for a job right now, you know.' I go to hand the card back to her, but she doesn't take it.

'I'm not offering you one right now either. Keep it though.' She nods at the card. 'You never know. You might change your mind. And so might I.'

7

London's sweltering under a temperature inversion as I walk across town to my flat. The air is still, exhaust fumes building up to dangerous levels. Sweat clings to my scalp, drips down my back and pools uncomfortably around my waistband. Black might have been appropriate for Pete's funeral, but it's the worst possible colour to be wearing outside today. Soon I'll be home though, then I can strip off and stand under a cold shower until the evening comes.

I could have caught a taxi, I suppose; they've all got air conditioning these days. But it occurred to me around about the same time as Veronica didn't offer me a job that I'm not exactly flush with cash right now. When I told her I'd quit, that wasn't exactly true, but it's only a matter of time before I'm either pushed or I jump. They want someone's scalp for Pete's death and the collapse of the whole operation. I know I'm the easiest target for that, even if I know just as well that I've done nothing wrong. Even if I can prove that, though, do I really want to work with a team that hates me? Tomorrow's interview with Professional Standards isn't going to be much fun.

There's a small tupperware pot by my front door when I finally arrive home, fretful and sweaty. Mrs Feltham has taken to feeding me now that I'm home all day and can drop by to chat. I peel the lid off and smell something wonderful and Jamaican that will probably blow the top of my head off when I eat it. Best not to ask what the meat in it is either. Goat, most likely.

The flat's too warm, so I go round opening all the windows. There's no wind to blow through though, just the noisy roar of the city. Popping the curry in the fridge brings a welcome flow of cool air, and for a moment I seriously consider just sitting on the floor with the door open.

Instead, I go to the bedroom to strip off my damp clothes, then stand in the shower for a while to cool down. I don't know how long I'm in there, but the tips of my fingers are all wrinkled by the time I step out and towel myself down. The afternoon light seems to be fading towards evening now, shadows lengthening. I stare at myself in the bathroom mirror for a while, not really seeing anything except maybe the puffy bags under my eyes. The same old careworn expression I've seen every day of my adult life. Perhaps it's time for a change, after all.

Loosely wrapped in a dressing gown, I wander back to the bedroom to get dressed. A thick towel wrapped around your pinky finger's never the best way to get water out of your ear, which is probably why I'm halfway to the bed before I notice there's a man sitting in the little armchair in the corner by the open window. His face is in shadow, but there's something very familiar about the shape of him. Then he moves, and I wonder whether I haven't caught a bit too much sun walking across town.

'Pete?'

'Hey, Con. It's good to see you.'

I still can't see his face, but there's no mistaking that voice. Except that Pete's dead. I know he is. I saw his body. The air in the bedroom is chill, goose pimples rising on my bare arms, but I feel no fear, sense no threat. If anything I'm angry, just not sure who I'm angry at.

'How can you be here?'

'Who says I am? I could just be a figment of your imagination.'

That sounds like the sort of rubbish Pete would say. He thinks it's clever and enigmatic, but it's just annoying. I slump down on the bed, unsurprised when his face stays in shadow. I know he's not there. It's just my grief and the stress of the past few weeks. My own guilty conscience taunting me.

'Seriously though. You're dead. I've just been to your funeral. Just spent an interesting hour talking to your ex-wife.'

'Roni? How is she? Taking everything in her stride, I expect.'

'She seemed fine. Sort of offered me a job.'

He tilts his head to one side as if considering the news. 'You'd work well together. You should consider it.'

'Yeah, well. Maybe. Let's see how tomorrow goes first. They might just throw me in jail.'

'I'm sorry. You should never have got the blame for what happened. If there's any justice they'll realise it wasn't your fault.'

I can't quite understand why I'm so calm, so rational. This is an impossible situation. There's no way I can be having this conversation with anyone but myself. And yet it's good to hear his voice, see him again. Well, most of him.

'I can't see your face, Pete. You trying to hide something from me?'

'You don't want to see it. Trust me on that, Con.' He leans back in the chair, fading into shadows that shouldn't be dark enough to swallow a man like that. 'Be careful. The people who did this to me, they won't stop there. Not if they think they're still threatened.'

I can hear the concern in his voice, and now I am scared. I stand up, cross the room to where he's sitting, but the closer I get, the more indistinct he becomes. I blink away the tears that have sprung from nowhere, and when my vision clears, he is gone.

★ ★ ★

The pub's full of people and noise, just the thing I want after whatever it was that happened in my flat. I didn't have a conversation with my dead boss, I'm sure of that. Fairly sure. I mean, ghosts don't exist, do they? Only on those rubbish telly programmes I've seen sometimes when night shift buggers up my internal clocks. Never mind the watershed, daytime television should come with a health warning.

I like this place. It's only five minutes' walk from the flat, and the usual crowd are young, carefree. London bohemians who don't take themselves as seriously as the hipsters in Peckham and Shoreditch. It won't last, property prices are pushing everyone who doesn't work in finance further and further out from the centre. Soon places like this will be no more than glorified wine bars, or worse yet gastropubs selling burgers for twenty quid and fries five quid extra.

But for now it's got a bit of life to it, and a band who aren't half bad. I'm almost tempted to get up and dance like some of the other customers in here, but maybe I'm a little bit old for that. And it's been a long day, a shitty fortnight.

'Connie? Connie Fairchild? No way!'

I thought I'd hidden myself well enough in the corner, nursing a bottle of Peroni with the wedge of lime left behind on the bar. I like this place because it's full of people, but people who don't know me and aren't trying to hit on me. The last thing I need is to be recognised. I risk a look in the direction of the voice and my heart sinks even further. It's been a dozen years now, but some people never change.

'It *is* you. Oh, this is just perfect. Shove up, shove up. I have to talk to my friend.'

Charlotte DeVilliers was always pushy. Back in school I learned early on just to go with the flow. It was always too much effort to try and thwart her when she decided she wanted something. We weren't really friends, but we're much the same age, and grew up in the same village. Her dad and mine were so close they could almost have been twins. It was inevitable we would become allies when we were both sent away to the same boarding school, even though we moved in very different circles there. I don't think I've seen her since I left that place, but she embraces me in the kind of hug a child gives her favourite aunt. I try not to be too rigid as she squeezes me tight.

'You're all muscle, Connie. What happened to the puppy fat?'

She's shouting to be heard over the noise of the band, more's the pity. I don't need a conversation right now, and really can't face a reunion. Much to my dismay the song ends and the singer announces they're taking a short break. I know deep down it's not going to be short enough.

'Charlotte. How have you been?' I think that's the right thing to ask. It's been so long since I've spoken to anyone like her I can't be sure. I left that life behind a long time ago. Happily.

'How have I been?' She rolls her eyes like an out-of-work actress. 'Is that the best you can do? It's been twelve years and not a word. I thought we were friends.'

I should just tell her the truth, that I never really thought much of her, that I tolerated her attention because that was easier than brushing her off the whole time. Some behaviours are ingrained though. I slip so easily back into old ways.

'What are you up to, then? You live around here, or are you stalking me?'

She stares, her face a picture of surprise at my directness, and I suppose I haven't quite slipped all the way back.

'I've just moved into a new place round the corner. Elmstead Road. You know it?'

I do. It's expensive, but then so's Charlotte. I say nothing, hoping she'll do all the talking for both of us.

'It's all a bit of a 'mare, really. I got divorced. Jack was shagging his secretary or some intern or something. Stupid idiot. I wouldn't have minded so much, but he got the poor girl pregnant.'

I tune out. It's an old survival mechanism I'd long since forgotten. I didn't even know that Charlotte was married, have no idea who Jack might be. Nor do I much care. She represents all that I've been running away from for the past twelve years, and yet here she is, in my local.

'Anyway, I was talking to Ben the other day. He said something about you working for the police, but that can't be right, can it?'

The words break through my mental noise-cancelling headphones. 'Ben?'

'Are you even listening to me, Connie?' Charlotte makes that face of hers that I really haven't missed. 'Your brother, remember? Benevolence? I never could get the hang of your family and its weird names.'

'I know who Ben is, Charlotte. Just wondering why it is you're talking to him. I thought you hated his guts.'

Charlotte's eyebrows are thin and painted on, but they still arch up in surprise. 'That was when we were like, seventeen? Come on, Connie.'

I try to shake off the fug of the day, the horror of Pete's death, the stress of his funeral and the weirdness of his ghost. It's too much of a coincidence Charlotte being here now. She has to have been looking for me.

'What is it that you want, Char?'

'Want?' She feigns innocence as badly as she rolls her eyes. 'I'm just pleased to see you. Is this your local? Are we, like, neighbours?'

I pick up my bottle of beer and neck what's left in it. I'd been hoping to stay put until they threw me out. Maybe find some uncomplicated boy to go home with. Looks like my plans for the evening have been ruined.

'Sure. See you round, then.' I thump the bottle down on the table a little harder than necessary. Push my way past protesting drinkers as I make good my escape. As if on cue, the music starts up as I step out into the night.

One bottle of Peroni's not nearly enough to give me a buzz, so the way I'm feeling right now probably has more to do with the chance meeting with Charlotte than any alcohol. Chance. Yeah. What's that Scottish expression? Aye, right. The only language in the world where two positives can combine to make a negative. She was looking for me, which means someone told her where I might be found. It doesn't take a genius to see the unhelpful hand of my brother in all of this.

At least the air's cooled now, a light breeze playing on my skin. The night-time city's never quiet, but it's hardly the bustle of traffic you get during the day. Not this far out anyway. There's only a few people about, and I lean back against a grimy tree for a moment, stare up through its branches and leaves and imagine I can see the stars.

My phone buzzing in my pocket ruins the moment. I pull it out to see a missed call from my brother. Of all my immediate family, he's the only one who has my number, the only one I'll even consider talking to. Right now I don't want to talk to any of them though. Not when my life is falling apart like this. I'd either get the cold shoulder I deserve or, worse, sympathy. It would be too easy to run home, tail between my legs, apologise for all the harsh things I said and beg forgiveness.

The hollow laugh that slips out of my mouth startles a couple walking past. Things would have to be a great deal worse than they are for me to consider going home.

I'm staring at the screen of my phone, wondering if I've got the energy to call my brother back and find out what he wants, when a text pops up on the screen.

Hey Con. You might get a visit from Char D.V. Soz about that. She's OK really. Speak soon, Ben.

I stare at the words until the screen cuts out, then slip the phone back into my pocket. At least it confirms my suspicion that bumping into Charlotte in the pub wasn't a coincidence. She wants something, and my brother's in on it. Nothing good can possibly come from that combination.

Trying hard not to sigh, I push myself away from the tree and walk back along the street towards my flat. In hindsight, it's probably for the best I don't get pissed tonight; I'm being interviewed by Professional Standards tomorrow morning, after all. That was always going to be a nightmare, but now I've got the added bonus of worrying what my brother's up to. Could things get any worse?

8

They're not ready to see me when I arrive at the station for my meeting with Professional Standards. I could go down to the canteen and drink bad coffee, but the looks I'm getting from all the other officers in the building makes the relative calm of my desk in the corner of the CID room more appealing. I grab a paper cup of equally bad coffee from the vending machine and head for the first floor.

I may be on suspension from active duties and likely to quit if I'm not thrown out, but that doesn't mean paperwork hasn't accumulated on my desk in my absence. There's stuff related to the operation that's gone so spectacularly badly, a few timesheets to fill in, even a neatly printed document from the union rep, telling me about all my options and how the union can help me. Nice of them to send me an email, or maybe even call.

Shoved under a stack of forms that are nothing to do with me whatsoever, I dig out something a bit more interesting. Initial pathology report on a dead body pulled from the Thames a few days ago. Not my case, not anyone's case as far as I'm aware. It's not the sort of thing we usually deal with, so it's probably been mislaid by one of the other teams we share this building with. There's a report number on file though, so I bring up the details on my computer. I could kid myself I'm just looking to see who it should be passed on to, but really I'm just naturally inquisitive. Sipping at the foul-tasting coffee, I start to piece together the story of the last few hours of someone who had an even worse day than me.

Steve Benson was apparently a freelance journalist. There's links to a few of his articles in major newspapers and magazines, so he must have been quite good at it. A quick look at the dates on his bylines suggests things weren't going so well for him recently. Still, enough to jump off a bridge into the Thames? That's what the initial conclusion seems to be. Suicide's not all that rare, especially in young men.

I tap a couple of keys, bring up the name of the detective who's prepared the report so far. I'm expecting someone from another unit, so it surprises me to see Detective Constable Dan Penny's name there. No wonder he's so grumpy the whole time if he's getting this sort of thing dumped on him.

With nothing better to do until Professional Standards arrive, I pick up the pathology report and start to read it. I'm not sure why it's been printed, rather than attached electronically to the case file, but someone's gone to the trouble. That they've then dumped it on my desk along with a load of other stuff is more of the kind of chaotic filing I'm used to in this place. The further I get into the report though, the more I wonder whether this wasn't put here on purpose, and my foul-tasting coffee goes cold and forgotten as I read on.

Steve Benson's lungs were filled with water, so he definitely drowned. Indications were he'd not been in the river more than a few hours though, which is a bonus. Get the tide right, and chances are you'll be swept out into the North Sea, never to be seen again. He was fully clothed when they found him, but his feet were bare. Again, not unusual for a suicide, oddly enough. It's habit to kick off your shoes before jumping in the sea, apparently. There's no indication as to whether he wore spectacles, and I click back to one of his articles to see the author photograph just to check. That's another thing people do, take off their glasses. He's not wearing them in the only picture I can find, and I reach out for some paper to scribble down a note to check that. Then I remember this isn't my case. Will never be my case. Old habits die hard, I suppose.

It's only when I get to the detailed pathology report that I open the pad and start to write. There are some unusual anomalies, faint marks around wrists and ankles that could be ligature marks, bruising around the ribs and thighs suggesting Mr Benson might have been punched and kicked not long before death. A puncture wound in the crook of his left elbow must be from a recent injection, but blood toxicology results have yet to come through.

I look at the page in my exercise pad filling up with notes for beginning an investigation.

Suicide/unlikely
Follow up path. report. More detail on markings. Drugged?
Tortured? Why?
Background – state of mind. What was he working on?
Last known movements
Speak to next of kin/colleagues

'What's that you're working on?'

I look up in surprise. My least favourite detective constable has managed to creep up on me, I'm so absorbed in this new mystery. Then I remember it's his case.

'Nothing. Just getting things straight in my head.' I shut the pad over the pathology report, even though I doubt he'd be able to read my handwriting from that distance. The computer screen's facing towards me, but I shut down the window anyway.

'Well, time's up. PS are here and waiting.' He sneers at me. 'I'd wish you good luck, but you don't deserve it.'

★ ★ ★

'You were a junior member of the team for Operation Undertaker, is that not correct, Detective Constable?'

I'm glad now of the interruption that stopped me getting wasted last night. If I thought it was bad being given a dressing-down by DS Bailey, the interview with Chief Inspector Jennifer Williams from Professional Standards is far worse. For one thing, she's being nice. I'm always suspicious of that. She's got a young constable with her taking notes. He keeps giving me a look that is half warning, half a little cartoon thought bubble with 'help' written in it in very small type. Nobody bothered to intro-duce him before we got started, which is another reason why Williams's niceness worries me.

'Junior as in my rank, or in my input into the operation, ma'am?' I've made an effort to look tidy today, which means I'm uncomfortable in my clothes as well as the whole situation.

'How would you define your role, then?' Williams has a smile that's all teeth and doesn't reach her eyes.

'I was first point of contact for Pe— . . . Detective Inspector Copperthwaite while he was undercover. Mostly he'd text me updates, occasionally phone. I was cleared to go to the office if necessary. We'd built an identity for me too should it be needed.'

Williams takes a moment to process this, ticks something off in her own notepad as the unnamed constable writes it all down. It's quite unnecessary. Everything's being recorded, after all.

'What was your relationship with Detective Inspector Copperthwaite?' Williams keeps her tone flat as she asks the question, but I can see the meaning behind it writ large across the constable's face. He's younger than me, early twenties if I'm any good at guessing. He knows how old I am, how old Pete was, and he's heard the station gossip. Is he shocked? Wondering what Pete had that he could hook a young thing like me? What kind of person I am who'd fuck a senior officer in the hope of an easy promotion? I know nothing about this young constable, not even his name, and yet he's so certain he knows everything about me.

'He was my boss. He gave me orders, I carried them out.'

Williams raises an eyebrow, the first readable tic I've seen on her face since the interview started. 'You worked together for a long time. Both of you moved over from the old unit when it was closed down.'

'As did half of the station, ma'am.' I hold her gaze. This whole set-up is meant to be intimidating, put me on the defensive, but I am utterly calm. I know I've done nothing wrong, but I also don't care if they try to throw the book at me. What's the worst that can happen? They can sack me, but I'm not going to jail for this. I'd be there already if they thought I was guilty of anything serious.

'Look, ma'am. I know what people say about me and Pete. Frankly I expected better from Professional Standards than just listening to the station gossip.'

The smile never falters as Williams ticks off something else in her book. 'Actually, this interview is only one small part of the investigation into DI Copperthwaite's death. Station gossip, as you so eloquently put it, is another. There are many strands to unravel before I get to the bottom of this, but one of them is determining whether there was more to your relationship than is professional. That would be a breach of conduct, after all.'

'Well, you can satisfy yourself on that score. Despite what a lot of ill-informed people might say, Pete and I were just friends.'

Another tick. 'So you wouldn't have any reason to blow his cover by making an unscheduled visit to the office where he was working, then.'

I can smell the smoke, see the blood and brains on the wall, the lifeless eyes and that horrible red spot. 'I've told Detective Superintendent Bailey, and it's in the statement I gave to DCI Bain, which I'm sure you've already read. I went to the office because Pete texted me asking me to. The phone records are all there to see. It wasn't a scheduled visit, but it wasn't unprecedented either.'

'I'm aware of the text. That's not the unscheduled visit I'm referring to.' Williams nods to the constable, who slides a sheet of paper from the back of his notebook, unfolds it and passes it to me. It takes me a moment to work out what it is: a list of numbers, dates and times arranged in a grid. A log of entry codes used to open the back door to the office, alongside the names of the officers allocated them. The back door I'd found unlocked and slightly ajar. The last number on the list is horribly familiar, but the date and time make no sense.

'I don't understand this. I couldn't have input that number at that time. I was here, in the office, in a meeting.'

'That much I know. Detective Superintendent Bailey and half a dozen officers have confirmed as much. Some more grudgingly than others, I'd add.' Williams speaks in a monotone, her body almost motionless. It's a very effective technique for putting someone on their guard.

'So how do you explain it?' I say. 'Someone faked the records?'

'I don't need to explain it, Detective Constable. You do. Perhaps you could start by telling me who allocated the different entry codes.'

I cast my mind back to the start of the operation, the endless meetings with IT nerds and surveillance geeks. 'Technical Services set the whole place up. There should be CCTV of the back yard too. Surely you can just look at that to see who used my code.'

'Do you think I'd be here if it was that simple?'

'Oh God. You're joking, right? Someone got to the cameras too?'

'Detective Constable Fairchild, Professional Standards are not in the habit of making jokes.' Williams puts her pen down carefully on top of her open notebook, looks me straight in the eye. 'In many ways it would have been easier if you and Detective Inspector Copperthwaite had been . . . romantically linked. It would have been a disciplinary matter, of course, but nothing more serious than that. You'd be back on active duty by next week. Earlier even. As it is, I can no longer eliminate you from the inquiry into how the operation was so badly compromised. You will remain on indefinite suspension, and I've no doubt the team investigating DI Copperthwaite's death will be wanting to speak to you too.'

9

Chief Inspector Williams's words echo in my head as I walk down the corridor away from the interview room alone. I can't blame her for doing her job, but someone's set me up big time. The story they're trying to paint's easy enough to see, me and Pete using the undercover operation to pursue some kind of clandestine affair. Somehow in our passion I forgot to follow protocol, and didn't lock the back door properly. The gang we're after found out Pete's a cop, tortured him for information and then shot him. Really sad, such a good cop, such potential for great things, blah blah blah. Stupid woman for letting her ambition and emotion get the better of her. It certainly explains why everyone in the team's treating me like I've got herpes all of a sudden.

The only problem is that none of it's true.

So what is true, then? Start treating this like an investigation, Con. Get together as many facts as you can before they either sack you or lock you up. I need to find someone on my side, but how? Everywhere I look I see that same expression of anger. They all think I did it. Maybe not actually pulled the trigger, but as good as.

I've always been a bit of a loner, I guess. It maybe doesn't help that I come from a posh background. Sure, I've knocked the corners off my accent, and I can swear with the best of them, but I've never really been part of the family. It's only now that he's gone, now that he's the root of the problem, that I realise how much Pete was my only friend here.

That doesn't mean there aren't other channels I can use. Police Sergeant Barry Thomas might be a bit of an old-school misogynist bastard with wandering hands and a prickly beard, but he's also the union rep in the station. If I'm going to be the target of a witch hunt, he's at least meant to be the one holding the key to the pitchfork shed.

'Wondered when you'd show up here.'

It's not the sympathetic greeting I'd hoped for, but at least he's speaking to me. As union rep, Sergeant Thomas has an office, and usually its door is open. I make a show of closing it behind me, but remain standing when he indicates the seat on the wrong side of his desk.

'What they're saying about me, about Pete. It's all lies.'

Thomas leans back in his chair and folds his arms across his chest. 'Pretty much thought that's what you'd say. The evidence doesn't look good though, does it?'

'What evidence? It's all circumstantial. Far as I can tell the only thing that points at me is the entry code log on the back door. We didn't choose those codes ourselves, we were given them. Mine would have been easy for someone to find out if they wanted to.'

'If you've done nothing wrong, you've nothing to worry about, then, have you?' Thomas unfolds his arms, leans forward as if trying to be comradely. 'Look, it's a very serious situation. I know that, you know that. Pete's . . . Pete was well liked and people are hurting. Give it time, lass. The truth will out and it'll all blow over.'

I can hardly believe what I'm hearing. I can feel a lump tightening in my throat, tears pricking the corners of my eyes. 'Blow over? For fuck's sake. Pete's dead. And what? I'm just supposed to man up and take it on the chin while everyone else works out their grief on me? That's the sum total of support I can expect from the union, is it? Sold down the river just to keep everyone else happy? Well, fuck that shit.'

Sergeant Thomas is on his feet almost before I've stopped shouting, his face red with anger to match my own. 'You want my advice, Fairchild? Then keep a lid on your martyr complex. I don't care how shitty you think it is. You're on suspension, so go home and take it easy. Let the process run its course and don't go screaming "unfair" like a spoiled rich kid.'

It's the last barb that tells me I'm on to a loser here. Stupid bloody emotions are making me irrational too, and the last thing I want to do is confirm everyone's suspicions that I'm just some hysterical woman. I take a deep breath and try to suppress the anger that makes me want to scream and break things.

'Fine. I'll do as you say. For now. But there's some serious shit going on here and if no one else is going to take it seriously, then I will.'

Thomas looks like he's going to say something else, but right now I don't want to hear it. I turn away from him, take two steps to the door, yank it open and leave. If he utters any more words at my back, they're lost to my seething rage.

'Oh, hello, Con. Thought you were home already.'

Mrs Feltham's on the stairs again when I get home, still quietly seething at the way I've been treated. This time she's got a well-thumbed paperback book and a big mug of coffee that smells divine. I know she roasts her own beans and makes it using some secret method passed down from mother to daughter over generations. I'd ask her how she does it, but I think she'd feel bad refusing to tell me. Then what she's just said sinks in.

'Actually I didn't think I'd be home for hours yet. What made you think I was here already?'

'I don't know. Just felt like there was someone upstairs, you know? Maybe I heard something? Didn't really think much of it.'

'No worries, eh?' I go to step past her, nervous now. Has someone broken in? Did I remember to close all the windows before I left this morning?

'Oh, thanks for the curry, by the way.' I'm about to lie and say it was delicious, even though it's still sitting in my fridge uneaten, but the frown on her face stops me.

'You don't eat proper, you gonna waste away, child. Get some meat on them bones or no man's going to want you.'

I smile, not sure whether Mrs Feltham's winding me up or not. It's nice that somebody cares though, even if she's just the old lady who lives in the apartment beneath mine. There's nothing happens in this block and she doesn't know about it though, which is why her thinking I was home already bothers me. I dart up the stairs before she can say anything more, hurry to my front door. Something's not right. Well, everything's not right, but this feels particularly wrong. I pause at the front door, wondering whether I should call for backup, listening as hard as I can for any sound that there's someone inside. I can hear only the noise of the city, the distant wailing of sirens and a radio blaring sickly pop music out of a nearby open window. The door looks no different to how it has always been: faded blue paint, chipped around the keyhole, scuffed kickplate and scratched handle. I'm being stupid, letting the events of the past few days get the better of my imagination. And how much worse would it look for me if I called this in only to find it was nothing?

It's cool inside, the air moving in a gentle draft from the open bedroom door across the hall. I remember opening all the windows last night to try and dispel some of the heat, but I was sure I'd closed them all this morning before leaving. Then again, I was distracted by the upcoming interview. Did I forget to go back and close the one in the bedroom? Shutting the front door,

I listen again, but the flat doesn't feel like there's someone else in here. There's a lingering scent though. Not a person, but something else I can't place.

I pick up the big old golf umbrella that lives in the hall, look around without moving. The flat isn't big, and I can see into the living room: no obvious sign that anyone's been there. Across the way the kitchen's as messy as ever; a burglar could probably turn the place over and I'd not notice. If anyone's hiding behind a door waiting to pounce on me, they're being very quiet.

Two steps take me to the bathroom door. I nudge it open with a foot, feeling more foolish with each passing moment. The bedroom door's partly open and I can see my unmade bed. I can't remember not throwing the duvet back over the sheets this morning, but I can't remember actually doing it either. The smell is stronger here though, sharp, almost like cigarette smoke, but distant. No, more like a struck match.

I push the door open, step inside, let out the breath I've been holding as I see there's no one here. The thin curtain riffles in a gentle breeze, so I must have forgotten to close the window. The smell is probably from outside, someone lighting up a couple of floors down.

Except there's something odd about the bed.

I haven't made it, but that's not unusual. The duvet's rucked up in the middle of the mattress, half covering the pillows, and for a moment I think there's someone sleeping there. Then I notice the marks on the patterned cover, dark spots like holes in the faded fabric.

My umbrella seems an ineffectual weapon as I reach out for the duvet with my free hand, poke a stupid finger into one of the holes. All at once I know what the smell is.

Brimstone.

Cordite.

Gunfire.

I'm still staring at the cover in disbelief when the folds shift, something moving beneath. I leap back in alarm, may even let out a little girl's squeal of surprise. Get a grip of yourself, Con. You're a grown woman. I reach for the bottom of the duvet, well away from the two black holes, and flip it over to the side of the bed.

Something long and black lies in the little dent in the mattress made by many years of my sleeping there. I can see one small hole beside it, where the bullet has passed clean through and presumably into the floor underneath the bed. The other one's nowhere to be seen. For a moment I can't understand why someone would put a dead cat in my bed, and then the poor beast moves again.

I drop the umbrella and lean over. That's when I see the other bullet hole, tinged with a small stain of dark-red blood, and a chunk missing from the cat's ear. I don't own a cat, although there's plenty that live around here. Some have homes to go to, but most are feral, I'd guess. Judging by the general condition of this one, and its lack of collar, I'd go with the latter option. It's fairly obvious what's happened. I must have forgotten the window when I left in the morning. This poor moggie's found its way in and crawled under the covers for a kip.

Then someone's put two bullets through the duvet thinking I'm still in there asleep.

10

'**D**on't think this is going to get you any sympathy from Professional Standards. You know that's not how they work.'

My tiny apartment is full of police officers and forensic technicians. Knowing that someone's been in here while I was out is bad enough, but this is a special kind of violation. I've worked with some of these people, and probably wouldn't have chosen to invite them around to my place for a coffee. Least of all Detective Superintendent Gordon Bailey. I'm frankly astonished that he's turned up, but I guess I'm on his radar right now. Either that or he's naturally nosey.

'What's all this fuss about anyway? I heard someone left a dead cat in your bed. Not sure we need all of this, do we?' He's standing in the hall, getting in the way of the fingerprint specialist and the firearms residue expert. Someone should have told him to put on a white paper coverall, but maybe they saw I wasn't wearing one and just assumed it wasn't important enough a crime scene to warrant it.

'First of all, sir, the cat's not dead. Someone from the RSPCA's taken it off to the vets. Second, it wasn't put in my bed. I reckon it must have crawled there itself, looking for somewhere to have a kip. Must have got in through the window.'

'You're a police officer.' Bailey manages to put a great deal of uncertainty in such a small observation. 'I'd have thought you'd know better than to leave a window open.'

I ball my hands into fists out of sight. The man's impossible. 'I know that, sir. Must have been a bit distracted this morning when I left for my interview with PS. The point you seem to be missing is that someone broke in here and fired two bullets into my bed, thinking I was lying there asleep.'

Bailey couldn't look less concerned if he tried. 'Not much of a hitman if he can't tell the difference between a sleeping woman and a cat.'

How I stop myself from lamping him, I've no idea. I always knew the man was a prize arse, but just because he doesn't much like me doesn't make it any less of an attempted murder. So soon after they killed Pete too, anyone with an ounce of sense would be all over this.

'You know how cheap it is to put a hit out on someone these days, sir. Any halfwit can get hold of a gun too. What I don't know is how the fuck they found out where I live.'

'Well, at least we know how they got in.' He finally moves, brushing past me and stepping into my crowded bedroom. It was a mess before forensics got here, but now it's chaos. Clear plastic evidence bags are filled with my duvet, sheets, pillows and some underwear that was lurking in the corner on its way to the laundry bin. Now a couple of technicians are studying the bare mattress. I've a horrible feeling they're either going to take it away for tests or cut out the bit they want to take away for tests and leave me with the rest.

'Give us a hand, will you?' one of the white-suited technicians asks me, nodding towards the mattress. I hesitate just long enough to annoy him. 'Need to turn it on its side. See what's underneath, right?'

I know what's underneath, but I help him all the same. The bed's an old wooden frame thing I picked up from a modern antiques place in Pimlico. One of the bullets has splintered a wooden slat passing through, but the other must have met the gap. Both have disappeared into a mess of old clothes and dust bunnies.

'Never seems to be time to tidy,' I say as the forensic technician draws in a sharp breath. I stand back as he carefully picks up my discarded tops, a pair of white jeans I'd forgotten I even owned, some underwear that at least isn't too kinky. He inspects every item closely, and though he says nothing I can hear the tutting anyway. He has to do it, of course. The bullets could be anywhere.

As it turns out, they're both buried in the floor. The technician goes down on all fours, prising at the carpet with a pair of tweezers, and comes back with a tiny lump of metal that once might have been a bullet. He drops it into a plastic evidence bag, I hope to be sent to the lab for analysis so they can identify the gun. The second bullet goes in another bag, then he stands up, back creaking as he stretches.

'Must've been using a cheap sound modifier or something. Took most of the force out of the bullets. The mattress will have done the rest.' The technician turns, points at Bailey. 'Judging by the trajectory, your man was somewhere by the window there, popped off two rounds and legged it. You sure the door was locked?'

'Positive.' I shove my hand in my pocket, pull out my keys. 'Had to use these to get in.'

The technician hobbles over to the window, pushes it as wide as it will go, and peers out. I don't need to follow him to know that it's a long drop onto a concrete path. There's a flat roof at the back of the next building just a bit higher than here, but the distance is too far to jump, surely. You'd have to be an acrobat to even contemplate it. Either that or mad. On the other hand the cat got in.

'Christ only knows how, but your man must have come in

this way. Probably off his face on something. If he'd gone out the way he came in we'd be scraping him off the path down there, so he must have scarpered out the front door.'

Back at the station I thought I'd left for good. I'm getting used to all the strange looks now, even if I still want to yell at everyone to fuck off and get on with their jobs. I thought some of these people were my friends, which just goes to show you never really know someone until you need their help.

Pete would have been on top of the situation. He'd have seen what was going on and had quiet words with the worst of the station gossips. He knew how to keep a team together even when one of them wasn't exactly Miss Popular.

But Pete's dead. And everyone blames me.

'Are you even listening to me, Fairchild?'

I register the change in Detective Superintendent Bailey's voice too late to fake it. 'Sorry, sir. It's been a long day and I—'

'You're a bloody disgrace, that's what you are. I don't know what Copperthwaite saw in you.'

That gets my back up. 'Disgrace? What the fuck are you talking about?'

'Don't take that tone of voice with me, Constable.' Bailey's anger flares as swiftly as my own, and I wonder what's fuelling it. He's lost a good detective, true, and a major operation's been flushed down the toilet, but this seems more personal than that.

'I'll take whatever tone of voice I fucking like, sir.' I lay extra emphasis on the last word. 'Ever since Pete's death I've been treated like shit. Like it was my fault. Like I was the only person working on that operation. Fuck's sake. How many other officers have been hauled up in front of Professional Standards? How many are suspended? Someone tried to fucking kill me this morning and all I get is "You're a bloody disgrace". Well, fuck that and the horse it rode in on.'

Bailey's always looked a bit like a toad, but now his eyes are bulging so far out of his face I think he's going to burst. I tense, ready for the shouting, but when he finally responds it's with a quiet, calm voice. That's somehow more frightening than the anger.

'You're suspended and under investigation because you're the only person who could have blown DI Copperthwaite's cover. You're the only person who's acted suspiciously since his death.'

For a moment I can't speak. Have I fallen through some weird time warp into a mad mirror dimension? Am I actually dreaming and soon I'll wake up and blame it all on late-night cheese? This man somehow managed to scrabble up the greasy pole to detective superintendent and yet his head is rammed so far up his own arse I'm surprised he can't see the back of his teeth.

'Someone tried to kill me today, sir. Just a day on from Pete's funeral. Please tell me you're at least going to have that looked into. Or do you think I set the whole thing up myself?'

Bailey stares at me like a man waiting for his constipation medicine to kick in, and I can't help thinking I've just planted an idea in his mind that wasn't there before.

'Of course we're going to investigate it. I don't like the idea of someone thinking they can take potshots at my officers, no matter how much of an irritant they are. We'll wait and see what forensics comes up with before jumping to any conclusions though.'

'At least tell me you're going to put a couple of officers on the door. In case whoever did this comes back for a second go.'

The pause before his answer isn't reassuring. 'I can't authorise that kind of manpower. You'll have a panic alarm and we'll get the patrols to concentrate on that area of town for the next few days. You're not going anywhere anyway. Maybe you'll remember to keep your windows closed now.'

11

I don't really want to go home. Forensics have been and gone, the locksmith's fitted a new lock and I know all the windows are closed. All the same, I can't help but feel exposed as I climb the concrete stairs to the second-floor walkway. Exposed and angry.

I stare out into the street for a while, hoping to see one of the promised patrol cars, but nothing appears. Who's out there? Who wants to kill me and why? Even Mrs Feltham's nowhere to be seen, and I miss her cheery hello. One hand in my pocket, I can feel the panic alarm nestling there like the useless piece of junk it is. Sure, if I press the button a patrol car will come rescue me. Chances are I'll be dead long before it gets here though.

There's plenty of light left in the evening as I fumble for the unfamiliar keys and let myself in. The flat feels all wrong, and not just because there are traces of fingerprint powder everywhere. This was my home for years, my refuge, and now that's all been taken away. I know it's just a transient feeling, part shock, part my brain dealing with all that's happened. Knowing it will pass doesn't make it any easier.

My trusty umbrella sits by the front door, and I pick it up as I drop my backpack in its place, hang my jacket on a hook. I draw the living room curtains before turning on the light. I wouldn't normally bother, but the insecurity is playing on my mind. The television isn't any solace as I flick listlessly through the endless channels of rubbish. Soap operas and reality TV, game shows where hopeful idiots vie with one another to see who can be most public in their stupidity. In the end, I stop on a wildlife documentary. Not because I particularly want to watch it, but because it's not as vacuous as everything else. David Attenborough's voice is soothing too.

'You don't need to stay here, you know?'

I should be startled by the voice, but instead I'm strangely calm. Over in the far corner I can see a man, his face shadowed, body still. I'd know him anyway, even if he hadn't spoken.

I mute the television, even though the volume is set low. 'Where would I go, Pete? I need to get through this. Find out who killed you. Who tried to kill me.'

He shakes his head slowly. I can't see his features at all.

'No you don't, Con. Nothing good will come of that.'

'So, what? I should just move on? Quit the force and find a rich man to marry?'

I can hear his silent laughter, the gentle chiding that was always his way. 'Why on earth would you want to do that? You hate all that stuff. Don't give in to it. Think about what you love.'

He's annoying when he's like this, but he's right. Accentuate the positive, as the song goes. Except there's one small fly in that ointment. 'But I love my job. I love helping people, setting the world to rights.'

'You don't need to be a cop to do that. Plenty other lines of work you could be in. And you've got training, hard-earned skills. Use them, why don't you?'

I don't know why I laugh at that. He's not really here, after all. This is just my guilty conscience talking. 'You mean go and work for your ex?'

'Maybe.' Pete's shadow shrugs. 'Or maybe just yourself. Think about it, Con. You don't owe those bastards anything. Except maybe a constructive dismissal claim.'

He has a point. I don't owe them. If anything, they owe me. But all I've got from them is suspicion and cold shoulder. That and the panic alarm I've left in my jacket pocket out in the hall where it's fuck all use to anyone. Maybe I should take his advice, make good on my threat to quit. Go and do something else with my life before I get too old to change.

I open my mouth to tell Pete's ghost he's right, but the light has changed in the room and now he's gone.

The door buzzer startles me out of a state of semi-stupor, Pete's parting words still echoing in my mind. I'm slumped in the armchair, umbrella across my knees as if it's the best possible weapon against intruders with guns. The television is still silent, but judging by the images flickering across the screen, turning up the volume wouldn't be an improvement. I wonder for a moment if I just imagined the noise, but then it goes again.

I approach the front door warily. The only way to see who's outside is to peer through the peephole, and that puts my body in the perfect position to be shot through the door. Christ, Con. When did you get so paranoid?

'Who is it?' The umbrella is still clutched in my right hand, raised as threateningly as a rolled up umbrella can be.

'RSPCA, mum. I've got yer cat.'

It's perhaps a sign of my poor state of mind that the thing that most annoys me is being called 'mum'. I take a chance and glance through the peephole. Sure enough, there's the young man who took the stunned cat away to the vet. I thought that would be the last I saw of either of them, but apparently not. Putting the umbrella down carefully by the door, I unlock it and open it wide. He's standing back a way, holding on to a black plastic pet carrier.

'I think there's been some kind of mistake. This isn't my cat.'

'You sure of that, mum? Picked it up here, din't I?' He hefts the carrier up, and inside I can see the poor creature staring at me with wide eyes. It's not that I don't like animals. We had cats and dogs when I was growing up, even a couple of ponies when I was a teenager, but I grew out of that quickly enough. Living in London and working the hours I do, it wouldn't be fair to have a pet.

'I know you picked it up here, but it's not my cat. It must have come in through the window. No idea who it belongs to.'

The young man's face drops in disappointment. He gently raises the pet carrier and peers in through the bars. 'Might explain why she ain't chipped, then. I was gonna suggest you get that done, but if she's not yours . . .' He lets the cage down gently again, shoulders slumped as much in dismay as from the weight of it.

'Sorry. I thought you knew when you picked her up.' I'm aware this doorstep conversation has been going on longer than I'd have liked, but I don't really want to invite a stranger in, even if he is clearly not a threat. 'She, you say? I had no idea. She'll be OK though? Someone'll claim her?'

'Don't rightly know.' He lets out a heavy sigh. 'No chip means we can't track her owner through the database. She'll go in the pen for now, but rehoming adults is a nightmare. Everyone wants kittens, right? And nobody wants black ones.'

'What happens if you can't find a new home for her?' I know the answer but ask the question anyway.

'She'll be put to sleep. Can't just let her loose, even if that's where she's come from.'

The cat takes that moment to move in the carrier. Either she's naturally placid or still drugged, but as her eyes peer through the front of the pet carrier I can see they've shaved a square of fur and stitched up her wound. One of her ears is split, although whether that was from the bullet or some earlier fight I've no idea. When she looks up at me with those wide, round eyes, I can't help but think my own problems are small in comparison.

'I'll look after her.' The words are out before I've begun to consider their implications. The young RSPCA officer's eyebrows shoot up in surprise.

'You will. But I thought—?'

'You thought she belonged to me, right? So who's to know she doesn't?' I glance down at the pet carrier again. Going to need to get one of them for myself. And a litter tray. And cat food. What the hell are you doing, Con? You don't need a cat. You can't have a cat. The lease on the flat says no animals.

'Well, if you're sure. It'd make things a lot easier.'

I'm not sure. Not sure at all. But I make the decision anyway, step to one side so he can come inside.

'It's the least I can do, really. Reckon she took a bullet intended for me, so I kind of owe her my life.'

You never have to go far in London to find a shop selling the stuff you need. Just as well, since I didn't know I needed cat food, a litter tray and litter until about half an hour ago. There's one of those retail units a mile or so from my flat, with a line of chain outlets and a far too small car park shoved into an old industrial site the council obviously decided was too contaminated for housing. A supermarket on the other side of the main road brings the punters in, and enough of them need to buy electrical goods, cheap clothes and pet food to justify the existence of small warehouses catering to each of them. I've never been in any of the shops before, but you can't miss them, especially on a Saturday morning when the traffic clogs up the high street.

I'm not quite sure how I feel about acquiring a cat just now. It's not something I'd have chosen, and yet the poor beast looked so downcast when the young man from the RSPCA let her out of her cage in my living room. She slunk around for a minute or so, crouched so low to the carpet I thought she was going to mess it. Then she more clambered than leaped into the armchair I'd been sitting in, turned around a couple of times and settled down to sleep. Apparently the sedatives she'd been given while they were stitching up her wounds would take a while to wear off, which gave me just enough time to pop out.

It's all too easy to spend money in these places. A new carry cage, bag of litter and a tray, selection of dry and wet foods, dish to serve them in, collar and a couple of toys – because why the hell not? – and soon enough I'm handing over fifty quid to the cheery-faced teenage girl at the tills. She tries to engage me in conversation, but I'm not in the mood.

Weighed down by my newly purchased cat-loot, I almost don't notice the car parked on the wrong side of the street, right outside my apartment block. It's a stretch limousine, but not the kind you usually get around here, with drunken hen party girls hanging out of the windows and screaming at the passers-by. This is a businessman's car, shiny, black and expensive. I've got my hoodie on, and clearly the two muscle-bound oafs in suits aren't looking for the bag lady I must resemble. Their gaze glides over me as I shuffle past on the opposite pavement. A hundred yards down the road, I cut across and around the back of the block and knock lightly on Mrs Feltham's door.

'You in some kinda trouble girl.' She beckons me into her tidy hallway, closing the door swiftly behind me. I can't help but notice it's not a question.

'Expensive car out there? Two goons in suits?' I jerk my head in the direction of the road.

'They gone to all the flats in this block now. Banging on the doors like they debt collectors or something. Heard them talking to Mr Johnston at number two there. They were asking for you, girl. Only they don't use your name. They just say nice police lady. He told them he don't know nothing about no police and sent them on their way. What you gotten yourself mixed up in now?'

'I wish I knew, Mrs F. It's nothing good though. I can tell you that.'

'Well, you can wait here till they gone. You see them from the front room here. No lights on, they don't see you back.'

She leads me through to a darkened room, the window covered with a lace curtain. Twitching it aside affords me a clear view of the street, just in time to see the suits get back into the car and drive off. I watch the tail lights as they brake at the corner and then disappear from view.

'You want a coffee while you wait?' Mrs Feltham asks. I'm sorely tempted; her coffee is very fine indeed and the chances of me sleeping tonight are minuscule anyway. I don't need to bring whatever trouble's seeking me down on her head though.

'No. Thank you, Mrs F., but I should go.'

She looks disappointed, although that might just be the way the street lamps cast insufficient light on her dark features. 'You know best, girl. But if you ever need anything, you just ask, right? I won't stand for no hoodlums messing with the people in my block now.'

Back in the hallway, I scoop up my bags. Mrs Feltham says nothing about the cat litter and carrying box, but insists on stepping outside to check the coast is clear before seeing me off. I scurry away up the concrete steps like an overburdened land crab, hardly daring to breathe until I'm safely back in my flat, the door locked and bolted behind me.

'What the fuck is going on?' I ask the darkness. It doesn't answer, but hearing my own voice calms my nerves a little. I can't keep running and hiding for ever. Maybe it's time to start acting like a detective again.

12

The cat stares at me with supreme indifference as I pace back and forward in front of the television. I could just be imagining it; that car might have a perfectly legitimate reason to be loitering around here. Yeah, and the couple of heavies Mrs F. saw were probably just Jehovah's Witnesses too.

I've got the number plate though. Normally I'd call it in and get the details of who it belongs to. But that would start a paper trail that would lead back to Bailey. Chances are I'm already registered on the system as suspended. Not worth taking the risk of yet another bollocking. Likewise I can't see much point in calling it in to the station. They all think I'm either nuts or bent, or both.

So I guess I'll just have to do this the old-fashioned way.

There's a couple of pubs near here I reckon I'm safe enough to go into even if someone's out to get me. Sticking to public places is probably the best idea anyway, but I need to find out what the hell's going on. And that means talking to the sort of people who don't answer phone calls from police officers, suspended or not.

'You going to be OK if I just pop out?' I ask the cat. She looks up from my chair, eyes still droopy from the anaesthetic, then tucks her head around and goes back to sleep. I can see we're going to get on just fine. Grabbing a coat and my keys, I leave the flat, making sure to lock the door properly behind me.

I don't hold out much hope for the Three Tuns. It's a dive, frequented by the local lowlife, but they're slowly being edged out by the young affluent Londoners who've decided this little corner of the city is the new place to be. I shouldn't be so dismissive, really. I'm one of them, after all, except for the affluent bit. I grab a drink anyway, more money going out and no good idea how much longer I'm going to have a wage. I'm not exactly skint, but rent takes up more than its fair share of even a detective constable's earnings in this city.

The evening's not got started properly yet, which works to my advantage. The afternoon drinkers are still here, the old men who make their money where they can and spend it on the lonely camaraderie of bars like this one. I glance at each in turn as I make my way from bar to small table by the door, but none of them are who I'm looking for. None of them pay me much heed either, which is a good sign. I take my time over my drink, watching for anyone making surreptitious phone calls to tip off some unidentified mob boss as to my whereabouts, but all they do is get up, one by one, and shuffle to the door for a smoke or the loo for a piss.

I don't get any joy in the Green Man, and switch to soft drinks at the Wellington Arms. The evening's wearing on and I'm getting desperate, which is why I chance my luck with the Ivy. Not to be confused with its posh namesake in the city centre, this place is a dark and forbidding basement, low-ceilinged and with its one light-well window painted out. Several televisions play different sports channels, and I know that many an illegal bet is placed here, away from the eyes of the law. It's also the place I should have come first; I'd have wasted a lot less time that way, and might have avoided using the rather unsavoury toilets.

Wee Jock probably has a surname, but it's been lost in the distant past. Actually, I don't think Jock's his real name anyway,

NO TIME TO CRY

but he's Scottish and small, so he's Wee Jock. Nicknames can be crueller.

I spot him almost as soon as I walk in, lurking in the corner and nursing a pint of something dark. He doesn't acknowledge my presence, but I know he's seen me as I lean against the bar. I order a couple of pints of Guinness, one for him, one for me. I don't really want it, but there's some things you have to do if you want people to be cooperative. This is a pub where men drink, so anything less than a pint's not going to cut it.

'Surprised to see you in here, lassie.' Jock barely catches my eye as I push the chair opposite him aside with my foot, place our drinks on the table and sit down. He claims his pint though, gnarled old fingers wrapping possessively around the glass.

'Not my usual watering hole, I'll admit. Still, hard times make for hard choices.'

'Heard about that DI of yours. Not good.' He's still not meeting my eye, but he shakes his greying head all the same.

'Any idea who did it?'

'Also heard you'd got yourself suspended.' He ignores my question. 'Pretty sure that means you're not meant to be talking to me.'

I take a sip of my beer. It's cold and wet, and tastes of burnt toast.

'You always were good at keeping an ear to the ground, Jock. You hear anything about someone wanting me dead?'

Finally he raises his head and looks straight at me. I've no idea how old he is, could be forty and had a hard life, could be pushing seventy. His face is lined, slightly grubby and sporting a couple of days' worth of grey stubble. His eyes are bloodshot and yellowing, and when he opens his mouth there's more gaps than blackened teeth. He probably smells like a tramp, but this pub's so foul it's hard to tell where the stench comes from.

'Way I hear it, there's a price on your head, aye. Someone

reckons you saw too much. Don't matter if you did, ken?'

'Who?' I know as soon as I ask it that he's not going to answer that.

'It's no' enough cash for any serious players. No' yet anyways.'

'What do you mean?'

'Means only an idiot would try to cash in right now. But see, if the price went up, mind . . .' He trails off, eyes focusing past me to something else in the pub. I resist the urge to turn around and look, even though that leaves my back vulnerable.

'Is that likely?' It's not often I catch Wee Jock in a talkative mood, so I'm going to get as much from him as I can.

'Mebbe. And mebbe some young loon'll have a go just to prove hisself.' Jock lifts his pint, drains it in a succession of deep gulps, his Adam's apple bobbing with each one. He thumps the empty glass down on the table, wipes foam from his mouth with the back of his hand, then nods towards the bar. 'I've a powerful need to be somewhere else right now, lassie. Reckon you might too.'

I look around as Jock struggles to his feet and sidles out from the table. A couple of young lads are talking to the barman. He's taking his time to serve them, and I get the distinct feeling he's keeping them distracted while the old man departs. Will he keep them occupied until I can get away too?

'You want my advice, lassie? Get out of Dodge. Far away as you can.' Jock lays a heavy hand on my shoulder as he squeezes past, pushing me towards the opposite end of the pub to where I came in. 'Back door's that way.'

The back way out of the pub's through a door marked 'Staff Only'. I take it anyway, and nobody seems to notice as I step through into a narrow corridor piled high with boxes full of bottles of spirits. A fire escape puts me in a dark alley running parallel with the main street, home to wheelie bins and a couple of parked cars. I half expected Wee Jock to follow me, but he must have gone the other way. Not sure why he and the barman are protecting me, if that's what they're doing. More likely Jock doesn't want to be seen talking to a cop, and the barman probably doesn't need the hassle of cleaning blood off the furniture, or the unwanted attention having someone shot in his pub would bring. Still, I'm not going to look this gift horse too closely in the mouth right now.

It's a tense few minutes walking down the alley and round onto the main road. I'm glad of my hoodie and the anonymity it gives me as I join the flow of people going about their business as if none of them had a price on their head. I feel safer in a crowd, but only a bit. Every young man with his hands in his pockets and slouched against a bus stop, a shop entrance or a street bin is a potential killer. I'm sure I'm being followed, even though my training and experience tell me that's not the case. Paranoia will get you that way.

The walk home takes longer than it should as I constantly double back, plot a route that will keep me in busy, well-lit areas. I wish I'd paid more attention to the locations of all the CCTV cameras in this part of town, but they wouldn't be much help if someone decided to attack me. I should really call it in, let someone know what I've discovered. Hard to believe they don't know it already though. If Wee Jock was willing to speak to me, someone else's informant will have spoken to them too.

So why aren't I being given protection? Why have I been fobbed off with a panic alarm and a promise of a patrol car outside my flat once an hour?

That thought stays with me all the way home, bothering me almost as much as all the other ways I've been shafted by my so-called colleagues since Pete's death. I can't forget my angry conversation with Detective Superintendent Bailey this afternoon, his none-too-guarded suggestion that I was responsible for what happened to Pete, maybe even pulled the trigger myself. I know that's not true, so why can't he see it? Unless he's protecting someone else. Shit, maybe that's why I'm being sidelined, because they're worried I might be onto something. But Bailey? He's a detective superintendent, for Christ's sake. He can't be bent.

What the fuck have I stumbled into?

Normally a long walk helps to calm me down when I'm angry, but this time it just stokes the flames of fury. I know the world's a shit place and fair is just a lie we peddle to children for a second of peace and quiet, but you'd expect a little bit of sympathy from fellow police officers, a little bit of understanding. Get out of Dodge, Wee Jock said. He's a scumbag criminal, minor gang member and probably responsible for many an unsolved disappearance down the years, but I can't help thinking he's right. And he's been far more helpful than any of my colleagues in the Met. Go figure.

The expensive car is long gone when I finally make it home, no sign that it was ever even here. Evening has surrendered to night, the sky as dark overhead as it ever gets in the city. I climb the concrete steps slowly, ears straining for any sign that someone is following, or lying in wait. I don't think anyone is lurking up on the walkway, but then my Spidey sense never fully developed no matter how much I wished it would when I read my brother's comics as a kid. There's no point putting this off any longer. If they're up there, then I'm just going to have to deal with them.

I thumb the screen on my phone until the camera comes to life, making sure the flash is enabled. It's dark up there, so a sudden bright light should put me at an advantage over any would-be assailant. Taking the steps slowly, I crouch low and use the concrete rail as a barrier, keeping out of sight until the last possible moment. I needn't have worried; there's no one on the walkway, no one hiding in the stairwell to the top floor.

Relieved, I hurry to my front door, shoving my phone in my pocket as I scrabble for the new keys. There's an odd chemical smell to the air that brings me up short, like industrial solvent. It prickles the corners of my eyes, and for a moment I can't work out where it's coming from.

And then I see it, plain as the day. A wide X painted across my front door in aerosol spray. Still wet, the red paint drips slowly down the faded blue like blood from a slit throat.

13

A cat carrier box is surprisingly heavy when it's got a cat in it. I managed to coax the beast in without too much difficulty; I think she likes the security of it, although it's equally possible the bullet that grazed her skull did more permanent damage. It didn't have any effect on her digestive system though, if the empty dinner dish and mound of half-buried shit in the litter tray are anything to go by. I'll likely regret having left that where it was when I go back to the flat, but at that moment all I wanted to do was gather up a change of clothes and a washbag, get the hell out of there.

And so I'm lugging this box down the street, heading somewhere I never thought I'd go to ask a favour of someone I really don't need to be beholden to. At least I'm unlikely to be recognised. Anyone out looking for me's not going to be expecting a mad cat lady.

They won't be looking for me in Elmstead Road either. It's way out of my pay grade for one thing, and the people who live here put my back up. Rich bankers, hedge fund managers, music industry leeches, people good at making money off other people's hard work. Most of the houses are huge by London standards, a mixture of semis and detached. They sit close to the pavement, suggesting large gardens at the rear. Somewhere for the Tarquins and Hermiones to play in relative safety. It's a far cry from the used-needles-and-broken-glass-strewn tarmac yard at the back of my block, even if the two aren't even a mile apart.

The address I've got is halfway down the street, where the semi-detached houses end and the larger places begin. Some of them might be split into apartments, but from the look of the front doors they're mostly single-occupier residences. You can almost smell the stench of money and I nearly turn back. Nothing can be so bad that I have to look to these kind of people for help. Then I remember the men in the pub, the blacked-out car and the red X on my front door. I don't really have any choice.

For a moment, as I stand on the doorstep waiting for the bell to be answered, I wonder what I will look like to Charlotte when she appears. A scruffy young woman in jeans and a hoodie, rucksack thrown over one shoulder and a cat carrier box in the opposite hand. Perhaps I'm enjoying her anticipated look of horror too much, as it takes me a while to realise someone else entirely has come to the door. I recognise him of course, how could I not? The look on his face suggests it's taking him a little while longer to see his own sister.

'Can I help?'

'I bloody well hope so, Ben. What the fuck are you doing here?'

'Con?' His eyebrows disappear underneath his floppy ginger fringe and he stands there motionless, mouth half open like the door.

'Who is it, sweetie?' I hear Charlotte's voice from the hall and a few pennies begin to drop. I should have seen it earlier, of course. The text, the surprise meeting in the pub, the hints in the conversation.

'How long's this been going on, then?' I lift the cat carrier up slightly, feeling the dead weight of my new responsibility as it tries to pull my shoulder from its socket. 'And are you going to invite me in or what?'

Benevolence steps back at the exact moment Charlotte appears in the hallway, and the two of them collide in best comedy fashion. My brother's always been a clumsy oaf, and making it past twenty-seven doesn't seem to have improved that much.

'Connie? Is that you?' Charlotte's smile is wide, but I can see the way her eyes track over me, the hint of distaste at the sight I must present.

'Sorry to drop by unannounced. I'm in a spot of bother and couldn't think of anywhere else to turn.' I hear my voice and wonder who's speaking. 'Spot of bother', for fuck's sake. It's like I've stumbled into a P. G. Wodehouse novel.

'Come in. Come in. Anything for Ben's sister.' Charlotte pushes my hapless brother back down the hall, opens the door fully and ushers me in. Only once the door's closed behind me does she seem to notice what I'm carrying. 'Is that a cat?'

I heave the cat carrier box up, catching sight of angry eyes in the darkness behind the bars. 'It's a long story. Couldn't leave her behind.'

Charlotte looks unconvinced, but some deeply ingrained sense of hospitality stops her from speaking her mind. Had I been Mrs Feltham, dark-skinned and common, I've no doubt I'd have been turned away. But I'm one of her clan, for all that I've tried to distance myself from it for the last ten years and more. And she's fucking my brother, so that counts for something too.

'Come through to the living room, why don't you?' She leads me down a hallway big enough to sleep a dozen illegal immigrants and into a room bigger than my entire apartment. 'Ben. Get your sister a drink.' She turns back to me. 'There's a nice Pinot in the fridge, or we've some beer if you prefer?'

'Actually, I'd kill for a coffee. Milk, no sugar.'

★ ★ ★

I know it's wrong, but I could get used to this. Charlotte's house in Elmstead Road is everything pre-teen me aspired to, after all. The only thing missing is a rich and handsome husband, but then I guess he's the one who paid for all of this. The cat – I've still no idea what else to call her – seems to like this place better than my flat too, but that might have something to do with the many half-unpacked boxes lying around. It's clear that Charlotte's not long moved in and the living room is a feline paradise. At least she's unpacked the coffee machine. Years of being catered for by the station canteen have dulled my palate; it's a revelation to enjoy a cup of something that doesn't have an aftertaste of styrofoam.

'So how did you two hook up, then?' I'm sitting on the floor beside an empty fireplace, back to a leather armchair piled high with yet more boxes. How can a thirty-year-old woman have accumulated so much stuff? Charlotte has draped herself over my brother on the matching sofa, the distance between us marked by an expensive Persian rug.

'Funny story, that.' Ben has a glass of wine, not his first of the evening. He waves it around like some theatrical prop as he speaks. 'Char had this horrible break-up with Jack going on. Messy, you know? Expensive? She's gone home to sort herself out and decides to go to the pub. You know, the Green Man?' Like I don't know the only pub in the village where I grew up. 'I was there with Joel and Christopher, and it was like this great moment of truth, you know?'

My brother is full of shit at the best of times, but this is turning into one of his taller tales. 'This how it really went, Charlotte?' I ask before he can go into full epic bard mode.

'Something like.' She pushes herself up from the couch and runs her hands through her long blonde hair. I hate to think how high-maintenance that barnet is, and what my short crop must look like to her. 'I know we were all horrible to each other when we were kids, but we're grown-ups now. There's a difference.'

The way she says it makes me wonder whether she really is, but I'm not about to protest. For the first time in days I feel reasonably relaxed, if not exactly safe. This is the last place the people who want to kill me will look. Undercover detective constables don't hang out with high-society types as a general rule. I'm still sober though, whereas both of them are at least a glass of wine the wrong side of drunk. And I can't forget the way Charlotte tracked me down. Or more accurately the way Ben pointed her in my direction.

'Why were you looking for me anyway?' I wince at the awkwardness of the question, but this isn't an interview room and these aren't suspects. They're my little brother and a girl I've known all my childhood. And there's something they really want to ask me but don't know how. Christ, I hope it's not something stupid like permission to get married.

'You remember Isobel?' Charlotte asks after a long enough pause for her to muss up her hair again.

'Izzy? Of course. Not all that easy to forget, really.'

She narrows her eyes at me with an accusing glare, and I remember the faux-scandal that rippled through the village fifteen, sixteen years ago.

'I never understood why nobody could believe she was your sister, Char. Just because your mum was – what? – forty-five when she had her.'

I've clearly said the right thing, as Charlotte relaxes, slumping back against my brother. He starts to play with her hair, and for a moment I'm filled with irrational jealousy, remembering how he used to do that to me.

'Forty-three, which isn't so old. Not nowadays anyway. But she wasn't planned. I mean, nobody plans to have a kid at that age, right? It came as a total surprise. Last thing I expected on my fifteenth birthday was to be told I was going to have a little sister.'

It all comes flooding back. The gossip, the innuendo. I only understood half of it at the time, but even I could see how much my parents and the other adults in our tight-knit little community enjoyed the frisson of scandal. Charlotte's mum and dad are much the same age as mine. She was an only child, spoiled rotten by wealthy parents. Half the village thought Izzy was Charlotte's child, but I never quite believed that. We were at school together in the months leading up to Izzy's arrival, and that's not the sort of thing you can hide. Still, no one could quite believe Mrs DeVilliers might possibly have fallen pregnant at her age. Rumour had it that Roger DeVilliers was more interested in younger flesh anyway.

Of course, there was always the possibility that Roger wasn't Izzy's father, but I'd kept that suspicion to myself. I babysat her a few times, remember her being a quiet kid, a bit sad maybe. Like with all of those people, I lost touch when I left home and joined the Met.

'She must be . . . what? Fifteen now? Sixteen?'

Charlotte nods. 'Sixteen last month. She's at Saint Bert's. Harriet House, the little swot.'

The names bring back memories, not all pleasant. I can only imagine our old school was split into six different houses to foster competitiveness among the pupils. Whoever came up with that idea was probably a man. Teenage girls are the most competitive creatures on the planet; they don't need any extra encouragement. Charlotte was in Galliard House, which was full of sporty types. Harriet girls were more cerebral, so I've no idea what I was doing there.

'The thing is, Connie, she's gone AWOL, walkabout. Whatever.'

Charlotte says it so matter-of-factly that at first I don't quite take on board what she means.

'You mean she's missing?' I ask.

'Sort of. Yes. She was meant to be getting the train home at the end of term, but instead she came down to London and then just disappeared.'

I've been half dozing, but now I'm wide awake. 'Disappeared? You've informed the police, I take it? People are looking for her?'

Charlotte shrugs. 'It's not like she's been abducted or anything. She's phoned mum a couple of times, even called me once. Just won't say where she is.'

I've not seen Izzy since she was about eight, so it's hard to square what Charlotte's saying with the quiet little girl I remember. Even so, the casual reaction to her disappearance feels deeply strange. 'You seem very calm about this, Char. How can you be sure she's not under duress? Have you spoken to the police?'

'I rather thought that was what I was doing.' She takes a long drink from her glass of wine. 'Besides, it's not the first time she's done it. She's always been independent-minded anyway, and the 'rentals don't seem to care much what she does. Pisses me off when you think how strict they were with me.'

'Christ, Char. If it was my little sister missing I'd be out there looking for her. Hell, I'd be breaking down doors.'

'You always were more forceful than me. But it's like I said. She's done it before. They caught her on a train to Edinburgh without a ticket when she was twelve. Last year the police found her in Dundee, of all places. This time they're less interested. She's sixteen now, so technically old enough to do her own thing. Every time I try to bring it up with Father he just tells me it's none of my business.'

'So you've not done anything to try and find her?'

Charlotte shakes her head, tugging her hair out of Ben's grasp.

'The thing is, Con,' he says. 'We were rather wondering if you might be able to help track her down.'

There are some things you can get away with when you're

speaking to a stranger that just don't work with someone you've known all your life. Charlotte's been working her way around the subject all evening, but Ben's never been so subtle. This is exactly what they were trying to set up before. Only they can't have known I've been suspended for the past fortnight, will probably be out of a job by the end of the month. Can they?

'You do know I'm not a private detective, right?'

'Yeah, but you are a detective. And it's not like you've got anything else to do now, have you?'

14

The used car trade's not what it used to be. Rules and regulations, fairly regular checks by the authorities and a largely functional nationwide database of registrations has seen to that. There's still plenty of old-school dodgy used-car salesmen out there though. I've arrested a few in my time, investigated even more. I never thought I'd need to turn to one for help.

Sammi Khan's probably more trustworthy than most, mind you. He works out of a lot that used to be a petrol station, back in the days when cars could only go a couple of hundred miles before needing a refill. At least that's the way Pete always used to describe them. I can drive, passed my test as soon as I was old enough to take it, but living in London a car's more of a liability than an asset. Most of the time. I've managed without one until now.

There's maybe a dozen cars parked so closely together on the forecourt you can barely slide between them, let alone open the doors. They're bland, old, a mixture of Fords and Vauxhalls well past their crush-by date. Pride of place goes to a lowered BMW, tricked out to look like an M3. Its windows are tinted so dark it must get pulled over every time it's driven. The wheels are too small for an M too. More likely it's got a wheezy four-cylinder 1600 diesel engine in it. The sticker price is as optimistic as a dog tied up outside the butcher's.

'Detective Constable Fairchild. This is a pleasant surprise.'

I turn to see Sammi appear from the single-storey block that once must have been where you went to pay for your petrol but now serves as the headquarters of his automotive empire. He's almost as bling as the BMW, immaculately dressed like a man who has just stepped out of the 1970s. I'm impressed both that he recognises me and that he remembers my name. I didn't think our last meeting was that memorable, and Pete did most of the talking.

'Mr Khan.' I shake his hand as he offers it, watch as his gaze drifts past me to see if there is anyone else about.

'The detective inspector not with you today?'

The question is genuinely innocent, but it cuts through me all the same. Pete's loss is still raw, the truth that he will never be with me again hard to accept. Not today, not any other day.

'No. This isn't a police matter. Actually, it's fairly simple. I need to buy a car. Preferably reliable, definitely cheap.'

A beat of hesitation, perhaps a wrinkle of confusion across his brow, and then Sammi beams a wide smile. 'Of course! Of course! Well, you have come to the right place. All my cars are reliable.'

I notice he's said nothing about being cheap. 'Even this one?' I nod my head towards the BMW and he has the decency to look if not embarrassed then at least a little chastened.

'Maybe, maybe. But this is a car for a young man trying to impress his lady friends. You, I think, are needing something a little less . . . noticeable?'

'And cheaper. That price is at least two grand more than the car's worth, and you know it.'

'A man has to make a living, Detective Constable.' Sammi shrugs. 'But for my friends in the Met, I think I can do something. In fact, I may have just the very thing. Come. Follow me.'

He sets off towards the workshop at the back of the lot without looking to see if I'm following. For a moment I think he's leading me to the close-parked repmobiles, but he slides past the far one and leads me through a small gate into a larger compound at the back. Most of the cars here are in various stages of disassembly, wheels stacked up in one corner and a couple of whole engines on oily pallets. Over at the far side, by a wire mesh gate opening up onto the back lane, a lone car cowers as if in terror of being taken to pieces. It's filthy, but underneath the grime is white paint. Boxy sides designed with a straight edge and square.

'A Volvo? A Volvo estate?' I can't quite keep the disbelief from my voice.

'Just came in today. A . . . friend owed me money. Gave me this to settle the debt. It's all above board. Paperwork's in order, year's MOT. She's ready to go.'

We're closer to the car now, and as my initial shock wears off I start to take in a bit more detail. Through the grime, it looks pretty straight, no sign of rust or damage. The seats are black leather or something that looks a lot like it. Alloy wheels have taken a lot of damage from the city's kerbs, but the tyres are all the same manufacturer and look to have a bit of tread still on them. The badge has gone from the boot lid and the number plate tells me it was first registered before I was old enough to drive. It's anonymous though, and Volvos are pretty bulletproof.

'How much are you looking for?' I hear myself ask before my brain has time to catch up.

'If I put her through the workshop, clean her up a bit, maybe some new wheels, I'd be asking for three thousand.' Sammi must see my raised eyebrows. 'But like this, for you, to take away now? Fifteen hundred.'

Realistically I don't think I'll get something worth bothering with for less, but I haggle anyway. 'A grand. Cash. And if it breaks down before I get home I'll send some of my mates round to see you about it.'

Sammi hesitates just long enough for me to know he's faking it, then holds out his hand again. 'Deal.'

And just like that I've bought myself a car.

There's nowhere to park near my flat, but I'm not going back there anyway. Chances are it's been staked out by someone keen to make some cash from whichever mob boss wants me out of the way. Elmstead Road is a bit easier, although navigating the complex one-way system means I get more of a drive in my new car than I'd expected. For all that used-car dealers have a well-deserved reputation, I think Sammi's done me OK with this one. It's old, and has done well over 100,000 miles already, but its engine is sweet and surprisingly powerful.

The biggest joke is that it's obviously an ex-squad car, probably Motorway Patrol from Essex Constabulary. Someone's swapped the interior to cover up the more obvious modifications, but there's holes in the dashboard where some of the kit's been fitted and removed. That would explain the high mileage, and at least I know it's been well cared for early on in its long life.

Charlotte opens the front door about five minutes after I first press the buzzer. Her long blonde hair looks perfect even when it's mussed up with sleep, and her confused expression as she stares at me with bleary eyes reminds me of a lifestyle I quit years ago.

'Connie?' She stares at me, then turns and looks over her shoulder. 'I thought you were in the spare room?'

'There was some stuff I had to do. Probably should have asked for a key or something.'

Charlotte follows me through to the kitchen and starts making coffee. I look around for the cat, find her lying on a cushion beside her cage. She looks up at me warily, almost as if she knows what's coming next.

'Don't suppose you want a pet.' I bend down and offer a hand to the creature. She sniffs me, then rubs the side of her face against my finger and starts to purr. I think it's the first time I've heard her make any sound at all. The wound on her head is starting to heal already, but it'll be a while before the hair grows back, and she'll always have one split ear.

'You're not really serious, are you?' Charlotte looms over me, a mug of coffee in each hand and a look of horror on her face.

'No. Not really.' I stand up a little too swiftly, take the offered mug. 'She's my responsibility, after all.'

'What's the plan, then? You going back to your flat?'

I considered it, early this morning when I first woke up. Cosseted by the luxury of this substantial house, the threat to my life felt less serious than it had when Wee Jock had told me about the price on my head. There must be loads of Met detectives who've pissed off criminals enough to become a target; that's why generally speaking we don't live anywhere near our beat. But something like this is taking it a step further, and however small the bounty might be, someone's already been willing to give it a go.

'No. It's not safe. Can't hang around here any longer either. I don't want to be seen by the wrong people.'

Charlotte's face is a picture of alarm as the implications of what I've just said settle in her mind. 'Oh my God. You don't think—'

'Don't worry, Char. No one's going to come breaking down your door. I'll be gone just as soon as I've finished this coffee.' I lift the mug in her direction, enjoying the aroma and not rushing to drink. 'And I'll take the cat too.'

'Where will you go?'

It's an innocent enough question, although part of me thinks it would be better if as few people as possible knew.

'Thought I might do you a favour and go looking for Izzy. Not officially, mind you. I can't do it as a cop, and I'm not a licensed private detective either. But she's near enough family that I've got a good excuse if anyone asks me what I'm up to.'

Something flickers across Charlotte's face as I speak. Not relief or anxiety, but an expression I can't quite read. And then it morphs into a big smile, as genuine as I've ever seen her give anyone. She puts down her own mug and grabs me into a hug that's rather more intimate than I'm expecting. I manage not to spill coffee all down her back, but it's a close call.

'Oh, that's so wonderful, Connie. I don't know how to thank you.'

'Let me find her first, OK? I'm not making any promises. This whole suspension nonsense might blow over in a couple of weeks, and then I'll have to go back to my real job.'

Charlotte seems as unconvinced as I am. I've pretty much told my boss I quit and he was happy with that. I can't see myself back with that team any time soon.

'Where will you go first?'

'Back to where she was last seen. That's how we always do these things.' I drain the dregs of the coffee and put the mug down beside Charlotte's. I knew as soon as I even started to contemplate looking for Izzy that I'd have to do it, but it's only now I've said it out loud that the truth hits home.

I'm going to have to go back to my old school.

15

The cat glares at me from her cage, sitting on the front passenger seat of the Volvo as I pull onto the A1 and drive north out of London. It's been a while since I've come this way. I like the car though. It has a solidity to it, and despite its many, many miles the engine is as sweet as a nut. The last time I owned a car was not long after passing my test; that wonderful feeling of freedom you only get in your late teens, before the reality of life comes crashing down.

I fiddle with the ancient radio, trying to find something that isn't Radio 4. Maybe if I had some actual CDs I'd be able to slot them in one by one and listen to some music, but I'm not even sure they make them any more. Perhaps seeing my hand through the bars of her carrier box, the cat yawns wide, reaches out a paw towards me. I'm not sure if it's helpful to be reminded I'm not entirely alone.

'What are we going to do with you, puss?' I don't expect an answer, so I'm not disappointed when I don't get one. It's a good question though. I don't even know where I'm going to sleep tonight, and sooner or later I'm going to have to let her out to do what cats do. I probably should have bought a harness and lead; she's bound to run off as soon as I let her out of the cage. On the other hand, that would solve the problem of what to do with her.

Who am I kidding? I could no more abandon her by the

NO TIME TO CRY

roadside than I could refuse to look for Izzy. That's not how I work.

'There must be some way to get some music out of this shit piece of—' My frustration with the radio is cut short by the trilling of my phone. It's wedged into a cheap stand suckered to the windscreen, and a brief glance tells me that Detective Superintendent Bailey is trying to get in touch. I'm tempted to ignore the call, but sense prevails. A tap on the screen brings up the speakerphone mode. If he can't hear me over the noise of the car, that's his problem.

'Where the fuck are you, Constable?'

So it's constable now, not Fairchild. At least he's not calling me Connie, like Charlotte insists on doing. Christ, but I hate that name.

'Good morning to you too, sir. I'm on the A1, northbound.'

'Are you driving?' As if that's not obvious from the sound quality of the call.

'Hands-free, sir. All above board.'

'Didn't know you even owned a car. What are you doing leaving London?'

The lie comes easily to my lips, even as my brain knows I'm going to pay for it later. 'Thought I'd take the opportunity to go home for a few days. See the old folks, catch up with friends. Been a while since I had any real leave.'

'Home?' Bailey manages to make the word sound like he's unfamiliar with the concept. It wouldn't surprise me.

'Harston Magna, sir. Little village in Northamptonshire.'

There's a pause, and I almost convince myself I can hear pages being shuffled as the detective superintendent looks through my personnel file. 'I know where it is, Constable. Just surprised. Way I heard it you never really got on with your parents.'

Way you heard it I was responsible for Pete's death too. Idiot. 'They're not the only family I have there, sir.'

Another pause, and I realise that he's not yet come to the point of the call. 'Well, it's a bit irregular, dashing off and not letting anyone know.'

I consider telling him that it's a bit irregular not posting a uniform officer outside my flat after someone's broken in and tried to kill me, but I realise the irony would be wasted. Concentrating on the road and not answering seems the better option. Sooner or later he'll get to the point.

'I need . . . Professional Standards need to know where you are. They're not done questioning you yet, you know?'

'I'll be a couple of days tops, sir. It's not like I'm trying to flee the country or anything. Besides, last time I spoke to PS they said they were done with interviews for the foreseeable.'

Something that might be a grunt but might equally well be a glitch over the wireless filters out of the tinny speaker on my phone. I jiggle the charging lead I bought for it, just in case it's not working.

'Would it help if I phoned in my location every day?' Annoying, I know, but at least it will keep him off my back.

'Better if you stayed in London where we can keep an eye on you.'

'I'd believe that more if you were actually doing it.' I speak the words under my breath, and yet somehow the phone picks them up. I can almost see Bailey's face reddening even though this is only a voice call.

'With that sort of attitude it's no wonder you're under investigation. I want regular location updates, and I expect you back in London by the start of next week, understood?'

'Sir.' I keep my tone flat, a little rebellion that's no doubt completely lost on him. He says something that might be 'Good' and then the line goes dead. Call ended, my phone reverts to its satnav function, flashing to tell me my junction is coming up in a few hundred yards. I indicate, pull off, slow down for the roundabout, all the time aware that DS Bailey never told me what he was calling about. It doesn't matter. The fact that he knew I wasn't at home is enough to set me on edge. There's only one way he could have known that.

There are few places I'd rather visit less than Saint Humbert's School for young ladies. It sounds like the scene for jolly japes and making friends for life, but in truth it nearly broke me. My parents sent me there as a bewildered seven-year-old, and I grew to both fear and hate its cold corridors and capricious staff. A third of my life, ten long years, I spent in a state of constant, nervous tension. You could never relax there, and home wasn't much better. It's hardly surprising I fucked off out of there at the earliest opportunity. I'm not surprised Izzy did the same. She was always a smart kid.

Originally a priory, the oldest buildings on the site date back to the fourteenth century. Or at least that's what the teachers used to tell us. Usually with a sneering tone that suggested we'd never amount to anything much, and certainly nothing as venerable as the stone and mortar around us. I loved the grounds, perhaps because they were extensive, heavily wooded and easy to hide in. The rest of it I would happily have seen burned to the ground, a sentiment I wasn't alone in if the regular fire alarms were anything to go by.

Thirteen years since I finally left, swearing I'd never go back, my first impressions are of a driveway shorter than I remembered and a collection of buildings less impressive and forbidding. Long before I reach the bleached stone steps leading up to the front door, it opens and a rather sour-faced woman appears from the shadows. There's no one particular thing about her, but her clothes seem somehow old-fashioned, her hairstyle a little too contrived. She looks no older than me, but at the same time ancient as the hills. I imagine she fits in here perfectly.

'Can I help you?' At least her voice is modern, not clipped and nasal like some extra from a *Carry On* movie. Her question leaves me momentarily dumbstruck though. I hadn't really thought through what I was going to do once I got here.

'Umm. Constance Fairchild. I was a pupil here a few years back.'

She gives me a look exactly the way Matron used to, back when I was ten. It almost works.

'Look, I'm a police officer, but this is unofficial business. I've been asked to look into the whereabouts of Izzy – Isobel DeVilliers. I'm a friend of the family.'

'Isobel. Yes.' Somehow she manages to put a lifetime of disdain into those two words.

'Look, I know she's run away. I know it's not the first time either. I'm not here to judge whose fault that is, just to find out where she's gone.'

I'm beginning to feel a bit annoyed by this woman with her slightly sneering expression. If she wasn't two steps higher up than me I'd be a head taller than her and the peering over the spectacles look wouldn't be half as effective.

'Not sure how we can help, really. Isobel was put on the train along with a number of other girls. It's not uncommon once they're her age, as I'm sure you know. We have no control over her once she's left the grounds.'

'What about her housemistress? Is she not concerned?'

The young woman draws herself upright, nostrils flaring as if I've insulted her and all her family. 'I am her housemistress, and I can assure you Harriet House cares deeply for all its girls.'

That's not the Harriet House I remember, but I keep that to myself.

'As it happens, I have just been discussing Miss DeVilliers with the headmistress. It's not a happy situation at all. Quite apart from the girl herself, we've the parents of all our other pupils to think about.'

Of course they do. That's who pays their salaries, after all. It's time to take a hold of this situation and start treating it like a proper investigation. Stop acting like the teenager who left here in disgrace. Two quick steps bring me face to face with the woman. 'If the headmistress is in, I'd probably be best talking to her, then. After that I'll drop by Harriet if that's OK?'

I know the way to the headmistress's office, of course, but there's still that ingrained feeling of wrongness about going there. You only ever went because you were being punished, because you had been sent. Still, I square my shoulders, take a deep breath and only pause a few seconds before knocking lightly on the door.

'Enter.'

One word, one simple little word, and I'm a teenage girl again. Sweat forms on my scalp and under my arms, a clamminess in my hands as my body responds to years of conditioning. It's stupid, I know. I'm thirty years old, not thirteen. Until a week ago I was a success in my chosen career, someone the pupils here might have looked up to. I've interviewed men and women who have murdered people in cold blood, but obeying that command fills me with far greater terror. I'd assumed Mrs Jennings would have retired by now too. It's been a dozen years since I left this place, after all, and she was ancient then.

Deep breaths, Con. I grasp the familiar brass handle, shiny with the fear of many thousands of miscreant girls, turn it slowly and push open the door.

She's sitting at her desk, horn-rimmed spectacles perched on the tip of her nose as she peers over them to see who I am. It's definitely Mrs Jennings, but she's smaller than I remember her, shrunken in on herself. Her hair's more white than grey now, thin like spider silk and clinging to her skin as if she died several years ago but didn't notice. I wouldn't put it past her to be so spiteful, even to death.

'Constance Fairchild. Of all the girls I might expect to turn up unannounced . . .' She doesn't finish the sentence, instead pushes back her heavy wooden chair and levers herself upright. Her frailty is obvious, as is the way she fights it. There's a walking stick leaning against the side of the desk, but she leaves it where it is and walks slowly across the room towards me. Then she extends a bony hand, trembling slightly, to be shaken.

'You'll be here about the DeVilliers girl, no doubt.' Her touch is warm and dry, almost waxy, like the shed skin of some reptile. Her grip is strong though, and she tugs me towards the far side of the room, where a couple of old high-backed leather armchairs sit either side of an unlit fire. 'Come, sit.'

I do as I'm told, remembering these chairs from many a previous visit. I was never allowed to sit in them before, mind you. That was a privilege reserved for prefects and adults.

'They tell me you joined the police force. Service. Whatever they call it these days.'

'That's true. I'm a detective constable in the Met. Part of a specialist team dealing with organised crime in the capital. It's . . . interesting work.'

Those grey eyes might be a bit more clouded than I remember, but they still cut through me as if they can see my thoughts before they form. 'And Isobel DeVilliers has been abducted by the Notting Hill Mafia?'

'Ha. No. Not exactly. It was her sister, Charlotte, who asked me to look into it. She's concerned their parents aren't perhaps as worried as they should be.'

'And the Metropolitan Police are fine with you conducting an informal investigation.' Mrs Jennings nods like a doddery old lady, but I'm not fooled.

'This has got nothing to do with them. I'm on leave and just asking a few questions. It's fine if you don't want to help.'

Mrs Jennings sits a little more upright, a frown spreading across her lined face, and for a moment I wonder if I'm going to be sent to the changing rooms for a cold shower.

'It's not that I don't want to help, Constance. It's just that there's very little I can do. Isobel is a gifted child, but troubled. I seem to remember another young girl in my charge who was much the same, and I didn't get very far trying to control her either. That little stunt you pulled the day you left is still talked about, you know.'

I expect chiding in her words, but instead there's something else. Is it pride? 'Well, I guess we're both Harriet girls. I see the new housemistress is just as spiky as her predecessor.'

'Daphne? Yes. She can come across as cold, but she's good at her job. She worries more about Isobel than she should. Certainly more than her parents seem to care.'

'That's something I find strange too. I mean, I don't know the DeVees all that well, but even so. You think they'd have called the police or something. Seems like nobody's done anything to find Izzy until Charlotte came looking for me. And Char's never cared about anyone in her life except herself.'

Mrs Jennings gives me one of those infuriatingly knowing smiles of hers. 'Oh, I think you do Charlotte a disservice. People change. They grow up and accept their responsibilities. Look at you, after all. Who'd have thought the girl who once smuggled teenage boys into the dorm for an illegal end-of-term party would end up as a pillar of society? A police officer?'

16

Mrs Jennings's parting words echo in my ears as I walk past empty classrooms and across the concrete yard where we all played during break. I can't stop wondering at how small everything feels, how close together. Yes, I was only little when I first arrived, but by the time I left I was pretty much fully grown. Was my spirit so crushed that only the intervening years have allowed it to grow back to normal size? Is that why it takes just moments to reach the house common room, rather than the age it always seemed to take before?

I have no answers as I stare up at the line of trophy boards in the common room. Harriet was never a sporting house, but we were good at debating. It's nice to see that tradition still holds. It looks like we've won the cup almost every year since I left. Not that I ever had anything to do with the debating society. None of the names from my years ring any bells either.

'You should really report to the housemistress before wandering around here, you know.'

I know who's spoken even before I turn. Daphne, Mrs Jennings called her. She's less intimidating now that we're on the same level and I know her name.

'Sorry. It doesn't feel like trespassing when you grew up in a place. Mrs Jennings said I'd be OK to have a nosey around. It's been a while, but some things never change, right?'

I was meaning the long list of winning teams for the debating cup, but Daphne clearly has other ideas.

'They still talk about it. What you did.'

'What they think I did.' I shake my head at the memory, quietly pleased that it's turned into one of the legends of this place. There can't be too many girls who are expelled from school on their last full day. For a moment I think Daphne's going to call me a liar, tell me to leave, but she just sniffs, turns and walks out. I'm tempted to follow her, but there's another way to get to where I want to go.

The tiny back stairs lead up to dormitories on the first floor, the iron bedsteads empty. At the far end of the corridor are the bedsit studies, where the more senior girls sleep. It doesn't take long to find Izzy's room. The name tags are still attached to the doors, although I'm sure they'll be reassigned soon. I'm surprised at how pleasing I find it to see that Izzy had my old room, even though generations of pupils must have passed through it in the intervening years.

The door's not locked, and when I push it open I can see why. Izzy's things have been packed up and taken away. The cleaners have been through here too, and the bed's been stripped to a bare mattress, hairy blankets neatly folded at one end, pillow at the other. The first time I saw this room it was almost exactly the same, a blank canvas awaiting my teenage creativity. Thinking about the posters I Blu-Tacked to these walls makes me blush. Where are those boy bands now?

But I'm not here to wallow in the past. I'm here for clues. Time to act like a detective, even if I'm not likely to be one for very much longer.

I start with the bed, checking under the mattress for anything that might have been tucked away there. It's the same basic wooden frame I slept on, a large storage drawer built into the base. That's empty, but pulling it right out reveals a useful hidey-hole at the back. Either Izzy never realised it was there or she cleared it out before she left.

None of the other hiding places I remember have anything in them either, which makes me suspicious. Standing on the bed, I reach up and run a finger along the top of the hanging cupboard. No dust at all; this place has been deep-cleaned.

'Were you looking for anything in particular?'

I'm not easy to spook, but Daphne's voice startles me. I hide it in a swift turn and stare. 'This was my room when I was here. It's not changed much.'

'How . . . apt. I've heard you weren't really a team player either.'

'I'm still not. Not really.' I pull the chair out from the desk and sit down, leaving the housemistress standing in the doorway. 'So what's the real story with Izzy? This isn't the first time she's done a runner, is it?'

'Isobel is a difficult child. She's bright, quick on the uptake, but she lacks motivation. And everything is a personal insult, no matter how innocent or insignificant.' Daphne leans against the door frame. 'I've seen it before in children with . . . older parents. They grow wise young, but it's not true wisdom. They rail at the world because the story they're told doesn't fit with the facts they see.'

A psychology student, I'd bet good money on it. I change the subject. 'This room is very clean.'

She shrugs. 'All the rooms are clean. I don't like paying someone to do half a job. This will be reassigned for the autumn term. Only fair its new occupant doesn't have to put up with the mess left behind by last year's girl.'

'So you don't think Izzy's coming back? I had this room for two years here. Left half my stuff in the drawers over the summer holidays.'

'I know she's not coming back. Her father called and explained to me in great detail exactly why, and every single word of it was a lie. Doesn't matter though. If he wants to withdraw her from school there's nothing I can do about it. She's sixteen, education's no longer compulsory. It's a shame, but I can't help being a little relieved too. Disruptive pupils are hard work.'

There's the ghost of a smile in Daphne's eyes as she makes her final statement, but it soon enough disappears. I recall the headmistress's words. 'You worry about her, don't you?'

'I worry about all the girls placed in my care. But, yes, Isobel especially. For all her faults, she deserved better. It might surprise you, but I even tried to offer her a scholarship.'

'Why would you do that?' The question's out before my brain catches up. 'Wait, you thought Roger DeVilliers pulled her out of school because he couldn't afford the fees?'

She shakes her head. 'I know. Stupid, really. But you're right. Girls who're coming back next year can leave their belongings here over the summer. This room's only clean because Mr DeVilliers instructed that all Isobel's things be packed and shipped home. Her trunk's still waiting to be picked up.'

There's something about the way she drops this piece of information into the conversation that makes me think she's been trying to tell me all along. I glance out of the window, see my car parked far away across the main lawn, white and boxy and with a huge space in the back. Sooner or later I was going to have to speak to the DeVilliers anyway. It's only an hour or so's drive.

'You know, I can probably help you with that.'

Cat isn't happy with me. While Daphne's finding the caretaker to load Izzy's trunk into the back of my car, I let her out of her cage, stick her on the grass in front of the main school building for a leg stretch. When I carry her drinking bowl over to the water fountain to fill, she just follows me like she's a duckling and I'm her mother duck. A couple of ineffectual laps at her drinking bowl and then she stalks back into her carry-cage, turns around a couple of times and settles down to sleep.

'Be like that, then.' I close the cage door and strap the box back on the front passenger seat.

'T5 Estate. Don't see many of them around these days. Used to watch them doing the Touring Car races back in the day.'

I turn to see a grey-haired man in loose brown overalls wheeling a sack barrow with an old school trunk strapped to it. It's only when he gives me a cheeky wink that I recognise him.

'Mr Bradshaw? I'd have thought you'd be retired by now.'

'I only work part-time these days, Miss Constance. Mostly tending to the grounds, you know. Better to keep busy than sit at home mouldering away.'

Between the two of us we manhandle the trunk into the back of the car. It's surprisingly heavy, but how much of that is down to the tooled leather and how much is the contents, I can't tell. I'm still trying to decide whether I'm going to go through it before I deliver it to Izzy's parents or ask her mother when I get there. With any luck her father will be in the city.

'They tell me you're a policewoman now,' Mr Bradshaw says, proving that gossip is still the lifeblood of the private school. I haven't the heart to tell him that 'policewoman' is frowned upon nowadays.

'Detective constable no less. Hence the plain clothes.'

'Always reckoned you'd make something of yourself. Even before . . . Well, you know.'

Mr Bradshaw has the face of a man who spends most of his life outdoors, but even so I can see the blush spreading from his neck upwards. Such is the power of a reputation, however ill-deserved it might be.

'I really don't know what you're talking about, Mr B.' I close down the back door of the car and walk round to the front, passing the passenger side and the cage on the seat. 'You wouldn't like a cat, would you, by any chance?'

'A cat?' Mr Bradshaw's face wrinkles in confusion, then he shakes his head slowly and sniffs. 'Not with my allergies. Mrs B's not a fan of them neither.'

'Ah well. It was just a thought.' I open the door, look around, surprised neither house- nor headmistress has come to make sure I'm leaving, or to remind me of the responsibility I've taken on with Izzy's trunk. They're probably just glad to see the back of it, her and me.

'You take care now, Miss Constance.' Mr Bradshaw holds the door for me while I climb in, then closes it gently as if I were some society debutante. I start the car and wind down the window at the same time. He's got his head cocked slightly to one side, and for a moment I wonder if there's something wrong with him. Then I realise he's listening to the rumble of the engine. A couple of blips of the throttle has him smiling wistfully, even if I'm worried that the exhaust might have more holes in it than the manufacturer intended.

'Porsche did a lot of the development work on that, you know.' He nods at the bonnet and the lump of metal underneath. I know a bit about cars, but I never knew that until now. The chances of my remembering it are slim too, but that was always the way with me and school.

17

I don't stop all the way from Saint Humbert's to Harston Magna. The drive always felt interminably long when I was a child, but aided by the satnav on my phone it takes just over an hour. With each mile closer, I debate whether or not to pull over and open up Izzy's trunk, go through the contents for clues as to where she might have gone. There's never a suitable place to stop though. All the lay-bys have trucks parked in them, or sales reps eating service station sandwiches. I know a couple of places near the village where I could probably park up unseen, but then I run the risk of a local dog walker stumbling across my crime. Worse still, they might even recognise me.

The closer I get to the DeVilliers home, the more nervous I become. If I thought going back to school was bad, then coming here, coming home, is even worse. There's little more than a couple of fields and a small bit of woodland between the Glebe House and Harston Magna Hall, where my parents live their uncomfortably separate lives. If I'm lucky I can get in and out without them ever knowing I was close by. I don't much like trusting to luck though.

It's been five years since I was last here, and not much has changed in the village. Not much has changed in the past five hundred years, for that matter. It's an odd little place, tucked away out of sight in the rolling arable fields of Northamptonshire. No more than a couple of dozen houses and cottages, clustered around the hall and the church, it's a lasting monument to a distant feudal past, with my father the lord of the manor, looking down on the serfs beneath him. Except that the farmland is all tenanted these days, and worked by huge machines rather than gangs of forelock-tugging men. Most of the houses have been sold too, the estate dwindling down the years as the more reckless heads of the Fairchild family have squandered their inheritance.

There are no cars parked outside the Glebe House when I pull up by the front door, and it occurs to me I should probably have called ahead to make sure someone was in. That would have meant calling Charlotte for the number though, and the fewer people who know where I am the better. I'm reaching in through the open passenger door to let Cat out when I hear a voice behind me.

'This is private property, you know. And we're not interested in buying anything.'

'Just as well I'm not selling, then, Mrs DeVee.' I turn to face her and give myself a hell of a shock. I remember Margo DeVilliers as an elegant lady, always well presented; indeed, the sort of person who might have a daughter like Charlotte. The woman staring at me now looks haggard, there's no other word to describe her. She's also unsteady on her feet and as she comes closer, head bent forward to get a better look at my face, I can smell the gin on her breath. I resist the urge to check my watch, but it's early to be hitting the sauce hard.

'Constance Fairchild. As I live and breathe. What in heaven's name are you doing here?'

At least she's recognised me. The last time I was here I had hair down past my shoulders and the ugliest pair of spectacles my parents could find for me. Laser eye surgery's a godsend, and I found long hair to be quite a hindrance when I was in uniform.

'I brought Izzy's trunk home. You couldn't give me a hand getting it out of the back, could you?'

Something like panic sweeps over her face at the mention of her daughter's name. I'm not sure that's the reaction I was expecting, and neither am I sure she's in any fit state to lift a designer handbag, let alone a heavy-tooled leather trunk. Perhaps I'd be better leaving it in the back of the car. I could take it away with me, except that right now I'm not entirely sure where I'm going.

'What are you doing with Isobel's trunk?' Margo's voice wavers between slurring and alarmed, as if it was a bomb I'd brought her and not her youngest daughter's worldly goods and possessions.

'I know she's missing, Mrs DeVee. Run away. Charlotte told me. Asked me to try and find her. I swung past Saint Bert's on my way here.'

'But you can't. You mustn't.' Margo shakes her head and the motion makes her stagger sideways. Acting on instinct I reach out to steady her and she all but collapses into my arms. I knew she dieted too much, but there's nothing to her. And this close up I can smell something more sour than the alcohol on her breath. She's not well.

'Why don't we get you inside, eh? Have a sit down and a cup of coffee. It's been ages since I've seen you. Must be loads of gossip to catch up on.'

I'm all too aware I've left Cat in the car as I steer Margo up the shallow steps and in through the front door. Nothing much has changed in the Glebe House since I used to babysit Izzy half a lifetime ago, although the kitchen is messier than I remember it ever being. A bottle of gin sits on the counter beside an empty tin of tonic water and a glass with a wilted slice of lemon in it. I ignore them and look for the kettle, the cupboard where the coffee lives and the little wooden stand with the mugs on it. Instant's not my favourite, but it'll have to do.

Margo's slumped down in one of the mismatched wooden

chairs around the old kitchen table by the time the coffee's made, her eyes locked on the gin bottle but her body lacking the strength to fetch it. I can only imagine what's happened to her in the past few years to turn her into this shadow of her former self.

'Here you go. White, one sugar. That's how you used to like it, right?'

She looks up at me as I place the two mugs on the table beside her, pull out another chair and sit down. Then she buries her head in her hands and bursts into tears.

'You're not married, are you, Connie?'

It's taken a whole mug of coffee, several sheets of extra strength kitchen roll and far too many longing glances in the direction of the gin bottle for Margo DeVilliers to recover her composure enough to speak. My training makes me give her the time she needs, even as I worry about Cat stuck in her cage in the car. At least the windows are open and it's an overcast day.

'No. I'm not married.'

'Boyfriend?' Margo hesitates, then adds, 'Girlfriend?'

That brings a slight smile to my lips, soon wiped away by the realisation that there's been no romance in my life for a very long time indeed. I shake my head. 'Not right now, no. Police work doesn't mix well with having a social life. Or any kind of life at all, I guess.'

'That's right. I remember Charlotte telling me. You joined the police. Can't imagine your father was best pleased about that.'

'The only thing that would please him would be marrying me off to some titled chinless idiot with a vast estate somewhere so I could provide him with grandchildren to brainwash.'

'Such bitterness in one so young.' Margo takes a drink from her mug, steals another look at the gin bottle. 'But then I guess Earnest always brings that out in people. In the end.'

There's an almost wistful quality to the way she says my father's name that sends an involuntary shiver down my spine. Time to change the subject.

'Do you know where Izzy's gone?'

Margo stiffens. 'That child. How she can be so different from her sister? How she can be so difficult when we've given her so much?'

Not a no, then. That's a start.

'Charlotte told me she phoned you. Did she use her mobile, or was it a land line?'

'I really don't remember.'

'Well, did she phone the house, or your own mobile? I assume you have one?'

Margo looks across the kitchen table and I see a slim smartphone lying there. She doesn't complain when I pick it up, and neither is it password-protected. The call log only goes back a few days though, so either it's a brand-new phone or someone's deleted the records. I put it back down on the table, just out of her reach.

'Did you know she was going to run away? Did you suspect she might? What about her father?'

She opens her mouth to answer, but says nothing. Closes it again and shakes her head.

'Is he the problem, then? Has Roger been abusing her in some way?'

'You really shouldn't be asking these questions. I know you mean well, Connie, but it's none of your business.' She looks away from me, but not to the gin bottle this time. Now it's the kitchen window with a view out to the front drive that calls to her. It doesn't take a genius to work out that she doesn't want to be seen here with me. Can I be bothered pushing this investigation further when it's clear nobody involved wants me poking my nose into it?

I drain the last of my coffee, regretting it as I feel the rough texture of the limescale from the kettle. Before I can get up and leave, Margo reaches out with a wiry hand to grab my arm. For a moment I think she's going to say something important, but she's transfixed by the tattoo circling my wrist, revealed as she inadvertently pushed up the sleeve of my jacket.

'What have you done to yourself?' She pushes the sleeve further up my arm, twisting it around to see patterns inked into my skin. I haven't the heart to tell her there's more, but instead gently pull my arm away and roll the sleeve back down.

'Charlotte's got my number, Mrs DeVee.' I stand up and push the chair back under the table. It scrapes on the flagstone floor with a loud squeal until I remember the technique beaten into me as a child. 'Give me a call if you want to talk, OK? I'll see myself out.'

She doesn't say anything as I leave, and by the time I reach the car, I can see her through the window still sitting where I left her. Poor woman, I almost feel sorry for her, but I can understand why Izzy might have wanted to run away.

My phone beeps as I leave the house: two missed calls, both from Detective Superintendent Bailey. I should probably check in, but right now I can't face up to speaking to him. Cat looks up at me from her cage on the passenger's seat as I climb into the car. The clock on the dashboard tells me it's almost four in the afternoon and I finally have to face up to the dilemma that I've been avoiding ever since I fled London this morning. I need somewhere to stay, but there's no way in hell I'm going home. I don't even consider Harston Magna Hall my home any more, but sooner or later Margo DeVilliers is going to speak to my mother or father. Or someone else will let slip I was in the village and didn't stop by. This is precisely why I didn't want to get involved.

'Come on, then,' I say as I reluctantly start the engine.

'Looks like we're going to introduce you to my aunt.'

It's not until I'm half a mile away from the Glebe House that I remember I've still got Izzy's trunk in the back of the car.

18

Unlike the Glebe House, or Harston Magna Hall itself, Folds Cottage is exactly what my idea of an English country house should be. Ramshackle and a little the worse for wear, its rattly wooden sash windows need paint and someone should cut back the wisteria before it starts to pull the roof off. It's set away from the bulk of the village too, in a small clearing surrounded by mature oak woods. I used to walk here on my own as a child, and as my relationship with my father deteriorated I'd spend more and more time here. Perhaps the only reason I'm hesitant to come back is the small matter of the blazing row I had with the woman who lives here, that day I left home for good. My father's older sister, Aunt Felicity.

I cringe every time I think about it. If anyone in my family deserves unconditional love and thanks it's Aunt Flick. In my defence, I had a lot to be angry about back then, but in hers she'd been a far better parent than either of mine.

It's been almost five years and I've never dared come back. Not after the things I said. We've spoken on the telephone and exchanged the obligatory annual Christmas and birthday cards, but there's always been a nagging sense of shame that's kept me away. And perhaps some of my father's stubbornness too. We don't back down, us Fairchilds. Not easily.

An elderly black Labrador is asleep on the doorstep, and barely moves as I park a few paces away. He only deigns to lift his head when I climb out of the car, raising his nose a little to test my scent on the air. Only then does he start to thump his heavy tail against the ground. He still doesn't get up though.

'Surprised you're still with us, Treacle.' I crouch down and ruffle his greying head as he looks up at me through cloudy eyes. I remember him as a puppy, then as a young dog racing through the woods to greet me. Seeing him like this brings a slight lump to my throat. Five years is a long time for the likes of him.

The front door opens while I'm still crouching down, fussing Treacle's ears the way he always loved. From this angle it's hard to read Aunt Felicity's expression as she stands there, flour-dusted apron around her middle and what looks like a half-kneaded loaf in one hand.

'Well, well. If it isn't my favourite niece.'

It's an old joke, since I'm her only niece, but the fact she's made it sets me at least partially at ease. Treacle complains a bit as I stand up, then lets rip with an unapologetic fart, wafted around by his tail. We can't help but laugh, and all the tension is gone.

'Seriously, Con. Why didn't you call? If I'd known you were coming I'd have had this done hours ago.' Aunt Felicity waves the ball of dough around as we walk through to the kitchen.

'It's been a long day.' I hear the words too late to stop them. 'Sorry, that's a crap excuse. I think I've just been trying to hide from reality. Stick my head in the sand and hope that all the problems go away.'

'Sounds like the Constance I know.' She slaps the dough down on the table, sending a cloud of flour in all directions, and then starts to knead at it industriously. 'Stick the kettle on, dear. Make us both a cup of tea and tell your aunt all about it.'

I've just had a mug of unpleasant coffee with Margo DeVilliers, but I do as I'm told. The familiar routine settles my nerves almost as well as the dog farting, and, as if on cue, Treacle shuffles into the kitchen as the water comes to the boil.

'He's grown old,' I say as I make the tea in a pot that takes me right back to my childhood.

'He's not the only one, dear.' Aunt Felicity thumps the dough down one more time, places it in a bowl and pulls cling film across the top. 'What's it been? Three years? Four?'

'Five, actually. I've not been back to Harston Magna since . . . Well, you know.'

She says nothing while she places the bowl with its rising dough on a shelf above the range, then fetches a cloth and wipes down the table. Only once all is cleaned and squared away, the tea poured and the tin with the biscuits in it prised open does Aunt Felicity answer my unspoken question.

'We were both angry that day, Con. And we both had good reason. The same reason, I think. Best let bygones be bygones, eh?'

I take a sip of proper tea, a bite from a home-baked biscuit that is better than anything I've tasted in years. Unlike the rest of my family, Aunt Felicity calls me by the name I prefer. Not Constance, like my mother, or Girl, like my father. And certainly not the horrible Connie that almost everyone else uses. I've always been Con, and she knows that it's important to me.

'I couldn't beg a bed for the night, could I? No way I'm going back to the hall, and the only hotel round here's a dive.'

'Actually it burned down a couple of years ago. Council's still debating over a plan to build two hundred and fifty houses on the site. Guess whoever set the fire didn't grease the right palms.' Aunt Felicity's humour is infectious. 'Course you can stay. And I won't speak a word of it to your father.'

'Thanks. I really appreciate it. Just need a little time to work out what to do next.'

She reaches out with a hand much thinner, more wrinkled and liver-spotted than I remember, pats me gently on the arm. 'It's no problem, really. I'll get some supper on the go and then we can crack open a bottle of wine. A problem shared's a problem halved, that's what I always say.'

Her smile is so genuine and welcoming I almost burst into tears, and that's when I realise just how tense I've been since everything went to hell in London. It also reminds me of something else.

'There is one thing,' I say, unsurprised when she raises a single eyebrow.

'Yes?'

'I seem to have acquired a cat.'

'Why are you not at home, Fairchild?'

I'm surprised there's a mobile signal at Folds Cottage, but I guess that's progress for you. The spare room up in the eaves even gets half-decent 4G. The downside is a slew of emails from work I spent the best part of an hour dealing with, and now a call from Detective Superintendent Bailey I can't ignore.

'I told you I was heading out of London for a few days, sir. Remember?' It was only this morning, after all.

The drawn-out silence suggest that he's forgotten our conversation earlier. Hardly atypical behaviour for most of the senior officers I've worked with, but it's annoying all the same.

'It's no matter. I want you back as soon as possible. There's been a development.'

'A development?' I suppress the urge to add 'What the fuck is that supposed to mean?' My aunt frowns upon cussing.

'Yes. Forensics have matched the bullet that killed Pete Copperthwaite to the two found under your bed. They were fired from the same gun. So you'll understand why we need you back here urgently.'

I had been standing at the window, staring out across the clearing towards the woods, painted in that orangey-green you only get as the sun sets on a fine summer's day. Now somehow

I'm sitting on my bed, back against the headboard, knees drawn up to my chest. I don't remember moving.

'Not meaning to be funny, sir, but wouldn't it be safer if I kept well away?' I want to tell him what I heard from Wee Jock, about the price someone's put on my head, but something stops me. The fear of his inevitable ridicule, perhaps.

'It wasn't a suggestion, Detective Constable.' Bailey pauses, as if using my rank wasn't hint enough that he expects me to obey his orders, however unreasonable. 'And, besides, Professional Standards aren't done with their investigation yet. You can't expect them to come to you.'

Given that I'm the one whose life is under threat, it doesn't seem that unreasonable to me at all. I don't really want to leave this house right now, let alone drive back down to London. Not if there's someone out there trying to kill me.

Then another thought occurs to me that's almost as bad as being hunted down by a professional hitman. 'Hang on, you asked me why I wasn't at home, right? You didn't mean the flat, did you?'

'No, not there. Your folks' place, like you told me you were going to this morning.'

'You phoned my parents?' I don't even ask how he got the number. It's my own fault for ignoring the missed calls.

'Naturally. Spent fifteen minutes talking to your mother, as it happens. She was very surprised to hear your name. Said the two of you hadn't spoken in years. Had no idea you were coming home.'

So much for getting in and out of the village without the wrong people finding out. And if Mother knows I'm here, it can't be long before Father does too. Going back to London and a potential hitman suddenly feels like the lesser of two evils. They're still both evil though, and Bailey's sudden interest in me doesn't sit right.

'Is tomorrow morning early enough for you, sir? Only, if I leave now it'll be well after eight before I can get to the station.'

Another long pause, and the line goes so quiet I think Bailey's hung up. Then it occurs to me he might have put me on mute while he talks to someone else. Straining to hear what's going on a hundred miles away is daft, but it doesn't stop me from trying.

'My office. Tomorrow morning. Ten o'clock sharp.' The detective superintendent's voice comes back so suddenly I almost drop the phone. It wouldn't have mattered if I did. He's hung up before I can say anything else.

19

I don't know how long I sit there on the bed, staring at nothing and with the phone hanging loosely between my fingers. At some point Cat comes in and leaps up, nudging at me before curling into a ball at the end of the duvet and starting to purr. It was light when I first came in, but now the evening shadows begin to darken the room.

'You can't go back, you know.'

The voice doesn't startle me the way it perhaps should. There's an old armchair sitting in the far corner, my jacket thrown over the back, and now it's dark I can imagine a man sitting there. Almost smell the reek of charcoal and burnt carpet.

'I can't not go back, Pete. That would mean disobeying a direct order from a senior officer. Given all that's happened recently, they'd sack me on the spot.'

'And would that be so bad? Thought you were going to resign anyway.'

I lean back against the headboard, drop the phone and stare at the ceiling. 'I thought I was as well, but that sounds too much like quitting when the going gets tough to me. And, besides, what would I do? I can't come crawling back here.'

Pete says nothing, but I can imagine him tilting his head slightly to indicate that I appear to have done just that.

'It's not the same. This is about tracking down Izzy.'

'And what are you going to do when you find her?'

I notice he doesn't say *if* I find her, and I'm grateful for that. 'I'm not sure. I need to see what kind of state she's in. Who she's with, whether she's being held against her will, brainwashed, that kind of thing. She's phoned her mum and sister, so it doesn't look like she's been abducted. Can't rule out some kind of cult though. Or maybe she's been groomed online. It'd be much easier if I had access to her computer.'

It's only as I speak the words out loud that I remember the trunk still sitting in the back of my car. I should probably have tried harder to leave it at Margo's, but I don't much fancy going back there. If I'm really unlucky, her husband will be home from the City or wherever it is he works these days. Dealing with a gin-soaked middle-aged woman is one thing; dealing with the man whose arm I nearly broke the last time he groped me at a dinner party is quite another.

'You never told me that story,' Pete says, as if he can hear my thoughts. As if he's actually here. 'What stopped you?'

'I don't know. Some last vestige of self-preservation, I guess. Roger DeVilliers is obscenely wealthy and used to getting his own way. He could have made life very difficult for me if he'd wanted to.'

'You going to look in the trunk, then? Start acting like a detective instead of moping around up here like a teenager? There's better ways of wasting your time than picking at old memories like they're scabs.'

I know that chiding tone well enough. Pete always was good at getting to the heart of the problem. 'OK. OK. I'll go look in the trunk.'

My legs are stiff from sitting cross-legged, and Cat complains when my ungainly movements disturb her. I pause for a moment, head a bit light from standing up. Pete says nothing, and when I flick the light switch by the door he's gone. Just an empty chair with my jacket draped over the back of it.

★ ★ ★

'There's casserole in the oven if you're interested.' Aunt Felicity is too polite to shout, but she has a way of making her voice carry so it can be heard from a distance. I reckon she'd have been good on the stage, if the very thought of acting wouldn't have sent my grandparents to an even earlier grave.

'I'll be there in a minute.' My yell is less ladylike, but then that's to be expected. Outside, the evening air has cooled enough to be pleasant. My car's where I left it, illuminated by a bright floodlight that comes on as I trip a sensor by the front door. I open the back to reveal Izzy's trunk where old Mr Bradshaw left it. Two leather straps and an unlocked brass hasp are all that keep me from the contents inside.

Opening the trunk is yet another reminder of school days. Everything is tidily folded, neatly arranged to make best use of the space. I find it hard to believe that a sixteen-year-old girl's entire school possessions could take up so little room, but everything is here. I'm hesitant to start unpacking the top layer, unsure now whether I'll be able to get everything back in again once I've disrupted whatever arcane magic has been used to pack it.

'Looking for something in particular, dear?'

I stand up too swiftly and almost brain myself against the tailgate. Either I'm out of practice or Aunt Felicity is very stealthy. I should have heard her feet on the gravel at the very least.

'It's Izzy's trunk. I picked it up from Saint Bert's this morning.'

'And she's fine with you going through her things?'

There's a chiding in her words, but when I look at her face I can see my aunt is smiling. There's a glint in her eyes that's more than the reflection of the spotlight overhead. Something mischievous.

'Probably a waste of time. This will have been packed by one of the matrons, most likely. If they'd found anything useful they'd have told me.'

Aunt Felicity shoulders past me, closes down the lid of the trunk. For a moment I think I'm being scolded, but then she reaches for one of the handles and drags it from the back of the car. 'You'll not find anything out here in the cold and dark. Come on. Let's get it inside where we can see properly.'

Between the two of us, we manage to carry the trunk to the front room and drop it on the floor in front of the sofa. I'm about to suggest that I go through the contents, since I've been trained in investigation, but before I get the chance Aunt Felicity has begun taking out neatly folded clothes. She inspects them one by one before placing each carefully down on the coffee table. There's nothing unusual about Izzy's uniform; every girl at Saint Humbert's has to wear the same. Her casual clothes, for visits to the town, show a liking for black that I can sympathise with, and her shoes are eminently sensible.

'Not one for sports,' Aunt Felicity says as she unfolds a lacrosse skirt that has clearly never been worn. The price tag still hangs on a little bit of string from the hem.

'She was in Harriet, what do you expect?'

'I'll have you know I was in Harriet, and I was captain of the hockey team.' Aunt Felicity folds the skirt back up again and places it on the table. There's not much left in the trunk now, just a few text books and notepads, a synthetic fur pencil case Izzy's probably had since primary school, and there, nestling at the bottom, an elderly laptop computer.

'Bingo.'

I open it up, click the power button and wait as it whirrs into life. I'm expecting to have to try and hack the password, so when it doesn't even prompt me for one I know I'm not going to find much of use on here. Izzy's left a few documents and folders on the desktop, so I click swiftly through them first. Homework assignments and music files mostly, my eye is caught by a scanned, handwritten document referring to somewhere called Burntwoods, near Dundee.

'Charlotte said they found Izzy in Dundee the last time she ran away. You know anything about that?'

Aunt Felicity's blank stare is answer enough.

'What about this place? Burntwoods?'

She shakes her head. 'Never heard of it.'

I tap and swipe, but there's not much here, at least after the briefest of casual glances. A more thorough analysis will take time though.

'I thought teenage girls lived on their phones these days anyway,' Aunt Felicity says helpfully. 'Surely all you'll find on there's her chemistry homework.'

'Actually I was more interested in her browser history, but you're right. Most of the stuff that might point to where she's gone will be on her phone if it's anywhere.'

'You should really be talking to her friends, you know.'

I stare at the screen without really seeing it. Aunt Felicity is right, of course. The first thing I should do when trying to trace a missing person is speak to their known associates.

'I would, if I knew who they were. They weren't all that forthcoming with names when I spoke to the staff at Saint Bert's. It's hardly surprising, mind you. I couldn't exactly flash my warrant card.'

'Not her school friends, silly. Her friends in the village. The girls she grew up with.'

'She still speaks to them? I hardly exchanged a word with any of my old primary school chums once I got sent off to boarding school. Except Charlotte, of course.' It's a possibility, I suppose, but I've no idea where to start. 'How would I even find them if I wanted to? I don't know who they are.'

Aunt Felicity looks at me like I'm a fool. 'I'd have thought that would have been obvious, wouldn't it? Not as if there's anywhere else to go in this village when you're too young to drive.'

20

I don't recognise the barman in the Green Man, Harston Magna's only pub, but then that's hardly surprising. He's cheerful enough as he serves me a pint of local bitter though, and gives me a lot more change from ten pounds than I'd get in London.

'Passing through?' he asks over the general noise as he drops a fiver and some heavy coins into my hand.

'Kind of. I grew up here. Hoping to catch up with some old friends.'

'Oh right. Anyone in particular?'

I try to think of some names. I spent most of my childhood either at Saint Humbert's or bored out of my skull in the north of Scotland. Dad being the local landowner meant I didn't get to mix much with those few villagers my own age, but there were a couple of farmers' sons I knew.

'Keith Spencer still around these parts?'

'Keithy? Yeah.' The barman looks at his watch. 'He'll probably be in around nine, half nine. If his missus lets him out, that is.'

'Keith's married? When did that happen?'

'Two, three years ago?' The barman shrugs, then loses interest in the conversation as another punter waves his empty glass for a refill. I sip from my pint, scanning the room for likely underage drinkers. At first it looks like I've drawn a blank, but then I notice a couple of coats stuffed into a corner bench, two bottles of something sickly sweet on the table in front of them. I wind my way through the crowd of strangers, take a seat at the next table along, and before long two young girls come stomping back in from the beer garden, the smell of cigarette smoke clinging to them like cheap knock-off perfume from the local market. One of them stares at me in a manner my Aunt Felicity would probably describe as rude, then they slump back onto the bench and grab their drinks. I give them a few minutes to settle, listening to their incessant bitching about someone called Johnny who's apparently a waste of space and probably has STDs. It brings back happy memories of my own misspent youth.

'It's Kathryn, isn't it?' I say to the taller of the two when the conversation drops for a moment. Both pairs of eyes turn to me like I'm some kind of sick paedophile or something, but I know I'm right. Babysitting was just about the only job I could get when I was in my teens, and eyelash extensions or not, I recognise the petulant child in the near-adult nursing her oh-so-grown-up drink.

'Who the fuck are you?'

I feign surprise. 'You don't remember me? It's Con. Con Fairchild. I used to babysit, remember?'

The scowl remains on Kathryn's face, but it softens a little. I can see the thoughts whirring. If I'm who I say I am, then I not only know who she is, but also how old she is. I haven't the heart to tell her the barman knows full well she's underage. Her dad's probably told him to make sure she doesn't get too plastered too often. Either that or he's just glad she's out of the house.

'What you doing here? Heard you'd gone off to work in London or summat.'

'Yeah, I did. Just passing through. Thought I'd have a drink in the old place. It's changed.'

Kathryn's friend sniffs. I don't recognise her, but the fact she's talking to me is a good start. 'Seems like the same as ever.'

'Dunno. It's cleaner than I remember. Folk go outside to smoke too. They never used to bother.'

'Fucking freezing.' Kathryn's friend sniffs again, reaches into her pocket and brings out a pack of ten. I can't tell the brand as the packaging's all white these days. Seems odd that these two smoke though. I thought it had gone out of fashion. Everyone's into those e-cigarettes that smell like toilet cleaner.

'Get you guys a drink?' I indicate their bottles, close to empty. It's almost too early into our conversation to ask, and I get a wary look in response. Then Kathryn shrugs. 'Sure. Why not?'

'Yeah, I'll have another.' Her friend shuffles around the table and stands. 'Be back in a minute.'

Whether she's off for another smoke or to the toilet I don't much care. It'll be easier to talk to just one of them anyway.

'Same again?' Kathryn nods, so I weave a course to the bar, thankful that the barman's not busy despite the crowd. He pours me another pint, puts two opened bottles down beside it. This time a tenner doesn't go so far.

Kathryn's still sitting there when I get back, but there's a look on her face I don't like. She still takes the drinks, necks one to claim it as her own and leaves the other for her friend.

'I remember now. You joined the police, didn't you?'

I shrug an ambiguous acknowledgement. 'See me in uniform?'

'Why'd you do that, then?'

'If you really want to know, it was to piss off my dad. Stupid old twat wanted me to marry some chinless wonder with a big estate and lots of money. Fuck that for a game of soldiers.'

Perhaps it's the casual swearing, or the offhand manner in which I refer to the man most people in this village still pay their rent to. Or it might be that a bottle and a half of alcopop is all it takes to loosen Kathryn up. Either way, she relaxes a bit.

'What you doing back here, then?'

'Honestly? I'm trying to find Izzy DeVilliers.'

She stiffens as she hears the name, the bottle halfway to her lips for another swig. I watch as she scans the room looking for her friend, uncomfortable in my presence again.

'Look, it's not a police matter. I'm not even doing it for her parents. Charlotte asked me to see if I could find her. Not to bring her back, just so that she knows she's safe.'

Kathryn gives me that look I first mastered as a teenager too. The one that says don't take me for an idiot, I wasn't born yesterday.

'What about Dundee?' I dredge up the name from the laptop. 'Burntwoods?'

She shrugs perhaps a little too swiftly for my liking, but she's clearly far more skilled at lying than the average scumbag drug dealer I come across in my day job. There's no point pushing it if she's just going to clam up though. Instead I go to fish out a card from my pocket. I've got some with the Met logo and office contact details on, some just with my name and mobile number. It's the latter I place on the table beside Kathryn's bottle.

'See, if she calls you, tell her I was asking after her. Give her that number if she'll take it, OK?'

'An' you just wanna talk?' Kathryn reaches out and slides the card towards her, palming it before shoving it in her pocket.

'If she wants to talk to me. She knows me. I looked after her when she was little. Same as I looked after you, remember?'

Kathryn opens her mouth to say something, but then her gaze darts away from my face. I follow, and see her friend pushing through the crowd of drinkers. She grabs her bottle, takes a swig and then thumps down into her seat with all the grace of a baby elephant.

'Some bloke over at the bar asking for you,' she says, nodding in the general direction. I remember my earlier conversation with the barman and wonder if Keith Spencer has arrived, and whether I really have anything to say to him anyway. We might

NO TIME TO CRY

have had a thing once, but it was as much my rebellion against my parents as anything else. And if he's married, well, that could be awkward.

Then a group of people move slightly, giving me a view of the bar and the people leaning up against it. I see him for only a split second, but there's no mistaking that face. Not Keith Spencer at all.

'I have to go.' I half stand, half crouch, sliding around the table in the direction of the back door and the beer garden. The two young women stare at me as if I'm mad.

'Someone I'd really rather not see.' I pull my last tenner out and put it down where the business card was. 'Get yourselves another on me, but I wasn't here, OK?'

Kathryn's eyes are wide, but her friend nods and palms the money much more quickly than the card with my number on it went. I duck through the crowd, keeping an eye on the bar and hope I can make it to the back door without being seen. There are many people I might have expected to meet in the Green Man on a Friday evening, but Detective Constable Dan Penny is not one of them.

A couple of smokers eye me suspiciously as I close the door carefully behind me. I don't know either of them, which is a relief; the last thing I need is to be dragged into a conversation. More cars have slotted into the narrow parking spaces out here, the street filling up too. I must have timed things just right when I came in.

It's fully dark now, and the night air chills me. I can sympathise with Kathryn's friend about the cold, even if it's her own bloody fault for smoking in the first place. At least I'm certain the two of them know Izzy, and well enough to be in touch. Kathryn's reaction to her name was all the tell I needed. Now I just need to hope they'll pass my number on to her, and that she'll give me a call. It would make life a whole lot easier.

I slip out of the beer garden and back into the street, keeping as much to the shadows as possible. What the fuck is Dan bloody Penny doing here? In the Green Man? Looking for me, obviously. Kathryn's friend said as much. But why? I told Bailey I'd see him in his office tomorrow morning. When I said it, I even meant it. So why come all this way to find me? Are they really that worried I might do a runner?

I'm fairly sure I've not been seen as I quicken my pace across the village green, heading for the gate that opens onto the path through the woods. Hands shoved deep in my jacket pockets and hugged against my sides, I'm not sure if I'm shivering from the cold or from anger and shock. If it had been any other officer, I'd have assumed there'd been some development. Maybe they needed to get me to a safe house or something. But they'd have phoned, and not sent someone out here from London. A couple of local bobbies in a squad car would have done the job just fine.

The sky is clear, moonless and speckled with stars. I follow the old path between tall hedges as it winds down the hill towards the woods. It's been too long since I last saw a proper night sky, not the orange glow of streetlights and the flashing strobes of planes on their noisy descent to Heathrow. As I put more distance between myself and the Green Man, so my initial surge of adrenaline wears off and my anger burns more slowly. It's not hard to see that there's something off about this whole situation. Everything that's happened since Pete's death all points at corruption in our team. Someone's been feeding information to the mob we were supposed to be gathering intelligence on, and that same someone has managed to deflect all the suspicion onto me.

But Dan Penny? Sure, he's the biggest arsehole I've ever met. He's so full of himself I'm surprised he can even breathe, and his attitude towards women belongs in the Stone Age, preferably weighed down with actual stones and thrown into a deep lake. He's lazy, not that good a detective and frankly about as attractive as root canal surgery, despite his claimed string of conquests among the women PCs in the station. Corrupt? Well, maybe. But not on his own, and not in charge. He doesn't have the imagination.

So why the fuck is he in the Green Man?

The looming trees give me no answer, and all the owls can do is hoot. I clamber over the stile, feel my feet sink slightly into the soft loam. It's maybe half a mile to Aunt Felicity's house from here, along a well-defined path. I walked these woods most of my life, know them like the back of my hand. Some people might be scared of the dark, but I've always welcomed it. I have no fear as I set off deeper into the forest, just the cold anger burning in my breast, the questions that have no answers, that make no sense.

Which is probably why I don't notice the two men until it's too late. The first one steps out from behind a tree, and with hindsight I know he's just a distraction. I'm trained for shit like this, tensed and ready to take him on even if he looks wiry as fuck. Then someone else grabs me from behind. Something clamps over my mouth and nose, a whiff of chemicals, and everything goes black.

21

A rhythmic shaking drags me up from the depths of sleep and into a world of pain. It takes me a while to work out that I'm in a car and being driven somewhere, a while longer to remember how I got here. I almost open my eyes before my brain starts to catch up with what's happened. The two men in the woods, someone using chloroform on me. Christ, do they still use that stuff? Judging by the way my head hurts, it would seem they do.

The car rides smoothly, its engine a muted distant drone. Big and expensive is my best guess, coupled with the fact that I'm belted into a reasonably comfortable seat. It would be better if my hands weren't tied behind my back, but beggars can't be choosers, I guess. I risk a glimpse through slitted eyes, then wince as the bright headlights of oncoming traffic lance through me like lasers. In that micro-second I am able to make out two people in the front seats, a driver and a passenger, leaving me alone here in the back. Where they're taking me is anyone's guess, but they don't know I'm awake. It's a slim advantage, but I'll take it.

The throbbing in my head eases as the minutes slip past, leaving me with a raging thirst and a horrible taste in my mouth. Keeping my movements to a minimum, I try to do something about the binding around my wrists. It feels like a cable tie, so I might be able to get it to loosen a bit, if I can just get a fingernail into the little ratchet.

The car slows, turns sharply and thumps over some kind of ramp before I can even get started. The noise changes, and I realise we've gone into some kind of building. I hope it's an underground car park and not some disused warehouse where I'll be tortured and killed like Pete.

When the car stops, I fake being still out cold. It must work, because rough hands grab me, unclip the seatbelt and haul me out of the car. He's strong, whoever he is, and smells of mothballs. I let my head loll forward onto my chest, then risk another peek through slitted eyes. It's darker here, and I have time to make out a polished concrete floor, doors to either side. There's a tray outside one that looks like nothing so much as room service in a hotel. A plate with the remains of a half-eaten meal on it, plastic knife and fork, empty Coke bottle. Maybe not a very upmarket hotel.

We pause, and I feign stirring. The man carrying me merely tightens his grip, and then a ping announces the arrival of a lift. Inside, the lights are brighter and my groan not faked. I feel sick to my stomach. How would my captors feel if I threw up in here?

'Come on. No messing around.'

It's the first words I've heard spoken since they captured me. Not the man holding me, but the other one. I stumble slightly, taking my weight on unsteady feet. It's still painful to open my eyes wide enough to see properly, but I can see we've gone from polished concrete to marble tile, and the skirting boards are dark wood.

We stop, and my captor knocks on a door. There's a moment's pause and then another man speaks.

'Bring her in, Adrian.'

I know that voice, and as he speaks those words so it all begins to make sense. Sort of. I mean, a telephone call would have been easier and less prone to later prosecution for abduction. It wouldn't have made me less disrespectful though. Chances are

I'd have ignored it, so maybe the chloroform and cable tie seemed the better option.

I'm guided into a room dominated by a view of London's night-time skyline seen through two vast window walls, led towards a chair and forced down with my hands still cable-tied behind my back. I squint through cigar smoke painted green by an old lamp, to the man who sits on the other side of an antique desk large enough to land a helicopter on, see that horrible face that I was expecting as soon as I heard him speak.

Charlotte and Izzy's father.

Roger DeVilliers.

'It's good to see you, Constance. Been far too long.'

My hands are still tied, and I'm still a little groggy from the chloroform, otherwise I'd probably get up and walk out. I had nothing to say to this man the last time we met, just a glassful of very expensive claret to the face. Now that he's gone to all this effort to see me, I've even less desire to be in his presence. Strange how being drugged, abducted and brought to London against your will can colour your impression of a person.

'Brandy?' He hauls himself upright, walks stiffly across the room to a black lacquer cabinet that probably cost more than a year's fees at Saint Humbert's. Opening it up reveals a row of crystal decanters and glasses. He unstoppers several, sniffing at the contents in a manner that puts me in mind of a dog investigating street lamps. Finally he decides which one to drink, pours himself a stiff measure, slightly less for me. The walk back from the cabinet to where I sit clearly gives him pain, and I take comfort in the knowledge that he almost certainly has trouble with gout. That would explain the size of him too. He looms, head haloed by a chandelier, then offers me a glass. My hands are still tied behind my back so I shrug my shoulders instead of taking it.

'Of course. Silly me. I should have asked Adrian to undo that.'

He puts the glass down a little too heavily on top of the desk and I watch the liquid swirl before settling. Looking over my shoulder to the door, I see that my abductors have left, so quietly I didn't notice before. They're well trained, probably ex-SAS or something. But then Roger DeVilliers always did insist on the best.

He shuffles back around the desk and drops himself into his chair. It squeaks in protest, and for a moment I picture him tipping over backwards onto the floor. Alas, my hopes go unfulfilled. The initial terror at being abducted has long since subsided, and now I know who's behind it, my anger is growing ever hotter. I don't know how yet, but I'm going to make this smug bastard pay for what he's done.

Now I know I'm not being watched, I swivel my hands so that I can get the tip of my pinky in the plastic catch of the cable tie. Just a pity I tend to chew my fingernails when I'm stressed. It's not been a good fortnight. Still, I work away at it while he prattles on. Always did like the sound of his own voice.

'You dropped round and spoke to Margo this afternoon, I understand. After you'd been to Saint Humbert's and harassed poor old Mrs Jennings and Ms Spungeon for information about Isobel.'

I think I can feel the cable tie loosening, although all the circulation to my hands has been cut off now and my fingers are still numb. A more observant interrogator, Adrian perhaps or his silent friend, would see what I was doing in an instant. Roger DeVilliers is not observant, and doesn't even seem to notice when I shift in my chair. I use the motion to cover myself as I twist at the cable some more. When it finally gives I suppress the urge to moan in relief. I just about manage to palm the tie so that I don't drop it and give the game away. Then the pins and needles come.

'I have to assume you didn't find anything useful at school, or you wouldn't have been hassling people in the pub. Or did you just go there for old times' sake?'

Hands still behind my back, I flex my fingers to get some life into them, mostly ignoring what the old man is saying. He always was full of himself, but I didn't understand quite how much until my seventeenth Christmas. It was a family tradition for people to come to the hall after midnight Mass, drink my father's booze and eat my mother's inedible Christmas cake. I'd mostly managed to avoid the mistletoe hanging in almost every doorway – a lesson I'd learned the hard way a few years earlier. Even so I couldn't avoid the drunken bull in a china shop that was my father's oldest friend as he steered me towards the nearest frond. He smelled of body odour, brandy and cigars then, much as he does now, and I'll never forget his loathsome, wandering hands. I'll never forget how funny my father thought it was either, his utter lack of concern as his oldest child was sexually molested in his own house. His braying laughter at my tears.

I got my own back though. The next time Roger DeVilliers tried to cop a feel I threw a good hundred pounds' worth of Château Pétrus in his face and broke two of his fingers. From the way he holds his brandy now, I suspect they never really set properly.

He drains the glass and struggles to his feet again, limps over to the decanter for a refill. When he comes back, it's not to his chair but to my side of the desk, resting his ample backside against the walnut veneer as he looms over me.

'Why exactly is it that you're so interested in finding my daughter?' He leans forward and I'm once more engulfed in that horrible smell. It doesn't terrify me like it once did though. Now it just annoys. And this close I can see the bloodshot yellow of his eyeballs, the crazed network of burst capillaries that cover his bulbous red nose and cheeks. His hair is thinning awkwardly, leaving a trail of greying fringe on his forehead as the bulk of it retreats towards his ears. He's dressed like some caricature of a country squire and looks frankly ridiculous.

'Why are you not?' I finally deign to answer while at the same time bringing my untied hands around from behind my back. I rub my wrists again to help the circulation, shove the cable tie into my pocket and then take up the brandy glass. I'm not a huge fan of the stuff, but at least it's not cheap. It takes away the taste of the chloroform too.

'Ah, so you do talk.' DeVilliers smirks as if he's just won some great battle of wills. 'Let me guess. Charlotte came to you with some kind of a sob story, did she? Or was it that waster of a brother of yours?'

Another jibe I find easy to ignore. This man thinks he's in control, but really all he has is wealth. 'Izzy walked out of school and disappeared. She's sixteen years old, there should be a nationwide hunt for her, all the newspapers and TV stations showing her picture to the world. A man of your resources, I'd have thought you'd have got all the tabloids running the story. They loved all that stuff about Char when she was fucking that Saudi prince, after all.'

The smirk disappears. This round to me. DeVilliers hauls himself upright, leaning on the desk as he limps back to his chair.

'I spoke to a chap by the name of Bailey this morning. Detective superintendent in charge of one of the Met's organised crime special task forces. You know what he told me?' DeVilliers pauses for long enough to take an unhealthy swig from his glass, then the smirk is back.

'He told me that you, a lowly detective constable, were currently on suspension from active duties pending investigation into corruption within your team. Corruption that led to the death of a Detective Inspector Peter Copperthwaite.'

Now I know he's just trying to wind me up, and that I'm

not about to get shot in the head, it's easier to ignore Roger DeVilliers' prattling and try to work out what's actually going on. I'd not really thought about it until he started all this, but the fact there hasn't been a big hue and cry about Izzy's disappearance is almost more noteworthy than her going missing in the first place. As far as I'm aware, Roger is one of the wealthiest men in England. Judging by his actions this evening, he's used to getting his own way and considers himself to be above the law. And yet for whatever reason, far from using his considerable resources to look for his missing daughter, he's actively suppressing any search.

'You don't want her found, do you?' I still can't bring myself to use his first name, and I'm damned if I'm going to call him Mr DeVilliers.

'Isobel is her own person. I've made enquiries, and I'm assured she is in no physical or mental danger. I see no reason in trying to track her down right now.'

I don't need to be a trained investigator to know that he's lying, and I can hazard a guess as to why. It would explain why Izzy ran away too. Far from putting me off, it only makes me want to find her more. If only to give her a big sympathetic hug.

'Are we done here? Only I've an important meeting tomorrow morning I don't want to miss.' I stand up and place the glass down on the desk, the brandy inside barely touched. For all my bravado, this encounter's rattled me more than I'd care to admit, and all I want to do now is escape. Rolling up the sleeves of my jacket covers my shaking, but it also exposes the colourful swirl of patterns inked up both my forearms. When I fold my arms across my chest, DeVilliers looks at me like I'm something he's just found on the leather sole of his thousand-pound handmade shoe.

'I'm serious, Constance. Stop looking for Isobel, or next time I won't tell Adrian to be so restrained.'

There's something in the threat that lends me strength. I'm sure he means it, and I've no doubt DeVilliers is both ruthless and resourceful enough to get rid of me should I become too much of an inconvenience to him, family friendship or not. But there's something else behind his bluster, something I never expected to see. He's afraid. Not as much as I am, but it's there all the same. I stand up straight and stare him down.

'It's Detective Constable Fairchild to you. And if I so much as see Adrian or his silent friend I will have them, and you, arrested for abducting an officer of the law.'

22

The lift takes me to a marble-clad lobby, and a smartly dressed concierge buzzes me out of the tower block. Two things occur to me as I stand on the pavement and look around. First, this is the exclusive private entrance to an ultra-modern development of designer boutiques, hotel, conference facilities and incredibly expensive serviced apartments, and, second, I really need to pee. I turn, and tap on the glass door, but the concierge ignores me. No doubt he's been told to make sure I leave and don't come back.

There's probably a way into the hotel part of the development, but that will likely be around the other side of this enormous building. It's late, and all the swanky wine bars and gastro-pubs around here are closed or closing, so it's not easy to duck into one and use their facilities before anyone notices. I'm in a part of the city I don't know well either, otherwise I'd be able to find somewhere easily enough. As I look around, trying to get my bearings, I notice a group of people standing outside what looks like the entrance to a basement. I can hear strains of music, ebbing and growing as if a door is being opened and closed on a live performance. Sure enough, when I wander over I discover a jazz club I've never heard of.

It costs me twenty quid to get in, along with an odd look from a doorman I'm sure I recognise but can't quite place. The club is tiny, a stage shoehorned into the back corner and crowded by the four musicians playing something that may or may not be music. It could be that I'm early and they're just tuning up, but judging by the earnest looks on the faces of the audience, this is what people have paid to hear. At least the toilets are easy to find, and clean. Relief was never more blessed.

I check my phone while I'm in here, surprised that no one's tried to contact me. It's too late to call Aunt Felicity, so I ping off a text and hope she's not worried about why I never came back from the pub. My stomach growls as I remember the promised casserole, most likely now in Treacle's dinner bowl. It's way too long since I last had anything to eat.

The noise from the band mimics my digestive tract, growing first loud, then shrinking away again as someone comes in. I hear the door on the next cubicle slam, the tinkling sound as someone else finds relief. It reminds me that I can't stay here, but I've no idea where to go. There's my flat across the city, but I've no idea if it's being watched, and as far as I know the bed's still got two bullet holes in it; not sure I could sleep easy there. I could go back to Charlotte's, but given the run-in I've just had with her father, I'm not sure I want any help from the DeVilliers family right now.

There is one place I could go. Somewhere nobody would expect. If my city geography's right, Pete's house isn't too far from here, and it should be empty. I've still got my key and I know the alarm code. I can hole up there for the night, then get out of London on the first train north. Back to Harston Magna for my car and Cat, then who the hell knows where?

The flushing toilet in the next cubicle reminds me that I'm not alone. Whoever's in there clatters the door on her way out, and doesn't wash her hands before leaving, the dirty cow. I take a bit more time over my personal hygiene, trying to do something with short-cropped hair that's not enjoyed such a long day. It's only when another woman comes in that I realise I've been staring in the mirror for too long, listening to the asynchronous noise of the jazz and trying to psych myself up to go outside. Time was I'd take something like today in my stride, punch my way out of it and stay smiling. Now I feel weak and small and overwhelmed.

'Know how you feel. Not my idea of a night out either.' The other woman smiles at me before going into the cubicle I've just vacated. Her words are well intentioned, and I take a strange succour from them. Not everyone is out to get me.

The door swings open again as I'm approaching it, the noise from the tiny auditorium washing over me in a wave. I'm expecting another bored woman, brought here on a date by some well-meaning bearded hipster. What I'm not expecting is the hipster himself.

'Wrong door, mate. This is the Ladies'.' The words are automatic, but even as I'm speaking them I can tell this isn't a simple case of misdirection. There's the look in his eyes as he sees me, for one thing, but the real giveaway is the short knife in his left hand.

'Who sent you?'

As opening gambits in a potential knife attack go, I suppose it's not the most obvious, but I'm more pissed off than scared at the moment. Sure, this is an enclosed space and the way he's holding his blade suggests to me it's not the first time he's done it, but my brain's had enough shocks today. He doesn't answer, of course. I never expected he would, and I'd probably not hear him over the noise coming in through the open door.

I take a step back, then another as he advances towards me slowly. I've no idea who he is, but his intentions are fairly clear.

'No, really. Who the fuck sent you? And how did they know I was here? Even I didn't know I was here until ten minutes ago.'

He pauses, head cocking ever so slightly to one side as he tries to understand what I've just said. I shrug my shoulders a little, hoping to loosen my jacket enough to whip it off and use it in the inevitable fight that's coming. I hate knives. Well, to be honest, I hate all weapons, but knives are nasty, unpredictable things. Nine times out of ten if you go out with a knife you'll end up being the one who gets stabbed with it. Just my luck if this is the tenth time.

The noise of a toilet flushing comes out loud and clear. I risk a sideways glance, trying to remember whether the cubicle doors open inwards or outwards. It doesn't really matter; my new friend who's just relieved herself has nothing to do with this fight and I'm not about to drag her into it. She's still behind me, so I have to act now. Luckily my bearded attacker thinks the same.

He lunges forward, bringing the knife up in a sweeping arc that would slice across my arms if I held them up to protect myself. Instead I duck backwards, grab the cubicle door and swing it open as hard as I can. He lets out a dull grunt of pain as the knife smacks into wood and skitters out of his hand. I wait until he's grabbed the edge of the door with his free hand, then pull it back as hard as I can, step forward and punch him in his exposed throat, bring my foot up into his groin. He crumples to the ground, smacks his head against the door, and falls still. The whole fight has taken just a few seconds.

'The fuck?'

I glance around to see the other woman standing in the open door of her cubicle. Wide eyes track from me to the man gasping on the floor and then back to me again.

'I told him this was the Ladies'. Some folk just won't listen.'

'Ummm . . . Right. I'll just be . . . going.' She steps carefully around me, looks down at the comatose man on the linoleum floor, then bolts out of the room. I locate the knife, kick it well out of reach, then place a foot in the small of the bearded man's back and roll him over.

'OK then, arsehole. Who sent you?'

He says nothing, eyes firmly closed. I reach a careful hand to his neck and check for a pulse. It's there, but weak. He's not faking it but really out cold. Just my luck. Going through my pockets, I find the cable tie Adrian used on me earlier, and press it to the same use as before. Then I haul my assailant up and drag him into the cubicle, sit him down on the toilet. He moans a little, but doesn't look like he's going to come around any time soon.

A quick search brings up nothing. He's got a fold of ten-pound notes in his jacket that I feel I've earned, a mobile phone that's locked with a PIN, so I can't even use his limp hand to open it. I shove it in my pocket anyway, then close the cubicle door on him. Too many questions, not enough answers, but I know more than anything else it's time I got the hell out of here.

23

I don't feel at all safe leaving the club, but then I don't feel safe staying there either. I suppose I could call the police; that's what I'd tell anyone else to do in the circumstances. Right now I'm not sure I trust even them though. I can't get the image of Dan Penny talking to the barman of the Green Man out of my head. What was he doing there? Why was he asking for me when he's got my mobile phone number and our boss spent the afternoon chatting to my mum?

My London geography's not as good as I thought it was. I know where I'm going, and I know I'm going in the right direction, but it's a lot further than I thought. I might have flagged down a taxi near the jazz club, but now that I've put a few minutes' walking between it and me, they're nowhere to be found. Nothing to do but shove my hands in my pockets, keep my head down and walk like someone who's meant to be here. I just hope that news of my little altercation hasn't spread too far. The last thing I need is gangs in cars roaming the streets looking for me.

Get a grip, Con. That's not going to happen. You don't even know if that bloke back at the jazz club knew who you are or was just a psycho out to cut someone. Maybe if you hadn't knocked him senseless he'd have been able to tell you.

But he was coming for me, not anyone else. And I can't help but remember the way the doorman looked at me. I still can't place him, even though he looked vaguely familiar. The more I think about it, the more I think he recognised me. But that's nuts. I don't live or work in this part of town. I'm not some kind of celebrity everyone thinks they own a part of. The only people who knew I was in that area were Roger DeVilliers and his two goons, Adrian and the silent one.

Wee Jock said someone had put out a contract on me. Not enough cash to attract the professionals, but maybe enough for wannabe amateurs. People who might panic and shoot a stray cat that was under my duvet? People who'd get a tip-off from a bouncer friend of theirs and try their luck with a switchblade in the Ladies' loo? What the actual fuck is going on?

I'm still pumped up on adrenaline and fear, walking too quickly not to attract attention. Forcing myself to slow, I take out my phone and chance the battery for a quick reminder of where I'm going and how long it should take to get there. Just as well, or I'd have missed my turning. I've been on a major road most of the way, but now the streets are tree-lined, more shadow than street light. It's late enough for a lot of the front windows to be dark, adding to the sense of unease. I can't see well enough to be sure I've not been followed, or there's nobody lurking a few paces ahead, ready to jump out at me as I pass. It's hardly reassuring that the darkness means nobody can see me either.

The closer I get to Pete's place, the more I begin to recognise things. I'm still on edge though, almost shaking, and I nearly forget to stop at the end of his street. There's always a chance that his house is being watched. If it's someone from my unit, chances are they'll be asleep by now; the night's too warm for a stakeout. If it's someone from the mob who we were trying to shut down, then I'm screwed. I don't think I've the energy left to fight them.

Just paranoia, Con. There's nobody watching Pete's house.

I approach it slowly nevertheless, constantly scanning the

street for any sign I've been spotted. Of course I haven't, but I can still feel the cross hairs on my back as I fumble with the keys and let myself in. Only once I've got the door shut firmly behind me do I finally begin to relax.

It's dark inside, but I daren't turn any lights on. Not at first anyway. I go straight to the alarm console, tap in the code to disarm it and only then realise it hadn't been bleeping, hasn't been set. Did nobody do that the last time I was here? Seems a bit lax. I double-check, but it's definitely off.

The house feels empty as I creep around it in the dark, check that no one is lurking in a small cupboard ready to jump out and knife me while my back is turned. It's not just the emptiness of no one being here, but a kind of deathly hollowness, as if all the life has been sucked out of it. The air outside was warm, my skin is sticky with sweat from my march across town. But in here it's cold enough to make me shiver. I pull my jacket tight around me, continue through the house until I'm certain there's nobody here and all the doors and windows are locked.

Only once I'm sure I'm alone do I collapse on the sofa in the front room. There's enough light from the street lamps outside to see by, now that my eyes have accustomed themselves to the darkness, and I stare up at the shadow patterns on the ceiling, wondering how I've got myself into this mess and how I'm going to get out of it. The first rule of any inquiry is to define the parameters; get to the heart of the problem and the solution will often present itself. If there is just one problem to deal with.

'Well, then. Deal with the most pressing problem first.'

I glance over at the armchair in the corner, fancy I can see a dark figure sitting there. The voice of my conscience come to haunt me again.

'What would you consider most pressing, then? The price on my head? The fact that I was abducted by one of the country's richest men and dragged back to London against my will? That there's clearly something very rotten in our unit and they're trying to pin it all on me?'

I'm staring at the ceiling again, but even so I imagine the shadowy figure shaking his head.

'Come on, Con. You're better than this. I can't help you if you won't help yourself.'

'What's that even supposed to mean, Pete?' I ask the darkness. It doesn't answer.

'OK. I suppose the fact that people are trying to kill me is probably most important right now. I need to put a stop to that, but how? As long as there's a price on my head there's going to be some idiot in a ninja suit coming after me wherever I go.'

'It's not the idiots you need to worry about. They more or less take care of themselves.'

'You think there's someone a bit more professional out there after me?'

'Someone shot me in the head. Reckon you need to be more worried about them than your bearded friend with the knife.'

I listen to the words in the darkness. Pete always did have a way of seeing through the rubbish to the important things. I guess that's why he was a detective inspector and I never made it past constable.

'So what? I should run away?'

'Well, you're not planning on walking into Gordon Bailey's office tomorrow morning, are you?'

Deep down, I know that Pete's not really there. I've never believed in ghosts and I'm not about to start now. I'm exhausted, hungry, under far more stress than any sane person should have to endure. Is it any surprise I'm seeing things, hearing my thoughts as the voices of the departed?

And it's true, I had no intention of going back to the station, even if my superior officer has ordered me to do so. I might have done, had I not seen Dan Penny in the Green Man.

'Penny's a stooge. There's no way he's behind all this.' Pete's voice might be only in my head, but it's scathing.

'I know that. I mean, it doesn't surprise me that he's bent as a nine-bob note, but he's never been a leader. No, my bet's on someone higher up the food chain. Maybe much higher. Fuck me. What have I got myself into?'

I stare across the darkened room, waiting for Pete to speak. But he's not there. He never was there. And I've no more answers than before.

24

The blaring of a car horn wakes me suddenly, and for a moment I can't work out where I am. Then it all comes flooding back, along with a deep pain in my wrists from the cable tie, a nasty chemical headache and a horrible stiffness in my neck and shoulders.

Pete's ghost is nothing but a memory, the armchair clearly empty in the pale morning sunlight that filters in through the trees outside. I struggle to my feet, stretch and shuffle upstairs to the bathroom. The shower is very tempting, but I've only dirty clothes to put on afterwards, and I don't think I feel safe enough to undress even here. Christ, I used to be a grown-up.

There's a text from Aunt Felicity lighting up the screen of my phone when I get back down to the living room.

Your father came round wanting to speak to you. Told him he can call you himself.

Short and to the point, much like my aunt herself. I text her back.

Heading for the train, can you pick me up from the station? Couple hours. Will call when on way.

The answer comes back swiftly, a smiley face emoji. Who says the over-sixties don't get technology?

I reset the alarm code to a new number before I leave, my own little act of rebellion. For a moment I consider posting the keys in through the letterbox. This isn't my house and I have no right to come here. In the end, I slip them back into my pocket, just in case.

It occurs to me as I walk up the street towards the nearest bus stop that I've no idea what will happen to all Pete's stuff. It's inconceivable that he didn't write a will, so I guess it will all be sorted out eventually. I suppose it'll all go to his parents. Unless he left it to his ex, Veronica. Having met her, I find that the thought doesn't bother me. I'm sorely tempted to turn to her for help, in fact.

No one pays me any attention on the bus; this is London, after all. I feel happier in a crowd, but still nervous knowing that people are looking for me, people want to kill me. In my line of work that's always been an occupational hazard. I've understood the risks and minimised them as much as possible, but if the job's not going to protect me, then I'll just have to do it myself.

Trundling up the Tottenham Court Road, I gaze out at the cheap electronics stores and remember Izzy's laptop. I want to have a more thorough look at it, but I can't keep hold of it for ever. I know a way around that, though, and the fat wedge of cash in my pocket, courtesy of last night's would-be hitman, will make it a lot easier. Jumping out at the next stop, I step into the first computer store I find open, and spend almost all of the stolen money on a new laptop and all the other things I'll need. It's frustrating to know that in my flat across town I have most of this kit already. Unless, of course, someone's been through there and taken it all as evidence.

'You planning on setting up as a hacker, eh?' The young lad who watches me counting out ten-pound notes tries to make it sound like a joke, but it's clear he's half serious. I give him something that's part smile, part sneer in response, then notice the line of neat padded rucksacks hanging behind the till.

'How much?' I point at the least garish, and he pulls it off the rack.

'Thirty. But seeing as you've bought all this, and it's cash, you can have it for twenty.'

'Cheers.' I peel off another two tens, hand them over. Not much of my ill-gotten gains left. Ah well. Easy come, easy go.

I reach Euston station around the time I'm supposed to be meeting Detective Superintendent Bailey in his office. It won't have gone unnoticed that I've not even checked into the station, so it surprises me that no one bothers trying to call. I spend the half-hour before my train leaves nursing a cup of coffee and going through my emails, all the while expecting some kind of communication from work. And yet it never comes. Not even a text.

The train's pulling out from Watford Junction when the door at the end of the carriage swishes open and a man walks in. I hardly give him a glance at first, go back to staring out of the window, but then something about him sets off my internal alarms. I only caught a brief glimpse of him before, but I'm almost certain he's the man who grabbed me in the woods last night. Without thinking, I rub at the sore marks on my wrists left by the cable tie, but before I can do anything else, another man slides into the seat opposite me.

'You've left town I see, Miss Fairchild. Very wise.'

This one I have less trouble remembering. I never had a chance to study his features before, but his short-cropped hair and angular face confirm my suspicions of him being ex-military. It takes me a few moments, but then I remember his name.

'Have you been following me all this time, Adrian?'

'Keeping an eye on things is what Mr DeVilliers pays me to do.'

'Didn't work out so well in the jazz club across the road though, did it?'

'I'm not your bodyguard. Just making sure you're doing what you're told.'

'And I suppose dear old Roger had a word with my boss. That'd be why no one from the station's tried to find out where I am.'

Adrian doesn't answer that, and it occurs to me that this is simply him trying to frighten me. It's hard to be scared by someone who's just following you around when there are people out there who are trying to kill you.

'You can assure Mr DeVilliers that I'm no longer interested in tracing his daughter,' I say. 'I am very interested in why he's so keen she not be found though, and I can't promise that it won't come up in conversations with some of my friends. So many of them are journalists, too.'

Another pause, and he taps a finger lightly on the table. He's well dressed, but casual, a fleece jacket over jeans and a plain T-shirt rather than a suit and tie. His silent friend is still standing in the aisle, swaying gently with the rhythm of the train.

'It would be . . . unwise if you were to talk to the press about any of this.'

'A bit like it was unwise to abduct me and bring me to London against my will?'

'Would you have come if we'd just asked?'

He has a point, but I'm not about to admit it. 'Was there any reason for you being here, or were you just showing off your tracking skills?'

'Just letting you know where we stand, that's all. And passing on a message from Mr DeVilliers.'

'I'm sure he's got nothing to say I want to hear.'

'Which is precisely why he asked me to be the messenger. That, and you stormed out of his office before he could say it last night.'

I've met Adrian's type before. Full of shit and taking pleasure in exercising what little power they have over you. With his background in the armed forces, I can imagine him fitting right in at the Met, although private security doubtless pays a lot better. I almost get up and walk away, but then he'll just follow me until he's carried out his orders. Trained dogs are like that. 'OK, then. Get it over with. What does the old lech want to tell me?'

'Mr DeVilliers is used to getting his own way, Miss Fairchild, but he acknowledges that carrot works better than stick some-times. He understands that there's been some . . . difficulty at your work recently. A colleague died in awkward circumstances. Awkward for you as much as for him, I should say.'

'There was nothing "awkward" about Pete Copperthwaite's murder. He was tortured, then executed, and I will find whoever's responsible and see they rot in prison for the rest of their lives.'

'Of course. I'm sure you will.' Adrian's words are condescending, but strangely enough his tone is not. 'But, in the meantime, Mr DeVilliers has asked me to tell you that as long as you stay away from London and don't try to find his daughter Isobel, then he will use his not inconsiderable influence with the Chief Commissioner of the Metropolitan Police to make sure that no charges are placed against you in the matter of Detective Inspector Copperthwaite's death. You leave us alone, and all that nonsense goes away.'

For a while it's all I can do to stare out of the window at the countryside rushing past. The sheer brass neck of the man leaves me speechless. To his credit, Adrian doesn't press me for an answer, simply waits patiently while I seethe.

'You do realise there's nothing for me to be charged with, don't you?' I say eventually. Not that truth or logic seem to count for anything these days.

'That's not what Mr DeVilliers has heard. And, let's face it, they're looking for a scapegoat and you fit the bill nicely. It's just fortunate you have influential friends and a wealthy family to fall back on.'

'Christ. You really mean that, don't you? You have absolutely no idea—'

'Just consider it, Miss Fairchild. Leave Isobel alone and this all goes away. Continue to pester the DeVilliers family and, well . . .' He leaves the sentence unfinished, shrugs his shoulders and then stands up. His silent friend moves aside to let him pass, and then the two of them walk away down the aisle.

25

Aunt Felicity meets me at the station and has the good grace not to ask any questions on the half-hour drive back to Folds Cottage. I can see that she wants to, and I'd be happy enough discussing it with her, but first I need to find whatever device Adrian and his friend have planted on me to make me easier to track. I can't believe for a moment that they've been tailing me all the while; I'd have surely noticed that.

'Have you any idea how long you'll be staying this time?' she finally asks as she pulls on the handbrake and kills the engine outside the rickety wooden garage. My Volvo is still parked on the driveway in perhaps the most awkward spot imaginable, the keys in my jacket pocket.

'I don't know. I don't want to be an imposition.' And I don't want to be this close to my parents either.

'You're never an imposition, Con, dear. I get few enough visitors as it is. The spare room's yours for as long as you need it.'

Neither of us has undone our seatbelt yet, let alone got out of the car. With the engine off, it's quiet and secluded. Private, even, although I can't shake the nagging feeling Adrian and his silent friend have bugged me and are listening in.

'I'm not going back to London. At least, not for a while. I'm not sure I want to stay here though.'

Aunt Felicity raises an eyebrow at this. 'Really?'

'Harston Magna, I mean. Not here here.' I indicate the cottage with a loose flap of both hands. 'We're too close to the hall, for one thing.'

'What about your job? Will they not complain if you don't turn up for work?'

'I rather think Roger DeVilliers has put an end to my career in the Met.' As I say it, I realise that it's true. Well, half true. Pete's death and the clusterfuck of our operation put an end to my career as a detective, and I'd pretty much decided I was going to quit anyway. Blaming Charlotte and Izzy's dad makes it slightly easier to accept though.

'Roger? What's that old scrote got to do with all this?'

'Old scrote?' I can't help but laugh. 'What a wonderful expression. Haven't heard it in ages but it sums him up perfectly.'

'Is he why you went back to London last night? Have to admit I was a bit worried when you didn't come home from the pub.'

'I didn't go to London, I was taken.' I tell Aunt Felicity a little of the story of my abduction, her face narrowing into a scowl with each new word.

'Horrible, horrible man. You know he tried to feel me up at one of our Christmas parties?'

'You and me both. I'm guessing you weren't underage at the time though.'

She shakes her head. 'Probably for the best he spends all his time down in the City these days, though I feel a certain pity for poor old Margo, rattling around in that big old house of theirs.'

'That might explain why she was on the gin in the middle of the afternoon. Guess that's the price you pay when you sell your soul to the Devil.'

Aunt Felicity stares at me, her expression even more startled than when I told her about being abducted. 'My dear child, I'd no idea things were so bad.'

'What do you mean? Margo and the gin?'

'No, silly. You. I thought you were just a bit shaken up about work, but it's much worse than that.' She reaches over and gives me as good a hug as is possible in the confines of a car. 'Come on. Let's get the kettle on and have a cup of tea. Things are always better with a cuppa, and your cat will be pleased to see you.'

I'm about to protest that it's not my cat, but before I can speak she's out of the car and almost at the door. I follow reluctantly; Aunt Felicity is right about the tea, and I could use a shower and change of clothes, but there's something warm and safe about the interior of her car. Bad things can only happen if I leave it.

The crunch of wheels on gravel breaks the silence as I reach the open front door. A couple of seconds earlier and I'd have been inside, could have ducked out back and into the woods. Escaped. As it is, I know I've been seen, and really there was no way of avoiding this, so I wait patiently as the shiny new Range Rover parks alongside my shabby old Volvo. The man I want to see even less that Roger DeVilliers climbs out and looks up at the cottage, slowly taking it all in before resting his gaze on me. He's balder than I remember, but my father's sneer is just the same.

'Constance. What the devil's happened to your hair?'

To say that the atmosphere in Aunt Felicity's kitchen is tense would be something of an understatement. My father has never been all that fond of Folds Cottage, and his relationship with his sister can best be described as strained. His earlier comment about my hair surprised me until I realised just how long it's been since last I saw him. I've had my boyish crop since I made detective constable, but it was short even before then. The last time we spoke face to face, it still hung below my shoulders. His has long since departed.

'Your mother's not been well. Are you going to come and see

her?' It's the first thing he's said since accepting a cup of tea, and while I'm halfway down mine he's not taken so much as a sip.

'I'm not sure I want to set foot inside Harston Magna Hall ever again. Perhaps we could meet in the pub.'

'What's this I hear about you upsetting poor Margo DeVilliers, chasing young Isobel around?' His sigh is far too passive-aggressive for my liking, but I can hear the petulant teenager in my own voice too. This is why I stay away.

'Have you spoken to Margo? Or has Roger been bending your ear?'

'Both, actually. Roger tells me you've quit the police.'

'Well, he's full of—'

'Cake, anyone?' Aunt Felicity cuts through our conversation before it gets too heated.

Father takes a slice, even though he clearly doesn't want it. I pick mine up with my fingers, shove it into my face and take an unladylike bite just to spite him. He toys with his with a fork, not actually eating anything. It takes about two minutes before the silence breaks.

'Why do you have to go chasing off after Isobel? I'm sure she's just fine wherever she is, otherwise her father would have called the police.'

I lick my fingers one by one. It's an excellent cake, and I know it will annoy my father. 'Isobel's just turned sixteen. She doesn't have to go to school any more, but she's not an adult. The police should have been informed the moment she didn't turn up home at the appointed hour, but nobody seems to give a shit what's happened to her. All I've heard is that apparently she's called her mother, only when I asked Margo about that she flew into a panic. And your best buddy Roger had a couple of his goons abduct me and take me down to London against my will. Now he's threatening my boss and me if I don't back off. And all I've done is ask a few questions about the whereabouts of his

156

daughter. So tell me, Daddy dearest. What would you do given the circumstances?'

It's the 'Daddy dearest' that ruins it. For a moment, I thought I'd got him, if not on my side, then at least considering there might be more than one side to the story. No doubt his old pal Roger has been on the phone to him, but my father trained as a lawyer. Once upon a time he was able to think critically, at least about things not affected by gender. On the other hand, he considers women to be inferior beings, quite incapable of functioning without the firm guidance of a male hand, and everything he will have heard about my recent misfortune at work will only have bolstered that opinion in his mind. I called him 'Daddy' ironically; inevitable I suppose that he will have taken it entirely straight.

'I would do precisely what the girl's father asked me to do, Constance. And that is what you must do. Of course.' He smiles as beatifically as any pope, wipes at his thin lips with a napkin even though as far as I can tell he's neither eaten any cake nor drunk any tea. I hope he is finished, but then again I learned long ago not to have any hopes where my father is concerned.

'And you must come home. Straight away.'

I'm still seething at my father, even though if I was being rational I'd have to admit he's not done anything too terrible this time. Watching from the relative safety of the living room as the Range Rover pulls away, I'm even more determined not to stay in Harston Magna. He won't leave me alone, and sooner or later I'll have to face up to Mother. At least my father doesn't really do emotional blackmail. He's just a dinosaur.

'I need to pop into town for an hour or so. Want to come?'

I can tell from the tone of Aunt Felicity's voice that she's only asking because she feels she should. Tea and cake with her brother is obviously something that doesn't happen often. I expect like me she finds the easiest way to deal with him is to keep her distance.

'If you don't mind, I'd rather stay here and sort some stuff out. You've got broadband, right?'

'Password's on the fridge door. Make yourself some lunch if you want it.' My aunt's relief at being able to get some time to herself is well concealed, but I'm trained to read people. I know she said I could use the spare room for as long as I needed, but it's another reason why I'm going to have to find somewhere else to go.

I wait until she's gone before I dig out Izzy's laptop and the bag of goodies I bought with purloined cash this morning on the Tottenham Court Road. I know that sooner or later someone's going to come around for the trunk, but I've got a plan that should buy me some time.

Unscrewing the cover on the underside of the computer, I extract the hard drive, relieved to see that it is the specification I thought it was. I've another one, identical but unused, in my bag, along with a couple of external cases and a shiny new laptop of my own. It takes a while to set everything up, and longer still to download the relevant software from the web, but eventually I've got a brand-new, cloned copy of Izzy's hard drive alongside the original. I put the clone into her computer, screw the cover back carefully so as not to leave any obvious sign it's been opened, and then put the whole thing back in its place at the bottom of the trunk. Then I drag it out into the hall, where it can wait to be collected.

I'm tucking into a sandwich when Aunt Felicity returns, laden down with what looks like therapeutic shopping to me. She dumps a bag of food from something that describes itself as an artisan delicatessen onto the kitchen table, then hands me another, larger bag from the local department store.

'You didn't have much in the way of luggage when you

arrived, dear. So I took the liberty of buying you a couple of outfits. Nothing flash, I know what you're like.'

I open the bag and the first thing I see is a box of underwear. Not the sort a man might buy me, but sensible stuff that's actually comfortable. The rest of the clothes are as close to perfect as I can imagine, and as I go through them I can't help the tears that prick the corners of my eyes. It's a long time since anyone's shown me such kindness.

'You really shouldn't have.'

'But I wanted to.' Aunt Felicity embraces me in the kind of warm hug I imagine most children get from their mothers. She's always been a better parent than either of mine. Perhaps because she never married, never had kids of her own. I've often wondered about that, but never dared to ask. Now's not the time either.

'Look at me. Battle-hardened detective constable and I'm crying over a three-pack of Sloggi knickers.'

We both of us laugh at that, and for a while everything's OK. It's Aunt Felicity who speaks up though, says the thing I need to say.

'You're going to keep poking at this until it explodes, aren't you, dear.' It's not a question.

'I have to. You know that. Otherwise they win.'

'I know.' Her smile fades, a look of regret passing over her face as she accepts what we both knew was inevitable. 'And Fairchilds never back down from a fight.'

26

The address on Veronica Copperthwaite's card takes me to a small business park off Coventry Road on the way into central Birmingham. It's just as well I've got satnav on my phone otherwise I'd never have found the place. Even with it I spend twenty minutes wandering around looking at doors with no numbers or name plates on them before I reach the right one. A bored-looking receptionist asks me if I've got an appointment, then directs me to an uncomfortable chair in the corner while I wait to be seen. There's half a dozen dog-eared *Cosmopolitan*s and a couple of *National Geographic*s on the table beside me, and a distinct lack of offers of coffee while I wait.

I'm halfway through an article about the Nile Delta with photographs far better than its prose when I catch sight of a door at the other end of the room opening.

'Constance. This is a surprise.'

Veronica Copperthwaite is dressed almost identically to the way she was when I met her at Pete's funeral. Business-like dark suit, sensible shoes, a stack of folders in one hand. She dumps these on the receptionist's desk, then crosses over to greet me. Her smile is genuine, but there's a hint of worry in her eyes.

'Sorry. I should have phoned ahead, but it was all a bit spur of the moment. I was wondering if I might beg a favour.'

'If I can help, of course.' She turns to the receptionist. 'If Reg

160

shows up, tell him I won't be long.' Then back to me. 'Come on through.'

It's only as the door behind me closes with an electronic click that I begin to notice the security about the offices. It's not a big space, just the reception area, then a corridor with half a dozen doors off it and a window at the back looking out onto yet another car park. Veronica leads me into the last room on the left, a small office piled high with boxes, surveillance gear, wet-weather clothing draped over a chair back and a couple of sorry-looking pot plants gathering dust on the windowsill. She indicates an empty seat, then scoots around the desk and sits down.

'If you're looking for a job, you've come at a good time. We're crazy busy right now and could use some help.'

Now I feel bad for bothering her, but the offer is welcome all the same. 'I'd love to take you up on that, but right now there's something else I need to deal with.'

'Pete?'

'In part, yes.' I hesitate a moment, unsure how to begin. Then decide to just leap in anyway. 'I think the people who killed him are trying to kill me now. Seems there's a price on my head.'

'I take it that you're coming to me because your colleagues in the Met are being less than helpful.'

'Worse. I think at least one of them's in on it. Possibly more. But I'll deal with that. I've another little problem that may or may not be related.' I pull my bag off my shoulder and root around in it for my phone. 'I think someone's using this to track me. Either that or they've got tech I can't even begin to understand, let alone find.'

Veronica looks at me for a moment, then pulls open a drawer and takes out something that looks like a wand with attitude. She stands up, comes back around the desk and waves it over me. Nothing happens, at least not that I can see.

'Well, you're not bugged, that's for sure. Nothing active anyway, or this would have picked it up.' She puts the wand carefully back in the drawer; it's either very expensive, very illegal or both. 'Let's have a look at your phone, then.'

I hand it over, having thumbed the button to unlock it. She taps away at the screen for a while, clearly in her element, then shuffles some things around on her desk until she finds a lead, plugs it in and fires up her computer.

'You'll need to let it know it's OK for me to access it.' She hands me back the phone, now asking for my PIN.

'What do you reckon?' I ask as I hand it back.

'Have you let anyone else access this recently?'

'Not knowingly, but it might well have been taken off me for a while.' I think about the journey from Harston Magna down to London, and how much of it I spent out cold. It would have been simplicity itself for Adrian or his silent friend to take my phone at the start, unlock it with my thumb, and put it back when they were done.

Veronica says nothing, staring intently at her computer screen, one hand holding up her chin, the other expertly guiding and clicking at a mouse with the tiniest of clear spaces on her desk to work in. I leave her to it, not quite sure when I first decided I could trust her more than any of my colleagues at work.

'Ah, now that is sweet. Very high tech. Ian would love to see that.'

'Ian?' I lean forward, but can't see the screen.

'Our IT guru. He's much more into this stuff than I am.' Veronica looks away from the screen and back to me. 'You're right though. Someone is using this phone to track you. Listening in when they want to as well. And they can access the cameras, front and back. All without you having the faintest idea. Damn, this is GCHQ-level stuff. You've some powerful enemies, Constance.'

'Umm . . . Do they know we've found it? Are they listening to us?'

Veronica smiles at me like a hungry tiger. 'No. It's dormant right now. I can delete it, if you want. Or better yet, make it so you can see it, so you can control it. I'd still advise you get another phone for day-to-day stuff, but this could be much more useful if whoever put it on here doesn't know, wouldn't you think?'

If I thought Birmingham was difficult to get into, it's ten times worse to escape. There seem to be roadworks and diversions every half-mile, and I get bored of the tinny electronic voice on my phone's satnav programme telling me she's recalculating the route, or to turn around and go back the way I came. On the plus side, the convoluted journey confirms my initial suspicion that I'm being followed.

I clocked them in the car park when I left Veronica Copperthwaite's offices, two blokes sitting in a car for no good reason. They're not particularly skilled, but have perhaps had a little training. The car they're using is suitably anonymous: a dark metallic-grey Ford Focus that's a couple of years old and has probably been stolen, its plates swapped. If I was on active duty I'd call it in, have a check run on the number, but I know that as soon as I do that Detective Superintendent Bailey will hear of it and I'll get an earful or worse. It's always possible they're some of Roger DeVilliers' men keeping tabs on me. What they'll make of me going to the offices of a close-protection and private-investigation firm is anyone's guess.

When we finally reach the motorway, I accelerate hard into the traffic, keeping up with the fastest idiot commuters in the overtaking lane for a good five miles. Then I slow down and slot in between two trucks doing a regulated sixty miles an hour. Sure enough, my dark silver shadow drops back, tucked in a few lorries behind me and just occasionally pulling out into the middle lane to check I'm still there. We stay like that all the way to the A14, and when I pull off at the Harston Magna slip road, they're still following.

Damned if I'm taking them home, I turn instead towards Kettering and the local police station. I might be suspended, but I've still a few friends on the force. A formal complaint should at least get the number checked, and I suspect whoever's tailing me won't want to hang around once they know they've been rumbled.

There's a certain inevitability when tailing someone on minor roads that you're going to end up right behind them eventually. The little Ford has been a couple of cars behind for a few miles, and then both of us take a turning at the same time. Before I can react, they have accelerated, pulled alongside. I know this road, know how difficult it is to overtake, and having seen them follow me all the way from Birmingham, I immediately understand that overtaking's not on their minds.

Even so, it's a shock when the Ford swerves hard and sharp into the side of my Volvo. My vision sharpens, and time seems to slow down. The road verge here is a narrow strip of grass, a hedge that's seen better days and then a sharp drop into a recently harvested field. At the speed I'm going, ending up down there's not an option, so I steer hard the other way, mashing my foot to the floor as I do.

It's simple physics, really. The Ford Focus weighs considerably less than my Volvo estate, and has a smaller, less powerful engine. They might have had momentum on their side to begin with, but their strategy was based on knocking me off the road with the first hit. Now we're side by side, almost locked together and speeding up towards a blind bend. A glance sideways and I get a glimpse of two young men. One has his hands fixed firmly on the wheel, the other stares through the open passenger window at me, eyes narrowed in concentration as he aims a gun in my direction.

I slam on the brakes as he fires, the gunshot sounding strange over the noise of the engine. I'm thrown forward against my seatbelt as the car comes to a surprisingly swift stop, the bullet disappearing somewhere over the bonnet. The Ford carries on towards the corner at speed. I see the tractor first, and remember what it was that was niggling me about the recently harvested field. The straw's been baled, and neatly stacked in piles ready to be carted off to a barn somewhere. It's that time of year when the country lanes around here are filled with massive farm machinery.

The Ford doesn't lock up as the driver brakes hard; all modern cars have got ABS now. What they don't teach outside of an advanced-driving course of the kind the Met put me through a few years back is that you're meant to steer out of the way of danger while standing on your ABS-equipped brake pedal. Most people freeze up and plough straight on into whatever's in the way. There's nothing I can do but watch as the dark silver car smashes right into the front of a lump of metal the size of a house, with wheels bigger than I am and a fork lift on the front sporting twin spikes. It's not a fair fight.

27

'You say the other car overtook you and tried to force you off the road, Ms Fairchild?'

To be fair to them, the first local squad car turned up within five minutes of my making the 999 call. They set up roadblocks either side of the accident and had a diversion in place in double time. Against all expectations, both the driver and passenger in the Ford Focus were alive when the first ambulance arrived. One died during the wait for a fire crew to come and cut them out of the crumpled mess which was all that was left of the car. The other lasted a little longer, but not much. The tractor barely had a scratch on it. Now I'm leaning against the front of my Volvo giving a statement to a grey-haired sergeant who looks like he's seen far too many RTAs in his long career.

'It's—' I'm about to say Detective Constable Fairchild, actually, but then I remember I'm suspended, my warrant card probably still in Detective Superintendent Bailey's desk drawer. If he hasn't binned it already. 'Yes, Sarge. They'd been following me for a while, then they pulled past and slammed into the side of me.'

He's seen the Volvo, its none-too-pristine white paintwork now dented and scratched, but he raises an eyebrow at 'Sarge'. Not many civilians would know one uniform rank from another.

'You'd be related to the Fairchilds of Harston Magna, I take it.' The sergeant notes something down and I can't help thinking this would be much better done at the nearest station, perhaps with a warm cup of tea and a biscuit.

'Yes. I grew up there. Left for London a few years back.'

'And where were you going when this happened?'

Do I tell him the truth? If I do, then there will be more questions. They'll find out that I'm with the Met and then that I'm suspended pending an investigation into possible corruption within my unit. Word will get back to Bailey, and then Christ alone knows what will happen. On the other hand, the passenger whose body is being stretchered into a waiting ambulance right now had a gun and fired it at me. Sooner or later someone's going to find that; I don't believe he had the presence of mind to toss it out the window before they hit the tractor.

'I was going to Kettering to do some shopping.'

The sergeant looks at me in that way sergeants do to young constables who are being economical with the truth. I open my mouth to tell him what's really going on, but a noise distracts us both. A horribly familiar looking Range Rover inches past the poor uniform constable tasked with keeping the road closed. The sergeant mutters something under his breath that just about sums up my own feelings about the situation.

'Wait here,' he says, before setting off towards the Range Rover. I ignore him and follow, catching up just as he's reached the driver's side and its slowly opening window.

'You can't come in here, sir. This is a crime scene.' I almost pity the poor fellow as he looks up into my father's angry face.

'Do you know who I am, officer?'

'I am well aware of who you are, sir. And it makes no difference. This is a crime scene and you can't come in. Please reverse back to the cordon and wait. We won't be long.'

'I'll have your name and number, officer. I'll be taking this up with the Chief Constable, you know.'

It's been a long day, a long week. My nerves are frayed, the adrenaline rush of the latest attempt on my life subsiding to leave me twitchy and irritable. I step past the sergeant before he can respond, hold my father's imperious stare for the first time in a while.

'You won't be taking this up with anyone. You'll move your car back beyond the cordon or I'll have it impounded and you'll be walking home.'

'Constance? What the devil—'

'That's Detective Constable Fairchild. And don't pretend you didn't know that I was here. Or are you in the habit of visiting Kettering of an afternoon?'

'I . . .' He starts to protest, but I can see the confusion in his eyes. It gives me a warm glow, even as I realise he has come here because someone has told him I'm in trouble. Infuriating as it is that he feels he needs to rush to my aid, it's not been an hour since the crash. Who's told him, and how did they know?

'I'm not hurt, but I need to help the police with their enquiries. You're getting in the way.'

He stares at me, uncertain. Yesterday's conversation has had some small effect on his attitude towards me, but I'm not so naive as to think he's worried about my welfare beyond the point at which it reflects badly on him. He's not a man who backs down easily though.

'I'll call you as soon as I get back to Aunt Felicity's, OK?' It's as much of a bone as I'm prepared to throw him. Far more than I'd have given him a week ago. He stares a moment longer, then nods almost imperceptibly before reversing slowly back the way he came.

'Detective Constable, eh?' The sergeant takes no time to get back to business.

'Met. Special Task Force for Organised Crime. I'm off duty, on leave.'

He gives me that special sergeant's look again, then relents.

'And the old man's your father, eh? Can't see him being too pleased about that.'

'Until yesterday I'd not spoken to him in five years. I'd be quite happy if it was another five before I had to again.'

'Yeah, well. There's still the matter of this.' The sergeant nods in the direction of the mangled Ford Focus. 'I might not be a high-flying detective in the Met, but I can see there's more to it than meets the eye. You want to come back to the station and give us a full statement?'

I look at the crash scene, my scratched and dented Volvo, and finally back to the cordon where my father's Range Rover is backing and performing a poorly executed three-point turn.

'Lead the way.'

There's nothing quite like a mug of tea to settle the nerves. And if there's biscuits too, then all is fine in the world. I think I might have visited Kettering police station once as a primary school pupil on an outing, although that might have been the fire station now I think about it. Whichever, it's an unmemorable building, but surrounded by uniformed officers and the bustle of police administration I feel calmer than I have in days. Sergeant Colin Jacobs, he of the greying beard and suspicious nature, directed me to a comfortable interview room and arranged for a cuppa before going off to make some calls. I know at least one will be to my station in south London, and now I'm intrigued to see how far Roger DeVilliers' influence reaches.

'Sorry to keep you waiting,' he says as he comes back into the room. He's alone, I can't help but notice. I'm not being charged with anything, just giving a statement.

'It's not a problem.' I lift up the last of a plateful of chocolate digestives, raise my mug. 'I don't get this kind of treatment at my own station.'

'Yeah. I had a word with your boss. Seems you weren't

entirely honest with me about being on leave.'

I put the biscuit back again. I've had too many already, but lunch was a long time ago. 'I don't know what he told you, but I'm not here to cause any trouble.'

'And yet somehow you have. We've two men in the mortuary, a stolen car on false number plates and a gun found lying in the grass at the verge. Forensics are looking at that, but they tell me it's been fired once, fairly recently.' Police Sergeant Jacobs leans back in his chair and folds his arms across his chest. 'Tell me, Detective Constable Fairchild. Should I be calling in my friends from CID to interview you? Maybe under caution?'

I take a sip of tea before answering. 'If you were going to, you'd have done so already. Look. I know this is a mess, and not the sort of thing anyone wants happening on their patrol, but those two idiots who died? I couldn't give a shit about them. They were trying to kill me. They're not the first, and I doubt they'll be the last. I'm more worried about that tractor driver and what he's going through right now. Poor bastard didn't deserve any of this.'

He looks at me in silence for a while, and I reckon he must have been plain clothes at some point. A beat copper wouldn't be taking this much interest just for an RTA report. Maybe this posting was his way of winding down towards retirement. If so, I've kind of ruined that for him.

'So, if you're not here to cause any trouble,' he says eventually, 'what are you here for?'

It's a very good question, and one I don't have a ready answer to. 'Nowhere else to go, I guess. I left London because someone broke into my flat and put two bullets through my mattress. If you've spoken to Gordon Bailey you'll know he thinks I did that myself to divert suspicion and get Professional Standards off my back, so I'm not exactly getting much support from my team.'

Jacobs nods at this. 'Any idea who the two loons in the Focus are?'

'Not a scooby. They started following me in Birmingham. Didn't want to take them home, so I was coming here, actually. Reckoned if I pulled into the staff car park they'd back off. I thought they were just tailing me. Seems they were actually waiting for a suitable spot for a hit.'

'Do I need to know what you were doing in Birmingham?' Jacobs shakes his head, lets out a deep sigh. 'No. Not really. You've done nothing wrong, Ms Fairchild. At least not here, anyway. I'm sorry it happened, and it's possible one of my plain-clothes colleagues might want to speak to you at some point. You weren't planning on leaving the country though, were you?'

'Not until I've cleared my name. Found out who wants me dead and dealt with that too. If you need to get in touch, you've got my number. I'm staying at Folds Cottage in Harston Magna at the moment. My aunt will know where I am if I'm not there.'

'Not at the hall?' Sergeant Jacobs raises a laconic eyebrow that suggests he's dealt with my father too often before.

'No. Not at the hall.'

'Well, that's probably enough to be going on with, then.' He gets up with a weary sigh. 'We'll be in touch in due course.'

I take the cue, rise to leave myself. It's only when he opens the door for me that Jacobs speaks again.

'Thanks, by the way.'

'For what?'

'For telling your father to leave the scene. He's a pain, but he's a very well-connected pain too.'

I shrug. 'That's kind of why I left home in the first place. Never could stand bullies getting away with it.'

28

Rain clouds have gathered and it's getting dark by the time I park outside the front door to Folds Cottage. I had to take a diversion on the way back from Kettering police station, the road still closed where the accident happened. I'm lucky they didn't impound my car, I guess, but it's looking very sorry for itself. At least it still works.

Cat twines herself around my legs as I open the door and let myself in. I find Aunt Felicity in the kitchen, peering over the top of her spectacles at a copy of the *Daily Telegraph*. Nobody's perfect, I guess.

'Earnest told me about the car crash. You OK?'

It occurs to me as I pull out a chair and sit down heavily that she's the first person to ask me that. None of the police or paramedics at the scene seemed concerned about my wellbeing, and my father was clearly more worried about the damage that might happen to his reputation than that which had happened to me and my car.

'Truth be told, I'm a bit sore. My neck feels like it's cricked, but that's hardly surprising.'

Aunt Felicity puts down her paper, takes her spectacles off and folds them carefully before letting them hang from the cord strung around her neck. She stands up slowly, a little arthritis in those hips, then walks around behind me and begins to massage my shoulders.

'That's not what I meant, and you know it, Constance.'

'Only my mother calls me Constance.'

'Would you prefer Connie?' Aunt Felicity pauses her pum-melling for a moment, then moves to the small of my back. 'From what I heard, the two idiots in the other car tried to overtake on a blind bend. Why do I get the feeling that's not exactly how it happened?'

'I told you before. About the price on my head?'

The hands stop. 'Yes. And you said it was a London thing. That they'd leave you alone if you moved out of town.'

'That's what I thought. That's what should have happened. I don't even know how these two knew where I was.' Except that I do. My phone with its hidden surveillance app. Adrian and his silent friend. Roger DeVilliers. Only that doesn't make sense. DeVilliers wouldn't want me dead, would he? And if he did, then why not yesterday when he had me abducted?

'It seems to me that Northamptonshire is not far enough away, dear. You need to disappear for a while, wouldn't you say?'

I'm enjoying the neck massage, but Aunt Felicity's words surprise me so much I break away from her touch and look around to see if she's joking.

'Are you serious? Fairchilds don't duck and run when there's trouble.'

'Now that's your father talking. And truth be told he's the most terrible coward.' Aunt F. flexes her fingers, knuckle joints popping like a street fighter. She walks over to the Aga and puts the kettle on, massage over. At least my neck and shoulders feel a bit more loose now, although how I'll feel in the morning is another question altogether.

'You reckon it's that easy? I mean, what if they follow me? That's three times someone's tried to kill me now.'

'And none of them have succeeded yet, but there's nothing to suggest they won't keep trying. You need to disappear for a while.

Long enough to take stock at least, work out what's going on.'

'I can't disappear. I need to sort this out. I need to clear my name and find out who killed Pete. Quite apart from anything else, I'm going to be out of a job soon, and then how am I going to pay the rent?'

Aunt Felicity pours boiling water into the teapot, swirls it, then chucks it down the sink. She spoons three teaspoons of tea leaves into the warmed pot, then follows up with more water from the kettle. There's something very calm and soothing about the action, far more so than dumping a tea bag in a mug and mashing it around until its stewed enough. There's also something quite aggravating about her calmness.

'You worry about the little things, Constance. I know you will never stoop to asking your father for money, but he's not the only one who can help. Ben has far more than he needs, especially now that he's courting that DeVilliers girl.'

'I can't ask my brother for money. That's as bad as asking Dad.'

'Then I'll stand you a loan. I'll lend you my car too.'

Now I'm confused. 'Your car? Why? I've got a car.'

'And the people you don't want finding you know what it looks like. You'll need something less recognisable or you won't get far.' Aunt Felicity pours a cup of lightly stewed tea, checking the colour beneath the light over the worktop before handing it to me. There's a jug of milk already on the table, but no bowl of sugar. Such desecration would be frowned upon by the Tea Fairies.

'You make it sound like I've a long way to go. I'm not running away from this problem.'

'Of course not, dear.' Aunt Felicity brings her own cup to the table and sits down opposite me. 'But you need a bit of time and space to think things through. You can't do that here, and you can't do that in London. There's really only one other place you can go, don't you think?'

I stare at her maddeningly smug face for a whole minute, trying to work out what she means. I don't have anywhere else to go. And then it dawns on me with a sense of both excitement and dread. The far north of Scotland, grouse moors, salmon fishing and the sort of deep boredom that can turn a child to a life of crime.

'Newmore? But won't Dad be going there—' I stop mid-sentence, remembering the date. He should be up there now.

'Your father hasn't been back to that place in years. He lost interest in the shooting and fishing a long time ago. It's all let out to the neighbouring estate now, except a couple of beats on the river I use from time to time. The house and land belong to me anyway.'

'They do? But I thought . . .' Again the words dry up on me. I never really thought at all.

'Harston Magna Hall and all the farms of the estate here went to your father when your grandfather passed away. I'm the eldest, but that's the way it's always been.' Aunt Felicity frowns for a moment as if lamenting the injustice of a world where the male line is all-important. 'But Newmore came to me, as did this house and a few other things besides. I let your father use the lodge because he's my little brother. It's my house though, and if you need somewhere to hide, I can't think of a better place.'

I open my mouth to protest, but I can see the logic in Aunt Felicity's suggestion. Dropping off the radar until the heat has died down a bit might be no bad idea, and there aren't many places further off the beaten track than the old family estate in the Highlands. Another thought occurs to me too. Newmore's not all that far from Dundee, where Izzy was caught after the last time she ran away, certainly a lot closer than here. And she was on a train to Edinburgh the time before that. There has to be a reason she was going to Scotland more than that it's a long way from home. Where better to start looking for her without anyone knowing I'm doing it?

'OK. I'll go to Newmore. Just for a while.' I take out my phone – my old phone with the tracking app on it – and place it on the table beside my tea. A quick swipe and a couple of taps shows me that it's not being monitored right now, but was checked just an hour ago. They're still watching me.

'But first I need to do something about this.'

The woods are no longer a place I feel safe; Adrian and his silent friend have ruined that part of my childhood for me. I've never been one to curl up in the face of my fears though, and there's a job to do. I've raided Aunt Felicity's wardrobe for the darkest outfit I can find, surprised to see that she has a taste for black jeans and men's linen shirts in an assortment of dark colours. At least I assume they're her shirts; in truth there's a great deal to my aunt I know nothing about.

I do know that she's a little bit larger around the waist than me, and her legs aren't as long. It's a discomfort I'm prepared to put up with as I pick a path as silently as possible through the trees back towards the village green.

There are no attackers, silent or otherwise, lurking in the dark woods. I may have put up a deer at one point, but, whatever it was, it bounded away more startled even than me. I paused then, barely breathing, straining to hear anything over the dwindling noise of broken branches and trampled undergrowth. When the dull roar of the distant A14 finally reasserted itself, I moved on.

And now I'm back in the village, staring at the lights of the Green Man. Cars line the road and people are clustered around the door despite the on-again, off-again rain. It's not cold, so a little damp isn't enough to drive them inside. I can hear the dull thrum of music, and as I approach through the shadows I make out the sound of a live band. That's new, and surprising. Back when I used to drink here as regularly as school holidays allowed, the only music was a jukebox crammed with scratchy seven-inch singles from the 1970s. Some of them were OK, in a cheesy kind of way.

This band are reasonably tight, but the singer's awful. I pause a while in the shadows, listening and cringing. It's only when a couple stumble out into the night, him unsteady on his feet, her scowling as only a sober person in the presence of a drunkard can, that I remember why I'm here and move on. I still don't know what Dan Penny was doing in my old local, but I'm not going to see whether he's there again. That's a mystery for another time.

The old post office has gone, not even a shop to mark where it once stood. The post box is still there though, and the little marker on the front of it confirms it won't be opened again until Monday at noon. I slip the padded envelope from my jacket – well, Aunt Felicity's jacket, but I'm keeping it now – and check the address again. My own address, in London. Inside, my fully charged phone is in standby mode, plugged into a backup battery that the manufacturer claims is good for over a week of charge. It should be still trackable by Adrian and his silent friend, but it's not going anywhere for a while. And when it does, it will lead them a merry dance. I've manually transferred all the important contact numbers into my new phone, uploaded all the music I've collected over the years. Even downloads of some of those cheesy seventies tunes. I'll miss that old phone though. We've been together through a lot.

I'm still nervous as I make my way through the shadows, back across the village green and through the woods to Folds Cottage. At one point I think I can hear voices, and I freeze for a moment before stepping close to the nearest tree. It's not Adrian and his silent friend I can hear though. Not unless they're into dogging.

The clock in the kitchen says half past ten when I finally make it back in. Aunt Felicity looks up from her chair by the Aga, her spectacles once more perched on the end of her nose.

'Success?'

'Yes. It's posted. The battery should be good for a long while, so if they're tracking me they'll think I'm still in the village.'

'Good.' Aunt Felicity stands up and walks across the kitchen, envelops me in a warm hug, then takes a step back. 'Black suits you.'

It's that awkward moment when I just want to get on the road. The car's packed, and I'm as ready as I'll ever be, but there's also so much I still want to say. I opt instead for a simple 'Thanks, Aunt Flick. For everything.'

'Nonsense, dear. That's what family are for. Call me when you get there, won't you? I've let the Robertsons know someone's coming, but not who.'

Outside, the sky is clear and a few stars outshine the glare from the spotlight above the door. Aunt Felicity's car sits on the gravel, waiting. Mine is parked up in the garage out of sight. Yet another part of the cunning plan that I can't help thinking is far too complicated already.

'I should take the Volvo. You'll need this to get around.'

Aunt Felicity holds up a hand to stop me going on. 'I'll take your car to Bill Jenkins in the morning. He'll fix it up, bash out all those dents and things. Won't take him long, and while he's at it I'll just bully your father into ferrying me around.'

I know there's no point arguing with her, and in truth her car's a lot nicer than mine. Far more comfortable for the long drive ahead. I give her another quick hug, then open the door and climb in. It smells of leather and newness, and something else that doesn't quite fit in with the ambience. I look around to the back seat, empty save for a cat carrier. Glistening black eyes stare out at me from the depths.

'You didn't think I was going to let you leave her behind, did you?' Aunt Felicity leans in through the window, kisses me lightly on the cheek. 'One other thing. There's an old friend of mine staying at the lodge just now. Don't worry, she's only there for a day or two. Besides, I think you'll like her. Take care, dear. And drive safely.'

29

When I was young, the trek north to Newmore for the season seemed to take for ever. My father tells of it being even more of an epic journey when he was that age, in the days before motorways. Then it might take two or three days to get there, and the family would stay for the whole summer. Having suffered the torment of being stuck there for weeks during the holidays, I can't imagine how terrible that would have been. Maybe that explains why he's as insufferable as he is.

The downside of leaving at night is that it's much more difficult to spot whether or not someone is tailing me, but all the way from Harston Magna to the motorway I'm fairly sure I'm not being followed. Aunt Felicity's car has cruise control, built-in satnav and a radio so complicated I probably should have spent the afternoon learning how to use it before setting off anywhere. For the first couple of hours, north up the A1, I'm happy enough to listen to the distant drone of the engine, the whistle of wind around the doors and the thrum of tyres on tarmac. It's a good space to think in, to try and work out what the fuck is going on and just how I'm going to put it all right.

A couple of things occur to me somewhere around Grantham. First, it's clear that the people who have tried to kill me so far have all been fairly amateur. That's to be expected if the price on my head's low, and it's worked to my advantage since I'm still alive to have these thoughts. Second, the only way the pair of idiots from Birmingham could have found me and followed me is if the tracking information on my phone was passed on to them. That doesn't make any sense though, if the tracking app was put there by Adrian and his silent friend, acting on behalf of Roger DeVilliers.

A few more miles and I've still not found a way to square that circle. DeVilliers is a piece of shit, it's true. But he's also my father's oldest friend. There's no way he'd try to have me killed, would he?

'That depends entirely on how badly he doesn't want his daughter to be found.'

I glance up at the rear-view mirror, seeing nothing but dark shadows in the back of the car. Even Cat is asleep, curled up in her carry cage and snoring.

'You're not really here, Pete.' I fix my eyes on the road, searching for a sign that will tell me how far it is until the next service station. I need coffee if I'm going to make it all the way to Newmore without a kip.

'None of us are really here, Con. That's the nature of life. Doesn't change the fact that someone's trying to kill you.'

It's the voice of my own thoughts, I know. Pete's dead, buried, gone. On the other hand, I always did find it easier to talk things through with him than puzzle them out on my own.

'So you think Izzy's the key to this, then?'

'I don't think anything. I'm dead, remember.'

'I liked you better when you were being helpful.' A sign flashes past, the logo of a fast food chain and a number. Twelve miles.

'OK, then. Why would DeVilliers be trying to stop anyone from finding his daughter? Why would he go to all that trouble to keep you from finding her? He's got the resources to track her down easy, and yet he spends all that effort on keeping tabs on you instead.'

'Yeah, tell me something I don't already know.' I let another mile pass under the wheels. The darkness makes a cocoon of the car, my own little sanctuary.

'She's got something on him. It's the only logical explanation.'

'Makes sense, I suppose. But what? What could make him so paranoid he'd kidnap me and drag me down to London? People like him, they're not afraid of the law. Don't really give a shit about public opinion either. It's all about money, right?'

Pete says nothing, but then that's hardly surprising since he's not really there. A few more miles disappear behind me as I follow threads of thought, each one unravelling for lack of hard information. It's like an investigation in its third week, when the initial excitement has worn off and the trails of evidence have all gone cold. I need to attack the problem from a different angle.

The distant glow of lights turns into a cluster of buildings, a covered footbridge over the motorway and the promise of hot coffee. Aunt Felicity's car has barely used a quarter of a tank of fuel yet, but I need a boost. I indicate, pull off into the service station, glad to see that no other car follows me. Even by the time I've found a space to park, no one else has come in.

It's late, the service station still busy but not the mad mêlée that I'd expect during the day. I locate coffee and an enormous pastry plastered in sugar and icing, pay a king's ransom for a small bottle of water that's probably come out of a tap in Slough, then take my swag back to the car. Cat looks up from her cage, but gives me no indication she wants to come out. I wonder how she'll adapt to the Scottish Highlands. Who knows? Maybe she'll meet a local wildcat and the two of them will go off together to have a family. Chance would be a fine thing.

My mind's doing that thing it does when I've not had enough sleep and am relying on caffeine and sugar to get through. Flitting from thought to observation and on to moaning about the unfairness of life. I need sleep, but the ever-helpful satnav tells me it's another 350 miles or so. It'll be early morning before I get there.

I shove the coffee into the cup holder built into the central console, lick the last of the sugar off my fingers and then wipe them on the front of my shirt. Aunt Felicity's shirt, if I'm being honest. Or possibly some long-forgotten boyfriend's. A quick check around the car park and I can't see any particularly suspicious-looking vehicles, so I set off on my journey once more. I'm a good few miles up the road before I realise why I'm wondering whether there's broadband at Newmore; the house didn't even have a phone the last time I was there.

I'm going to need some kind of internet access if I'm going to track down Izzy DeVilliers.

The pale dawn light has been growing ever stronger since I skirted past Edinburgh and over the shiny new Queensferry Crossing. By the time I reach Perth, the day is getting into swing, early traffic building. I don't remember it being quite so well developed or busy when I was here last, but then that was a while ago.

Aunt Felicity's words come back to me as I take a half-remembered turning off the A9 and head into wooded hills. I always assumed my father loved this place so much he didn't think twice about inflicting its boredom on his children. But then I always assumed he owned it, too. Like he owned the hall, half the houses in the village, all the farms I used to visit in the hope of a glimpse of one of the young farm lads. So much of that life I just didn't understand, because I wasn't told and because I never asked. I can see the bubble I grew up in for what it was now, the purest distillation of privilege, yet bound with chains that said I must wear dresses, speak properly, marry a man with no chin, bear him children and beat those same terrible values into them. Well, fuck that sideways.

The trees thin out as I go further up the glen. I know I'm getting close when the road narrows to a single track, passing places marked by little white diamond-shaped signs. Or more often just the rusted metal poles on which they were once fastened. Tufts of grass grow up through the middle of the tarmac, the car rumbles over a cattle grid, and then I round a shoulder of the hill and Newmore opens up in front of me.

The lodge sits high on a rocky outcrop above the loch, painted in shades of pink by the dawn. It's so still that the water reflects the sky, the flanks and peak of Beinn a'chruach Mhor mirrored perfectly. As I get closer, a flock of geese fly just a few feet above the surface, and for a moment it looks like there are twice as many of them in a perfectly symmetrical double V.

The track to the house takes me past the old stone steadings of the home farm, unchanged in my lifetime and quite probably my father's before me. I remember a few adventures in there: Ben and me pretending to be pirates or cowboys and Indians or whatever politically incorrect thing was in vogue for six- and eight-year-olds with nothing better to do. Behind the steadings, there's a light on in the old farmhouse. I can't believe Tam Robertson is still alive, so it must be his son, George, who's getting up early to go and do whatever it is livestock farmers do. Christ, I can't believe how many things I can remember about this place, and there's no denying that view is something to make you stop and look.

I park Aunt Felicity's car next to something that looks like it was made a hundred years ago. I don't know much about cars, but I know art nouveau, and this is Rennie Mackintosh on wheels. Aunt F.'s friend must be minted if she can afford to drive something like this. I'm not even sure what make of car it is, just old.

The air tastes clean when I climb out of the car and stretch, a wonderful change from the second-hand smoke and car exhaust particulates I've been breathing for too many years. There's the gentlest of breezes bringing scents of water, heather and something else I can't quite place that nevertheless calms me. The sun is breaking through the narrow pass at the far end of the loch, but it's the utter silence that takes my breath away. How could I have hated this place so much?

Turning to face the house itself, I remember why. Once-white harling has been turned grey by centuries of Scottish weather. The three-storey facade is built to withstand that battering wind and flaying rain rather than with any particular aesthetic in mind. The windows are small, deep-set into the walls, and the central tower is a rich man's affectation that doesn't sit well with the earlier building. There's a light on over the front entrance that I don't remember from before, and one of the two outer doors has been left open for me.

It's been such a long drive, I almost forget Cat, quiet in her cage on the back seat of the car. I lift it out, place it on the gravel and open the front, expecting her to emerge nervously and sniff the ground before sticking close to my legs. Instead, she goes straight to the open door, tail high and stride purposeful, then disappears inside as if she's always lived here. Closing up the car door and leaving the cage where it sits, I set off after her.

Inside, the house is both different and the same. It doesn't smell as dusty and damp as I remember it, but the furniture is unchanged: solid, functional, more carved than crafted. The dark wood panelling in the hall absorbs what little light makes it in through the narrow windows, but I'm pleased to see a modern telephone handset on the sideboard. At least that much technology has made it here.

I glance at my watch as I step quietly across the chequerboard floor tiles and gaze up the stairs to the two landings and the glass light well high above. It's not quite seven, early for some. Is my aunt's friend a late sleeper? I know nothing about her at all.

The long corridor from the front hall to the kitchen at the back of the house is a lot shorter than I remember it. Memory plays tricks, and the world shrinks as we age. The door is slightly ajar, and as I approach I can hear the quiet sounds of someone inside. Cat saunters up to me, purring gently and nudging my leg as if she wants me to hurry.

A wonderful aroma of coffee greets me as I push the door wide and step into the kitchen. Of all the rooms in the house, this was always my favourite. Probably because it was always warm, but possibly because it was Margaret the housekeeper's domain. What little domesticity I have I learned in here: how to bake bread; how to prepare vegetables and make a stew big enough to feed an army; how to darn socks, sew buttons back on trousers, and knit simple things like hats and scarves. All skills I've long since forgotten, or maybe consciously rejected, but I learned them all the same. I also learned how to make porridge properly, and it's that smell which wins out over the coffee as I see a person standing over the stove, stirring a pot.

'Hello?' I'm not sure I meant it as a question, but that's how it comes out. There's no mistaking this person for Margaret. The housekeeper was a tiny woman, and she'd be about a hundred by now. From behind, all I can tell is that Aunt Felicity's friend is enormous. At least six foot and change, and broad-shouldered. Her greying hair hangs neatly around her shoulders and she's dressed in a tweed skirt and jacket, a white apron tied neatly around her wide midriff.

'Ah. Lady Constance. You've made good time. I'm so pleased to finally meet you. I'm Rose.'

She turns as she speaks, one hand clasping a wooden spurtle like a weapon. I can't say anything, am aware that I'm staring and that it's rude, but there's nothing I can do about it. When Aunt Felicity told me an old friend was at the house, I assumed some school friend, spinster of the parish or suchlike. The woman who smiles at me now is something quite different.

The woman who smiles at me now is quite clearly a man dressed in drag.

30

I know it's bad of me. I've been through the diversity training, lived alongside all manner of colourful individuals during my years in London. There was even a teacher at Saint Bert's who all the girls were convinced was a man in drag, although in truth Mrs Staunton was just unfortunate to have a husky voice and a bit too much facial hair. I shouldn't really be bothered by Aunt Felicity's friend, Rose, and yet I can't help staring at her. I don't feel threatened, don't sense any kind of hostility in that patient gaze, which is perhaps even more unsettling.

'You look exhausted, girl. Sit you down and I'll get you some coffee.'

Her voice – his voice? – is strange. There's a soft Scottish accent about it for one thing, but it's also a bit like old Mrs Staunton's voice, not so much deep as coming from the wrong part of the throat. It takes a while for the words to sink in, and that's when I realise she's right. I am dog tired.

'Sorry. I'm staring, aren't I?' I pull out a chair and thunk down into it. Rose simply smiles, fetches a mug from the draining board and pours coffee into it from a large cafetière warming on the back of the stove.

'Milk's on the table.' She points to the jug. 'And I'm used to it.'

I cradle the mug in my hands; just the smell of the coffee is enough to give me a boost. 'I have to admit, you're not quite what I was expecting when Aunt F. told me an old friend was staying.'

'How very like her to be so mysterious. She does love to tease. Hang on a mo.' Rose turns her back on me, and I hear the sound of frantic stirring as she tries to stop the forgotten porridge from sticking to the bottom of the pot. 'Think that's done, right enough. You want some?'

I remember eating porridge in this kitchen as a child, watched over by Margaret, who tutted at my adding sugar and cream. It was always served in wooden bowls and eaten with a wooden spoon. Don't ask me why, it just was. 'If there's any going spare. I'm starving.'

Rose goes to the cupboard and comes back with two bowls. They're not the ones Ben and I used to use, they'd be tiny now, but they're made of wood. I watch as she spoons a generous portion of gloop into each, then passes one over to me.

'I always think it's best with a sprinkle of demerara and a knob of butter, but some people prefer cream.' Rose pulls out a chair and sits down opposite me, her imposing bulk even more obvious. I'm sure there was only a milk jug on the table before, but somehow there's a little bowl of sugar, a butter dish and a pot of cream in front of me now. I'm just tired, I must have dozed a little.

'How long have you known Aunt F.?' I spoon a bit more than a sprinkle of sugar over the porridge, then drown it in cream. It's not often I get to indulge. Rose ponders a while before answering.

'I think I must have first met Felicity in about nineteen sixty. Or was it fifty-nine? She was just a little girl then, of course. Looked a lot like you, actually.'

I do the maths in my head. In 1959 my aunt would have been about four years old, I think. Dad hadn't even been born.

'Yes. I remember now. I used to have a little bookshop in the

189

Grassmarket. Your grandfather came in looking for a copy of Aleister Crowley's memoirs, brought little Felicity along for the trip. She was a very serious young girl. Not at all interested in the children's picture books.'

Having just taken a mouthful of porridge that's an almost perfect trip down memory lane, I have to stop myself from spitting it out laughing. The thought of my aunt as a serious little girl is too much. How did she grow up into the adult who took such delight in letting me and Ben do things my father disapproved of whenever she could?

'Hot.' I wave a hand over my mouth in the universal gesture in an attempt to hide my rudeness, swallow the mouthful and take a sip of coffee before speaking again. 'The Grassmarket? In Edinburgh?'

'Of course, you know the city.' Rose's face breaks into a smile, and it occurs to me that she's probably as uncertain about me as I am her. I took my jacket off when I sat down, forgetting the twining patterns of the tattoos on my arms. A well-to-do lady like her probably finds them a bit common, maybe unsettling.

Except she's not a well-to-do lady. Well, she's not the stereotypical Edinburgh matron. She's transgender, for one thing, and a lot older than I first thought if she knew my grandfather. And yet after just a few minutes in her company I have accepted her as just a normal late-middle-aged woman. Strange. I always notice when people put me on edge, but Rose is the complete opposite.

'I went to university there. Four wonderful, wasted years.'

'And now you're a police officer. A detective no less. How very exciting.'

'Maybe a little too exciting sometimes.' I wonder how much Aunt Felicity has told her friend about me. 'Hence my trip here.'

Rose takes a few thoughtful spoons of porridge, concentrating on her food rather than me for a while. I'm happy to do the same; it's very good and I'm starving. In surprisingly little time we have both finished.

'I should have made more. It's not often I have an appreciative audience.'

'I've not had such a good bowl of porridge since I was a little girl.'

'Sure you're not just tired and hungry from a long drive?' Rose tilts her overlarge head to one side as she asks the question, and I find myself ever so slightly mimicking the action. With the motion comes the realisation that she's right. I'm utterly knackered, and the weight of creamy porridge in my stomach isn't exactly waking me up. I stretch and yawn, eyeing the cafetière warming on the back of the stove, the precious black stimulant swirling within.

'I'll be fine. Maybe have a bit of a nap once I've got myself settled in.'

'Will you be staying long? Only I'll be leaving later today. Heading back to the city.' Rose frowns, perhaps misinterpreting my own expression. 'Not because of you, my dear. I was only going to be here for the week, and the week is done.'

'Oh.' It's all I can think of to say as she puts the pot in the sink and fills it with cold water, fusses around tidying things for a while. Finally she brings the cafetière over and fills up my mug.

'I shan't be leaving till the evening, and I would love to talk some more. But that can wait. Drink that down, then go get some rest. You look all done in, dear. I'll let your aunt know you've arrived.'

And with that, she strides out of the room, leaving me to my thoughts.

★ ★ ★

191

I don't have much luggage, but what there is I carry up to the tower room where Ben and I slept when we were children. Like everything else, it seems smaller, but it's still more than twice the size of the bedroom in my London flat. There aren't any holes in either of the two mattresses either. It's a long time since last I slept in a single bed, but it's worth it for the view across the loch to the mountains beyond. Although perhaps if I was being sensible I'd take one of the guest rooms looking out over the drive and any unexpected and unwelcome visitors.

Checking my phone for the time, I'm surprised to find both a clear signal and Wi-Fi. The connection isn't password protected, and I'm halfway through composing a stern talk to my aunt about cyber-security and identity theft when I remember where I am. The nearest house is well out of range, and that's occupied by the farmer and his wife. They've probably got their own connection anyway, and the thick stone walls of Newmore won't let much of a signal out. You'd have to be parked at the front door to use it, and that would be fairly obvious. It's a far cry from the old days, when the nearest telephone was a red box in the village, a three-mile walk away.

The old dresser makes a passable desk for my new laptop, and I spend a while plugging it in and getting it fired up. It's much quicker than my battered computer back in London, or any of the rickety old machines in the station, but as soon as I sit down and stare at the screen I'm yawning. I'm fighting the weariness when Cat comes in, sniffs the air and twitches her tail before leaping onto Ben's old bed. A couple of turns, and she's curled up tight, purring herself to sleep.

It's light outside, still morning, but I can't fight the lethargy any more. I lock the computer down, pull off my boots and clamber onto my own narrow bed. A twenty-minute nap will clear the cobwebs, and then I can get down to work. The old springs protest at a weight much heavier than the pre-teenage girl who slept here last, but the mattress is surprisingly comfortable and the pillows freshly plumped. As I stare up at the spider-webbed ceiling, I barely have time to wonder who's done that before the warmth and the silence and the calm drag me down into sleep.

31

I wake up to dreams of choking, and find myself staring into the face of a monster. Cat sits on my chest, her nose inches from mine, studying me with the sort of intensity that would have a hardened criminal spilling all in the interview room. It takes a while for reality to reassert itself, my head thick with sleep. The silence is total, and for a while I can't remember where I am. Then it all begins to seep back in. The long drive north through the night, Newmore house and its strange guest.

'Give me some space, won't you?' I struggle to remove Cat from on top of me, then lever myself upright. My mouth tastes like something has crawled in there and died; never a good idea to have coffee and then sleep. My phone tells me it's late afternoon, at least eight hours since I lay down and stared at the ceiling for a quick power nap. I hadn't realised I was so tired, can't remember the last time I slept that long uninterrupted. It's hard to get any kind of peace in the city; out here it's hard to find any noise.

I grab my washbag and stumble across the narrow landing to the tiny washroom on the other side of the tower. There are baths and showers down a floor, but this is all I need right now. The face that stares back at me in the mirror is mine, I've seen it often enough, but I don't recognise the puffy bags under the eyes or the pallid skin.

Brown peat water fills the old ceramic basin, and I can smell the earthiness in it as I wash my face and damp my hair to get the worst of the spikiness out. The toilet bowl reflects the same dark colour. Instinctively I reach for the chain on the old cistern hung high on the wall above it, then stop myself. No one's dropped a depth charge and then forgotten to flush, Con. You're in the Highlands now, remember? This water's purer than anything you'll find coming out of a London tap. No one else has drunk it since last it was a cloud.

Back in my room, I stare through the window and out over the loch. Four storeys down, Rose's impossibly elegant car still sits next to Aunt Felicity's more modern motor, so the strange house guest is still here. As if my thoughts had summoned the spirit, I hear the sound of heavy footsteps on the narrow wooden stairs, slow and measured. They stop every so often, a heavy sigh punctuating the silence. By the time she appears at the bedroom door, I've more or less composed myself.

'I thought I might find you up here.' Rose fans her face as if she's just climbed the north face of the Eiger, not a steep set of rickety wooden steps.

'This was always my room. Well, Ben's and mine. Back when we were forced to come here as kids.'

'Forced?' Rose raises a perfectly drawn eyebrow. 'Why on earth would you need to be forced to come here? This is paradise.'

I manage to suppress my laugh, more or less. 'I'm guessing it's been a while since you were a teenager.'

She smiles, comes into the room and sits heavily on the end of Ben's bed. 'Aye, well. You may have a point. Still, did you not have adventures here? Boat out to the wee islands at the far end of the loch and pretend to be pirates?'

I want to say, 'It's the twenty-first century, not the nineteenth', but I've had manners beaten into me by my father and, more effectively, the staff of Saint Humbert's.

'We were never allowed to use the boats. They were for the fishermen. I walked out to one of the islands once. The year there was a drought. Took me pretty much all day to get there and back, and I got a beating from my dad for the trouble I'd caused not telling anyone where I was going. He said they'd been searching for me all day, but I saw the boats out the whole time. Nobody'd even noticed I was gone until I came back.'

It's another of the wonderful memories I have of this house, of the utter misery it used to bring me. And yet, for all that, I feel safer here than I have at any time since I found Pete's body. Since before then, really.

'Your father never comes here any more. His gammy leg can't cope with stalking deer or walking up grouse, and he lost patience with fishing around the time I first met him.'

'You know him? My dad?' I'm surprised. My father is so tightly wound he'd never cope with meeting a transgender person. I kind of wish I'd been a fly on the wall at their first meeting; his discomfort would have been a delight to watch.

'I'd hardly say know. Earnest Fairchild does not entertain the likes of me.' Rose shakes her head sadly. 'A shame, really. His father, your grandfather, was much more open-minded. Your Aunt Felicity takes more after Fortitude. I think you probably do too.'

I'm not sure how to take this intimate telling of my family history. Quite how I've made it to my age without ever meeting this strange woman who seems to know all about the Fairchild lineage puzzles me too. I'm sure I'd have remembered her if we'd crossed paths before.

'How is it you know so much about me? About the whole family?'

'Not the whole family, Lady Constance. Just the important people.'

It's the second time she's called me Lady Constance. No one's called me that in years, although technically speaking it's the correct way to address me. Not something I encouraged in the Met, of course.

'Just Constance is fine. Or Con. I really can't be doing with this Lady business. You've no idea how much my colleagues at work would make life hell for me if they knew.'

Rose smiles, nods her head in understanding. 'Ah yes, the rough humour of the police force. Your family were for a long time defenders of the common people; I'm pleased to see you have chosen that vocation. But tell me . . . Con. Are you still looking for Isobel DeVilliers? Please tell me that you are. I know her father doesn't want you to, but she's very important. Far more than you can know.'

Hearing Izzy's name spoken brings me up short. How much has Aunt Felicity told her? How much does she trust this man who knows herself a woman?

'You know about her?'

'But of course. Why else would Felicity send you here to meet me?'

I open my mouth to complain that this is wrong on many levels, but something about Rose's directness stops me from speaking.

'Isobel is very like you. Stubborn, resourceful, but also struggling with her fear. I think you will find each other soon enough. I hope so, for all our sakes.'

'Have you any idea where she's gone?'

Rose pauses a while before answering. 'I see you haven't asked me if I know why her father doesn't want anyone looking for her.'

'Do you know that?'

'I have my suspicions.' She struggles to her feet with much theatrical huffing and puffing. It's all an act, I can see now. I'm

197

just not sure who it's meant to be for. I don't have time to ask before she speaks again.

'Well, my dear. It was lovely meeting you, albeit briefly. I have no doubt we shall meet again, and soon.' She pauses a moment, then produces a business card from the pocket of her tweed jacket. 'If you find yourself in Edinburgh any time, do drop in.'

I take the card, glancing briefly at the words. Antiquarian Books, Occult Curios. It seems somehow apt. Rose is already out of the door, crossing the narrow landing to the stairs. I stand up, go after her. 'You never answered my question. Either of them, for that matter.'

'No. No, I didn't.' She doesn't turn to face me as she speaks, her gaze on her feet as she steps carefully down. 'But don't let that deter you. Keep searching, my dear. The truth won't hide from you for long.'

A part of me wants to chase after the old woman as she thumps down the stairs, but instead I let her go. My brain hasn't really woken up properly yet, and sleeping through the day has left me feeling oddly disconnected. The conversation plays over in my head: her in-depth knowledge of my family is one puzzle, but perhaps not so surprising if she knew my grandfather, and has been friends with Aunt Felicity for almost sixty years. More worrying are her words about Izzy, and Roger DeVilliers, or rather her lack of words. I can't help but feel I am being manipulated, although why someone would try to influence me into doing something I was going to do anyway, I can't begin to understand.

The strangest thing, perhaps, is that I feel I would like to spend more time with this mysterious Rose. She strikes me as the sort of person who would be fascinating to talk to at length, someone with deep historical knowledge. And, truth be told, I know little about the family history of the Fairchilds, just the biased account my father used to tell when Ben and I were still small. I learned early on that those tales were more for my brother's benefit than mine. What was it that Rose said? That we were defenders of the common people? That doesn't sound like the knights and chivalry I was taught.

Staring out of the window, I see Rose finally leave the house. She's wearing a long overcoat and carries a small leather Gladstone bag, which she puts carefully into the boot of her ridiculously beautiful car. She can't possibly see me, but she turns, looks up and waves before opening the door and climbing in with surprising agility. The engine bursts into life, then waffles and burbles away into the distance as she leaves. Only once the quiet has reasserted itself do I finally move.

The house has changed in the years since I was last here. Aunt Felicity must have spent a fortune on rewiring it, for one thing, and all the rooms are freshly decorated. I wander from guest bedroom to guest bedroom, sticking my nose into things in a manner I'd never have dared when I was a child. It's all so clean and tidy, I can only assume someone comes in regularly to keep it that way. Not like my tiny flat in London with its archaeological layers of discarded clothing and general detritus. But then I could only just about afford the rent on my detective constable's salary, so no chance of employing a cleaner. Not much chance of keeping the place at all unless I find a way to earn money soon.

The main living room – the drawing room as my father insisted on calling it – used to be damp and dismal on those cold autumn days when the fog never lifted and the sun was just a slightly brighter patch in the grey. Now it's been transformed. The open fireplace has been replaced by a large cast-iron stove, piles of logs and peat bricks to either side. It's too warm to light right now, but the thought of it churning out heat when the rain is beating against the windows brings a smile to my lips.

Through in the smaller living room, I'm surprised to find a

television. I shouldn't be, given the telephone and Wi-Fi, but it still seems out of place. Switching it on, I'm presented with the evening news, and absent-mindedly check my watch to find that it's gone six o'clock already. I'm about to turn it off, uninterested in the endless machinations of our elected so-called representatives, when a familiar face appears on the screen behind the newsreader. The sound's muted, but I find the volume button soon enough.

'. . . inquest into the death of freelance investigative journalist Steve Benson, whose body was found floating in the Thames. Initially thought to be foul play, police now think Mr Benson may have taken his own life. CCTV footage of the journalist approaching Tower Bridge the night he died, and revelations concerning his private life, suggest he may have committed suicide.'

I stare at the screen, hoping for more, but the report ends and the newsreader moves on to another piece about school exam results. I switch off the television, and still I can see the face in my mind. I never knew Benson alive, only spent an hour scanning his case file, but nothing about it spoke of suicide. The man had ligature marks around his wrists and heavy bruising where he'd been either punched or kicked repeatedly in the ribs. There was absolutely no doubt that it was foul play. Without thinking, I pull out my phone and thumb the screen awake, then realise that I can't call the station to discuss what was never my case anyway.

'Bloody Dan Penny.' I speak my frustration to the empty room as I remember his gurning face. He was the one who wrote up the initial report, likely the one who dealt with all the forensic and pathology results. Unless there are two dead journalists called Steve Benson in London right now, then this is a cover-up. The question is why?

★ ★ ★

I swing past the kitchen, pleased to find that Rose has left a well-stocked fridge and a large jar of her excellent coffee. The light outside is taking on that evening tinge, but it's nowhere near dusk. That's something I'd missed about Scotland, the way the summer light fades so slowly into a night that's never truly dark. It's maybe a bit late for coffee, tempted though I am. Instead I opt for a heavy mug of tea, and trudge back up the many flights of stairs to my tower-top lair. It's time to get to work.

The first thing I notice is the complete lack of emails from anyone at the station. Nothing from my fellow detectives, no messages from the HR department about my being suspended pending investigation. There isn't even anything from Professional Standards, which surprises me. I'd thought they were more or less incorruptible and took pride in being as awkward as they possibly could.

There is a message from Charlotte though. Much like herself it's short and sweet and rather lacking in substance.

Hey Connie,
    just spoken to Dad about Izzy and everything's fine. No need to bother looking for her, she'll be home in a week or two. Just went off with a school friend and forgot to tell anyone. Tried your phone, but it's just taking messages. Hope everything's OK. Benno says hi.
    Char.

I read it through a few times, looking for any evidence of a coded message explaining her change of heart. It could be that the message isn't from her, that Adrian or his silent friend have hacked into her email account and are just trying to reassure me. But the way she calls me 'Connie' and the reference to my brother by the nickname he also hates is typical Charlotte.

There's no way that I'm going to stop looking for Izzy though.

Fairchilds never run from a fight. We're also a cussed bunch, contrary to a fault, and the very fact that Roger doesn't want me to look for her is enough to set me to the task. That Charlotte has fallen for her father's lies only makes me more determined.

Fishing around in my bag, I find the hard drive I took out of Izzy's laptop, still in its little caddy. I plug it into my own computer and search for another of the programs I downloaded while at Aunt Felicity's. It takes only a few moments to access all the files.

There's not much useful information. Mostly Izzy used her computer for writing bad poetry and homework assignments, but buried deep in the hidden folders most people don't know much about, the archived web browser history is a bit more revealing. Izzy spent a lot of time searching for information about refuges for battered women, as well as law firms specialising in domestic abuse. I can barely read any of the handwriting in the scanned document I saw before, but I find an entire folder labelled 'Burntwoods' that will take a while to work my way through for clues. Of course, the whole thing could be for a school project, but having experienced her father's attentions first hand I think there's rather more to the story than that.

I flick back to the poetry and things start to make a horrible sense. Sure, it's naive and painful to read, but the words between the lines speak volumes.

> Daddy, daddy. Dearest daddy.
> Why do you say you love me
> And yet hurt me so?
>
> I was your precious flower,
> Your littlest buttercup,
> Your perfect miracle.

I used to love the way you held me,
Your warmth, your solidity.
Now your stench makes me sick.

And on and on, line after line, page after page.

I close down the files with all the poetry, and start scanning through folders in search of more tangible evidence of abuse. There are very few images in the pictures folder: a couple of school trips; some blurred photos of a party that seem to focus on one particular girl; a few pictures I recognise as Izzy herself. Looking at the dates these images and folders were created, it soon becomes obvious that a lot has been deleted. There's nothing in the wastebasket, of course, but I've a few tricks up my sleeve. Nothing as sophisticated as I'd have access to if I was back at the station, and I'm sorely tempted to give Bob in the IT department a call to see if he can't help me out. I know that any contact will get back to Bailey though. And if I'm really unlucky they'll use it to trace me here.

By the time I've downloaded a free program for recovering deleted files and set it to analyse Izzy's hard drive, the tea is long gone. Outside, the sun has dipped below the mountains, painting the sky in blues, purples and yellows like the bruises on a week-old corpse. It'll take the program hours to finish its analysis, possibly even overnight. I leave it chugging away and step out into the gloaming for a bit of fresh air.

32

There's a stillness to the evening as I stand outside the front door. Not a gust of wind to be felt, and a silence so profound I think I might have gone deaf. Then some noisy bird screeches from the silver birches that line the boggy edge of the loch. As the London filters fade, so I begin to notice other sounds. The chattering of the burn running down the hill, the whistle of curlews and the contented munching as a flock of nearby sheep work their way through the tough grass. And then I hear a footstep on gravel, turn to see a lone figure walking down the drive from the farmyard. It takes a moment for me to realise it's a woman, carrying something in her arms.

'Would you be Mistress Constance?' As she comes closer, I see that she's probably about my age, although shorter and rounder. I'm tempted to say plump, but there's a strength about her that makes me think it's not fat that's shaped her, but long hours of hard work.

'Emily Robertson.' She nods her head, both hands already full of what looks like a heavy casserole dish. 'George's wife. Miss Felicity phoned and said you'd be coming, so I made a bit of mutton stew. I kent Madame Rose was leaving, but I wasn't sure if she'd left anything for you to eat. Thought I'd just pop it in the kitchen, but seeing as you're here.'

I can't help but be reminded of old Mrs Feltham, in her flat the floor below my own back in London, cooking fiery Jamaican curries for her family and making sure there's enough to leave a tupperware pot outside my door. The two women couldn't be more different physically, and yet the same basic, decent hospitality links them both.

'That's very kind. You really didn't need to.' I reach out to take the casserole dish, then realise that Emily is wearing heavy oven gloves.

'Och, it's no trouble. Here, let me take it in for you.'

I follow her back in through the front door and on towards the kitchen. I've not eaten in far too long, and the smell escaping from the casserole dish has my stomach rumbling. She puts it on the back of the stove before fetching a spoon from a drawer she's obviously opened many a time before.

'I usually cook for the hunting and fishing parties. That's if they don't bring their own cooks. A lot of folk do these days.' Emily goes to a cupboard and pulls out a large plate, slipping it into the warming oven with a practised motion. 'There's vegetables and dumplings in the stew, but I could boil up a few potatoes if you want.'

I realise too late that I'm being mothered. It's a bit odd, coming from someone who's probably not much older than me anyway. I remember George Robertson, Tam's son, as a young man. He drove the old tractor and looked after the sheep. Sometimes in the summer I might see him out in the hay fields without a shirt on, but I never found that particularly arousing despite what all my school friends might have thought had they been here to see it for themselves. He'd have to be forty by now, but there's no reason why his wife shouldn't be younger, I suppose.

'I . . .' I'm about to say I'm not hungry just now, but my stomach takes the opportunity to growl loudly at that precise moment. I'm not going to get away with it that easily. 'No. Just the stew will be fine. Thank you.'

I pull out one of the chairs from the large kitchen table and sit down, hoping that Emily will do the same. She doesn't, and neither does she say anything. I'm used to leaving silences for suspects under interrogation to fill, so I shouldn't fall for it myself, but I do. 'I've not been here for quite a while. How long have you and George been married?'

Emily smiles and leans back against the stove. 'Oh, it's coming up on ten years now. Wee Tam Junior's nine this Christmas, and his sister's nearly seven.'

Once I've made that initial show of interest, the floodgates open. I listen to her life history and all the things that have happened on the estate in the past decade and more. It's an easy conversation, although a little one-sided. Emily clearly doesn't get out much, and I suspect George isn't the most dynamic of company. Right now, he's either up in the mountains looking for a lost sheep or fast asleep in the front room of the old farmhouse, telly on and an empty glass of beer beside him. I listen, then listen and eat after Emily has spooned some hearty stew and dumplings onto the warm plate and set it in front of me.

She's not old Margaret the housekeeper who looked after me and Ben when we were children, but I like her all the same. If I'm going to be stuck here a while, at least I'll not lack for company.

I watch Emily walk away up the drive, back to the old farmhouse and her sleeping husband. It's been nice to have a little company to take my mind off things, and I can't deny her mutton stew was excellent. Looking out across the land as the darkness begins to settle, I can see the pale dots of hundreds of sheep, ranging over the moorland. Was it one of their brethren gave its life so that I could eat? Probably.

It's so quiet here, so still and peaceful. I can understand why Aunt Felicity suggested the place as a hideout, even if she had more nefarious purposes in mind as well. The events of the past week were threatening to overwhelm me, and even Harston Magna wasn't safe. Up here though, and with my phone being slowly tracked through the postal system back to my London flat, I've the luxury of space to breathe, to collect my thoughts, to plan.

I follow the narrow path that leads from the house down to the loch. The air is warm with the end of summer, and there's still light enough to see. It never gets truly dark here at this time of year, but then it never gets truly light in the winter. Gazing out across the still water, I can't help thinking there's something missing. The jetty's where I remember it, two wooden rowing boats tied up ready for anyone who might want to go out in search of salmon or trout. The stone boathouse with its rusty tin shed squats over the little inlet like some massive insect come down for a drink. There'll be outboard motors, oars and other boating stuff stored in there, I suppose. We were never allowed to play on the loch, the only concession to our boredom being permission to paddle at the water's edge, where the burn runs down from the mountain.

Unbidden, my feet take me there. I'm glad of my stout boots over the uneven and slimy rocks. The silver birches that can be seen from my tower bedroom loom above me, reaching out over the wall and deepening the gloom, but I feel no fear in this darkness.

'It's a nice place. I'll give you that.'

Straining my eyes, I can just about make out the shape of a figure a few paces away, mostly hidden by the overhanging branches. Why am I not surprised that Pete's ghost has followed me all this way?

'I never took you for a country boy,' I say, leaning against the drystone wall. Pete doesn't move, but then that's hardly surprising since he's not really there. Just a figment of my imagination, a trick of the shadows. My conscience talking. Either that or Emily uses some very strange herbs in her mutton stew.

'You're still looking for the girl, I take it.'

'Sort of.'

'Sort of, nothing.' Pete's tone is disparaging, and it occurs to me that if he's just in my head then anything he says is coming from me anyway. It's still nice to have someone to talk to about the case. And it is a case now, even if I'm not really a detective any more.

'There's something bugging me. Well, lots of things, but this one in particular.'

'The assassination attempts?'

'Yeah. Well, not the attempts themselves. Could do without that kind of stress, but it's no good moaning about it. I'm more concerned about how they happened.'

'How they knew where you were going to be, you mean?'

'The first one, OK. I live there, so it's fair to assume I'd be there at some point. But the other two? The only reason I was in that club was because it was close by Roger DeVilliers' penthouse, and the two idiots who tailed me from Birmingham had to have been told I was there by whoever put that tracker on my phone.'

'Adrian and his silent friend.'

'That's my best hypothesis. Can't think how anyone else could have managed. But that's the problem, see. Wee Jock told me the hit was put out by the same mob as did for you.'

'He also said it wasn't enough money for anyone professional to take it seriously, if I remember. I'd be a bit narked by that. It's like saying, I want her dead, but not so much I'm prepared to pay for it.'

'Tell me about it. Only something must have changed. The guy in the jazz club and the two idiots in the car must have been tipped off. Word must have got out, and it sounds a lot like the price on my head went up.'

'Still not pros after you though.' Pete's shadow shakes its head. 'Don't mean to sound disparaging, but if they were, we wouldn't be having this talk. Not here anyway.'

'Heaven has bars, does it? Or are we both destined for the other place?'

It's only as I say the words that I realise how crass they sound. How insensitive. I'm alive and Pete's dead. Tortured for information, then shot in the forehead. I'm meant to be trying to find out who did that. How else am I going to make them pay? But I can't do that if someone's laid out cold cash to have me killed.

'It's all connected though, isn't it?' Pete's voice thins as the night deepens, little more than the rustle of leaves in the gentlest of breezes.

'What do you mean?' I've been staring out at the black water, speckled with the reflection of the first stars, and when I look for the shadow shape my mind had decided was a person, I can't see it any more. Just rocks and trees and water.

'Think it through, Con. The pieces are all there.'

I can't be sure this last cryptic and unhelpful clue is only in my mind. Then again, this whole conversation has been in my mind. Me talking to the silent gloaming. I open my mouth to ask another question, then slap at my cheek as something tiny bites at my flesh. Too late I remember what was bothering me before. The loch, the long grass and trees, the damp, still air.

In an instant I'm surrounded by a cloud of whining insect bodies. Where they've been until now, I've no idea. Maybe they don't like ghosts. Maybe they were busy pestering someone else and have only now noticed I'm here, woefully under-dressed for a lochside summer evening in the Highlands. Too late I remember just how bad they can be, these dread Scottish midges.

Heedless of the uneven rocks and slippery shoreline, I fix my sights on the house and run.

33

The little buggers are in my eyes, my nose, my hair. I can hear them buzzing in my ears and crawling over every inch of bare skin. Not biting, at least not yet, but itching like crazy. It's a stupid, rookie error. I've been here enough times before to know that you don't go out at dusk or dawn without first dousing yourself in copious amounts of eye-watering and noxious chemicals. But, then again, I've not been here for going on fifteen years. I've lived in the dry south, and the depths of London, where midge is an ageing pop star who sang on a Christmas charity single before I was even born.

I spend a good ten minutes going round the house and making sure every window is shut tight. There aren't many lights on, but it only takes one small entry point and the bastards will get in. Only once I'm sure I'm safe do I climb the stairs to my tower bedroom. When I stare at myself in the washroom mirror, my hair is all spiky and askew, my face smeared with the crushed bodies of a million tiny insects. Black spots in the corners of my eyes are yet more of them, drowned in my tears, and still I can feel them crawling over my scalp. I can hear Pete's voice in the back of my mind, laughing at my discomfort. It doesn't help my mood.

Standing under a hot shower in the en-suite off the master bedroom brings a small measure of relief. I don't know how often Aunt Felicity comes here, but the cupboards are well stocked with toiletries. There's a towelling bathrobe on the back of the door too, and enough clothes in the wardrobe to suggest she spends more time here than I thought. For all that I hated coming here as a child, I can understand why. The south of England has become so busy, so frenetic. Everyone is running just to stand still, especially in London. There's never any time to just stop and think. Up here, with the silence so unnervingly total, and knowing there aren't any other people within a hundred yards of me, I can finally relax.

On the other hand, this is a luxurious house, inherited wealth and privilege. All the things I swore I'd never come back to when I finally faced up to my father's tyrannical misogyny and told him where to put it. How easy it is to slip back into a world where the little things are taken care of for you, where the bills are someone else's problem and it's more a question of what and where to eat than whether. I have to remind myself that this is a temporary thing. I sincerely hope that I'll clear my name and find out who killed Pete as well as tracking down Izzy to make sure she's safe, but when that's done I will move on from this. I made it for seven years in the Met, I can reinvent myself without falling back on the family for help.

Cat's curled up on Ben's bed when I go back into the tower bedroom. I could sleep downstairs, but somehow I feel safer up here. A quick check of the laptop shows that it's still working its way through Izzy's hard drive and will probably not be finished for a few hours yet. It doesn't matter, the hearty meal, fresh air and hot shower have worked their magic and now I'm way too tired to concentrate on any of that. It's late too. Far later than I thought. The bed I slept on top of earlier in the day beckons me, its springs creaking as I climb under the blankets. For a moment I wonder whether the utter silence will keep me awake, but the low mechanical whirr of the hard drive in its caddy is enough to drown it out. As I drift off, I can almost convince myself I'm back in my flat in London.

Something wakes me with a start, and in an instant I'm alert, eyes open. I can't hear any noise, not even the sound of the hard drive, so it was probably the program pinging to tell me it had finished. Either that or someone's crept into the house and is coming to try and kill me. Over on Ben's bed, Cat sleeps soundly, letting out the occasional whiffling snore, so maybe it's not that. I check my phone to see that it's not quite six in the morning, bright daylight outside. As good a time as any to get up.

I take the laptop and Izzy's hard drive down to the kitchen. The casserole dish is gone, last night's plate washed up and put away. Emily went back to the farmhouse when I stepped out for some fresh air, but she must have come back in and tidied. Unless she gets up even earlier than me and has been in this morning, which might explain the noise that woke me. When I open the fridge I can see that she's put the stew in a plastic tub to reheat whenever I'm feeling hungry, so much like old Mrs Feltham I'm struck with a weird pang of nostalgia even though it's less than a week since I last saw her. I stand there, the cold air falling from the open fridge door onto my bare feet, just staring at nothing as a horrible question forms in my mind. Will I ever go back to that flat? Is that life over?

The chill finally snaps me out of my fugue, and I close the door on the piles of food. I'm still too full to think about eating, but I find a cafetière and some of Rose's ground coffee, set about making myself a brew. I take a bit of time to savour the first mug, then unlock the laptop and click on the folder to see what secrets have been uncovered.

There are thousands of deleted files, each with a meaningless alpha-numeric code for a name. Useful information like when they were first uploaded or created has long since been lost, but

at least I can sort them by size. The largest files are most likely
video and images, the smaller ones documents or maybe thumb-
nails. The file recovery program has had a stab at classifying some
of them, but it was a freebie, nothing like as sophisticated as the
analysis software we use at work. I'm going to have to do this
the hard way.

The first few large files are indeed images, but nothing particularly worthy of notice. More of the party and the girl who
must be one of Izzy's school friends, a few pictures taken in and
around Harston Magna and the Glebe House. I recognise
Kathryn and her surly friend, the inside of the Green Man.
The first video file I click on is corrupted, just jagged lines in
multicolour. The sound is still there though, a curious huffing
and groaning that sounds almost like a farmyard. Until someone
screams.

I'm so shocked, I knock over the mug. Luckily for me it's
empty now, but my hand trembles as I reach out and set it
upright again. The scream has quietened down to sobs, a young,
high-pitched female voice muttering 'no, no, no, no, no' while
the farmyard noises continue in the background. Except they're
not farmyard noises, not animal but human. Male.

The file comes to an abrupt end, and I have to pour more
coffee, drink half of it before I can bring myself to open up
another. This time it's a still image, but it's not a school outing or
some innocent teenage party. I've worked in vice, and my
department in CID sometimes dealt with the more esoteric and
barely legal kinds of pornography. I've seen stuff that would
make you want to join a convent and devote yourself to Christ
rather than look at a man, and I've seen stuff that isn't pornography at all, even though sex is what drives it. The girl in this
image is far too young to have given consent for what is being
done to her, which makes it child abuse. The tears in her eyes,
the running black of her inexpertly applied mascara, make it clear

she isn't a willing participant either. I can't see the faces of the men; they wouldn't be stupid enough to let that happen, although someone, somewhere, knows exactly who they are. I can see the face of the girl though, and now the dreadful poetry makes horrible sense.

Izzy DeVilliers ran away because she was being abused and filmed while it was happening. And if she had these images in her possession, it doesn't take a genius to work out why her father doesn't want her found.

34

It takes me a whole day to come to terms with what I've uncovered. Finding out that your father's best friend is a serial child abuser is not something you can process casually, no matter how much the revelation is actually unsurprising.

My first instinct is to pick up the phone and call this in, but the knowledge of who I'm dealing with stays my hand. Roger DeVilliers managed to get even Professional Standards off my back, so his reach is far, his influence everywhere. I might have thrown them off the scent for a while by posting my phone back to London, but soon enough they'll work out what I've done. It won't take Adrian and his silent chum long to get my number plate on the NPR alert database, probably Aunt Felicity's too if they're even half competent at their jobs. Christ, I hope they don't drag her into this.

I spend the morning going through as many of the files as I can stomach, gathering together as much evidence as possible. It's harrowing work, even after I've downloaded a simple photo editing app to blur out the faces of the girls. I'm not interested in identifying those of them who aren't Izzy. Not yet. For now I'm trying to see recurrent features in the men doing the abuse. Their faces might never be seen on camera, but there are more ways to identify a person than that these days. I'm hoping Roger DeVilliers doesn't know that.

In the afternoon, I go for a long walk up the mountain. I

remember as a child being forced to hike over the moors, and hating every miserable minute of it. Now with only sheep and deer, rabbits and eagles, for company, it's the perfect antidote to the soul-sickening video footage I've been wading through. It gives me time to think too.

I really need to find Izzy. I understand now why she ran away, why she would have been difficult at school. It's hard to understand why DeVilliers would let her out of his sight at all, but then the kind of man who could do what I've seen today would surely believe he had total control of her. And if it started young, then maybe he does. Almost. He must have a contingency plan though, probably more than one. He'll have been seeding doubts about her mental stability for years, of course, but what will he do if he feels really threatened? How far would he go against even his own daughter?

When I get back from my walk, I can't really bear to go over the photographs again, even though I know there are clues in them that will help put Roger DeVilliers away for the rest of his life. Instead, I flick through the files Izzy hadn't deleted, and the folder labelled 'Burntwoods' that I'd been going to read through before I uncovered the horrible truth. I heat up some of Emily's mutton stew in the microwave, pour myself a beer and settle down to read.

It's not quite what I was expecting.

Burntwoods, apparently, was a large country mansion built in the early nineteenth century a few miles north of Dundee. Much like Harston Magna Hall, it was the centre of a large estate split up into several farms, but there the similarities end. Unlike the Fairchild way of passing the estate down the male line, Burntwoods came to a daughter of the family in 1875. Mirriam Downham, rather than finding herself a husband to run the place, took it on herself, and over the years it became something of a refuge for abused women and girls. Tragedy struck in 1930, when a fire all but destroyed the mansion, killing many of the women staying there at the time, Ms Downham amongst them. Various male members of the Downham family tried to press their case for inheriting what remained a sizeable and wealthy estate, but it appears Ms Downham had already transferred title to a trust, managed by her niece. The house was never rebuilt, but the Downham Trust still funds shelters for abused women to this day.

Izzy's research is far more meticulous than anything I would have cobbled together at her age. There's scanned images from old newspapers, copies of deeds and legal documents, endless articles about both the house and the trust, as well as plenty of photographs of Mirriam Downham herself. Burntwoods was an impressive building if the black-and-white pictures are anything to go by, but I can't work out why Izzy would be trying to get there, if that was why she ran away to Dundee before. From all I can see here, the house was never rebuilt and the trust funds shelters all over the country. One closer to home or Saint Humbert's would surely have been easier to reach.

I'm still puzzling that one out when my new mobile starts to ring. I stare at the screen as it shows a number I don't recognise. Not Aunt Felicity, who's pretty much the only person who knows this new number. Not any of the people I've added to the address book either, or it would show a name. Two more rings and it will go to voicemail, an anonymous welcome message that doesn't confirm anything. I should let whoever's calling speak to that. If it's something important, they'll tell me what, and if it's an attempt to trace me it will fail.

Except the only way someone could have got this number is through Aunt Felicity. And if they've persuaded her to part with it, then I need to know who they are, need to know that they're coming. I tap the screen to accept the call at the last possible moment.

'Hello.' I pitch my voice lower than normal, try to make it masculine.

'He— . . . Hello? Is that Cons— . . . Miss Fairchild?'

A young woman's voice, I can hear the fear in just those few words. I recognise it too. The Green Man in Harston Magna, a couple of underage drinkers. One who I used to look after when she was just a baby. I've not seen her in any of the photos or videos, so clearly she's not Roger DeVilliers' type.

'Kathryn? How did you get this number?'

'Oh, thank God. I tried to call you, but it kept going to message. And then it was answered and this man asked me who I was. I hung up sharpish. Didn't know what to do. But then I remembered your aunt. Figured you'd be staying with her, not up at the hall. Not after . . . well.'

'Is she OK? My aunt?' I cut through the babble before it can get properly started.

'Is she OK?' A moment's confused pause. 'I guess so? She gave me your new number anyway. Tried to explain it to her, but . . . she said it was easier if I talked to you myself.'

'What was easier, Kathryn? What are you trying to explain?' I've a horrible feeling I already know, but I need to hear it from her.

'It's Izzy. She hasn't called. I think something's happened to her.'

The silence that follows goes on for so long, I begin to wonder whether she's hung up.

'Kathryn?'

The air in the kitchen is still. Outside there's not a breath of wind. The utter lack of noise in this place used to freak me out as a child, and I can't help but remember those nights when I'd wake a few hours before dawn, terrified that Ben had died in his sleep, straining my ears to hear his shallow breathing. To hear anything at all.

'Kathryn? Are you still there?'

Something like a sob comes down the line, and with it I hear noises all around. The house creaks and groans as its walls and floors expand with the day's heat. Out on the edge of the loch a curlew is calling its low, bubbling whistle. A tractor chunters down the drive towards the old steadings.

'You said Izzy hadn't called. Is that something she'd set up? A regular contact with you?'

'I'm not supposed to tell anyone. She was right stern about that. 'Specially not the police.'

As I hear those words, it all makes a horrible kind of sense. If Izzy's father can pick up the phone and speak to Gordon Bailey, if he can have whatever misdirected witch hunt they'd set up for me called off, then of course he's got the police primed to jump on anything that might even smell like his daughter leaking incriminating evidence.

'If it helps, I'm not really police. Not any more.'

'Yeah. I know. That other one told me.'

'Other one?'

'The bloke in the pub. You remember, right? That's why you went out the back way?'

So much has happened in the days since I last spoke to Kathryn that I'd almost forgotten Dan Penny.

'What was the deal with Izzy, Kathryn? I know what her father did to her, what she was running away from. Believe me, if I can find a way to put Roger DeVilliers behind bars I'll do it. If I had my way, I'd be looking for a more permanent solution. Probably involving garden shears.'

Another pause, but it's shorter this time. Then when she finally speaks, the floodgates open.

'She said he was a monster. Showed me and Tina some photos and stuff and it was just horrid. I mean, proper want to throw up horrid. That man. Her own dad. How could he? But she couldn't just go to the press, see? It was a journalist came to her in the first place. Said he was working on an exposition or something like that. Only he turned up dead in the Thames a few days later. That's when Izzy said she'd have to hide. But she didn't just want to disappear. What if that . . . man found her? I mean, he must have raped her a dozen times. More. Why wouldn't he kill her this time? And she was scared. But she was also kind of angry at it all. And she had a plan, but it wasn't ready. She needed to get away.'

I've been fiddling with the laptop while Kathryn's been speaking, closing down images and randomly clicking on some of the other files in the Burntwoods folder. There's a lot of photographs of the house, and quite a few of the women who lived there in the first three decades of the last century. They all stare at the camera with the same accusing expression, angry at a world that could treat them like objects. How little things change.

'Did she give you a number?' I ask, half distracted by the latest image, the woman I've come to recognise as old Mirriam Downham standing on the stone steps leading up to the front entrance of the house.

'No. She didn't want me to get in trouble. Maybe didn't want me to know it so's I couldn't tell anyone.' Kathryn's gulp is audible down the line, her imagination working overtime even though it's doubtful Roger DeVilliers and his cronies even know she exists. Far too plebeian for his daughter to be mixing with. Just a local girl from the village. Not even attractive to a paedophile.

'So she said she'd phone you regularly. Once a week, maybe?' I click another file open, see another photograph of sombre-looking Victorian ladies, scowling at the camera as if it's trying to steal a piece of their souls.

'Once a week. Yes. She should have called two days ago, but

she didn't. I waited, just in case. But what if something's happened to her? What if he's got her?'

I don't need to ask who he is, but I'm momentarily distracted by the next picture, showing the old house as a burnt-out ruin, a couple of fire engines parked on the grass.

'What were you supposed to do if she didn't call, Kathryn?'

'There's an email I've to send out to a bunch of people. Nothing attached to it, just a simple message. "Let it be", whatever that's supposed to mean. What should I do?'

I don't really remember Kathryn that well. Not since I used to bathe her and put her to bed. Her parents lived in one of the old farm cottages, but didn't work on the estate. He was some kind of shopkeeper in Kettering, I think, and she cleaned people's houses. It wasn't that long ago, so they probably still do. And their only child's somehow got herself mixed up in something she really shouldn't. Except that she was Izzy's friend. And Izzy's gone missing. Gone more missing than she intended.

I click another filename while I'm thinking, my eyes quickly scanning the image that comes up on the screen. It's the scowling women again, this time in grainy colour. It's not that which catches my eye though, so much as the undamaged house. Colour photography wasn't unheard of before 1930, but it was rare and expensive. And this looks more like some of my parents' holiday snaps from the seventies. There's something else about it that catches my attention too. Mirriam Downham is there, which would suggest the photo was taken before she died in 1930. And yet cutting the blue sky above her head is a contrail from a modern airliner.

I know where Izzy might have gone. But if she's not called Kathryn when she said she would, then something's gone badly wrong. Looks like I'm going to Dundee.

'Send the emails, Kathryn. That's what Izzy wanted you to do, so that's what you should do.'

35

My instinct is to leave straight after I've finished speaking to Kathryn, but for once I let the sensible voice of my training hold me back. It means a night of little sleep after many more hours wading through the recovered files on Izzy's hard drive, and a hurried conversation with Emily as she catches me leaving at first light.

'Hope I'll be back before too late, but could you look after Cat if I'm not?' I ask her.

'Och, she's no bother, Miss Constance. I'd be more than happy to. The bairns love her too.'

It's only as I'm turning onto the single-track road at the end of the long drive that I wonder how it is the 'bairns' can have met my adopted cat, but if she's settled here then that's one less thing for me to worry about. It's got to be nicer than London, that's for sure.

Burntwoods doesn't show up on my phone's satnav, so I get it to take me to the nearest village instead. I should probably have looked at an old-fashioned paper map first, to get the lie of the land; there's plenty of them in the library at Newmore. As it is, I'm surprised to be taken through the middle of Scotland's third city. I don't know this part of the world at all, had always assumed Dundee was a backwater, trading on its past history. The reality is somewhat different. There's a lot of new development going on down by the waterfront, dominated by a vast black construction of angular concrete that looks a bit like a half-constructed boat and which a large billboard informs me is going to be a Scottish outpost of the Victoria and Albert Museum. I shouldn't be surprised at the appearance of such culture, but I am.

Past what I assume is the city centre and out towards the east, things start to revert to more of my assumptions. Lines of grey council housing, playing fields turned yellow-brown by the unusually dry summer. Twin wind turbines loom over an industrial complex, motionless in the still air. And then before I've really had time to take it all in, I'm out in the countryside again.

I have no idea what to expect. The articles on Izzy's deleted hard drive told of a large but ruined country mansion surrounded by landscaped gardens and mature woodland, but all I can see is fields either in the process of being harvested or littered with big round bales of straw. Massive, modern sheds mark the heart of each individual farm, and to my right as I drive, the North Sea glints in the sunlight.

Arbroath comes and goes, and with it the memory of those strange smoked fish my father would eat for breakfast on our interminable summer holidays. They were always too strong for me, burning my tongue and repeating all day. I much preferred the porridge and the wooden bowls.

Finally the satnav turns me inland, up a winding road that crests a shallow hill before dropping down into more rugged, wooded country. Before long I'm driving slowly through the tiny village of Friockheim, whose oddly Germanic name I have no idea how to pronounce and of whose existence I was blissfully ignorant until a day ago. The tinny electronic voice tells me that I've reached my destination as I slow down in what must be the centre of the village. A square-towered kirk stands sentinel at the crossroads, opposite a garage that doesn't look like it's been open for decades. All the houses are dark-red sandstone, imposing if rather sombre, and lifeless. I'd hoped to find a village shop or maybe a pub where I could ask questions, but this place is as lifeless as my parents' marriage.

Moving slowly along the high street, I finally see a person standing at the next crossroads, staring at me. By the time I get there, they've disappeared, but then I catch sight of them a hundred yards or so down the left-hand turning. Again, they're not moving, just staring. I drive towards them, not much else I can do right now, but as I reach the point where I was sure they were standing, they're a hundred or so yards further on.

'OK, Con. Not strange at all.' I speed up as the figure disappears around a bend in the road and, sure enough, once I reach that point, they're a hundred or so yards away, standing, staring.

I follow the mysterious figure for about five minutes, at the end of which I have to admit I'm hopelessly lost. The road here is narrow, with thick forest on either side. I've turned down that many lanes I couldn't even say which way is the sea and which the mountains. Then I take one final turn and come face to face with an impressive pair of gatehouses. They're built in that same dark-red sandstone, towering four storeys over a wide entrance to a long drive that curves away into the woods. Wrought-iron gates that must weigh several tons each stand open, almost beckoning. Of the person who has somehow led me here, there is no sign.

I've read this book, seen this movie, but even so I turn off the road and drive slowly through those gates, recognising them from one of Izzy's photographs. Glancing in my mirror, I fully expect to see them swing closed behind me, but they stay resolutely open. Ahead, the drive climbs a gentle slope, the trees on either side receding until I pull out into a wide clearing. Shaggy Highland cattle graze in well-kept fields, leading up to a house that is considerably less a ruin than the articles I've read might have suggested. It looks very much like the black-and-white photograph from the 1920s, a magnificent Victorian country mansion.

A couple of fairly new cars parked on the turning circle outside the front door reassure me that I've not fallen through some warp in time. The sun's shining and everything is brightly coloured, which helps as well. When I switch off the engine and climb out of Aunt Felicity's car, I'm greeted by a quietness that's almost as total as Newmore's, but underscored with a distant roar from some unseen major road. Then I hear a scrunch of booted feet on gravel and turn to see a tall woman approaching. From afar, she looks like the figure I saw at the roadside, leading me into this place. Closer up, I see that she's tall, thin, and with long flowing grey hair. She stares at me in a manner that isn't exactly hostile, but isn't exactly friendly either. She's dressed like a gardener, complete with muddy cotton gloves, but even so I recognise her from the photographs. Mirriam Downham. Strange enough that the house isn't the ruin I'd been expecting, but stranger yet to find it still inhabited by the woman who's supposed to have died here almost a hundred years ago.

'Constance Fairchild. You're late.' Her voice is high and thin, but not unfriendly. I can only stare at her, mouth slightly open in astonishment. I try to say something, but nothing comes out. She stops a good ten feet away, looks me up and down as if measuring my worth by the clothes I wear, shakes her head at something. 'Well, you're here now. You'd better come in.'

'The fire was never quite as severe as the newspapers made it out to be.'

I'm following the woman who may or may not be Mirriam Downham down a long, wide corridor through the middle of Burntwoods. The high ceiling makes it feel more like a hall, but we've already crossed a much grander entrance. I'm used to large houses; I grew up in one, after all. The whole of Harston Magna Hall would fit into just one wing of this mansion.

'And I suppose you just happen to look a lot like the original Mirriam Downham. A great niece, perhaps. Or great many times over, I should say.'

She stops, facing me with a gentle smile. With her long straight hair, narrow face and weather-beaten skin she reminds me of a nursery rhyme illustration of a witch more than anything, except that her nose isn't hooked, and doesn't sport a mole with tufts of wiry black hair sprouting from it. Maybe the black clothes don't help dispel the image, or maybe she doesn't want to.

'People always say I look like her.' She cocks her head to one side as if laughing silently at some unsaid joke. 'It probably doesn't help that I share her name either. But come. There is much to talk about, and we were expecting you some days ago.'

She turns away before I can say anything to that, setting off again at a swift pace. I catch up with her as she opens a door and ushers me through into a large drawing room. Full-height windows on the opposite wall open up onto a pleasant lawned garden, and beyond that neat parkland. Highland cattle seek shade under ancient oak and beech trees, the dark green of the forest smudging the distant horizon between land and sky. It's all very idyllic, perhaps too much so.

'Tea?' My host indicates that I sit, and I see a tray already laid out with teapot, cups and a rather fine-looking cake. I hope it's not been here for days awaiting my arrival too.

'What do you mean you were expecting me earlier?' I ask as I sit down. 'I didn't know I was coming here until yesterday evening.'

Mirriam pours tea, offers milk, slices cake, everything a polite host should do except answer my question.

'It's no matter. You're here now, and I must assume you're looking for Isobel.'

'Is she here? Can I see her?'

'Why are you so interested in the girl?'

Mirriam's defensiveness puts my back up. 'I'm not here to take her back to her father, if that's what you're thinking. Nothing could be further from the truth.'

'Her father?' Mirriam tilts her head to one side, the ghost of a smile playing on her lips. Her impossibly long hair falls from a centre parting on the top of her head in long thin strands that reach to the floor now she is seated.

'You do know who her father is, right? Roger DeVilliers? The billionaire hedge fund manager? Notoriously lacking in moral scruples?'

The smile widens, then turns hard and cruel. 'Roger DeVilliers? Of course. He has indeed spent many years abusing Isobel, and sharing her amongst his friends. Since she was too young to know it was wrong, and then with the usual threats should she tell anyone about their not-so-secret.' She leans forward in her chair, bony hands clasped together as she stares deep into my eyes. 'But she only wears his name. He is not Isobel's father.'

For a moment I think she's going to make some odd statement about the patriarchy and how no man can claim dominion over woman. There's something about Mirriam Downham, if that truly is her name, that reminds me of the more uncompromising feminists I knew at university. The ones who would have rid the world of all men if they could. I'm not entirely sure what put that thought in my mind, other than her physical appearance and the few scant and conflicting details I gleaned about the house before coming here. Then it occurs to me that she's actually being quite literal.

'He's not?' I picture Izzy's face, both the baby and small child

I knew and the few photographs I've seen since I began looking for her. It never occurred to me before, but she doesn't much take after her mother or sister, and neither does she have Roger's features. Certainly she's missed the DeVilliers nose. And now that I think about it, Margo and Charlotte are both blondes. Izzy's hair was always dark red. Darker even than my own.

Like my father's in those holiday snaps from the 1970s, before I was born. Before it all started falling out.

So many little clues slip into place. My face must be a picture as my brain rushes to process it all, but my hostess witch says nothing. Even her smirk is gone; no crowing here. I don't know how long I stare at her, unseeing. It might be seconds, might be long minutes. But eventually it all boils down to one simple question.

'Does she know?'

'Yes, she knows. Isobel has known her true parentage for a very long time. And so has Roger DeVilliers. He is a monster, but he would never sully his own daughter. I suspect in his own mind that makes him quite noble.'

I'm still reeling from this revelation, but it doesn't change the fact of why I came here. 'Can I see her?' I ask. 'Will she see me?'

Mirriam puts down her cup and breathes out a heavy sigh that makes me believe she might well be over 150 years old, despite what she told me earlier. 'I'm sure Isobel would be delighted to see you. But I'm afraid she can't. That's why it's such a shame you didn't pick up the trail we left you earlier. She's gone missing, you see.'

36

'Gone missing? When?'

The tea tasted excellent, and I'm sure the cake would have been just as good. I'm not interested in either any more. Perhaps sensing my impatience, Mirriam puts down her own cup and stands.

'Best if you talk to someone who knew her better than I did.'

I follow her back out into the vast corridor and further into the enormous building. There's a calmness about the place that reminds me of Newmore. Like my aunt's lochside lodge, it feels safe here, and yet I can't quite shake a feeling of unease.

'You'll have worked out by now that we don't exactly advertise our existence to the world. That's kind of the point of this place.' Mirriam pushes open a door that's twice as tall as she is, and ushers me through into a library. It's darker in here, slatted shutters closed across the windows in an attempt to preserve the endless rows of books. Lit bulbs hang on old cord flexes from a high vaulted ceiling. For the first time since my arrival, I see more people. More women, I should say. Maybe twenty of them, all shapes and sizes, ages and colours, they sit around a large refectory table in the middle of the room. Books and notepads open, they look like they're in the middle of a lesson of some kind, although I can't see any teacher. They all turn to stare at me.

'Jennifer?' Mirriam says, and one of the younger women puts

down her pen, stands up and comes to meet us. The others go back to their studies once they know they're not needed.

'Jennifer, this is Constance. She's looking for Isobel.'

A flash of anger passes across Jennifer's eyes as she stares directly at me. She's maybe twenty or twenty-one, but wears an expression that suggests a much longer lifetime of struggle.

'Not here, is she? She left, din't she?'

'We both of us know that, Jen. Perhaps you could show Constance to Isobel's room. The two of you were close, so you might have some insights as to where she has gone.'

Jennifer opens her mouth to argue, then closes it again. She shrugs, nods her head for me to follow, and sets off towards a door at the far end of the library. I pause for a moment, looking to Mirriam, but she just motions for me to follow the young woman.

'We've nothing to hide here, Miss Fairchild, but neither do we court publicity. As long as you respect that then our doors will always be open to you.' She turns and walks away, leaving me to hurry and catch up with Jennifer. I have a horrible feeling of being dismissed by the head teacher.

'She family then, Izzy?' Jennifer asks as she holds open the door. It leads onto a wide corridor that could be anywhere within the endless miles of this mansion. I'm usually good at keeping my bearings, but it won't take much to have me totally lost. My new guide is completely at ease here though, and clearly knows her way around. She sets off at a speed I struggle to keep up with. Conversation is harder still.

'No. Well, sort of. Not really.'

'Aye, I heard about that. Still not sure why you're here though. Izzy's gone, right?'

'But she was here, wasn't she? And recently.'

'Why you want to know?'

'Because her sister's worried about her. And because her

father's doing everything he can to stop me looking for her.'

Jennifer stops mid-stride so suddenly that I'm a couple of paces past her before I realise.

'That bastard's not her father. Evil—' Her face twists into an angry snarl, and she clenches both fists by her side. For a moment I fear she's going to explode, or attack me, but the pent-up violence slowly ebbs away. When she's calmed down enough to speak again, I can see tears glistening in the corners of her eyes.

'Izzy's spent her whole life trying to get away from that man. She finally does it, finally escapes for good, and then two weeks later she's gone. Why the hell did she leave here? It's safe here. They can't find us.'

It's the 'us' that makes me understand, and I kick myself for forgetting what this place is meant to be anyway. A refuge for battered and abused women and girls. A safe haven away from all male oppression. Yes, it's a coven, but the witchcraft practised here isn't something from Shakespeare or even a Stephen King novel. It's far purer than that.

'He abused you too, didn't he?' We're standing outside another double-height door. Jennifer doesn't answer my question, just turns the handle and pushes. It must weigh a ton, but it's so well balanced it swings easily and silently open to reveal a large, empty bedroom.

'This is Izzy's room. Was, I guess. Don't know if she left anything behind, but seeing as you're the detective, maybe you can have a look.'

Jennifer stands at the door, hesitant, as I walk in and over to the windows. The view is much the same as I had from the drawing room earlier, formal gardens leading to mature parkland. Only here it's easier to see the ha-ha wall that stops the cows from trampling the roses. The antique furniture fits in with the decor so well I can only assume it was commissioned at the same time as the house was built. There's no sign of anything personal though, no clue that anyone has slept in here recently.

'When did she leave?' I ask as I open drawers and wardrobe doors, hoping to find the smallest of clues.

'A little over a week ago. Didn't join us for breakfast, so I came to wake her up. This is what I found.'

It's not good that she's been gone that long. I've a horrible feeling I know what's happened to her.

'She not leave any stuff? Clothes, books, phone?'

'Mobiles don't work here. It's part of the magic that protects us.'

It's a strange word to use. Magic. Nevertheless, I pull out my phone and tap the screen awake. She's right. No signal at all, and no Wi-Fi either.

'How do you call anyone, then?'

'Why would we want to?' Jennifer looks at me as if the very thought is madness.

'Umm, I don't know. To let your family know you're OK? To talk to your friends?' I pull out a chair from in front of an elegant writing desk, sit down and start searching through drawers. Most are empty, and those that do contain anything look like it was put there before the last war. Unused envelopes turned yellow with age, writing paper thick enough to absorb ink from an actual quill pen, bunches of keys tied together with string, their brass dark and uneven, labels faded to obscurity.

'This is a refuge. We come here to escape the world outside, study, learn the skills needed to survive, maybe help others. It's always been the way. When you come to Burntwoods, you cut all ties.'

'But don't you want to go back? Don't you miss it?'

'Maybe, a bit. But I'm not ready to leave. Not yet.'

'You can though? Leave, that is.' I pull open the bottom-right drawer and finally see something from the current millennium. A colourful notebook and a cable for a mobile phone.

'Of course we can. This ain't a prison.'

I miss the anger in Jennifer's words at first, only hearing it as I pull out the notebook and flick through it. A few scribbled drawings, but nothing really significant. 'Sorry. I didn't mean to upset you. Just trying to work out what's going on.' I pull the cable out of the drawer and notice something else at the back. Reaching in, I pull out a half-empty plastic bottle of Coke. It sparks a memory, but not one I can place. I'm still staring at it, trying to get there, when Jenny interrupts my thoughts.

'So what is going on then, oh great detective?'

I put the bottle down on the desk. 'Izzy left instructions with a friend. If she didn't call once every week at a specified time, then the friend had to do something for her. If she couldn't call from here, she'd have to go somewhere she could. I don't know much about your – what did you call it? Magic? But let's assume it doesn't extend beyond those big iron gates at the end of the drive.'

Jennifer narrows her eyes at me. Not quite a scowl, but more than halfway there. 'Aye, you can get a mobile signal just out on the old Arbroath road. Sometimes in the woods up towards Coothies Farm. Dies as soon as you step back inside the gates though. Magic, see?'

I figure it has more to do with topography and a lack of cell towers, but if Jennifer wants to believe in pixies, who am I to argue?

'OK, so she has to leave the grounds to make a call. She sneaks out while no one's looking, walks to the boundary, phones her friend to let her know she's still safe, comes back. All good.' I pick up the bottle by its lid, shake it slightly. The memory's tantalisingly close, like having a word on the tip of your tongue. 'The thing is, the people looking for her have access to some

very sophisticated tracking equipment. They'll have been monitoring her mobile number from the moment she was first
reported missing, if not before. Soon as she used it they'd know
where she was. It'd take them a while to get to that spot though,
so if she came back here after the first call then they'd find
nothing. Assuming your magic really does keep unwanted folk
away.'

I maybe put a little too much emphasis on the word. Jennifer
breathes in sharply, and I can feel another tirade building.

'OK. OK.' I hold my hands up to placate her. 'They can't get
in, can't even find the place. But they're very patient. They set
someone to watch, and they wait. Next time she sneaks out to
call her friend, they grab her.'

Jennifer's face is a picture of horror. 'You really reckon he's
kidnapped her?'

'If not him, then who else? You said it yourself. She was safe
here. Why leave this place if you don't have to?'

'But . . . but what's he going to do to her? Where would he
take her?'

I stare at the wall behind the desk, the Coke bottle going out
of focus as I try to think. That's when it hits me, where I last saw
one like it. I've never been much of a Coke drinker myself, and I
certainly wouldn't have seen any at Folds Cottage or Newmore.
Still woozy from the chloroform Adrian and his silent friend
used to knock me out, I did see an empty bottle on a tray by a
door, deep in the bowels of Roger DeVilliers' tower block
though. Sitting on a tray alongside a half-eaten meal, plastic
cutlery. How many days ago was that? I cast my mind back, feel a
shiver of horror as I realise it all fits.

I spring to my feet so suddenly, Jennifer leaps back in alarm.
I don't know what trauma brought her here, but it must have
been bad.

'I think I know.' I pick up the bottle, shake it again and watch the dark brown liquid foam against the clear plastic like burn water in spate.

'But it's going to be a bugger to get in there and find out.'

37

Afternoon's fading into evening as I hit the border, driving south. It feels a little strange to be going back to London so soon, and there's still the matter of the price on my head. But Izzy's down there, and she's in danger. It's only a matter of time before Roger DeVilliers decides that she's too much of a risk to keep alive.

'You're forgetting "Fairchilds never run from a fight" too. I never thought you'd hang around up here for long. Not once you'd worked it all out.'

Pete's face is in shadow despite the headlights of oncoming cars and the glow from the instruments. I'm not sure I'd want to see it anyway. I know what he looked like after they'd finished torturing him, can still see the smear of his brains on the office wall behind his dead body.

'Charming, I'm sure.' His voice is in my head, but I turn down the music anyway.

'You're not really here, Pete. Just my mind playing tricks. Just my conscience getting the better of me.'

'And now I'm hurt, Con. We were partners. We worked well together, you and I. Besides, there's a lot more going on here than you realise.'

'What, you mean more than someone putting a bullet in your head? More than one of the country's richest men serially raping his stepdaughter and murdering a journalist who'd stumbled on

NO TIME TO CRY

the truth? More than someone putting a contract out on me?'

'A lot more than all that. Come on, Con. You're missing the big picture.'

'You reckon it's all connected?' The thought had occurred to me, but I'd discounted it almost as quickly. Occam's razor is an essential tool for any detective.

'Everything's connected to everything else. You just need to see the links. They're right here in front of you if you'll just look.'

Infuriating man. He was like this when he was alive. Purposely cryptic both to wind me up and to get me to think.

'Can you at least give me a clue?'

'I can help you with your reasoning, maybe. As you're so fond of pointing out, I'm just your conscience talking anyway.'

I mull that over as a few more miles of motorway rumble underneath me. It should be scary having a ghost sitting motionless behind you; that's what all the stories I was told growing up said. But knowing Pete's there, even if just in my imagination, is oddly comforting.

'It has to have been someone in the Met,' I say eventually. He says nothing back, so I continue. 'I don't think it's Bain. He's too new, and my gut says no. But he knows something more about the operation than I do.'

Saying it out loud, it seems obvious, and I slap the steering wheel in frustration that I've not had any team members to sound off against. 'That's what it's all about, isn't it? The operation. It wasn't about the gang at all. It was meant to flush out corruption in the team.'

'That's quite a leap.' Pete's voice is level, neither confirming nor denying, like a politician.

It makes a horrible kind of sense though. Only it backfired spectacularly. And once they'd tortured all the information they needed out of Pete, then I was really the only loose end. So they tied me up trying to work out who was after me while they shifted the blame for Pete's death my way as well.

'Bastards aren't going to get away with it.' I smack my hands against the steering wheel again, harder this time, then tug hard to stop the car veering into the middle lane. The movement gives me a shot of adrenaline, gets my blood pumping and wakes me up for the long drive ahead, but when I glance in the mirror to see if I've upset any other drivers, my ghostly confidant is gone.

It's getting very late indeed as I drive the narrow lanes from the main road back to Folds Cottage. At least I remembered to let Aunt Felicity know I was coming back. She'll have left the front door unlocked and a light on to welcome me. Chances are she'll be asleep in an armchair in the living room, even though I told her not to wait up. It'll be nice to have someone normal to talk to for a change, and I'll need something to unwind before I can sleep; ghosts and witches don't really do it for me, and I'm still raging at the thought some of my colleagues have been behind all the shit that's been going on recently.

I almost don't notice the car, tucked away in a gateway into the woods. I'm pressing on now, probably going a bit too fast for the road in my rush to get this interminable drive over and done with. I catch the swiftest glimpse out of the corner of my eye as I whizz past, but my senses seem to be enhanced right now. I play back what I've just seen as I slow for the turn onto the driveway, reach for the indicator stalk. It was a nondescript car, but new. I can see the number plate in my mind, the Vauxhall griffin on the front of the bonnet, the figure sitting in the driver's seat briefly illuminated by my headlights.

My initial thought is a young local and his lass, and I really don't want to think what she's doing. But that's not the best place, or even the most popular, for that sort of thing. It could be that the woods around Folds Cottage have become a haven for doggers, of course. I think both Aunt Felicity and my father would have had something to say about that were it the case though.

And then the image builds, the face forming impossibly in my memory. There's no way I could have actually seen what I'm seeing now, and yet I'm sure enough to pull my hand away from the indicator, gently press the accelerator pedal and speed up again, past the turning I should have taken.

The road curves round on its way to the village proper. I slow down and pull in once I'm sure I'm well out of sight and sound of the parked car. The more I think about it, the more I'm convinced. It's a perfect spot to sit and watch people coming and going from Folds Cottage. Time was I'd have scoffed at myself for being paranoid, but that was before three separate assassination attempts. Before my boss was shot in the head by one of his colleagues.

A chill in the night air tells me that summer is coming to an end. I'm still dressed for the Highlands, which is some small consolation as I quietly climb over the fence and tread as silently as possible through the woods, back to the parked car. I needn't have worried, the man in the driver's seat is fast asleep, and he certainly doesn't have a young friend giving him executive relief. I still crouch down low as I approach the door, ears straining for the sound of any approaching car that might light up the narrow track and reveal my presence. There's only the distant roar of the dual carriageway and the quiet screeching of owls.

Luck is on my side. If I was on a stakeout, I'd lock the car while I was in it. I wouldn't have my seat belt on either. He's forgotten both very important points taught to us as part of our CID training, along with the third one, which is not to fall asleep. He wakes as I open the door, but tangles up in the seatbelt as he tries to extricate himself. It's a moment's work to reach in and bang his head hard against the steering wheel. Even with the padding on most modern cars, that's enough to stun him so that reaching in, unclipping the seatbelt and dragging him out onto the forest floor is simple. In moments I've got his arms locked behind his back, a knee holding him down while I go through his jacket pocket and find the expected set of cable ties. His weak struggles suggest both that he was in a deep sleep and that I've maybe worked a bit too much of the day's frustrations out on him. On the other hand, he's as guilty of Pete's murder as the man who pulled the trigger. I know that just by his being here now.

'Wha—?' He blinks like a halfwit when I turn him over, struggles to sit upright until I place a heavy boot in the middle of his chest and press him back down into the loam.

'Looking for me, were you, Dan?'

'Are you sure this is wise, dear?'

It's taken me longer than I thought it would to drag Dan Penny all the way from his stakeout car back to Folds Cottage. He's fatter than he looks, and either faking it to make life awkward for me or still suffering from having his face clattered off his steering wheel. There's a bit of blood around his nose, and one eye doesn't seem to want to open fully, so maybe I was a bit more forceful than necessary. Pulling off one of his socks and shoving it in his mouth to keep him quiet was probably unnecessary too; it's not as if anyone would have heard him shouting for help on a quiet country lane surrounded by woods and in the middle of the night. It made me feel better though.

Aunt Felicity was awake when I arrived, and helped me get Dan into the garage, empty while my Volvo is away being fixed. I'm not entirely sure how I'm going to pay for that; I burned up pretty much all my savings just buying the damned thing.

'I reckon he's faking it.' The two of us stand over the wooden kitchen chair we've tied him to. Dan squints up at us, seeing us in silhouette against the bare lightbulb hanging from the ceiling. It's not as if we need to hide our identities, but it's nice to see him suffering.

'No. The poor dear's concussed.' Aunt Felicity has already brought a bowl of warm water, TCP and some cloths to clean up the grazes. I guess she can be the good cop if she wants to. I'm not sure I have the patience.

'Well, Dan. This is how it's going to be. You're going to answer my questions, and only answer my questions. If you say anything out of turn, or if I don't like the answers you're giving me, then the sock goes back in. Nod if you understand, OK?'

He tries to glare at me, but seems to be having trouble focusing his eyes. Eventually he gives up, drops his head a little in assent. I'm not so sure about the sock as I pull it from his mouth. It wasn't quite so damp before.

'You'll be sorry for this, Fairchild.'

'Ah, now, here I was thinking you were going to be reasonable.' I shove the sock back where it came from, then turn to Aunt Felicity. 'You couldn't make us a cup of tea, could you? And maybe bring the kettle back too?'

I'm standing behind Dan as I speak, so he can't see the wink I give my aunt. She plays a mean poker face, nodding her understanding, then leaves without another word.

'Are you going to be reasonable now, Dan?'

He nods, eyes a little more focused, a little more fearful. I remove the sock and drop it to the floor beside him.

'OK, then. First off. What were you doing sitting in your car up the road? And I don't mean having a quick kip.'

'Thought that would have been obvious. Waiting for you to turn up.'

'And what were you doing here a week ago? Back when you were spotted in the pub. Looking for me then too?'

Dan nods, then winces in pain.

'Under whose orders though? I know we're short staffed, but a lone stakeout well away from our normal patch. That's not a sanctioned expense, is it?'

He stares at me, non-droopy eye squinting. 'You think you're so fucking clever, Fairchild. But you're not. You're just a spoiled little rich kid who's got herself in far deeper than she knows.'

'Really?' I bend down and retrieve the sock, holding it as lightly as I can between thumb and forefinger like the manky thing it is. 'I know you were the one who tortured Pete for information. You used a baseball bat and kept those leather driving gloves of yours on so you wouldn't get his blood on your hands.'

Penny stares at me still, but the sneer has gone from his face. Is that a hint of worry I see there? I was just fishing. I knew he was involved, but not to what extent. His reaction is as good as a signed confession as far as I'm concerned. Time to up the ante a bit.

'So what I need to know, and I suspect the Crown Prosecutor will too, is who fired the gun? I don't believe for a minute you're the brains behind this operation, so I suspect it's someone quite senior, right?'

Penny's eyes are wide now, and he seems to be having difficulty forming articulate sentences. I've got him rattled, just need him to give me a name. I know it won't be admissible in court, but frankly I'm beyond caring about that sort of thing right now.

'I . . . I can't. They'll kill me.'

I make a gun with my fingers, reach forward and press Penny in the forehead. 'What? Like you killed Pete?'

'Very much like that, Miss Fairchild.'

Too late I see Dan's already fearful gaze slide past me. I spin round, recognising the voice of Roger DeVilliers' hired muscle, Adrian. His silent friend is there with him, standing in the open garage doorway, but they are blocking the main escape. There's only the door through to the house, where Aunt Felicity should be almost done making my cup of tea. Crap. I really should have thought it through before dragging her into all this.

'Mr DeVilliers is very upset with you, disappearing like that and not telling him where you went.' He nods at his silent friend, who steps into the garage, walks past me and begins untying Dan. I offer the sock, but he just ignores it, escorting the hapless detective constable out into the darkness. Good riddance to him.

'What are you going to do with him?' I ask more to distract Adrian from going into the house than anything. With luck, Aunt F. will see what's happening and keep well away.

'Nothing bad. At least not now. A tame copper's always useful, even if he is just a grunt.' Adrian tucks his hand into his jacket, comes out with a rather more substantial gun than the one I put to Penny's head. He doesn't point it at me, but the implication is clear.

'Let me guess. Old Roger wants a word?'

38

At least I'm not drugged and tied up this time, and I can see where we're going. Adrian's silent friend frisked me for concealed weapons and took away my phone, but other than that no one's laid a hand on me. I'm still not sure whether agreeing to go with them was a sensible choice. They could be taking me to see DeVilliers, or they could be making a beeline for the nearest construction site so that I can form an integral part of the foundations.

They haven't killed me yet though. And they left Aunt Felicity alone. I have to hope that she was listening in all the while, and that she's got the good sense to go as far away as possible until all this has blown over. I just hope that I'm around to apologise.

'He doesn't say much.' I nod my head in the direction of the driver's seat, cut off from where I'm sitting by a motorised glass partition.

'That would be difficult without a tongue.'

I say nothing, but my raised eyebrow is all the response Adrian needs.

'Secret ops in Afghanistan. Back in oh-two. Went spectacularly tits up, and Tommy managed to get himself captured by the towelheads, stupid bastard. They tortured him, but he wouldn't say anything. So they cut his tongue out. They were going to chop his head off too, but we got there first.'

In 2002 I was fifteen years old, worrying about exams, hating my school and trying to pretend I wasn't all that interested in boys. Sure, I knew about the Afghan war, but there's a big difference between that and being there, seeing action, getting injured in the line of duty.

'How'd you both end up working for DeVilliers, then?' I ask.

'My, aren't you full of questions?'

I shrug, lean back in my seat as if it's no matter to me whether he answers or not. 'Figure there's not much else to do. The way I see it, I'm either about to lose my head or Mr DeVilliers will offer me a job I can't refuse. Either way, I'd like to know as much as possible before it happens. Fair enough?'

Adrian says nothing, and for a while there's just the muted roar of tyres on road, a quiet whistling of wind as we speed down the motorway. This isn't the same car I was driven in before; that was much quieter and more luxurious. It's still a stretch limousine though, and I'm reminded of the car that was parked outside my flat in London.

'What did you have to do with Pete's death?' I ask. It's a question that's been bothering me since these two showed up in the woods a week ago. I can't see how they fit into the operation at all.

'Pete . . . ? Oh, right. Your boss. Yeah.' Adrian shakes his head. 'Nothing to do with us. That was all your mate Penny and that tit Bailey.'

'Bailey?' I can't make up my mind whether I'm surprised or not. I knew he was an obnoxious twat, but corrupt enough to kill? 'Detective Superintendent Gordon Bailey?'

'Here, have a look at this if you don't believe me.' Adrian pulls out a smartphone, taps at the screen a couple of times and then hands it over. There's a look on his face I don't like much. It reminds me of my uniform days, policing football matches. Most of the fans were decent enough folk, happy or sad depending on the outcome of the game. But there were some who only went for the fight, who delighted in causing as much mayhem and damage as possible, didn't feel it when it was dished out to them either. Adrian has that look on his face now.

What I see on the screen isn't much better.

The quality's not good, but it's clear enough to tell that I'm seeing one of the camera feeds from the office where Pete died. Only now I can see he's alive, frightened but defiant. He looks up at the camera, stares past the two men who are with him. One of them, wearing what looks like leather driving gloves, and holding a short wooden bat, follows his gaze. As he turns, I see the idiot expression of Dan Penny fill the screen.

'Fuck's sake. How did you get this?'

'It's not over yet,' Adrian reaches for the phone, clicks the volume button up and hands it back just in time for me to hear someone speak.

'This is getting us nowhere.' The voice is familiar enough, but I'd recognise that bald spot in a line-up any time. I know what's coming, but even so it's a shock when Detective Superintendent Gordon Bailey puts a gun to Pete's head and pulls the trigger.

'Fuck.' I don't think I'll ever get that image out of my mind. 'They told me the tapes had all been wiped.'

Adrian smirks as he takes the phone from my unresisting grip and slips it back into his pocket.

'The boss has his eye on many things. He didn't know anything about Bailey's little scam until you started looking for Isobel though. That's when we started looking into you, so in a way, you helped us out there. You never know when you might need a favour from someone high up in the Met.'

'What, like covering up Steve Benson's murder?'

Adrian's smirk turns into a scowl as something more like anger than irritation passes across his face, a tightening of the skin around those pale-blue eyes. I hold his gaze for as long as I can, but he's clearly more used to staring down death than I am. There's nothing to be gained from angering him, anyway, but that doesn't stop me from trying.

'I've seen the photographs, the video, all the stuff Benson dug up and passed on to Izzy. You happy working for a man who can do that to a child? To his own daughter? Happy to let him carry on doing it to other children?'

'She's not his daughter.'

'And that makes it OK, then? His wife has an affair with his best friend and he takes it out on the child? That seems reasonable behaviour to you, does it? He gets his kicks raping kids and sharing them with his sick friends. Filming it so he can blackmail them later. And you're happy to cover it all up just as long as he keeps paying you?'

'You talk too much. Either shut up or I'll have Tommy shut you up like he did the last time.' Adrian doesn't shout. Where there was excitement before at showing me the video of Pete's death, now there's no inflexion in his voice whatsoever, which makes it all the more terrifying.

I'd hoped I might be able to shame him, maybe make him question his actions, sow a seed of doubt in his mind that I could exploit later on. Divide and conquer, but first you've got to divide. I can see now there's no point trying to appeal to Adrian's better nature. He doesn't have one.

London never really sleeps, but in the small hours it slows down just a little. Instead of the black cabs and cycle couriers, tired commuters, delivery vans and construction traffic, the roads fill with street cleaners, delivery vans and construction traffic. There are fewer people walking the pavements, and fewer pedestrian crossings on red to slow the flow of traffic.

I assumed that I was being taken back to Roger DeVilliers'

penthouse apartment for another intimate chat, but Tommy the tongueless driver charts a different route through the city. It doesn't take long for me to work out where he's going though, and soon enough we're pulling up outside the concrete hulk that is my apartment block. Only once the car has stopped does Adrian speak again.

'Mr DeVilliers is otherwise occupied at the moment, but he will see you soon. In the meantime, you're to stay in your apartment and wait for us to come and fetch you.'

'Or else?'

'Or else you'll be investigated by Professional Standards, who will uncover irrefutable evidence of your corruption and complicity in the murder of your colleague Detective Inspector Copperthwaite. You will not only lose your job, but will spend many years in prison. You might not care much, but I suspect your family's reputation will suffer at the hands of the gutter press too.'

It's as much as I might have expected, and I can't deny the relief at not having to face DeVilliers straight away. Nodding my understanding, I unclip my seatbelt and step out of the car into cool night air. 'Can I have my phone back?'

'Your phone is in your apartment, where you posted it. We've taken the liberty of restocking your fridge and cupboards. There'll be no need for you to leave until we call for you.'

'What about keys? I left mine in my aunt's car back in Harston Magna.'

Adrian rolls his eyes, climbs out of the car himself. He takes a hold of my arm, not so hard that I might bruise, but hard enough that I know resistance is futile. Together we walk up the concrete stairs to the open air walkway and along to my front door. The first thing I notice is that it's been painted, covering up the mark left before. The next thing I notice is the shiny new lock. Adrian produces a key from his jacket pocket, slides it in and opens the door. He reaches in and flicks on the hall light with an ease that confirms to me he has been here before, then pushes me inside.

'You won't have to wait long. Forty-eight hours at the most. Mr DeVilliers needs to attend to some urgent business that's come up on account of someone sending off emails to various journalists and civil rights lawyers. As soon as that's dealt with we'll come and fetch you.' Adrian pulls the key from the lock and drops it back into his pocket. 'Don't try to leave. We're watching the door at all times. We will know if you misbehave again, and you know what will happen if you do.'

And with that he is gone, leaving me all alone.

I stare at the closed door, motionless, barely able to think. All that's going through my mind, on slow agonising repeat, is the memory of that short piece of video footage on Adrian's phone. First Dan Penny with his baseball bat and driving gloves, then Gordon Bailey oh so casually lifting a gun, pressing it to Pete's forehead and pulling the trigger. The sound on the recording was poor, muted by the noise of the car, but with each repeat the bang gets louder, Pete's death-spasm more violent. Over and over, faster and faster, the horror show plays in my mind, overlaid with Adrian's hooligan expression of delight, until my stomach heaves. Necessity drives me to the bathroom and before I know it I'm on my knees, retching into the toilet bowl, tears blurring everything.

I don't know how much time passes before I feel able to stand, flush, wash my face and hands. It's been a long day, I should be tired, but instead I'm shaking with barely controlled rage. How the fuck can they do this and get away with it? And that last snippet of information Adrian dropped on me. They know about Kathryn's emails. All Izzy's carefully worked-out plans are falling apart, the whole thing quietly swept under the carpet as if nothing had ever happened. Christ, I hope they don't hurt Kathryn herself. Bad enough they've got Izzy.

I walk back into the hall, open the front door and stare out at the building across the street, searching for any sign of being watched. As if expecting me to do so, a curtain pulls wide to reveal a man's silhouette in a brightly lit room almost directly opposite. He waves, slowly, then holds up a hand and taps the wrist, as if indicating the time. It's late. I should get some rest. I flip him the bird and close the door.

The flat doesn't feel like home any more. Nothing much is different, it's still the untidy pit it always was, but I have changed. The past week has left me jittery, unsettled and very, very angry. I want to break things, mostly Adrian's neck. And Roger DeVilliers'. I want to call up Professional Standards and tell them everything I've found out about Dan Penny. I'd tell them about Gordon Bailey too, but they're unlikely to take me seriously, especially if they ask me how I know. And, anyway, the suspicion is already on me. Anything I say will be dismissed as an attempt to shift the blame onto someone else.

Through in the kitchen, I find out that Adrian is as good as his word. The fridge is full, and they've not skimped on the luxury. There's a couple of bottles of champagne tucked away on the bottom shelf, packets of cold meats from Harrods Food Hall. I pick through a selection of prepared salad vegetables in tubs and little pots of pickles and preserves that must have come out of a very posh hamper. None of it's the sort of thing I'd ever consider eating, even if I hadn't just puked my guts out. Right now I'd kill for one of Mrs Feltham's goat curries and a bottle of Peroni.

Actually, right now I'd kill for a shower and bed, but I'm not so stupid as to think this place hasn't been comprehensively rigged with hidden cameras and microphones. Without scanning gear I could spend hours looking for them and not find anything, and there's no way I'm going to give whoever's recording my every move any kind of a peep show. There's also the fact my bed's still got two bullet holes in it.

The bullet holes get me thinking though. Cat must have got in through the window, and it's a racing certainty that's the way my would-be assassin did too. It's only when Roger DeVilliers got mixed up in all this that people started coming in through the door. If someone athletic and foolhardy enough managed to get in, then surely it must be possible to get out that way.

And then what? They'll see I've gone, track me down and throw me to the wolves. Stupid plan, Con. You're not thinking straight. Get some sleep, for God's sake.

I make a cup of tea with far too much milk and a couple of teaspoons of sugar, just how I used to drink it as a child. Mug in one hand and a ridiculously fancy tin of chocolate Bath Oliver biscuits in the other, I go through to the living room and slump down into the saggy armchair. Someone, Adrian probably, has collected all my letters and put them on the low table in front of the telly. They've all been opened, which is just another item to add to the hate list, even if it's only a bunch of bills and junk mail. There's the parcel with my phone and backup battery in it, too, both dead.

It takes a while to find the charging lead, but eventually it's plugged in. While I wait for it to come back to life, I sip sweet tea and munch biscuits that aren't nearly as good as their packaging promised. Or maybe I'm just too tired to eat, but too anxious to sleep. Reaching for the lamp beside the chair, I switch it off and plunge the room into semi-darkness. I need someone to talk to, and Pete's ghost, the projection of my feelings of guilt and hopelessness, is as good as anyone.

He doesn't come, however much I stare at the darkened corner where the other chair sits. How like a man to abandon me when all the chips are down.

39

Something wakes me with a start. A distant noise, perhaps, or a touch to the back of my neck. For too long, I don't know where I am. Then the sounds of London filter in, and bring with them the memories of last night. With a groan, I sit up and rub the sleep from my eyes. On the little table by the side of my armchair, a half-drunk mug of milky tea now has a scum of hard water on the top of it. The biscuits look even less appealing in the light of day.

A soft beep, and I realise what it was that must have woken me. Both phone and backup battery pack have fully charged. I pick them up, swipe the phone's screen awake and tap in the passcode. It takes a few seconds to connect, then the emails and text notifications start pinging in.

Groggy and stiff with sleep, it's not until I've stripped and am in the shower that I remember last night's worry about cameras. I find that I no longer care. It's my body, and I've never been particularly ashamed of it. Since I've every intention of bringing down Roger DeVilliers and everyone who works for him, karma will catch up with them soon enough.

I've just got to work out how I'm going to do that.

Through in the bedroom, I throw open the window as far as it will go, taking the opportunity to look out and see how a person might escape that way. It's not particularly encouraging, and I can't spend too long staring in case I'm being watched. I take my time choosing clothes and getting dressed, quite unlike my usual approach of grab what's at the top of the clean pile and get going. It gives me an opportunity to search the room without it being too obvious. Not that I find anything that might be a camera or microphone; Adrian's team will be far too good for that.

Breakfast is better than I could have hoped for. In among the many expensive ingredients left behind to keep me happy is a bag of fine coffee, and there are croissants in the bread bin. I'm most impressed to see that someone has even cleaned all the mouldy crusts and festering crumbs out before putting fresh produce in it. That's a level of attention to detail some of my detective colleagues could learn from.

It takes the better part of an hour to go through all the emails and texts on my phone, deleting most and responding only to those where no harm can come from the messages being intercepted. I'm about to make another pot of coffee when I hear a light tap at the door. Startled, it takes me a while to react. I wasn't expecting anyone to come until tomorrow at the earliest. Actually, I was counting on it.

The knocking comes again, followed by a familiar voice. 'Con, girl? You in there?'

I get up and hurry to the door, opening it wide to the welcome sight of Mrs Feltham. She's clutching a tupperware pot wrapped in tin foil, and I can smell the herbs and spices from where I'm standing.

'Thought I heard you come in last night. Been all types coming and going while you away.' She raps a knuckle on the freshly painted door. 'Done a nice job, mind you.'

'You want a coffee, Mrs F.? I was just putting the pot on.' I open the door a little wider, but she shakes her head.

'No time, child. My boys are all coming round this evening and I have to get everything ready. I made a bit extra curry goat for you though. I know you like it, and you need to put some meat on your bones.'

She thrusts the tupperware towards me, and when I take it with one hand she clasps the other between both of her own. 'You take care of yourself, girl. I was worried when you were gone so long without telling me.'

She's let's go of my hand, is about to leave. 'One moment, Mrs F. I've still got the empty pot from last time. Let me get it for you. Won't be a sec.'

It's a risk, and I don't want to involve anyone if I can help it, but I have to take the chance. I dash back to the kitchen and grab the clean tupperware box off the draining board where my kind abductors have left it. I can't waste any time, so the message is necessarily short and cryptic, scrunched up on a bit of paper torn from the corner of my notebook and dropped into the box. Lid on, I hand it to Mrs Feltham as she stands at the door.

'You're so kind to me, Mrs F. I just hope I can repay the favour some day.'

'Favour nothing.' She waves me away, tupperware box tucked under one arm as she sets off for the stairs.

The rest of the day is a nightmare. I want to call up people, Charlotte and Ben, Aunt Felicity, even Emily Robertson to see how Cat is doing. And yet I know I can't have any communication with any of them. My mobile phone is bugged and tracked, any call on the landline will be listened to as well. I spend a couple of hours searching for cameras, and find a few sneakily hidden within lightbulbs. I leave them where they are, except the one in my bedroom, which I make a big show of removing. They can come in and replace it if they want, or they can leave it to chance.

I make the bed before I remove the camera, even though the holes in the mattress are unlikely to be very comfortable to sleep on. And then I spend the afternoon cleaning. It's not as if I've got anything better to do, and it gives me an opportunity to look for any more bugs. What I wouldn't give for the sort of high-tech scanning gear our IT boys have.

The landline rings at about six in the evening. I consider leaving it for the answerphone, but pick up at the last minute.

'Mr DeVilliers would like to see you tomorrow morning. I'll send a car round at eight.' Adrian sounds bored. I would be too, if I was being expected to act as a secretary when my specialist training was in close surveillance and protection work.

'Should I wear my best party frock?'

'You don't own a party frock, Miss Fairchild. I know because I've been through your entire wardrobe. Trust me, I got no particular thrill from the experience.'

'Not you who put the camera in my bedroom, then, if girls aren't your thing.'

'I'm not—'

'It's nothing to be ashamed off. Lots of my friends are gay. You wouldn't believe how many serving police officers are these days too.'

'Whatever. We know you found the camera. I'd send someone round to put it back, but you're not going to do anything stupid, are you.' It's not a question, more a weary assertion of fact. I don't have the heart to contradict him.

'Eight o'clock sharp,' I say instead. 'I'll be waiting.'

Adrian hangs up, and I walk over to the window that looks out across the street. I can't see anything in the building opposite, where the cheery fellow waved at me early this morning, but that doesn't mean much. Checking my watch, it's still not time.

I'm not hungry, but I heat up the curry Mrs Feltham brought round. A couple of mouthfuls soon revives my appetite. I don't finish it all, even though I want to. Instead, I spoon about half into a bowl, pull cling film over the top and put it in the fridge. Then I make myself a cup of tea, all in full view of the camera mounted in the light bulb hanging from the middle of the kitchen ceiling.

I dump my dirty plate, cutlery and the teabag into the sink, knowing it will annoy whoever tidied up the kitchen while they were restocking it for my house arrest. Through in the living room, I try to watch the television, but it's all shite soap operas and weird reality shows, neither of which bear any resemblance to everyday life at all. The cop show I stumble upon is even more laughable. If only the job were that simple. I channel-hop like a teenager, keeping an eye on the little clock that appears each time I switch over. Killing time.

Around half eight, I make a big show of yawning and stretching, switch off the telly and take my mug through to the kitchen. I check the front door is locked, then switch off lights on my way through the tiny flat, into the bathroom. Teeth cleaned and face washed, I go through to the bedroom. And that's when the nerves kick in.

The window's still open from earlier, letting in the noise of the city and it's more unsavoury smells too. There's no bulb in the ceiling light any more, so I switch on the bedside light, clamber onto the bed fully clothed, and wait.

It doesn't take long.

First I hear a couple of voices arguing, loud but too far away to make out the actual words. A third voice joins in, then a fourth. More join the fray and soon there are other sounds too. Bins being kicked over, car alarms going off. Bless Mrs Feltham and her boys.

It takes a few minutes to strip the bed and knot the sheets together like they do in all those Chalet School adventures I read as a girl. I'm still not convinced it'll take my weight, but the alternative to falling to my death is being forced to serve Roger DeVilliers, so it's not much of a choice, really. The biggest problem is getting out of the window – it was designed specifically to stop people accidentally falling to their deaths, after all. There's a moment when I think I might be stuck, but the low whoop whoop of a police siren in the street spurs me on.

The sheets don't get me all the way to the ground, and the drop from the end looks too far. I have to risk it though. There's too much at stake.

Hitting the concrete walkway drives all the wind from my lungs. I crumple and fall sideways, narrowly avoid smashing my head against the concrete wall, and end up curled in a ball in the shadows by the bin store, wheezing and gasping. My legs hurt, and my ribs, but as I haul myself to my feet I can tell nothing is broken.

I left my phone behind. No point giving Adrian any help. Checking my watch, it's not quite nine in the evening. The car might not be here until eight tomorrow, but they'll know something's up if I don't show myself in the house by seven. I've got ten hours to find Isobel and enough evidence to clear my name.

No pressure, then.

40

I never thought I'd want to come back to this place. The concrete and glass monstrosity that is the tower block where Roger DeVilliers has his penthouse apartment isn't the tallest building in London, but it makes up for that with its ugliness. Approaching from the front this time, I wish I'd made a little more effort with my appearance. There's no point going to the private entrance, especially given that I don't want the wrong people to know I'm here, so I'm going to have to get in through the public side and somehow find my way past security. I have a plan, roughly worked out on the journey over here, but it's not a good one.

Nobody pays me any attention as I walk through the hotel lobby, which is a good sign. The Ladies' toilets are shiny clean and opulent to a fault. They're also unoccupied, so I don't feel too self-conscious studying myself in the mirror. I wouldn't say I was untidy, but there are far more glamorous women out there. There's not much I can do about my hair, but a little bit of concealer and some dark-red lipstick make it look like I've not just stepped in from working on a building site.

The door opens while I'm still deciding whether to try and do anything with my eyelashes. I don't really do make-up though, so chances are if I try too hard it'll look rubbish. I tense at the noise, only relaxing when I see that it's not a knife-wielding hipster who's come in, but a sensibly dressed woman about my age.

'You with the conference too?' She goes to the next basin but one, puts her bag down beside it and starts to rummage around inside. No doubt she's got much the same idea as me.

'Conference?'

She looks at me a bit more closely, taking in my clothes. It's only then that I see the lanyard hanging around her neck, a name badge I can't read at the bottom of it, hidden by the fold of her jacket. 'Thought you were a programmer, maybe. Sorry.'

'No need.' I shake my head slightly as she sets about making herself look even more perfect with a skill that suggests she's done it many times before. Finally she produces a tiny atomiser and sprays little puffs of scent at her neck. It's powerful stuff, most likely very expensive.

'Nice.'

She smiles. 'My boyfriend bought it for me. He's normally rubbish at that sort of thing, but just occasionally he gets it right. Want to try it?'

I'm about to say no, but my new friend didn't appear to be expecting an answer. Before I know it, she's sprayed more of the scent around my neckline. I can't help feeling as if I've just been claimed.

'Thanks.' I try to smile, and I have to admit that the perfume isn't unpleasant. It might even help.

'So what are you here for, then, if you're not a programmer?' It's an innocent enough question, but given recent events I can't help going on the defensive.

'Just came in for a drink. Chap I know's got one of the apartments here. Thought I'd see what all the fuss was about.'

It seems to satisfy her. She pops everything back into her little handbag, clips it shut and takes one last look in the mirror to check she's not missed anything. Then with a little nod and a smile, she leaves, high heels making her hips sway in a manner that's probably provocative and certainly uncomfortable. I wait for a while after she's gone, steeling myself for the task at hand, and as I finally make for the door myself, I can't help wondering if her boyfriend is here too – or if the effort is for someone else.

Now that I know there's a conference on, the hubbub in the public atrium of the hotel makes a lot more sense. I drift around as if I'm supposed to be there, taking in the electronic noticeboard at the bottom of a set of wide stairs. 'Hotel DeV welcomes the Federation of IT Security Consultants,' it proclaims, and then lists a number of function suites and what is going on in them. I hadn't really taken on board that this entire building was one of Roger DeVilliers' properties, but it makes sense. There are many branches to his empire, after all, some more legitimate than others.

The main conference hall is up the stairs, and the great and good of the IT security world are milling around at its entrance, slowly filing in for what must be some kind of award ceremony. It's far too late in the evening for it to be a conference dinner, surely? But then, don't all these computer types work late at night anyway, or is that just how they're portrayed on the telly? I take the lift, noting that the floor numbers go only so far before a resident's swipe card is needed to access the apartments above.

I catch a brief glimpse of my glamorous friend as she moves with the crowd into the big room. I have no lanyard, and don't want to go in there anyway. Instead I go to the bar, where a few people nurse expensive drinks. Their expressions are mostly of relief, which makes me think they're regulars here who hadn't got the memo about the conference and are only just now enjoying the peace they'd been expecting.

The glass of white wine I order costs considerably more than I'd normally spend on a bottle. The barman looks slightly aghast when I ask him for some tap water to go with it, but if they want me to drink more they're going to have to lower their prices a bit. And, besides, I need to keep my head clear.

Alternating sips of wine which is actually very good and London water which is at least 90 per cent ice cube, I look around the bar and the wide landing beyond. It's quiet now everyone's gone into the conference room, too quiet for what I was hoping to achieve. Then I sense more than hear someone to my side.

'This seat taken?'

I look round, pretending to be startled. A young man who looks like he ought to be in the conference room stares down at me. He's maybe mid-twenties, not bad-looking in a tousle-haired kind of way.

'Sure. I mean, no. Help yourself.' I give him a ghost of a smile as he settles into the seat beside me, waves at the barman for service.

'I'm David, by the way. You come here often?' He lets out a soft laugh which is surprisingly attractive. 'God, I can't believe I just said that.'

'Sometimes you've just got to go with the classics, right?' I take a delicate sip of my wine and try to remember how to act sophisticated. Ten years at Saint Bert's and all I can remember is how to climb out of a sports car without flashing my knickers. 'And no. I've never been here before. What about you?'

If he notices I've not told him my name yet, he doesn't let it show. 'A couple of times. I'm still finding out about the area. Not long moved in.'

'Here?' I raise both hands in a gesture that's meant to encompass the whole building. 'In a hotel?'

'Ha ha. No. There's apartments higher up.'

'Oh, I know that. It's just . . . Well, I heard the apartments in there started at a million and a half, so . . .' I let the assumption hang unsaid.

'You think I'm not worth that much, is that it?' David's voice is hurt, but he smiles as he speaks, a flash of perfect teeth that must have cost a fortune in private dentist bills.

'I've no idea what you're worth. That's the beauty of London, isn't it? A smart suit and a neutral accent, you can be anyone you want.'

'And you? What do you want to be?'

'Me?' I toy with my drink, lean closer to him and let him get a whiff of the perfume. Is it time to slur my words a bit yet? 'I always fancied being a detective, you know? Like those badass women on the telly?'

'Really? Like, here? In London?' His eyes widen in disbelief and he suppresses what would probably have been a belly laugh, reducing it to a slightly disdainful snort. 'I'd have thought that would be really dangerous, wouldn't it? Not much fun at all.'

'I guess so. Can't all be glamour and car chases.' I shake my head, wishing I had my perfume-sharing friend's tumbling locks. 'So what about you, then? What does someone have to do to be able to afford to live in a place like this?'

He studies me a little before answering. Not in a lascivious way, or at least not in the way my male colleagues at work tend to eye up the young female constables, which is my bench-mark for this kind of behaviour. It's been too long since I've spent non-professional time with a man who's not related to me or on the same payroll. I've forgotten what it's like, how to behave.

'The suit's a bit of camouflage,' he says, tugging at one lapel. 'I'm usually more of a jeans and T-shirt person, but I had a long and bruising meeting with my financial backers this afternoon. Hence the drink.'

It's the tiniest of tells, a flick of the eyes to the left as he speaks, but I see now he's lying about something. There's a little too much detail in his answer too. That's always a sign someone's making it up as they go along. Most people wouldn't notice, but then most people haven't been trained in suspect interview techniques. Most people probably aren't as jaded and cynical as me either. Ah well, it was always going to be too good to be true. Rich, handsome, available and picking up women in bars.

'Financiers? That sounds very . . . fancy.' I lean towards him, letting him get another whiff of that expensive scent. 'Let me guess, then. Not a suit-wearing job, so something in IT, I'd say. Some kind of fancy website? An app?'

'All three, actually.' David leans close too, forearms resting on the bar. His shirt is unbuttoned at the neck, and I can see a few wiry hairs escaping from the gap. Not a chest waxer, then.

'What's it like?' I wait just long enough for the confusion to show on his face, put on my best little-girl-lost voice. 'The apartment, silly. How high up are you? Bet it's got a killer view. Hey, you don't live in the penthouse, do you?'

'I wish. No. That belongs to the bloke who built this whole place, lucky bastard. I'm a couple of floors down, but you're right, the view's a killer.' He pauses just long enough for someone less suspicious than me to think this wasn't what he was planning all along. 'You want to see it?'

If I hadn't seen the view from Roger DeVilliers' penthouse a few storeys above me, I'd have been seriously impressed by David's apartment, although whether impressed enough to sleep with him is another matter. It's worth considerably more than a million and a half too. All of London is drawn out beneath us in twinkling lights, the Thames a darker band reflecting a fat moon. I'm not sure I'd pay that much to live here, but I can see why people would.

Clearly there's money in the app and website business too, enough for him to have been able to pay an interior designer to outfit the place anyway. I can't glean any useful information about him from the decor other than that he's singularly lacking in imagination. A shame, really. A bit more personality and he'd have been quite a catch.

I play the slightly drunk, simpering idiot until my skin begins to crawl. David doesn't seem to notice, plying me with drink and getting steadily more familiar. He used a swipe card to unlock the lift to bring us up to this floor, then shoved it back in his wallet. That's in the inside pocket of his jacket though, and he's still wearing it. I fear there's only one way I'm going to get him to take it off, but time's running out and needs must.

'So, how big is this place? I mean, you weren't just going to show me the view were you?' We're both on a leather sofa that's a lot less comfortable than it looks. Close up, he doesn't smell too bad, but it's a long time since I've been this familiar with a man.

'You want the full tour?' He leans in and kisses me lightly on the lips. In a movie, I'd probably grab him into a tighter embrace and we'd end up naked on the rug. This isn't a movie, so I settle for pulling away while at the same time gently easing his jacket off. I let his hands wander a little while I slip his wallet out of his pocket and tease out his security swipe card. Only once I've tucked it into my own back pocket do I reach up, take his head in my hands and kiss him hard. He tenses, then relaxes a little. I guess he's not used to being dominated. I give it a count of five, then pull away.

'Is there something . . . ?' His confusion works to my advantage.

'Bathroom?' I shove both hands into my lap, shrug and give him my best simper.

'Oh. Right. End of the hall. Last on the left.'

I lean forward again, brush his lips with mine as I stand up. 'Be right back. Don't go anywhere, right?'

41

I thought I'd feel bad about leaving David waiting expectantly for me to come back, but truth is he picked me up in a bar and took me back to his place without even bothering to find out my name. I can't deny his usefulness as I swipe his electronic passkey on the lift and hit the button to take me down to the basement car park. I was prepared to go a lot further to get hold of one. Desperate times and all.

There are cameras everywhere in this building though. I can see one here in the lift, a smoked glass dome set in the middle of the ceiling. Hopefully the fact that I've used an electronic pass will mean no one will pay me any attention. I doubt Roger DeVilliers has people keeping an eye on security for the whole building, just his part of it. Trying to take the lift to the penthouse might set off alarms, but going down to the basement should be fine.

Should be.

A glance at my watch tells me the pubs will be calling last orders now. I'm taking a huge gamble here, but I don't want to think too hard about how much could go wrong. I don't know if Izzy is even being held here. All I've got is gut instinct and an empty Coca-Cola bottle. I don't do hunches. Cases are cracked by logic and diligence, painstaking attention to detail, and above all the ability to recognise patterns in amongst the noise. On the balance of probability, Izzy's in this basement somewhere, locked away. She has to be. But I don't do hunches.

The lift comes to a halt almost imperceptibly, just a ping to let me know we've arrived. I hold the 'door open' button down while carefully looking out to see if there's anyone here, but it seems empty.

The car park's much as I imagined it would be, concrete pillars and a ceiling that feels low even though it isn't. I'm surprised how few cars there are here, and how cheap some of them are. This level appears to be all private parking, although I suspect the hotel has a few spaces it can charge guests an extortionate fee to use. Driving and London don't really mix, so maybe it makes sense this facility is underused.

I find two blacked-out stretch limousines parked together, close by the lift. I recognise the number of the Mercedes that brought me down to London from Harston Magna yesterday. The bigger car next to it must be the one they used the first time. It's a Bentley, of course. Roger DeVilliers' own car, at a guess.

A click of a door opening has me scurrying for the shadows, just in time to see Adrian's silent friend, Tommy, walk across to the cars. From a dozen paces away, he plips the locks and pops open the boot of the Mercedes. I'm positioned so he can't see me unless he knows to look, but even so it's unnerving to watch him. He's not as broad and muscly as Adrian, and he walks with a slight limp that suggests he lost more than just his tongue to the Taliban, but even so he's a trained soldier, ex-SAS, with plenty of combat experience. I'm no match for him in a fair fight.

Which is why I wait until he's bent double, reaching deep into the boot of the car to fetch something out.

I step swiftly from my hiding place and smash the boot lid down as hard as I can on him. He must have sensed me coming, as at the last moment he began to stand, but whatever he had picked up must have been heavy. Had he stayed down, the boot lid would have caught him painfully across the back. As it is, it smacks the top of his head with a satisfyingly meaty thunk, and he collapses unconscious.

My heart's racing, my arms shaking with adrenaline, and all I can think is how fucking stupid what I just did was. So many things could have gone wrong, so many still could.

I check Tommy's pulse to make sure I've not killed him, then fish around in his pockets until I find the keys for the car. There's another set in there too, presumably for the Bentley or Rolls or whatever it is, and an electronic security pass for the building, similar to the one I nicked from David. I'm half pleased, half disappointed to find he doesn't have a gun like Adrian, although I do find a couple of evil-looking knives, one big enough to gut an elephant. There's something else weighing down one of his jacket pockets, and when I pull it out, I find a fully charged Taser. Police issue and highly irregular for a member of the public to be carrying around, close-protection specialist or not. Never one to look a gift horse in the mouth, I shove it into my bag.

The heavy item that Tommy was trying to pull out of the boot turns out to be a faux-leather sports bag. I don't take him for the gym and squash set, and judging by the weight of it, he's stolen all the barbells anyway. I haul it out, wincing at the echoes in the car park as it clangs on the ground. No one comes running though, and soon the distant sounds of the city outside reassert themselves. I should be moving, but my curiosity gets the better of me.

Inside the bag are what can only be described as instruments of torture. Either that or Tommy moonlights as an orthopaedic surgeon with a sideline in joinery. Hammers in various sizes, bonesaws, hacksaws, a blowtorch, a neat little plastic box filled with hobby knives, all these and more are packed inside, rolled in clean cloths. There's some thin rope, and I take a moment to use it round his hands and ankles before hauling him into the boot of the car. It's big enough in there for him not to be uncomfortable.

I'm just about to shut the lid down on him and lock it, when I have a thought. Going through his pockets again, I take his phone and swipe it on. It asks for a thumbprint, so I use his tied hand to unlock it. I've no idea how long that will last, but it gives me a phone for at least a little while, and if anyone calls to find out where he's got to, I'll have some notice they're looking for him.

Tommy's security pass gets me back into the lift, but it also opens the fire door just beside it, leading onto the stairwell. I opt for this instead, since that's where he came from.

The concrete steps end one storey down, so I must be in the deepest depths of the basement. The door here has no security lock, most likely because you would need to pass through several to get here. It opens onto a wide corridor, half a dozen doors spaced equally along either side. They look a bit like my hazy memory, half drugged, from when last I was here, although I can't be sure they're the same, or why I would have been dragged past here from the car park on the way up to the penthouse. I've got to start my search somewhere though.

The first two doors have labels – 'Electrical Substation' and 'Communications Hub'. The next two are just numbered, as are the following four. The final doors have nothing written on them at all, but when I open the first it reveals a sizeable store room, stacked with maintenance equipment. Across from it, another room is filled with boxes of electrical equipment and metal shelving fixed to the walls.

Two more doors at the far end of the corridor from the fire door and the lift. The first is locked, so I go to the other one. It opens onto yet more storage space, this time empty, so I go back to the locked door. There's a keyhole, no fancy electronic swipe pad to accept Tommy's security pass. I've got all his keys though.

Pulling them out of my pocket, I go through the keyrings until I find something that looks like it might fit, slot it into the hole and turn. It clicks with a well-oiled ease, and I push open the door. Inside, there's a chair, a desk, a chemical toilet in the far corner beside a sink unit that looks like it's most often used for rinsing out mops. What there isn't is any sign of Izzy, until I catch a glimpse of movement in the corner of my eye.

Instinct kicks in, and I drop to the floor as something rushes through the air where my head had been. I try to roll before my attacker can come in for another try. On my back, I get a better view of the chair pulled up to the door, the young woman brandishing what looks like a bit of plastic pipe that might sting if she hit me with it but probably wouldn't do any actual damage. I shove myself backwards as she rushes towards me, arms up to fend off the frenzied blows. I was right, the pipe stings like fuck, but I don't think it's going to break any bones.

'Izzy!' The shout falls on deaf ears, so I time the next blow and grab the pipe. Slapped against my palm, it sends a jolt of pain up my arm that has me swearing like a navvy, but I manage to keep my grip, tugging it from hers. The initial frenzy of her attack has dissipated now, and she stares at me with wild, confused eyes.

'I'm not here to hurt you, Izzy. Quite the opposite.' I throw the pipe to one side, inch my way backwards until I can sit up and get a better look at her. She's bedraggled; there's no other way to describe it. Her hair's a tangled mess of spikes and mats, her eyes sunken and bruised. She looks like she's not had a square meal in a week or more, and her clothes are filthy. There's still a spark in her eyes though, and a strength in her voice when she finally speaks.

'Con— . . . Constance?' I try my best smile of confirmation, but she's not finished yet. 'What the fuck are you doing here?'

42

'Not quite the greeting I was hoping for, but I'll take it.' I scramble to my feet, rub at my palm, where a pipe-shaped red welt is beginning to show. 'You want to get out of here or what?'

'Are you . . . ?' Izzy seems to be having difficulty stringing words together. 'Aren't you . . . ? I mean, are the police here?'

'Not exactly. And we don't have a lot of time. Come on.' I step past her, open the door slowly and poke my head out to see if there's anyone about. I can't quite believe that I've not been spotted yet, and then I see the light above the lift doors click on, the arrow pointing resolutely down.

'No time to explain. We've got to go now.'

To give her her due, Izzy does what she's told. We both sprint down the corridor, pushing through the door onto the stairwell as the lift pings that it's arrived. I close the door as softly as I can behind us, praying we've not been heard. Through the reinforced-glass window, I see two figures, their backs to us, walk down the corridor towards Izzy's cell. Turning to face her, I put a finger to my lips even though she's not making a sound, then point it upwards. I wish there was something I could block the door with, but the only thing I've got is Tommy's phone. I bend down, jamming it under the door. It might keep them occupied for a minute, but then again they might just take the lift.

271

I catch up with Izzy at the landing, where she's about to climb further up. 'Out here,' I whisper, and we step out into the car park. The two stretch limousines are still parked close by. There's no sound from the Mercedes, so Tommy must be still out cold. I find I don't much care if he never wakes up again.

'Not that one,' I say to Izzy as she stares at the blacked-out car. Tommy's bag of torture implements is still on the ground where I left it. 'You could shove that in the back of this one though.'

I unlock the Bentley, pull open the driver's door. Izzy struggles with the bag, but manages to get it in the back, then climbs into the passenger seat beside me as I fire up the engine. It's an automatic, unfamiliar, but I've had enough police driver training to know the basics. As I pull out of the parking space and head for the ramp that will take us up to street level, I catch a glimpse in the wing mirror of the lift door opening, a blond-haired man stepping out. He sets off towards us at a run, so I floor the throttle. This thing might weigh twice as much as my elderly Volvo, but it's also got twice as much power. With a chirp of rubber on concrete floor, we lurch forward, picking up speed, and soon outpace him.

Another glance and I see him pull out his phone, slap it to the side of his face, and that's when I realise we've still got to get up to street level and out. If Adrian tells security to lock it down, we're going to be stuck in here.

I have to slow as we approach the gates. It's nothing as simple as a cheap barrier; that would let anyone walk in from the street. A swipe pad the same as those by all the doors is mounted on a stalk sprouting out of the floor like some improbable mushroom, and once I've found the button to operate the window, I reach out and swipe Tommy's card over it.

Nothing happens.

I swipe it again, and the little red light refuses to change to green. Fuck it. Now we're really screwed. I can imagine Adrian sprinting after us, waving that gun of his.

'What's the problem?' Izzy's worried voice reminds me why I'm here.

'They've shut the place down. This card doesn't work any more.' I wave it in her face, and then remember I've got another one. It's worth a shot, surely.

'Here. Chuck this out.' I throw Tommy's card at her, slapping at my pockets to find David's stolen one. An angry blond-headed figure appears in the mirror as I fumble with the slim sliver of plastic, reach out and slap it against the pad. Relief floods through me as red turns to green and the gates swing inwards. I hit the central locking button at the same time as I wind up the window, engage drive and surge forward before the gates have fully opened. The thump of Adrian's fist on the boot of the car is sweet music as we spring out of the building and into the night traffic.

I park the Bentley on a double-yellow line in a back street in Soho, unlocked and with the keys lying on the driver's seat. I was tempted to take it further out of town, leave it in a less savoury neighbourhood for the local youth to play with, but the longer we're in it, the more chance of its theft being reported to the police. Right now, I imagine Detective Superintendent Bailey is preparing the nails for my coffin, and there's almost certainly a warrant out for my arrest. How quickly things go from bad to hopeless.

The black cab back across the river uses up far too much of my remaining cash. I tell the driver to drop us off a few blocks away from Pete's house, and we go the rest of the way on foot.

'Where're we going?' Izzy asks, the first words she's spoken since we escaped the tower block. She sounds weak, exhausted and terrified. I can only sympathise.

'A friend's house. We can't go back to my place, and we really can't go to the police. Not right now.'

'I thought you were the police.'

'I . . . It's complicated.' I dig around in my jacket pocket for my house keys, glad that no one has realised there are two sets on the keyring and only one fits my own front door. Or at least used to fit my own front door before Adrian had the lock replaced. Nobody has changed Pete's locks yet, which is a relief. The new number I programmed into the alarm still works too. I lead Izzy through to the kitchen at the back of the house, but when she reaches for the light switch, I grab her arm.

'Best not to let anyone know we're here, OK?'

There's enough street light filtering in through the window for me to see her face, eyes wide with fear, but she nods once, then goes to the table and collapses into a seat. I chance a quick look in the fridge, the light making me squint. There's not much in there, and the milk's more than two weeks out of date. Go figure.

'Whose house is this?' Izzy asks as I turn my attention to the cupboards. Instant coffee or tea? It's a difficult decision. At least there's biscuits.

'My old boss in the Met.'

'Won't he mind?' It's a strange thing to be worried about, given all the other options, but then one of the things they beat into us at Saint Bert's is consideration for others above ourselves. Not that it sticks with most of the girls.

'Not really. He's been dead a month now.'

Izzy says nothing for a while, just looking around Pete's darkened kitchen. Finally she faces me again. 'How did you know where to find me? Why were you even looking?'

'As to how, well, that's a long story.' I'm not about to tell her or anybody else that it was a wild guess based on an unlikely coincidence. 'The why's easier. Your sister asked me to, and then your father threatened to kill me if I carried on.'

Izzy stares at me in the semi-darkness, her fear turning swiftly to anger. 'He's not my father.'

'No. You're right. He's not.' I put two mugs of black coffee and a packet of chocolate Hobnobs on the table, pull out the chair beside her and sit down. Izzy reaches for the biscuits first, fingers fumbling as she rips the packet apart and stuffs one into her face. I watch her eat for a while, cradling my mug as much for something to hold on to as any desire to drink it.

'Do you know who is?' she asks after a solid two minutes of concentrated munching.

'Yes. Do you?'

Izzy looks up at me in the half-darkness, and I see her unkempt dark-red hair, thin face and strong jawline. It's not quite like looking in a mirror, but not far off. She nods, then goes back to the biscuits, pausing only occasionally to slurp down some of her coffee. She doesn't speak again until they're all gone and she's cleaned the inside of the packet with a licked finger.

'So what do we do next?'

I'm really not sure. My career's down the drain, my reputation is about to be dragged through the mud, and if the police catch me I'll be going to jail for a very long time. It's small beer compared to what Izzy faces if she falls into Roger DeVilliers' hands again. I saw what was inside the bag Tommy was fetching from the back of the Mercedes, and I've no doubt at all who it was intended for.

'Get away from London for a start. Find somewhere safe to hide out. Burntwoods, maybe.'

Izzy scowls at me. 'That place? Christ no. They're all so wet. Hiding away from the world instead of trying to change it. The power they have, the knowledge. They could do so much.'

I'm surprised by the anger in her voice, but heartened by it too.

'You saw the photos, didn't you? The video.' Izzy holds my gaze as she speaks, almost daring me to make something of it.

'Yeah. Clever way to hide them, deleting them off the hard

drive and then not using it for anything else. I take it you sent copies to other people though?'

'Not me. Steve Benson. The journalist. He's the one who found all that stuff in the first place and worked out it was me. He came to school, pretended he was doing a piece on private education in England and how it was adapting to the new rich. Mrs Jennings thought it would be good publicity. Get Saint Bert's in the paper and the Russians would all start sending their daughters there. She's probably right.'

'Surely they didn't let him interview girls alone?'

'No. We were always chaperoned. But he slipped a note to me when no one was looking. Just a web address for a private file storage account. I thought he was coming on to me at first, only he didn't seem the type.'

I'm about to ask what she means by that, a habit from my interview training, but then I remember what she's been through, the years of sexual abuse. Of the two of us, she's probably got way more experience in these things than I have, even though she's half my age.

'This file store. Does it still exist?'

'Far as I know. Unless they managed to get the passcode out of him. Blondie told me he was dead.'

'Blondie? Oh, you mean Adrian. And yes, Steve Benson is dead. His body washed up in the Thames.' I tell Izzy about the initial forensic report, and the news item I saw suggesting suicide.

'Christ. He's everywhere, isn't he?'

I don't need to ask who 'he' is. 'That's what being a billionaire gets you these days. He's probably got film footage of any number of powerful people in compromising situations too. A bit of carrot and a lot of stick.' I remember Adrian's words on the train up to Northampton, about how if I did as they wanted, all my troubles would go away.

The clock on Pete's cooker glows red, telling me it's past

midnight. 'Why don't you get some rest? We'll have to try and come up with something, but apart from anything else I need to get hold of some cash. I'll give Charlotte a call first thing.' I remember my previous stay at her house on Elmstead Road, the late start. 'Well, maybe not first thing.'

'Why Charlotte? What's she got to do with any of this?'

'She's the one who asked me to look for you, remember?' Something occurs to me then that should have been obvious days ago. 'She doesn't know anything about her father, does she.'

'No. He's very careful about that sort of thing. I think Mum suspects, which is probably why she drinks all the time. Maybe why she fucked your dad, too. Although that might just have been her way of getting some small revenge. Cuckold her husband with his best friend? There's a certain pleasing symmetry about it. If only she'd been a bit more careful.'

I can hear the anger rising in Izzy's tone again. Maybe coffee and Hobnobs wasn't the best thing to feed her. I'm too wired to sleep either, but we both need rest if we're going to come at this problem with clear heads. The urge to jump on a train and flee back to Scotland is overwhelming. Sure, they could still find us there, but the distance would be reassuring.

'Look, there's a spare bedroom upstairs. First on the left. Bathroom's right next door if you need it. Try not to use a light if you can avoid it, OK?'

Izzy hauls herself out of her chair. 'Can't promise I'll sleep much, but I'll try.' She stops at the door, turns back to face me. 'Thanks, Constance. For coming to my rescue.'

'Hey, no problem. That's what sisters do, right?' She smiles at that, which is good to see. 'And it's Con, by the way. Only my mother calls me Constance.'

43

I hear light thumping noises upstairs for a few minutes, the flush of the toilet, and then everything falls quiet. Pete's house creaks and groans as all old houses do, and beyond it the city's mute roar reassures me that millions of people are going about their lives untouched by Roger DeVilliers and his sick games. Lucky them. I've still no idea how I'm going to extricate myself from this mess, and I'm all too aware that I'm running out of options.

Through in the living room, I take up my old post in the armchair facing the bay window. The blinds are half closed, just enough for me to see out without people on the street outside being able to see me. The nearest street lamp casts orange slats across one wall, highlighting the pictures and the carriage clock on the mantelpiece. It's stopped ticking since Pete's not been here to wind it, so I get up again, and pick it up. It's too dark to see the inscription to Pete's grandad engraved in the silver, but there's enough light to open up the back and get the key out. There's something else in there besides, a slim roll of paper that turns out to be several hundred quid in twenty-pound notes.

'Pete, you beauty.' I shove the money in my pocket, wind the clock and settle back into the armchair to its gentle ticking.

'Well. It's not as if I'm going to need it now.'

I'm unsurprised, if a little guilty, to hear his voice and see the shadowy shape in the other armchair across the room. There's something very calming about his presence; I feel as if nothing can harm me while he's around.

'I'm always around, Con. Or not. Depends on your point of view.'

'Really? And here's me thought you just turned up to annoy me when I'm trying to get some sleep.' I pitch my voice low, barely a whisper, all too aware that Izzy is upstairs and most likely staring sleeplessly at the ceiling in the spare bedroom. The last thing I need is for her to think I've lost my mind.

'She's a tough one. Has to be, to get through what she's been through and not be an utter basket case.'

'Can't help that DeVilliers is still out there. And he holds all the cards right now too.'

'Does he? I thought you still had video evidence of his crimes, a witness who can identify him. That sounds like more than nothing.'

I think about the hard drive, tucked away in the laptop case in my bag in the back of Aunt Felicity's car. Have they found that yet? Have they hurt Aunt Felicity? I should never have involved her in the first place. I should call, make sure she's OK.

'Think, Con. Stop just reacting and try to piece it all together.'

I'm already on my feet, halfway to the hall and the phone. Chances are it's still connected and working. Pete's words drop me straight back into my seat. Calling anyone from this number is a risk, but calling Aunt Felicity is just foolish. Even if she's fine, they're bound to be monitoring her line. It only takes a few seconds to trace a landline to landline call if you've got access to the sort of resources my old department has.

'Gordon Bailey.'

'That's more like the Constance Fairchild I remember. You think he's bent, right?'

'Think? I know he's bent. Just can't believe he got away with it for so long. He shot you in the fucking head, Pete.'

'And why do you think he did that, eh? Pretty drastic, don't you think? Unless we were on to him.'

It seems at the same time far-fetched and yet all too plausible. 'If he was under enough pressure. Maybe the noose was tightening and he needed a way out.'

'What about that operation though? You can't believe it was a coincidence we'd be trying to break up the same mob he was involved with, right? What chance of that?'

As he talks, so Pete's questions begin to sound more and more like my own misgivings voiced aloud. I was a minor part of the operation, right from the start. I ran the surveillance side of things, except for that one time when I'd been sent off on a training course. Dan Penny took over in my absence, and the next day Pete was dead. I've not really had time to sit still and think about that until now.

'So the operation was a deliberate set-up to smoke out Bailey? To get to the bottom of corruption in the team?'

Pete says nothing, but I imagine his shadowy form tilting its head to one side.

'And then Roger DeVilliers comes sniffing around because I've started looking for Izzy. He wants to get some dirt on me to use as leverage, ends up uncovering something far more serious. But how the hell did he get hold of that video footage in the first place?'

I stare up at the ceiling as if the answers are written there, but all I can see are the stripes of orange and black cast by the street lamps through the half-closed blinds. A flickering in the light disrupts the pattern. It's not unusual for cars to come down the street, even this late at night, but something about the way it moves sets me on edge. I get up as quietly as I can, creep towards the window and peer through the blinds. Two cars have double-parked about fifty yards up the road, one behind the other. They're not taxis, and there are no lights on in the house immediately alongside them. I'd thought we were safe, but of course bloody Dan Penny found me here the day after Pete died. If they've been casting the net as wide as possible to find me and Izzy, it was only a matter of time before someone remembered this place.

'Got to go, Pete,' I whisper as I turn from the window, but the shadows have shifted, and now the chair sits empty.

As if I was only talking to myself all this time.

As if he was never there.

'Wake up, Izzy. We need to get out of here.'

I daren't turn any lights on, but there's enough of a street glow filtering in through the spare-room window to see the tousled mess of the bed. Izzy's not in it though, she's sitting on a small chair in the far corner.

'Wasn't asleep. Who were you talking to?'

It's too late, I'm too tired and the adrenaline is making it hard to think straight, so I just answer her truthfully. 'Pete's ghost. He had some very interesting ideas about why all this is happening.'

'Pete?' Izzy stands, fully dressed.

'The man whose house this used to be. My former boss, Detective Inspector Copperthwaite.'

'Oh. Right.' I don't know if this means she believes me or believes I've finally gone mad. It doesn't really matter. 'Why do we need to leave? We've only been here, like, an hour?'

'There's two cars parked a way up the street I don't like the look of. And they might have guessed I'd come here.'

'OK. Where are we going to go?' Izzy moves slowly towards me and the door. I want to tell her to hurry, but equally I want to be as quiet as possible. At least for now.

'I'm not sure. Not got many options left, to be honest. Away from here is the first priority. Come on. We're going out the back.'

She follows me downstairs and into the kitchen. There's a door out onto the small garden. A gate in the high brick wall at the back leads onto a narrow lane. There's two bolts in the gate, but also a mortice lock. Luckily I know where Pete kept the key. I hand it to Izzy as I open the back door.

'Go down there. Listen carefully to make sure there's no one on the other side, then slide back the bolts but don't unlock the gate. I'll be right with you.'

'Where are you going?' She looks at me with wide eyes, gripping the key in nervous fingers.

'To the front door. I'm going to reset the alarm. If I remember right, I'll have fifteen seconds to get back here and close the door behind me.' I don't tell her that I want to have another look to see what the two cars are doing. I'll feel a bit foolish if they're gone. Izzy just nods once, then steps out into the night.

At the front door, I gently ease the bolt into position, hang the security chain back and deadlock the Yale. Peering out the spyhole, I can see the two cars still parked a way up the road. I wonder what they're doing. Waiting for backup? Circling around the building to come at us from both sides? I quickly reset the alarm, wincing as it beeps loud enough to be heard in Northamptonshire and lights up like it's the fifth of November. No time to worry about that now. I dash through the house and out the back door, closing it behind me as a London silence falls once more.

'Can't hear anyone out there,' Izzy whispers to me as I join her at the gate. I want to jump up and peer over the wall, but it's too high for one thing, and set with broken glass for another. The key's in the lock, so I ease it round and open the gate just a fraction, leaning hard into it to stop someone from pushing the other way.

There's no one in the lane. I step through swiftly, Izzy close behind, then pull the gate back shut again, lock it and slip the key into my pocket.

'This way.' I point to the end of the lane, where it opens onto a street at the far end from where the cars were parked. 'Keep to the shadows.'

It's hard to walk slowly and keep as quiet as possible. The lane is strewn with rubbish, and we have to tread carefully around every set of bins. Only the foxes see us though, and they don't care enough even to stop foraging.

I begin to wonder whether my paranoia has finally got the better of me. What if those two cars had a perfectly innocent reason to be double-parked there? A large party getting a couple of Ubers home, maybe. Or even a lift to the airport for a very early flight. By the time we reach the road's end, I've almost convinced myself that I'm just an idiot. Then light floods the lane behind us and an alarm starts wailing into the night. I grab Izzy's hand, pull her into the shadows behind a set of wheelie bins, peer around to see whether someone's seen us or not. I can't see a person, just a security light bathing the lane outside Pete's house. Bless him and his police-approved alarm system. I squeeze Izzy's hand slightly, pull her close.

'Run!' I bark, and we pelt off into the night.

44

Dawn creeps slowly into the sky as we walk across the city. I don't know London like a native, certainly not the parts around Pete's house, and Izzy's even less clued up about the bits beyond Soho and Covent Garden than I am. Country girls, the two of us. I'm tempted more than once to flag down a taxi. I've got Pete's cash, after all. But this far out and this time of the morning, there don't seem to be any.

By the time we hit the river, the commuter stream has begun to trickle and the coffee shops are opening. We're both tired, weary and scared, but somehow the fact that we've escaped again is reassuring. We're still free even if we're running on empty, and even if it sounds corny, we've got each other.

'Where're we going?' Izzy asks as we merge with a line of office workers pouring out of Embankment Tube station and slouching towards the Strand. It's the first thing she's said in well over an hour.

'We need to end this, which means we need to go public. Only every time you've tried to do that, Roger's shut it all down. He's got my name tarred so badly no one will believe a word I say, but you're his daughter—'

'Stepdaughter. Not even sure I want to be called that.'

'Yeah. Sorry. I can understand. Well, a bit. Still, as far as the world's concerned, you're his daughter. Use that while you can.'

'So, what? I phone up the BBC and say I want to talk to the

news desk? Could they just broadcast my allegations on the morning news?' She shakes her head in despair. 'Didn't work out so well for Steve Benson, did it?'

'Yeah, you're right. Allegations won't cut it. Not your word against his. He'll just pay a couple of doctors to section you. Maybe I'll tell you about Great Aunt Chastity some day, but the short version is it's not a good idea to let them think you're even slightly mentally ill. They'll lock you up in a private asylum and that'll be the end of it. But if you've got the pictures and video, it becomes that much harder for them to sweep it all under the carpet.'

We keep on walking, getting closer and closer to my flat. I'm not going back there, probably won't ever go back there except to give Mrs Feltham the biggest hug I can manage, but there's a little hipster café on the corner of Elmstead Road that will be just perfect for breakfast. I'm hoping that Charlotte thinks so too, or at the worst, Ben.

Food never tasted so good, even if it's mostly pastries washed down with strong black coffee. For all her skinny frame, Izzy has quite an appetite, and I'm happy enough to feed it. Pete's roll of notes won't last for ever, but if this plan doesn't work out there's enough for two tickets to Dundee. We'll just have to wing it from there. I don't mention to Izzy the possibility of going back to Burntwoods though; it's clear from her earlier talk that she doesn't much like the place, and I'm inclined to agree with her. Very much a last resort.

'We need to take the fight to them.'

I'd been thinking much the same thing, but it's Izzy who says it.

'How, though? I mean, I told Kathryn to send your email, but as far as I can tell it's had no effect.'

Izzy frowns at me. 'Kathryn . . . ? Oh God, yes. Good old Kat. She did what she was told, but they somehow managed to intercept all of the messages. Christ, I don't know how far their surveillance reaches but it's fucking terrifying how much they know. The way Blondie – what did you say his real name was? Adrian? – the way he gloated about how they'd tracked down and destroyed all the copies of those photos. Those videos.' She shakes her head again. 'Part of me's glad. In a way. You know what I mean? That's me in those pictures. Those men . . .'

I reach out across the table and place my hand over hers. I can feel the tension running through her, but I can't imagine the thoughts that are leading to it. I've seen a few photos, watched a few videos that make me wish mind bleach were a thing. She's lived through it.

We sit there for a little while, and I'm happy just to give her the time. Poor girl, I don't think anyone's ever done that for her before. Then the little bell above the front door tings the arrival of another customer. I look up and see a familiar face come in.

'Charlotte.' I speak the word quietly, to Izzy only. She looks around to see her sister – half-sister – approach the counter. Charlotte hasn't seen us sitting near the back of the café, and she appears too distracted to notice anything much. I'm half concentrating on the door, looking through the window to see if she's been followed, but she seems to be alone. No Ben with her today either, the lazy sod.

She's ordered her coffee and is waiting for it to be made when I finally stand, step quickly over to her. When I say 'Char', she almost jumps out of her skin, whirling around, eyes wide.

'Connie. What are you doing . . . ?' She focuses past my shoulder, then rushes past. 'Izzy! Oh my God!'

The hug is shorter and stiffer than I might have expected, given Charlotte's earlier concerns. Or maybe my view is coloured by my greater knowledge of the situation. I stand back and observe the two of them together, only approach when Charlotte's coffee is ready.

'We were kind of hoping you might drop in. Not quite sure how else I was going to get in touch.'

Charlotte raises an eyebrow at this. 'Erm, you've got my phone number, right?' She sees the look Izzy and I can't help exchanging. 'What's going on?'

'Have you noticed anything strange happening the past few days?' I ask.

Charlotte shakes her head. 'Not especially, no. Well, Ben didn't come home last night, but he's probably gone out on the piss with some of the lads from the office. Not the first time, won't be the last.'

A chill runs through me at her words. For her own part, Charlotte seems completely unfazed by the temporary disappearance of her boyfriend, but then she always was the epitome of self-absorption.

'What about your father? Have you spoken to him recently?'

'Daddy?' Charlotte manages to make the word sound utterly innocent and lovely, but beside her I see Izzy tense. 'Not for a week or so. He's always so busy.' She looks at her half-sister. 'He told me you'd gone off to the Continent with a school friend and not to worry myself about you. How come you're here? And why do you look like you've been sleeping in those clothes for a week?'

I ignore her idiot questions, it's always the best way to deal with Charlotte. 'You've got his number though, right?'

'Of course.' Charlotte takes out her phone, swipes the screen awake. 'You want me to call him now? What's this about, Connie?'

I take the phone from her unresisting hand, navigate to the contacts and hit the personal mobile number for 'Daddy'. I know what to do now. Izzy's right. It's time to take the fight to the enemy.

The call rings a half-dozen times, and I'm sure it's about to go to voicemail. I'm all set to leave a message, even if I'm not quite sure what I'm going to say, when the line clicks open.

'Charlotte, dear. What have I told you about phoning me while I'm at work?'

I can hear the background thrum of a car's engine, so it would seem they haven't recovered the Bentley yet. What surprises me more though is the tone of Roger DeVilliers' voice. It's not that I wasn't expecting him to answer; that was kind of the whole point in calling him on his personal number. It's the edge of tenderness in his chastisement of his daughter – his true daughter. The mental disconnect between how he treats Charlotte and how he has treated Izzy is too wide for me to begin to comprehend. But then I can't fathom how someone can find sexual gratification in the abuse of a minor either.

'Charlotte's busy right now, Mr DeVilliers. She let me borrow her phone though, so I could have a quick word.'

As expected, the line goes mute for a while, and I can imagine DeVilliers shouting instructions to whoever is with him. Adrian, probably. Maybe Tommy too, if I didn't hurt him too much. I've got an eye on my watch as I speak, but in truth I've no idea how quickly they can triangulate this location from the call. Hopefully they'll assume I'm at Charlotte's house.

'Miss Fairchild. I'm surprised to hear from you. I'd have thought you'd be busy fleeing the country right now. What with the arrest warrant out for you and everything.'

I don't rise to the bait. 'Nice try, Roger. You're the one going to prison, not me.'

'Really? And how do you suppose that will happen?'

'Oh, I don't know. Video and photographic evidence of your sick abuse, the sworn testimony of one of the victims. That sort of thing.'

DeVilliers lets out a low chuckle, as I was sure he would. Across the table from me, Charlotte's face is a picture of confusion, but then she's only getting one side of the conversation.

'Tell me, Miss Fairchild. Have you spent much time with your half-sister? Oh yes. I know about that. Your father's betrayal of his oldest friend. It's no surprise Isobel is the way she is, given her family history. The girl is quite clearly mentally challenged. I've psychiatric reports from several very eminent doctors. No jury will take seriously anything she says about me.'

'Isobel is fine, despite your depraved attentions. I think she will make a very compelling witness in your trial. And we have the photographs, the videos. I think you'll have a hard time playing them down.'

DeVilliers sighs down the phone as if my threats are more tiresome than anything to be taken seriously. 'If you're referring to the photographs on the laptop we found in your aunt's car, then I don't think you have them at all, do you? And I'd hate to think what would happen to poor sweet Felicity if the police were to find out what she had in her possession. Who knew the dear old lady had such unsavoury interests?'

'Nice try, Roger, but it won't wash. Threatening me and my family just confirms to me what a depraved monster you are. We still have a copy of those pictures in a secure cloud storage account. You could search for a thousand years and you'd never find it.'

'And what of it? These photographs, the video footage. I've not seen it myself, but I'm told it is only the girls who can be seen. You have no idea who is doing anything to them.' I can hear the edge of panic in his voice now, and it gives me a tiny thrill.

'Have you heard of vein pattern analysis, Mr DeVilliers? It's something they've developed up in Scotland. Quite fascinating, really. And just as revealing as a fingerprint. All you need is a clear image of the back of someone's hand, say. Or an erect penis. Actually, even a flaccid one will do.'

The phone goes silent again, and I check quickly to see he

hasn't hung up. It's only muted, no doubt while he speaks to his henchmen. My last barb was probably going a bit too far. It's true though.

'Let me tell you how this is going to go, Miss Fairchild.' DeVilliers comes back on the line, his voice strained as if he's trying hard not to shout. 'You will bring Isobel to me. You'll bring the web address for the so-called evidence you have too, along with any passcode needed to access it. Once any images are destroyed, you will walk to the nearest police station and hand yourself in. Isobel will come with me, and as long as she behaves, I'll see to it that no one else in your family suffers unduly from your criminal misbehaviour.'

Charlotte's phone pings at me to say a text has arrived. I ignore it, chilled by the cold malice in Roger DeVilliers' tone.

'Why on earth would I do a thing like that? Why would Izzy?'

'Adrian has just texted you a photograph, Miss Fairchild. Have a look at it. Closely. I think you'll find my demands aren't all that unreasonable. You have half an hour.'

He hangs up this time, and I flick through the menus on Charlotte's phone until I find the text. The photograph fills the large screen in all-too-high definition, and Charlotte gasps as she peers at it over my shoulder.

'Benno!'

My brother stares back at me from the screen. His eyes are wide with fear, his hands tied behind his back. But it's the hunting knife, big enough to gut an elephant, and held to his throat that makes my blood run cold.

45

My brother and I had a love–hate relationship growing up. He's a few years younger than me, and had all of the attention lavished on him from the moment he was born. I was old enough to notice this, but not old enough to know why. It was only later that I realised both that he was the male heir my father longed for, and that this wasn't Benevolence's fault. Despite a lifetime of conditioning in the Fairchild way, he actually grew up to be rather fair-minded. A bit spoiled, yes, perhaps feckless too, but hard-working when he finds the right motivation. He's my brother though, so I cut him more slack than I would most.

Even if I hated him as much as I hate my father, I'd still shudder at the image on Charlotte's phone.

'What the hell's going on, Connie? What is this?' She tries to take the handset from me, but I pull it away. Now's not the time for emotional reactions. We need to bring cold logic to this problem.

'Your father's not the man you thought he was, Charlotte. I'm sure if you ask her, Izzy will tell you exactly how little you know him, but right now I need to think.'

'What did he say?' Izzy asks, and I realise neither of them heard the other side of the conversation. I outline Roger DeVilliers' demands as swiftly and succinctly as I can, knowing it's just going to make Charlotte even more confused.

Izzy takes all of ten seconds to digest the information before saying exactly what I knew she would. 'I'll go back.'

'Like fuck you will. I didn't risk my life dragging you out of that place just so he could get away with it. And I'm damned if I'm going to prison for him either.'

'Prison? But you've not done anything wrong.' Charlotte's mouth drops open slightly, and then she raises her hands to her face as something dawns in her pretty blonde head. 'Oh my God. This is all my fault. If I'd not asked you to look for Izzy then none of this would have happened.'

I want to take her by the shoulders and shake some sense into her, only it would take too long. Years, probably. 'No, Charlotte. It's not your fault. This goes back way further than that.'

I expect more of an argument from her, but instead she just lets out a very quiet 'Oh' and then falls silent.

'So what are we going to do, then?' Izzy asks. 'You any idea where they're holding him?'

'I'd expect the same place they had you. Don't think I'll get away with another rescue attempt though.' I've still got David's security card, but I expect it will be disabled by now. Or worse, they'll have set it up to let me in but not out again. 'No. I think it's best if we get them to bring him to us.'

'You think they'll do that?'

'If we agree to their terms. But only to get them onto neutral ground. We're not letting anyone get away with this.' I see Izzy's confusion, Charlotte's face beyond even that. Not for the first time, I wish I had a friend I could call on, but pretty much everyone I know in the Met will think I'm a crook, and the only other person I can think of is two hundred miles away in Birmingham. She might be able to help though. And I think I know just the place to set up the handover.

'Charlotte. I need you to do something for me.'

She takes a moment to understand I'm talking to her now. 'You do? What?'

'First off, I need you to give Izzy any spare cash you've got. A credit card and PIN number would be good too. We promise not to bankrupt you.'

Charlotte has a good line in puzzled frowns, but she digs a slim leather purse out of her large handbag, pulls out a couple of cards and studies them for a moment. 'I think this one's got the most credit on it.' She hands it to Izzy, reciting the number twice so she doesn't forget it, then counts out a couple of hundred pounds in crisp, straight-out-of-the-bank-machine twenty-pound notes.

'I can get more, if you need it.' She hands them to Izzy as if they're nothing. How the other half live.

'Hopefully we won't need it, or the card. They're just a backup. Thanks, Char. Now there's one more thing.'

'There is?'

'Yes. I need you to go home. Not up the road home, but Harston Magna. I don't care how you do it, but get your mum away from there. Take her to a health spa or a holiday break some-where. Whatever you do, wherever you go, you need to be out of communication for at least a couple of days. More would be better.'

For once she doesn't argue. Just nods at me as if the full enormity of what's going on has finally sunk in. She gives me an apologetic smile, leans close and pats me on the arm.

'You be careful, Con.' She reaches for the phone, but I shake my head.

'Sorry, Char. I'm going to need this too. And the passcode.'

She shrugs. 'It's the same as the card. My birthday and month. Never was good with numbers.'

Both of us sit in silence for a while after Charlotte leaves. Izzy toys with her coffee, the half-eaten pastry no longer appetising.

I can't help but stare at the image of my brother, the fear in his eyes.

And then my training starts to take over.

I ignore his face, look at the other details. He's dressed much the same way as when I last saw him, a crumpled jacket over a shirt with no tie. He's sitting on an office chair, hands behind his back so I assume tied. They've not gagged him, and the fact there's not even a rag dangling around his neck suggests to me he's somewhere that shouting for help will do him no good. The photo's cropped too close for me to see much of the background. A bit of dark-grey wall that is almost certainly the same concrete basement where they were holding Izzy. I need to find a way of getting them onto my ground; there's no way I'm going onto theirs. If only I had any ground I could call my own.

Something's bothering me about the photo, and for a long time I can't work out what. There's a clue in there I should be seeing, but there's nothing visual I've not already noticed and discarded. Then it dawns on me. The photograph pinged onto Charlotte's phone while I was talking to Roger DeVilliers. It wasn't taken by him, and wasn't sent by him. It was sent by Adrian, and that's almost certainly his hand holding the knife.

'I think I might have an idea.' I thumb and swipe at the screen, confused by the operating system of Charlotte's unnecessarily expensive smartphone.

'What are you trying to do?' Izzy asks.

'Find the number of whoever texted me that image.'

'Here.' She reaches out, takes the phone off me and in seconds has the details I need. Bloody teenagers. 'Why's it important?'

'A couple of reasons. First, that's Adrian's number. You know, Blondie? We can speak to him independently of your . . .' I stop myself. 'Independently of Roger DeVilliers.'

'And how exactly does that help? He's hardly going to talk to us. Suddenly switch sides and dump the man who pays him.'

'Maybe. Maybe not. Depends how quickly he thinks the ship is sinking. I wasn't going to speak to him anyway. I'll get a friend to do that for me. Someone Blondie will more likely listen to. If we can use that to distract him, it's a start.'

'Why do we need to distract him?' Izzy scratches at her head, then shakes it. 'No, stupid question. What are we actually going to do? It's been twenty minutes now and you need to phone that bastard back before he decides he doesn't need your brother after all.'

'He won't hurt Ben. Not unless he really has to.' I say the words as much to convince myself as Izzy. I need to be right about this. It's true though. I remember the tone of Roger DeVilliers' voice when he thought he was talking to Charlotte rather than me. He's a heartless bastard who gets off on raping kids, but he loves his daughter – his true daughter. He wouldn't do anything to hurt her, and killing Ben would certainly do that. He's just a distraction. I hope.

'How can you be sure? You know what they did to Steve, what they did to me. He's got all the cards. We've got nothing.'

'That's what he wants us to think, but it's not true. We've got him on the ropes.'

'How do figure that, Con? He's got your brother and he's threatening to cut his throat open.' Izzy stares at me with disbelieving eyes.

'He wants the photographs and video destroyed. I know that's just common sense, given his position, but there's more to it than that. You should have heard him. The moment I mentioned the possibility of vein pattern matching, he snapped. Before that he was being his usual obnoxious self, but he was in control of the situation. He didn't think we could prove he was involved.'

'But I was there. It happened to me. I just need to tell people and—'

'And he'll have you sectioned, locked up in an asylum,

disappeared. He'll destroy your credibility before you've even opened your mouth. Hell, he's probably been doing that for months already. Years, maybe. But you're missing the point, Izzy.'

'I am?'

'He knows that identifiable parts of him appear in the photographs. He knows that we can prove to a jury beyond any doubt that he . . . did what he did to you, and those other poor souls.' I try to keep my voice level, even as my mind reels at the thought of it. Bad enough what was done to the poor girl, but knowing the identity of the man responsible makes it hard to hold her gaze and not break down in tears.

'It doesn't help though. Even if we can prove he's guilty, he's still got Ben. And you've got five minutes to phone him back and tell him we're coming in.'

'But we're not coming in. You're not going back to him and I'm not going to jail. We've enough to make him come to us. He'll do that now he knows we can identify him.' I wish I had my own phone, with all my contacts on it, but it's easy enough to find the number I need from a quick web search. I pause a moment before dialling it, thinking what I need to say. It's all about timing now, and time's running out.

'The important thing is to take back as much control as we can. That and to start trying to divide them. We need every bit of help we can get.' I hit the dial icon. 'Fortunately I know someone who might just fit the bill.'

46

I'm not sure I'm ready for this. It's still too soon since Pete's death, the memories too raw. One thing to see it on a phone screen, quite another to be here in person. I can't think of anywhere else to go though, not with the impossible lack of notice, not where I have the advantage. And I need to draw the right kind of attention to myself too. I don't like that there are so many variables, so many things to go wrong, but surely it's about time my luck turned? And anyway, this is where it all began; there's a pleasing symmetry about it all ending here too.

'What is this place?' Izzy asks as I lead her through the back alley to the door. She's remarkably calm, given how nervous I'm feeling. But then I guess she doesn't know what happened here. Nor does she know just how much I've bet on the set-up here being largely untouched since I was last in this building.

'We set this up as a fake office. Undercover cop work.' I pause before tapping Pete's code into the keypad; they'll have surely cancelled mine by now. It's only when the lock clicks open that I realise I've been holding my breath.

'Undercover?' Izzy's tone reminds me that for all the harsh life experiences she's had, she's still only a teenager. 'Cool.'

'Yeah, well.' I lead her up the stairs, but instead of going into the front room, where I found Pete's body, I key the code into what looks like a locked store cupboard and pull open the door. Behind it is a much larger room, lined with surveillance screens, wires trailing into server boxes in a rack on one wall. I'm relieved to see led lights flickering even though the screens are blank.

'Wow. What is this place?'

'This, dear sister, is the nerve centre.' I pull out one of the two office chairs that have been shoved under a long counter, reach for the nearest keyboard and bring everything to life. If I'm lucky, things will start pinging in the station soon.

'How good are you with computers?'

Izzy looks at me as if all her Christmases have come at once. She pulls out the other chair and drops down into it, flexes her fingers and reaches for a mouse. 'What do you want me to do?'

'First off, bring up your secure folder with all the video footage and photos on it. Give it a new name and copy it to the Met storage. I'm guessing that's the last place they'll look for it.'

'Sneaky. I like your style.' Izzy works her way through the various screens and menus as if she's been doing this all her life. I could do it myself, but having her preoccupied works to my advantage. I use the second workstation to review the surveillance on the building. This is the first time I've managed to look over anything since Pete died, and I'm not surprised to find that all of the recordings have been erased. Clicking back through the date-stamped folders, there's nothing to see at all. It's possible everything's been removed to another file store somewhere, but I somehow doubt it.

'What are you looking for?' Izzy asks. I can understand her eagerness to help.

'I need to make sure all these cameras are recording, all the microphone feeds too. Especially in the front room there.' I point at the window on the main screen showing a view of the office where Pete died. Where Gordon Bailey shot him between the eyes. 'It needs to record to the drive here locally, but it also needs to go here.' I switch on Charlotte's phone and bring up the text Veronica sent me. By now, Bailey will know we're here and fiddling with the equipment. I've no doubt he's got a plan to delete anything recorded today, just like he deleted everything around the time he shot Pete. I'm hoping he's not clued up enough to realise there's a second copy out in the wild where he can't reach it.

'Done.' Izzy's fingers finish tapping at the keys and she looks up at me expectantly. 'What next?'

'DeVilliers will be here soon. He should be bringing Ben with him.' I shove my hand in my pocket and bring out the Taser I stole from Tommy the silent bodyguard, place it down on the desk beside Charlotte's phone. I hope she doesn't think I'm completely insane. 'So. Here's the plan.'

There's nothing to do but wait now. I pace the room, close to the window overlooking the street outside, and try not to look at the chair where Pete met his end. I can still see him in my mind, the look on his face as he stared sightless into nothing. That tiny red dot in the middle of his forehead and the larger spray on the wall behind him. Someone's had a go at cleaning that up, but not very successfully.

'If it's any consolation, it didn't hurt. Was kind of a relief after what they'd already done to me anyway.'

He's there, but he's not there. It's daylight outside, coming up on noon. There's no sun as such, too much cloud and the threat of rain, but that just means there are no shadows in this room even without the lights switched on. Pete can't hide from me in the darkness.

'You're just my mind playing tricks on me. You know that?'

'And here's me thought we were friends. I'm here because you need me to be, Con. I'm here to help.'

'That's . . . reassuring.' I still can't look at the chair, concentrate instead on staring out of the window and up the street.

'They'll be here. Don't you worry about that.'

'It's who else they bring that worries me, Pete. And who gets here first.'

I pace the room a couple more times while he says nothing. Is this what it's come to? So wound up by stress I'm talking to myself, imagining the ghost of my dead boss is going to help me out?

'Sometimes you've just got to go with your instincts, Con. Even after all they drummed into you at training college, all the procedure and logic. Sometimes it's for nothing and you know it.'

'So, what? You're in control of the traffic lights between here and wherever DeVilliers is coming from? You're timing his approach through some eldritch means I can't even hope to understand?'

More silence, underlined by the ever-present roar of the city. On balance, I think I preferred it at Newmore. I go back to the door, open it and look out onto the reception area at the top of the stairs. Two desks, computers, chairs, filing cabinets full of random paperwork. We spent months setting this place up.

'If it means anything, I wanted to tell you what we were really up to.'

Marvellous. Pete's ghost has followed me out here now. 'What are you trying to tell me, Pete?'

'Operation Undertaker. Hah, there's a joke that's not so funny in the telling. If it had been up to me, I'd have told you from the start it was all a ruse meant to flush out Bailey. Except we didn't know it was him, of course.'

I don't need this shit. I should be in the office, waiting for DeVilliers. Doing all I can to save my brother. I leave reception and go back into the office, shaking my head even though there's no one here to see me. 'Why didn't you, then?'

'Not my call. Bain was in charge, and he said the fewer people who knew the better. He had a point. Just a pity one of those people had to be Bailey.'

I stare out of the window as a car slows down, looking for somewhere to park. I've been over this all before. Even so, I can't quite suppress the shaking in my hands, the horrible churning anxiety in my gut. Bailey's a detective super and he's been doing this for years. How the fuck am I supposed to go up against that? Christ, how many people are in his pocket? How many can he drum up to come and get me. Come and get Izzy?

'It's too late for him, Con. The cat's out of the bag now. One way or another the truth will out.'

Not exactly reassuring. One way could be Bailey going to jail, another me ending up with a bullet in my brain. I turn to face the empty chair, ready to tell Pete how reassuring his words aren't right now. It's empty, of course. It always was empty. Pete's dead, and Izzy's probably been watching me for the past fifteen minutes wondering whether I've completely lost my mind.

Maybe I have.

A car door thunks shut outside. It's no different from any other noise, and yet it drags my attention away from the chair and back to the window. I stand far enough away not to be seen from outside and peer down at the street. Detective Constable Dan Penny has a nice shiny bruiser from where I smacked him in the face a couple of days ago – I can take a certain amount of pleasure in seeing that. It's scant consolation as I see Bailey climb out of the car though. He's canny, I'll give him that much, but even he can't help glancing first up the street and then down it. I track his gaze each way, and it's not hard to see the backup he's checking is in place.

47

I'm at the intercom waiting for them. 'First floor. But then you know that already. It's not locked.'

I go back to the office, leaving the door open for them. Two sets of feet clump up the stairs. It takes them a while to cross the reception area outside, giving me plenty of time to arrange myself close to the window opposite the door.

'Have you any idea how much trouble you're in, Fairchild?'

As warm welcomes go, it's a bit lacking, but then I've come to expect no more from my boss. My ex-boss, I should say. Detective Superintendent Gordon Bailey looks ill, his eyes deep-set as if he's not had much sleep in the week or so since I last saw him. His hair's greyer than I remember too, what little is left of it.

'Trouble, Gordon?' I give him my best innocent-girl smile. 'I don't know what you mean.'

'Cut the crap. You were already under investigation for DI Copperthwaite's death.' Bailey gives the empty chair behind the desk a nervous glance. 'You should have been sitting at home waiting for Professional Standards to finish their investigation into that, but no, you had to go sticking your nose into other people's business. You're implicated in an RTA that left two people dead and you assaulted a fellow officer just a couple of days ago. Anyone would think you had a death wish or something.'

302

'Death wish? An interesting choice of words, coming from the man who put a contract out on me. The man who actually murdered Pete.'

'Oh come on. I'm a detective superintendent in the Met, not some cheap hoodlum.' Bailey is swift in his response, but not swift enough. I can see how hard he's working to suppress his startled expression, hear the edge of panic in his voice.

'And you, Dan. Quite handy with a baseball bat. I have to assume there's a fat wad of cash in it for you.' I turn my attention to Penny, who has been trying to edge surreptitiously around the room to a point where he might be able to launch himself at me in some kind of attack. Poor sod should have learned from his last experience, but at least he stops when he realises I've clocked him.

'You really are quite paranoid, aren't you, Fairchild?' He nods his head towards Pete's chair. 'You actually think either of us had anything to do with that?'

'Think?' I shake my head, catching a glimpse of movement out of the window as I do. 'No. It's not about thinking or believing. It's about knowing. Proof.'

'Now I know you're delusional.' Bailey laughs. 'There is no proof. How could there be?'

'Oh, you mean the CCTV recordings you thought you had deleted?' I wave my hand at the light fitting in the centre of the ceiling even as I take another glance out of the window. 'You know as well as I do there are copies. I've seen the footage myself. Admit it, Gordon. That's the real reason you came in person.'

'Enough of this nonsense, Fairchild. Is this why you called us here? To make wild and spurious allegations? Are you hoping to throw us off the trail, because, if so, it won't work. We know that the same gun used to kill Pete Copperthwaite was fired twice through your mattress. We know there was no break-in, so either you let the shooter in or you are the shooter. Given your behaviour over the past couple of weeks I'm inclined to believe the latter.' Bailey folds his arms, leans back against the desk and gives me a smug look of satisfaction. I already knew about the ballistics is useful information, even if he's spinning it to his advantage. More importantly though, I've just spotted what I've been waiting for out of the window.

'You know why I called you here, Gordon. Otherwise you wouldn't have come. This chat's been nice, but really it's just been about killing time.'

Roger DeVilliers' black stretch Bentley sweeps up the road and parks on a double-yellow line right outside the office. Adrian climbs out of the driver's side, then opens the passenger door for his boss. I hope that means Tommy's still incapacitated, but it's possible – likely even – that there are other operatives keeping an eye on the building.

'Looks like we've got company.'

I can almost hear Pete's ghost chuckling as the door downstairs opens and footsteps thump up the stairs. Dan Penny's at the office door before it swings open, and almost catches Adrian off guard. The close-protection specialist is too good for that though, turning the detective constable's attack against him. In a matter of seconds, Penny's on the floor, his arms behind his back and being pulled up so tight he screams like a little girl.

'What the fuck are you doing here?' Adrian loosens off the strain, pushing Penny aside with a foot as he stands slowly, scanning the room again. His gaze flits up to the ceiling rose too swiftly, almost as if he knows the camera is there. Then it comes to rest on me and he grins like a hyena.

'She's here, boss,' he shouts to the reception area behind him. 'The bent coppers too. Thought I saw some unmarked cars out in the street.'

'Tommy not with you?' I ask, pleased to see an angry scowl darken Adrian's face.

'Nearly broke his head open, you little bitch.'

'Language, Adrian.' Roger DeVilliers steps in through the door. He doesn't seem to notice the two detectives, focusing solely on me. 'Tommy's in an induced coma in intensive care, thanks to you. A quite unprovoked attack that I'm sure will be added to the list of your other violent offences.'

'Don't make me laugh. He was going to torture Izzy, just like he tortured Steve Benson. That's his speciality, isn't it? Could probably teach Dan there a thing or two.'

DeVilliers frowns, looks around as if only just noticing Penny and Bailey are here too. 'Detective Superintendent. I assume Ms Fairchild came up with some far-fetched story to drag you down here.'

'Yeah, I told him I knew who'd killed Pete Copperthwaite. Thing is, he knows already, but he's worried I might have some evidence he didn't destroy.'

DeVilliers looks at me like a dog whose owner has just made a funny noise. 'Pete . . . ? Oh yes. The detective inspector. Your boss, no less. And who did kill him, then?'

I point at Bailey's chest. 'He did it himself, of course. After his lackey on the floor there had spent a couple of hours torturing him to find out what he knew. You know that. Your man Adrian showed me the video footage. Must be useful, having that kind of hold over a detective superintendent.'

Bailey pushes himself up from the desk and takes a step towards me. 'Like I said, delusional. Sooner we get her out of here and in a cell, the better it will be for all of us.' He's reaching for my arm when his phone rings. I suppress the urge to glance at the hidden camera in the corner. The one Izzy's monitoring.

'You might want to get that,' I say, but Bailey's already on it. The moment he stares at the screen, it stops ringing.

'Unknown number. Come on, Fairchild. Enough of this nonsense.' He takes another step forward, and then his phone pings at him again. A text this time. He swipes at the screen in irritation at the distraction, then stares at the image on display. 'What the fuck is this?'

'You don't know him, but that's my brother Ben. The man holding the knife is Adrian there.' I nod in the bodyguard's direction, and as if by magic his own phone begins to ring. Veronica should be watching the video feed from the cameras in here too, piped through to her from the control room at the back of the building. Her timing is spot on.

'You'll really want to answer that,' I tell him. Ever the professional, he looks to his boss for permission first. DeVilliers was always florid, but his face looks like it's about to burst now, which would save us all a lot of hassle. Instead of exploding, he nods, and Adrian takes the call.

'Yes?' He goes silent as whoever is on the other end of the line tells him something very important.

I turn my attention back to Bailey, still staring at the image of my brother. 'As I was saying, sir. That's my brother, Ben. All of us in here are guilty of something, I'm sure. But he's as innocent as the day. The only thing he ever did wrong was being related to me, and that's hardly something he had any control over.'

'What are you blethering on about, Fairchild?'

'My brother was abducted by Adrian over there, on the instructions of his boss, Mr DeVilliers. Also over there.' I point at them, just in case he's not sure who I'm talking about. 'They threatened to kill him if I didn't bring Isobel DeVilliers to them and then hand myself in at the nearest police station. That sounds like a crime to me, so I expect you'll be wanting to arrest the two of them, won't you?'

'You're beyond insane, Fairchild. This could be staged for all I know. For all I care.'

'Ah, but it's not staged. I can prove that image was sent from Adrian's phone just a few hours ago. I can also prove that the hand holding the knife is his.'

Three pairs of eyes stare at me, and I don't think I've ever seen so much concentrated hatred. There's a fourth pair of eyes in the room of course, but Dan Penny was never all that quick on the uptake. Bailey can see the trap I've set for him though. If he doesn't at the very least arrest Adrian, then he's complicit in Ben's abduction. If he does, then DeVilliers will hang him out to dry.

'Clever girl.' It's DeVilliers himself who breaks the uneasy silence. 'It won't do you any good though. Nothing that happens in this room will get out beyond its walls. And, besides, you're wanted for the murder of Detective Inspector Copperthwaite. Nobody's going to believe a word you say.' He shakes his head in fake contrition, then turns to his bodyguard. 'Adrian. Put this woman out of my misery, will you?'

Adrian still has his phone to his ear, which I take as a positive sign. The look on his face is less reassuring. His frown has turned to an angry glare, and he ends the call, puts the phone away with slow, measured motion. Then he reaches into his jacket and pulls out a gun.

48

The office isn't large, maybe four yards by six. I'm at one end, by one of two windows that look down on the street outside. Adrian's standing beside the door, as far from me as he can get. It's still not far enough. He's a trained soldier, guns are second nature to him. And judging by the way he has this one pointed at me, not a shake in his hand or twitch around his eyes to be seen, killing doesn't worry him much either. Too late, I remember the look on his face when he showed me the video of Pete's death. It's back again.

'Sit.' He nods his head in the direction of the chair. I haven't really got much option but to comply, even though I can't help thinking about the last person who was in this position. I should be terrified, should be on my knees begging for mercy, but somehow the fear isn't there. Instead I feel nothing but calm.

'The thing I don't understand,' I say as I settle myself gently into the seat. 'The thing that's been bothering me ever since this started, really, was why you had to torture Pete before you shot him. Were you worried he knew more about your operation than you thought?'

Bailey opens his mouth to say something, then closes it again, glances up at the ceiling rose and shakes his head.

'Worried this is being recorded?'

'Tie her up.' Bailey ignores me, directing his order at Dan Penny. For a moment I think the detective constable's going to ask 'What with?' but he's come better prepared than that. Once more I suffer the indignity of having my wrists bound with cable ties. Penny loops them around the back of the chair so I can't stand. Close up, I can see the sweat on his scalp, smell the fear on him like body odour. I never much liked the man, but I feel a tiny bit of sympathy for him. It's clear he never imagined things would go this far.

'You really want to do this, Dan?' I whisper, stare past him at DeVilliers and Bailey. 'Those two are old. They'll be dead soon enough. But you're still young. A life sentence, no chance of parole. Reckon you'll go mad long before they let you out. Prison's not a good place for ex-cops either.'

He says nothing, but I can see from the way he shakes his head that I've got to him. When he stands up from tying my ankles together, he won't look me in the eye, either, so the lickspittle does have a tiny sliver of conscience.

'My guess is the girl will be in the control room at the back of the building,' Bailey says. 'Go fetch her.'

Penny nods, then disappears out the door, leaving just the four of us.

'You know this doesn't end well for any of you.' It's meant for all of them, but I stare at Adrian as I say it. 'Everything that's happened so far has been recorded, and I meant it when I said you could be identified in those photographs.'

'Divide and conquer, is that it?' DeVilliers almost laughs at me. 'You have no idea the kind of people who work for me. Reputation is everything for them. Adrian would no more turn against me than shoot himself.'

'I never thought he would. He's not the only one with his life at stake here though.'

From where I'm sitting, I can't see much of the reception area outside the open door, but I've been watching the play of shadows on the wall out there. Before I can say or do anything, a figure bursts in, smashing into Adrian, one hand reaching for the gun. The noise is deafening as it goes off. Then someone lets out a scream of pain. Tied to the chair, all I can do is watch as Adrian swiftly overpowers his attacker. I'm only half surprised to see that it's Dan Penny, but my surprise turns to horror as Adrian kicks him to his knees and shoots him in the back of the head. Blood spatters the window and the dead body slumps to the floor.

'Stupid fucker.' Adrian gives Penny a kick in the ribs, even though he's past caring.

'Never mind him. You fucking shot me.'

In all the noise and commotion, I hadn't noticed that Detective Superintendent Bailey has collapsed into the only other chair in the room. He's holding on to his chest, blood oozing between his fingers, face white as a sheet.

'Shouldn't have got in the way, then.' Adrian raises the gun, aims it straight at Bailey's forehead. I tense for the shot. This has not played out the way I hoped it would. Not by a long way.

'Not here.' DeVilliers reaches out and pushes the gun down so that it's pointing at the floor. 'Things are getting a little out of hand. Take him somewhere quiet and get rid of him. Bloody man's more of a liability than a help. You'll need to get a clean-up crew in here too.' He takes a handkerchief from his breast pocket, shakes it open and wipes his hands, even though I know he's not touched anything.

Adrian grabs Bailey, hauling him to his feet, then nods in my general direction. 'What about her?'

'I'll deal with Miss Fairchild. We have a great deal to talk about.'

I let my mouth drop open slightly, watching as Adrian escorts a weakly protesting Bailey from the room. DeVilliers paces back and forth for a while, pauses to stare out the window, then turns on me.

'None of this needed to happen, you know.'

I look past him, down at Dan's dead body. I hated Penny, but I still wouldn't have wished such a brutal execution on the guy. And it seemed like he was trying to come to my rescue at the last too. One futile, final shot at redemption. That's going to make me feel guilty for a while.

'If you'd just seen sense when I first contacted you, then this man would still be alive and there'd be no need to frame you for his murder.'

'You do realise this has all been recorded, right? There's half a dozen video cameras in this room alone and they're all active right now.'

DeVilliers smiles like a shark, leans on the desk with both hands and looms over me. 'The video cameras that recorded that idiot Bailey shooting your colleague? Have no fear, my dear. They've been taken care of. I own the company that supplies all the equipment.'

'Of course you do. That's how you found out all about Gordon Bailey so quickly once you started looking into me.' I'm playing for time, trying to distract him while I work away at the cable tie around my wrists. There's a metal edge on the back of the chair I can rub it against, hoping to break it, but it's hard to do that and not draw attention to myself.

'Yes, that came as quite a surprise. He has a very sophisticated operation running. Must have taken him years to set it all up. Who knows how many officers he's got on his payroll.'

'You know I had no involvement in his operation.'

'Of course. That was a bit of a disappointment, really. If you'd been bent, then corrupting you to my own ends would have been so much easier.'

'Is that why you increased the price on my head? Got a few

more crazies out there to try and have a pop at me?' I can feel the plastic of the cable tie stretching even as it cuts off the circulation to my hands. I still don't know what I'm going to do about the one around my ankles though. It's going to be hard to choke the life out of this fucker with useless fingers and my feet shackled.

'Oh, they were never going to kill you. Just chase you away. It worked, for a while. If you'd only stayed away, things would have been just fine.'

'For you, maybe. Izzy, not so much.'

'Ah yes. Isobel.' DeVilliers shoves his hand into his jacket pocket and pulls out a tiny pistol. The kind of thing they sell in American big-box stores as 'handbag guns'. The essential accessory every girl needs. It looks stupid in his fat hand, but lethally stupid all the same.

'I don't much like getting my hands dirty.' He holds the gun awkwardly, looking around it until he finds the safety catch and slides it off. 'But needs must. Isobel was a pretty little thing, when she was younger. Very willing once she learned what was good for her. I looked after her well too. It would have broken poor Margo's heart if something bad had happened to her. But now, after all the trouble you women have given me of late, I find I don't really care what Margo thinks any more.'

'And Charlotte?' I flex my wrists and feel the cable tie snap. Relief is tinged with pins and needles, but I need to keep this megalomaniac idiot talking while I work out what to do with my feet.

'She'll get over it. Poor brainless Charlotte doesn't have the intelligence to be sad for long. An expensive cruise with her mother, a couple of months in the sun. She'll have forgotten all about your feckless brother and you.' He raises the tiny pistol and points it at my head. 'You know, in a way I should be grateful. I didn't know about vein pattern matching until you told me. That's not a mistake I'll make again.'

I'm sitting in the chair that Pete died in, the same office that he died in too. With the grey light filtering in through the windows behind him, I can't really make out the details of the gun or the expression on Roger DeVilliers' face. I should be panicking, fearful, shaking even, facing certain death here. Instead that strange calm that's settled over me since I first walked in here a half-hour ago now coalesces into a clear, familiar voice speaking a single, simple word.

'Duck!'

Something flies across the room from the still-open doorway as I throw myself sideways out of the chair. DeVilliers tenses, spasms, his finger pulling the trigger. Another loud explosion sets my ears ringing, and I feel the heat of a bullet whip past me, through the space where my head just was. As I crash to the floor, the chair comes with me, cable tie still looped around my ankles and the central pole. I expect another shot any second now. Tangled up as I am, I'm in no position to avoid it.

Nothing happens, and as the ringing in my ears from the gunshot subsides, so I hear an odd gurgling noise. Then a thump on the carpet as DeVilliers falls to his knees. He's twitching and jerking like he's having an epileptic fit, but the rapid clicking suggests a more satisfying explanation. I kick out, breaking the last of the cable ties as he slumps onto the floor alongside Dan Penny's dead body. As I haul myself to my feet I can see the twin wires of the Taser stretching back across the room to where Izzy stands, a wide grin of triumph pasted across her face.

'Oh my God. That felt so good.'

49

I t takes me a long time to get my brain working. All I can do is lean against the desk and stare. Eventually the clicking stops as the Taser runs out of charge. I'm not sure you're supposed to keep on using it once the intended target's been incapacitated, but I can appreciate just why Izzy might want to give Roger DeVilliers more than the recommended dose.

'Ben?' I ask after what seems like an hour.

'He's OK. In the car. They'd locked him in the back.'

I'm unsteady on my feet, but I force myself first to stand, then to crouch down and put a finger to DeVilliers' neck. He has a pulse, but is unconscious, a bubbly smear of drool leaks from the side of his mouth, and he smells like he's let go in the trouser department. The gun's still in his hand, one pudgy finger stuck in the trigger guard. I'm about to reach for it and disarm him when it occurs to me that leaving him in very obvious possession is a much better idea. There's a fresh hole in the wall behind where I was sitting that the forensics experts will find fascinating. He might still find a way to wriggle out of the child abuse charges, but I'll settle for possession of a handgun and attempted murder just now. It's all on tape anyway.

'Where's Adrian?' I remember the short, one-sided fight. The way he casually executed Dan Penny. Looking over at the dead body sprawled on the floor I can feel the puke rising in my throat and fight it back. This crime scene's messy enough as it is already.

'Blondie? He's gone. No idea where. There's a man tied to the chair outside though. Looks like he's been shot.'

I stagger across the room, push past Izzy and see Gordon Bailey sitting on one of the receptionist chairs. The way his head's lolled to one side I can tell he's passed out. There's a fair slick of blood on the floor beneath his drooping hand too, every chance he might bleed out. It's tempting to just let him, but then I wouldn't get to see him in the dock. A quick check shows the bullet has gone through his arm, not his chest as I'd initially thought. More's the pity. I search around for something to use as a tourniquet, settle for his belt in the end. Cinching it tight brings a grunt of pain, but Bailey stays unconscious. I'm surprised the police aren't here already. Suppose I'm going to have to call them.

'You were meant to use the Taser on the driver, not your— DeVilliers there.' I point back at the office.

Izzy shrugs. 'There wasn't a driver.'

It takes a moment for my brain to catch up. 'What?'

'It was weird. I was watching you on the cameras. Making sure it was feeding to the address you gave me. I waited like you said, then went out and tapped on the car door. But there wasn't anyone in the front of the car, and it was locked. I came back and shut myself in the control room. Watched what was happening. Then Blondie shows up, opens the door like it's just an unlocked cupboard. He still had that gun on him. You know, the one he used to . . .' Izzy's got her back to the office door now, the Taser still in her hand, its wires trailing behind her and into the man who used to be her father.

'He didn't shoot you though.' I hear how stupid it sounds as the words come out, but I'm still trying to understand what's happened and how different from my hastily concocted plan it is.

'Well, duh.' Izzy drops the Taser and raises her hands in an unhelpful gesture. 'Thought he was going to, mind. But he just looked at me, said, "You win" and chucked me a set of keys.' She shoves her hand into a pocket and brings them out. There's a security swipe card for the tower block on the keyring too, which will come in very handy.

'He did a runner? I guess that makes sense if he knew the game was up.'

'"The game was up?" Have you any idea how lame you sound, Con?' Izzy shakes her head like I'm some old fogey or something. I certainly feel like one just now. 'Anyway. I went and unlocked the car and Ben was in the back. Hands tied, duct tape over his mouth. I gave him Char's phone and told him to call the police. Came up here to see what was happening. Just as well I did, really.'

I can hardly keep up with the stream of consciousness that's Izzy's overexcited babbling, but one thing sinks in. 'You told him to call the police.' As I say it, so the sound of sirens wafts in on the background noise of the city. 'You have to go, then. You know how to drive?'

'Drive?' Izzy looks at me like a spaniel told not to eat the pheasant it's just retrieved.

'Ben knows how. Just take the Bentley and go, OK? You don't want to be here when my colleagues arrive.'

'But . . . You're coming with us, right?'

I shake my head. Back through in the office, Roger DeVilliers groans and begins to stir. Someone's going to have to make sure he doesn't get rid of that gun before the forces of law and order arrive to arrest him, even if that means they arrest me too.

'Not this time, Izzy. You go. Get Ben back to Charlotte. She won't even have made it to Harston Magna yet. Then the lot of you take off somewhere far, far away.'

It's going to take a very long time to explain this all to the powers that be.

I can't quite believe the officers who came here with Bailey and Penny didn't rush in when they heard the first gunshot, but by the time the real police arrived, they'd all mysteriously disappeared. I've no doubt Professional Standards, by which I mean the real Professional Standards and not the inspector in Bailey's pocket, will track them all down. How deep the rot goes is anyone's guess. I'm not sure I want to be around to find out.

'Tell me again how you even came to be in here, Detective Constable.'

I'm just about ready to believe DCI Bain's not bent. The look on his face when he saw Dan Penny sprawled on the floor, Roger DeVilliers semi-conscious beside him, was enough to convince me he really had no idea what was going on all around him. That doesn't say much for his promotion prospects, mind you. I'll be very surprised if our entire division doesn't get disbanded, promoted sideways or pensioned off.

'It will all be in my report, sir.'

'Your report? For fuck's sake, Fairchild. You're suspended from active duties. You're not supposed to be here. Don't talk to me about reports.' Bain turns a circle around the room, taking in the space where Roger DeVilliers almost died of a heart attack, the dark stain where Dan Penny's blood and brains mixed together in the carpet. 'Just tell me what the fuck happened.'

I try my best, but every time I get two or three steps into the story he stops me with yet another question. I can't blame him, it sounds unbelievable and I lived through it. Unlike Pete, and Dan Penny. Gordon Bailey? Well, that's still to be determined. He lost a lot of blood.

'I should really take you into custody. Lock you up in a cell until we can get to the bottom of all this.'

I hold my breath. There's nothing I can do if he decides that's the best step. I'm done running from shit anyway.

'But I'm not going to do that,' Bain continues. 'Go home.

Get yourself cleaned up, get some rest. You look all done in anyway.'

'Have you had a call from Birmingham yet, sir?' I chance the question even though I know I should keep out of it. So much hangs on the footage from my carefully staged meeting making it to another police force. That's what I asked Veronica to do. After she'd made a copy, of course. That and get one of her ex-military friends to call Adrian at exactly the right moment and let him know just how bad things were.

'Yes. Can't say the Deputy Commissioner's too pleased with them being involved, but given the circumstances it was probably the right thing to do.'

'And Adrian?' I see Bain's confused frown. 'The blond-haired man. DeVilliers' chief of security and bodyguard. The one who killed DC Penny.'

Bain's frown deepens into a scowl. 'All ports notified. He won't get far.'

I doubt that. He's got a head start and strikes me as the sort of man who knows how to pass through borders unseen. The thought of him out there after what he did makes me shudder. I've seen dead people all too often; hard not to in my line of work. Today was the first time I watched someone be executed.

'Go home, Fairchild.' Bain puts enough emphasis on the words for me to know it's an order. Best to do what I'm told before he changes his mind and has me locked up.

'Yes, sir.' I nod, take one last look at the place where Pete and Dan died, then turn and walk out of the room. I'm almost at the top of the stairs when Bain calls out for me to stop.

'One last thing. Before you go.' He's at the door, sticks his hand into his jacket pocket as he crosses over to where I'm standing. When he pulls it out again, he's holding a warrant card. My warrant card.

'Here. This should never have been taken off you in the first place. If everything you tell me's true, I dare say you'll be a DS soon.'

I reach for the card, tucked neatly into its slim plastic folder. It represents everything I wanted to be when I first signed up to join the Met. All the years of training, the work on the beat as a uniform officer, being cut off by my father and shunned by my mother. This was the life I intended to pursue until it was time to retire. Or I met someone attractive enough to consider having a family of my own. All that changed though, in that room I've just left, when Pete Copperthwaite died at the hands of a fellow police officer.

I let my hand drop, DCI Bain still clutching the warrant card.

'No.' I shake my head. 'Thank you, sir, but I don't think I want that any more.'

He looks at me with a slightly surprised expression, then shrugs his shoulders, tucks the card back into his pocket.

'We'll discuss it later. It's going to take months to sort this all out, and you'll be on suspension while that's ongoing. With full pay, of course.'

It's something, I guess. There's still the small matter of my reputation though. 'You really think anyone in the Met will want to work with me? After this?'

'I guess that depends on who they think they're working with. You're resourceful, Fairchild. You think on your feet. I'd hate to lose those skills. Not all police work is about teams, you know. And there are other forces beside the Met.'

'You offering me a job, sir?' Bain doesn't answer, just stares at me until I feel uncomfortable.

'I'll think about it,' I say.

Then I turn away and walk slowly down the stairs.

50

'   ore news about disgraced financier Roger DeVilliers,
. . . M who has been implicated in the murder of journalist
Steve Benson. Benson was investigating allegations that
DeVilliers was involved in a paedophile ring and had serially
abused his own daughter. We go live now to the Old Bailey . . .'

It takes me longer than I would have liked to locate the remote
and click off the television. I don't need to hear it all over again,
nor do I particularly want to see that sneering face. I take some
small comfort from the knowledge that he's in prison awaiting
trial, but I know too that he's enormously wealthy and has access
to the best legal defence that money can buy. There's already an
appeal lodged against his bail refusal.

That bigger story has completely overshadowed the arrest of
Detective Superintendent Gordon Bailey and half a dozen less
senior officers in the organised crime team. I've not been back
except to give a series of long and rambling statements to DCI
Bain and Inspector Williams. Bain keeps on dropping hints about
a promotion and some new job in the Met, but I'm still
undecided what I want to do. Pete's death and the fallout from it
have left me bruised and cynical. I'm not sure I'm ready to do it
all again. At least I won't have to think about it for a while yet.

A light knock at the door interrupts my musing, and when I
peer through the spyhole it shows me the ample form of Mrs
Feltham, clutching a large tupperware pot to her bosom.

'Saw you on the news, child. That's some trouble you got yourself into, now.' She beams at me with a broad smile as I open the door. I glance past her nervously, looking for reporters, but for now the coast seems to be clear.

'I hardly think it was my fault, Mrs F. Trouble has a habit of coming looking for me though. You want to come in? I was just packing up some stuff.'

'You moving away?' Mrs Feltham doesn't move, but she does look over my shoulder and into the narrow hallway. I pack light, usually, but there's still two large suitcases behind me.

'Just for a while. There's too many people know my face in London right now. When the trial starts it's going to get even worse.'

'Shame on them, chasing you out of your own home. Who am I going to find to eat my curry now?' She proffers the tupperware pot as if only then remembering she has it. When I take it from her it's still warm, and a wonderful spicy smell leaks from the lid.

'Thank you, Mrs F. I'm going to miss these for a while, but I'll be back. I'm sure those boys of yours will eat everything if you let them. I never got the chance to thank them, and you, for what they did that night.'

'Ah, that was nothing. Just them venting a little frustration. Better them do it there than somewhere they get in trouble with the police.'

I turn slightly and wave my free hand towards the doorway again, hoping the old lady will come in. I'm almost certain there will be paparazzi with long lenses trained on my front door, and the last thing I need is for them to start hounding Mrs Feltham too. 'Sure you don't want to come in for a coffee or something?'

'No time, child.' She shakes her head. 'But thank you for the offer. You been a good neighbour. I'll be sorry to see you go. Don't you be a stranger now.' She steps forward then, and sweeps me up into a bear hug so tight I fear the pot of curry still clutched

NO TIME TO CRY

in one hand will burst open and cover us both. A few moments, and then she releases me, wipes a tear from the corner of one eye, and walks away.

Slate-grey clouds scud across a wide-open sky, the wind from the north bringing with it a promise of winter even though it's barely autumn yet. It's taken me hours to find this place, but in many ways the effort seems worth it. I left the car down in the village, outside a pub that I hope will give me a warm meal when I get back in an hour or so.

I don't know how many times I've travelled through Yorkshire, but I'm fairly sure this is the first time I've stopped. Wrapped in a thick coat, a garish yellow fleece hat keeping my head warm, I trudge up a steep and narrow track towards what looks like a set from a Hammer horror film, but is actually the remains of an abandoned church. I remember Pete telling me about it, but I never thought I'd come here.

The wind whistling through hawthorn bushes and rattling the tops of nearby trees is almost as loud as being in London. That's where the similarities end though. I can breathe freely here, and the scent on the air is of coming rain, not unwashed bodies and diesel fumes. I haven't seen another soul since I parked the car either.

It doesn't take long to find what I'm looking for. The grave-yard is surprisingly well tended given the state of the church itself, and a neat path leads to a freshly dug plot. It's a good spot, sheltered from the worst of the wind by a drystone wall. Beyond that, the hill rises to the moors, where I'm reliably told you shouldn't venture without your hat. I'm not going any further than here, Pete Copperthwaite's grave.

'It's not a bad place, really. Even if I couldn't wait to get away.'

I don't turn, there's no need. It's enough to know that he's there. I can sense his presence like a calming influence, and even the wind seems to die down as I read the weather-faded names on the surrounding gravestones.

'They disbanded the unit. Half of the officers were corrupt or knew about it and did nothing. Everyone else is either taking early retirement or moving to a different region. Start again from scratch, I guess.'

'You're a bit young to be retiring, aren't you, Con?'

'I'm still suspended on full pay. You know, I never imagined how boring that can be.'

A thoughtful pause is punctuated by the distant screaming of a buzzard.

'What'll you do next?' Pete's ghost finally asks. It's a good question. Exactly the sort of thing my subconscious would ask.

'Short term, there's a couple of trials I'm going to be involved in, a lot of media attention I could do without.'

'And long term?'

The buzzard's shrieking comes closer. I look up to see it swooping and diving, a couple of jet-black crows harrying it for whatever reason crows need.

'DCI Bain keeps dropping hints. I think he wants to set up a new unit. Not just London-based though. More a National Crime Agency thing.'

'You going to take him up on it?'

I stare at the gravestone, then up at the clouds.

'I don't know,' I say to the sky. 'Maybe.'

There's a point around Newcastle when I think the old Volvo's going to die on me. Aunt Felicity's mechanic's done a good job on the bodywork and sorted out a few other bits and bobs, but it's a twenty-year-old car with almost 200,000 miles on the clock. It can't live for ever. The detour around Yorkshire involved a lot more twisty bends and steep hills than its previous life as a motorway patrol car ever saw too.

NO TIME TO CRY

As it turns out though, all it needs is fuel. That and another appointment with a garage to get the petrol gauge fixed. I take the opportunity to wake myself up with a coffee before setting off north again and over the border.

If you'd told me a year ago I'd not just be going to Newmore but actually looking forward to it, I'd probably have laughed in your face. A month on from watching Izzy Taser her stepfather insensible and I can hardly wait to get there, even if the weather's turning more wintry and the nights are going to be fair drawing in.

Visiting Pete's grave felt right, even if I doubt that's the last I'll hear from him. I don't much believe in ghosts and spirits, but it's nice to think that someone's got my back. It's good to have someone I can trust to bounce ideas off too. Even if it's just the voice of my imagination. He has a way of getting to the heart of the matter. I can kid myself I've not made up my mind about Bain's offer, but I know I'll be reporting for duty just as soon as the dust has settled.

These and other thoughts occupy my mind as the car slowly eats up the miles. I'll have to go back down south again soon enough, give evidence at more than one trial. I can't say I'm looking forward to it, but I know I'm not going to be alone.

The sun's almost set by the time I crunch to a halt on the gravel outside the front door, park alongside Aunt Felicity's car. Light spills from half of the windows, making the house feel far more welcoming than ever it was when I was a child. I turn my back on it for a moment as I stretch and ease out the kinks from the long drive. Out across the loch, the dusk paints the sky in a riot of oranges and pinks, mirrored perfectly in the still water.

'Thought I heard a car.'

I turn to see the front door open, and Izzy steps out into the gloom. As she walks across the driveway to where I'm standing, Cat trots out behind her, doing her best to trip my half-sister up, tail held high and bullet-torn ear healed. I reach down, offer a hand to be sniffed. I'm rewarded with a deep rumbling purr that's the loudest noise in all the surrounding silence. And for the first time I can remember, I feel like I'm home.

Acknowledgements

It's always a struggle writing acknowledgements at the end of a book. So many people have helped me along the way, it seems somehow unfair to pick out just a few to mention by name. There's the worry that I might forget someone important too.

Having said which, I'm going to go ahead and name some names regardless. If yours isn't here, it's not that I don't care, just that my brain is full.

I am eternally grateful to my agent, the indispensable Juliet Mushens, and her assistant, the amazingly organised Nathalie Hallam at Caskie Mushens. So much more than just a literary agency.

No Time to Cry is the first book I've written in a decade that's not part of an already established series. I don't think it would have happened without the support of Alex Clarke, Ella Gordon and the rest of the team at Wildfire. Their energy and enthusiasm have been a much needed impetus for me to try something new. I've enjoyed the experience, and I hope you do too.

Many others have helped mould my wayward words into something readable, and special thanks must go to Mark Handsley for once more preventing me from heading into disaster. Thanks must go as well to the crime writing community, a bunch of misfits and ne'er-do-wells I'd not trust at a crime scene, but whose kindness, support and capacity for drinking never cease to amaze me.

But the biggest thanks of all go to Barbara, who keeps everything running while I'm away in my own head. Without her holding the fort, I doubt any of this would have happened.

And lastly, a specific thank you to Vincent Holland-Keen, who may well have forgotten the conversation, many years ago, about naming a character Constance because she was anything but. My Constance has turned out rather more steadfast, I feel, but it was from that spark of an idea that the character was born.

THRILLINGLY GOOD BOOKS
FROM CRIMINALLY
GOOD WRITERS

CRIME FILES BRINGS YOU THE LATEST RELEASES FROM
TOP CRIME AND THRILLER AUTHORS.

SIGN UP ONLINE FOR OUR MONTHLY NEWSLETTER AND BE THE FIRST
TO KNOW ABOUT OUR COMPETITIONS, NEW BOOKS AND MORE.